Dead Gods

A Hell and Heaven Novel

By Darren Walker

Introduction

"What's the difference between Hell and the Civil Service? One is a place of absolute pain and ultimate agony, and the other is Hell."

All civil servants – Sat at every desk, in every office, every day.

"Challenge accepted!"

Satan.

1 - And Gods were born...

The origin of Earth and the abundant forms of life that seethe on it, is something that is often contested in a far too hot manner. However, when discussed in a civilised way, with only voices and eyebrows raised, rather than weapons, the subject has kept deep, and shallow thinkers alike employed for millennia. As no side will back down it will probably also keep them busy for many more centuries to come. Accepting the differences of opinion there is one theory which demands just as much respect as any other and it is this...

In the time when man had just learnt the trick of walking, which could be roughly described as an upright way, allowing knuckles to be raised enough so that they didn't drag across the ground, and before they could even talk to express their emotions, there were fears. Vague terrors of indescribable things far beyond their inarticulate ability to explain. People living simple and uncomplicated lives, undoubtedly existence was basic but with oh so many complicated terrors. Deep dreads that filled their hearts and the covered the rest of their bodies which no washing could remove – even if they had invented washes. These feelings usually resulted in bowel releasing side effects, but soiled fur skin clothing was the least of their worries. Unexpressed emotions existing in minds before they had even learnt to understand the concept of fire and how to make it the first of many slaves.

They lived in a world where the nocturnal darkness of the African plains, or the thin strip of coastal land on the tip of the Arabian Peninsula, were all they knew. There were no concepts such as states, countries, or continents to complicate things. There was the small bit of land they were stood on, the bit of the planet just in front of them and then the mysterious places beyond the next hill or, perhaps, the hill after that. If they looked the other way they might see the vast rivers, oceans or seas, stretches of water that could be drunk and assist with life or drunk and be detrimental to it. A saline death making the finding out, which was which, a steep and often harsh learning curve. Their limited vocabulary of grunts, groans and snarls punctuated by gesticulating hands assisted by their secret weapon that differentiated them from the other wild animals, opposable thumbs. This first tool, taken for granted as much then as it is today, enabling them to pick up and manipulate simple stones, rocks or pieces of rough wood to use as their second tools. As wheels and the internal combustion engine, to make them move in the optimum way, were still many millennia away, they had to make do with what they found on the ground or in the trees.

For what was to become known as the human race there was no safety in the dark for these primitive creatures. Despite the schoolboy image of them all living in caves, such safe domiciles were not always available in what would become the Rift Valley and the southern part of Arabia. This meant that they had to cling to their ape ancestry and find safety in the long branches of trees. It was a time of primal and impenetrable darkness of not only the real world but also of their minds. Each gloaming delivering a horror magnified by imagination and lack of tangible information. Empirical thought has never been man's greatest asset and even in modern times there is the preference to embrace dogma, prejudices and opinion instead of accepting some idea or concept that might make them use their brains or accept change. Homo-erectus was more than just an excuse for modern childish sniggering and for them, along with Homo-Sapiens, and Homo-Neanderthals, the use of scientific reasoning was non-existent.

The few basic priorities of life were known even if they were

not fully understood. There was the need to eat, the pleasures of fornication and the requirement of surviving. Although surviving and the fornication soon became interlinked; after all what was life without sex? All of these were performed within the never-ending cycle of night following day and the unpredictable, and nebulous, vagaries of the weather. There were patterns but not recognised by the proto humans and definitely not understood. As far as they were concerned if it rained, they got wet, and it could rain forever. If it was sunny, they'd be dry, and it might never rain again. And as for fog, well that was something that couldn't make up its mind. Water that wanted to be air or perhaps air that thought it was water, either way it was cold, wet and didn't put them in the mood for love making. But they would still do that as a way of keeping warm, so that excuse never has never changed.

Over and above the basic acceptance of the regular switching from light to dark, and back again, along with the fact that weather happened, there was little in-depth thought. The furthest they got to analysis was the instinctive knowledge that if they didn't eat, they would die and, therefore, cease to be able to fornicate; and that was the only one true pleasure that existed and actually allowed them escape from the dangerous grind of life. Life was very simple, if you don't find some wild fruit, or hunt some animal, and devour it, you would die. Get eaten by a Sabre-Toothed Tiger or a Dire Wolf, then you don't get to have sex, ever again! The wild animals might have changed but it is a prerogative that has changed very little since then. Death preventing the act of physical union, or limiting the enjoyment of it, for at least one of the participating parties.

Vacuums were concepts not to be understood for many thousands of years, but they existed all the same and the ignorance that they had inside of minds was abhorred by nature. The emptiness of facts in their small brains had to be filled by other ideas. The distant noises of lion snaring an antelope and then ripping its flesh, to sate a raging hunger, had to be explained away in the all-pervading tenebrosity. A warthog digging in the dirt, searching for tuba roots, or foraging for grubs made all the more frightening thanks to a made-up image to make sense of the strange sounds. Even a passing elephant breaking wind could induce panic accompanied by the desire to run away and hide. Perhaps if the animal was close enough for them to smell the offending fart, they might have taken flight even faster? Ignorance was certainly not bliss, it was a prison that they carried with them and gave little opportunity to ever escape it.

Slowly, as a simple defence mechanism, they began to create images to brighten the nights. Vague greys to replace the blackness as these faint, and dull, shades began to metamorphosis into shapes. At first unclear they eventually adopted forms that made sense to the primitive and ignorant brains. Then, once they existed, they began to change even more. Colours added to the dull monotone. These shapes became almost, but not quite, recognisable animals and humans that stalked the unexplored edges, and the wastelands, of their knowledge and imagination. These fantastic forms were given their own private histories to validate their existence and make them superior to the made-up people of their brothers and sisters. Actions became stories, first basic but becoming more detailed over time. Language created and evolved with these tales first bouncing about in heads before being released and shared. Organic, growing, changing slightly and evolving over time with each repeated telling.

As they were told time and time again, in an attempt to fill the long and empty nights, these fabrications became *facts*. Unbreakable truths that must be real. How could they be anything but facts? In the mysterious night who could prove otherwise? Their fictional actions became legends and the perpetrators imbuing these creations with powers far beyond the weak and vulnerable human storytellers. The first superheroes soon became gods, only ones that didn't need capes, or masks, to hide their true identity. Without writing, to enable them to record the tales, word of mouth became the first Holy Scripture. Entertainment for the masses when the total population of the planet wouldn't have filled a modern small town. The earliest version of television entertainment was devised, showing nothing but re-runs of the same made-up stories.

Eventually the first true great invention came along, fire. Perhaps, more accurately, it was accidentally discovered, but it was quickly harnessed. Where there had been pitch black, there was heat, the orange glow and the dancing shadows as the flames gave warmth and protection with these strange lights punching small holes in the darkness. Answering some questions about the night but also adding to the mystery. The sources of the strange and previously inexplicable sounds faintly exposed and revealed for what they really were, with the basic understanding not making them any safer but at least freeing them from having to create fantasies to explain them away.

But even as the true nature of the outside world was revealed to them the need for the stories grew. The lure and the all-encompassing excitement of people able to control their own destinies, and those of others, was too strong. And for every mystery revealed by the light there were further questions created, new tales to be told to fill in the blanks in knowledge, providing believable, if not accurate, answers. Where did the sun go at night? Why do animals keep eating us? Where did the elephants come from and what was that awful smell that seemed to appear when they did?

Then the ultimate questions were found, ones those were slightly more than the basic answers required to ensure that body fluids could be donated, or received, in a recreational and fun way. Questions that have been asked ever since and still can't be agreed on. The philosophers, religionists and scientists all taking a stance and refusing to accept anything that might contradict their convictions that they are right and everyone else must be wrong. The fear that if they did concede anything then their own private worlds would come tumbling down on their heads and leave them lost, alone and in a darkness not experienced since the pre-fire days of their ancestors.

Where did we come from? Why were we here? Where did people go after they were Sabre Tooth Tiger lunch? There had to be a meaning, over and above having intimate body contact with someone else by firelight. If not, then what was the point? Surely there was more to life than sex? A question still asked today with many still coming up with 'No' as the answer.

Thanks to creative imaginations the new gods could take animal or human forms, or even be hybrids of both. Jackals, cats or snakes it didn't matter. If there had been platypuses in that part of the world, they would probably have made them into gods as well. Originally unsophisticated creatures they evolved and became beings that ruled the mere human's world, moving people around as it they were early versions of chess pieces. No knights, just a board full of pawns with invisible kings stood doing nothing.

These early humans simply couldn't exist anymore without these fictional super beings. Despite what had always happened before, thanks to the new religions, the night now wouldn't end, and the dawn would not arrive unless gods made it happen. Bits of sharpened flint stuck on the end of long sticks would no longer provide sufficient protection from animals with bigger, more numerous and sharper teeth than they had, and love making would be unbearable without the blessings of their newly created deities. Simple acts, which had previously been natural, suddenly became impossible. A new word was created for this – *sin*. Without the gods there was no hope or future and to question that was a heresy. Talk to them in prayers and tomorrow will come and the faithful just might live through it. Ignore them and there would be eternal darkness and no sex.

Eventually when the demand for their protection, in the here and now, was established the perceived facts about the future had to be changed, a bigger purpose over and above life's sole pleasure. After death they couldn't just become a steaming pile of sabre tooth tiger, primitive wolf or crocodile excrement. There must be another, greater, world where they went after life. One where they didn't have to hunt, wait for trees to bear fruit, hide from animals looking for a snack and where elephants didn't smell so bad. A place where they went to be safe, eat as much as they wanted and only stop so that they could philander. So, in the hunt for meaning, the newly made gods were given a home. Far more spectacular than anything the mere mortals could ever achieve in life, but a location for them to aspire to.

Each human group, huddled around their respective fires, giving this magical place their own private names. Take your pick - Heaven, Paradise, Swarga - as many names as there were campfires. And the price for entry into these places was total and utter unquestioning belief, worship, faith, and obedience. The person with the biggest club, or sharpest stone, ensuring their version of religion became the *truth*. The first high priests were now there to populate the metaphorical chessboard and move diagonally instead of just small steps forwards. Obey their rules and continue to live, disobey, and pay the price. When the gods finally decided that it was time to die the reward was a trip to a better place. Refuse to bow to the self-important priests and they ensured a brief skull crushing meeting with a solid and fatal object, a sacrifice to appease an unhappy super-being. No longer just failing to exist, the punishment had to be an opposite of paradise. A Hell where they would be punished for refusing to tell the story properly, bend a knee or to give their food to the biggest guy, often wearing a fancy headdress, who was too lazy to hunt for himself but strong enough to make others do it for him.

As the stories were passed from generation to generation the words began to solidify. The concerted powers, of the growing number of worshippers allowed the gods to become real, filling the moulds and adopting the shapes set out for them. These new beings forced to suffer the emotional states of those that prayed to them. Base feelings stripped bare while the raw power was magnified. Anger and love taken to extremes with no half measures for the supreme beings and their human interpreters. Jealousies and hatreds became their biggest strengths and as these became amplified so did their carnal lusts. If humans enjoyed sex, then the gods must absolutely thrive on it. Able to seduce and copulate with anyone that took their eye. It might mean adopting the shape of a bull or swan but if humans were into that sort of thing, then why not?

Soon the gods, who had been created by man, became the masters. The puppets lost the strings that held them up and used them to hogtie or whip the humans in the linear process of becoming the puppet-masters, seemingly controlling all elements of life. As the believers increased the volume of worship then the new beings grew stronger. Powers, freely given to them, were exercised with carefree alacrity as formerly natural occurrences became acts of gods being played out on a human stage. The planet full of fire spewing volcanoes and shifting tectonic plates causing the Earth to quake as they became vents for the rage of vengeful and vicious gods.

But even the immortals suffered their own natural life cycle. They were given birth by humans, fed by unquestioning prayers and, as they grew old, they were replaced by newer and more virile entities, leaving the old gods to grow ever weaker. Supplications that had nourished them lost, forcing them to desperately cling onto a feeble existence. Occasionally they'd receive a spurt of newfound energy as their cult became temporarily trendy again but eventually the fires that burned, and lit their faces, burnt out, like the fires on the stone alters in the temples, the embers of faith burning out and turning to cold grey ashes. And, lacking supplicants, that was the end of them. A death which their original creators, and blindly devout adherents, would have never accepted. Blasphemies and heresies that, in the god's heydays, would have been rewarded with death for even suggesting such an idea was even possible. Ever fading echoes of what were glorious, mountain shaking and sea moving, roars. Stories, fables and myths left to entertain children but no longer backed by the power of true belief. The withered, undernourished and empty remains transmogrified into statues and transported to a place where they could be eventually forgotten, mounted proudly and imperiously on plinths but not seen or remembered. An unknown art gallery celebrating forgotten ideas and ideals, superseded by newer gods that delivered differently worded messages wrapped in the same threats and punishments. Dust and cobwebs the only things to disturb the eternal peace that dead gods seldom gave to humans when they had lived and been at the peak of their theological powers.

Although no visitors came, it was a long chamber of statues lit for all to not see. Until, one day, they were accidentally visited. Two travellers came but only one of them looked and understood what was before his eyes. He knew some and, remembering, held back a gentle tear for one the dead gods. An apostasy of a first love, given freely but finally betrayed and lost. But, even then, he moved on so that he could try to forget again…

2 – The Earth Speaks Once More

The clouds over the town were forming, slowly at first, but gradually they became thicker, darker and increasingly ominous. They blocked out the sun and, with the ensuing darkness, turned the midday sky to night, all summer warmth lost under the impenetrable menacing blanket. Stray, dirty and emaciated dogs could sense the imminent danger and cleared the streets in an attempt to find shelter, and safety, wherever they could. Even the children playing together looked up, saw the impending storm, and decided to go home until it blew over. Mothers rushed to collect their washing from the lines and bring it inside and still the cloud grew and grew like a nebulous sword of Damocles. Anyone that saw it thought that they knew what was coming but they didn't know when or how destructive it would be. The whole town seemed to grow silent in anticipation of the hurricane. There had been storms before and the population of San Ignacio de Moxos, in Bolivia, were used to them, but this was the dry season. Now was the time to enjoy the weather, not hide from it. The tropical floods had receded, and the town was supposed to be able to relax. With even the old people of the place having never seen anything quite like this before, it was as if the whole sky had become viscous, vengeful and enraged. A semi-solid wall separating the land from the clear blue sky above it. The air itself seemed to become electric making the hairs on arms, or necks, stand on end. Then, in the distance, the inhabitants of the town heard the first leaden, doom-laden, rumble of thunder. An avalanche of noise making the branches of the trees sway reluctantly in supplication to the force thrown against them. Sceptical and devout alike crossed themselves as if that action alone would keep them safe from any forthcoming danger.

Finally, it struck but it was not the expected lightning or flood of water as the giant cloud released its contents; this was something else. The land shook throwing people to the ground and sending birds, in the surrounding jungle, flying into the air. Their senses unsure if they would be safer higher up or near to the ground. Bridges over rivers, unaccustomed to the buffeting of the land and the elements, surrendered their anchoring to the embankments and collapsed into the agitated waters below.

Neat and tidy white plaster coated brick houses fell, leaving solid corners to support nothing - air where there were previously homes. Rubble, dust and death replacing places full of love, joy and memories. Although buildings belonging to the poorer population were demolished their destruction was less fatal than those of the more affluent. Corrugated iron sheets and wood causing less permanent damage than bricks as gravity pulled them to the floor. Huddling together in terror under tables or beds many of the occupants were able to find shelter. Safety in poverty-stricken numbers as the earthquake continued. Screams lost in the noise of the moving ground. Trees falling, destroying telephone lines and overhead power cables, with insane dancing sparks briefly illuminating the darkness.

Then the rumbles in the sky grew closer and ever louder. Like a snarling tiger on a weak and straining leash the ominous threats there, alongside the obvious destruction still to strike and deliver its full potential, leaving people left on the streets unsure where to run to. Buildings were now in ruins, with the newly created open spaces providing no protection from the impending lightning and rains. Then the cloud was lit up as if a giant blue lightbulb had momentarily been switched on inside it. The panic in hearts not calmed by the brief light show. Then the lightning, that had initially been rolling about inside the mountainous cloud, escaped. Released it struck but there were no indiscriminate or random targets hit before moving on to other locations.

These bolts of destruction had one single target which they hit time and time again. The one solid building with thicker walls and which had managed to survive the initial onslaught of the earthquake was the Jesuit mission building, San Ignacio's, the sacred church and social centre of the town. A hoped-for sanctuary given to those that couldn't make it to the assumed safety of their own homes. Prayers offered to God, asking for protection in His sacred temple. The brown, unpainted, wooden veranda at the front of the building blown to pieces more efficiently than any explosives could ever accomplish, while the tall white tower was demolished, sending the bell crashing to the ground in a rain of debris. Next it was the turn of the walls of the building itself, taking hit after hit, like a giant fist striking a defenceless body, before collapsing under the electrical bombardment. As they gave way so did the once sturdy wooden roof, with the devout supplicants finding no answers to their invocations to God. Statues and paintings, bearing an uncanny resemblance to someone that looked nothing like the real saint, were crushed and destroyed, along with the humans on the ground uttering words to the images. The only reward, or punishment, was entry to Heaven for the good and damnation for those using religion to hide their sins.

Eventually, after what seemed like an eternity to those stuck in the middle of it, and as suddenly as it had started, it ended. The silence almost as frightening as the noise, ears expecting more, waiting for the next rolling barrages of death and destruction. But there was one last salvo to be unleashed on the building. A small section of the wall had managed to survive the assault, thick bricks coated with still pristine white plaster. A lightning bolt was loosed, and it struck but it didn't recede straight away, instead the twisting and turning link from the sky to the ground constantly danced against the remnant of the once proud symbol of a town's unshakable and devout faith. The fiery rod arcing across the blank space, leaving black singed scars in the once virgin surface. Smoke escaping from something that shouldn't burn. Super heat charring the surface and, in the process, ionising dust.

Finally, as if the whole thing had been a dream, the cloud evaporated into nothingness. Brilliant sunlight returning in a cloudless and pale blue sky, the light returning and revealing a scene of desolation. Where there had been a town full of life there was little left, with so many lives lost in a place now absent of safety and protection for bodies or souls. Basic existence replacing security and happiness.

Bewildered, those that had survived and were able to walk made their way to what was left of their church, an ingrained homing instinct drawing them to the one place where everyone else could gather. The opportunity to find brethren that had made it through the day and to take stock of those that hadn't. Prayers could be offered for both.

Once at the holy site they looked at the pile of stones and bricks that had been their spiritual sanctuary. Many fell to their knees when they saw the destruction and the lifeless limbs protruding from the rubble as all hope escaped their souls. Others stared blankly at the former building, trying to process all that had just happened. What had they done to deserve such a punishment? Was this a fair test of their faith?

But thankfully, there were a few that could focus on the reality. There were people trapped in buildings that needed to be rescued and such religious questions could wait. Emergency triage for the injured, with limited medical resources shared out to those that had a chance of surviving until help from the outside world eventually arrived. And for those with worse injuries, they could be comforted until their life candles burned out.

But one mind was focused on something else, a sight that shouldn't be there and he didn't understand its existence. Staring at the tiny section of mission wall still upright, he concentrated on writing etching into the surface. Black scorched graffiti, a sacrilege against the building and all that worshipped there. Like a challenge or taunt to the God that owned the church he saw the erratic symbols, undecipherable pictograms unread by human eyes since the early days when people had first settled there. He had no idea what they said but he did know that the marks were no coincidence or accident. Even the ancient and indigenous language, *Ignaciano,* was not that old. Whoever, or whatever, had put them there had meant to do it. This was deliberate and was no freak of nature. It might have been an act of god, but which god, what were they saying and why?

Surrounded by chaos, destruction and despair, his heart was full of sadness. He'd only been there a relatively short time yet so much had happened. A visitation for the festival named after the patron saint of the town. Days of joyous drunken pleasure full of music and dancing now a memory of happier times. If this had happened a few days earlier the town's population would have been swollen by the tourists and visitors from nearby villages determined to celebrate life and the year ahead of them. Fortunately, they had moved on and it was just the local residents that were paying the price for this strange phenomenon. He would soon help the sick and injured, where he could, but first he had a far more important call to make. Walking to the shade of a tree, that had managed to stay upright, he disappeared unseen by any local residents. One second, he was there, the next he was gone. He would return with help, but some things were even more important than alleviation of transitory pain and suffering.

Unlike many saints in the vast register of Christian doctrine, St. Ignacius had actually once existed on Earth and deserved his title. Having founded the Jesuit order in the 15th century he had tried to spread the word of God to those that had not previously heard it. Whether they wanted to listen was immaterial to him, in his heart he had a calling and the concept of a race of people living happily in ignorance of the teachings in the Bible was an anathema. His idea of teaching also involved leading by example, but wasn't totally "Do as I say, not as I do". He followed the Ten Commandments and the sword he carried in life was only for self-defence against those that were strong enough to defy his idea of faith and deemed his words to be heresies against their own gods. It was only after his death from malaria in Rome that his order began to take holy orders far too seriously and used harder weapons than The Book to enforce their message of love and peace. Their credo becoming *accept the love of a peace-loving Jesus or die'*. But such facts embarrassed the saint and he had done all in his power, ever since his entry into Heaven, to make up for the perversion that had corrupted his original vision and destroyed the dream.

His current return to Paradise, after one of his frequent trips to earth, was not its usual joyous occasion. What he had just witnessed had upset him and the words burnt into the side of his church had also had the same effect on his brain. He had no idea what they meant but he knew he had to find out. If Satan was up to something, then this was outside of his usual modus operandi and such crass and wanton destruction was not normally his style. The Dark Lord was not averse to sacrilege, cold blooded murder and indiscriminate mayhem but it was usually targeted at those that deserved it or were an obstacle to him achieving some goal. As far as the saint could see, the town named after him, was harmless and insignificant. The innocence of the place might possibly have annoyed Satan, but such minor things were usually ignored. There were bigger targets for his attention and evil machinations.

Deep in thought he made his way through Heaven, oblivious to anybody else as he walked. Greetings from angels and fellow saints, unaware of the catastrophe he'd just witnessed, were met by deaf ears. He needed answers and felt sure that only One could help him. Answers might not be obvious but there had to be some, and he felt sure that whatever the truth was he wouldn't like it. When he reached the outer office of God, he entered without knocking. His confused mind was preoccupied with too many thoughts to even notice his minor social faux pas. It was only

13

when he realised that he had reached his destination did he look up. Seeing God's secretary, Angelica, sat looking at him with a concerned expression on her face, made him snap out of the dramatic play being performed inside his head, a show where characters that had become his friends meeting terrible ends which they didn't deserve. He would meet them again in Heaven, but first he needed to see God.

"I'm sorry Angelica, I should have knocked first. Please forgive me. But I need to speak to God. It is important."

Angelica could tell from the look on his earnest face that he had genuine reasons for wanting to speak to her Boss and any questions to verify, and clarify, his request would be futile and just a waste of time. "Of course, Ignacius, He's in His office, do you want me to announce you?"

"Yes please. I really need to speak to Him." The repetition of his urgent words was redundant as, even without anything being spoken, she would have known that he shouldn't be delayed.

Pushing the intercom button on her desk she waited for a reply and then she spoke into the machine. "Sire, I have St. Ignacius here. He needs to see you urgently".

"Of course, send him straight in."

Despite the direct instruction he still went to the door, knocked and waited for the command to enter before walking into God's inner office. Once inside the private room he paused. Although he had met and spoken with God many times, it always filled him with awe and reverence whenever he was in His company. God was currently in the form of a 12-year-old boy but in His own office the disguise did nothing to hide His true identity. Forming his thoughts into what he hoped would be some sort of sensible and coherent order the saint proceeded to describe everything that he had just witnessed. Long ago he'd had to accept that God wasn't omniscient or omnipresent, so facts had to be given to Him and there was no assumption that He would already know everything in advance. Words flowed from the saint's mouth and God sat at his desk, listening with a rapt expression, taking everything in. Eventually the recounting of the day's experience was completed and the final description of the black words on the wall were spoken in a quivering voice but, having no Rosetta stone to translate them he couldn't tell God their meaning. Once he'd finished, he looked at God with expectant eyes, hoping for some answers that would make some sense; reasons or justification for such seemingly pointless destruction.

When God had allowed all He'd heard to sink in He spoke, His voice strong and confident, a total contrast to the prepubescent form He was currently adopting. "I need to read the message Myself. Please excuse Me." With that He disappeared, but His absence was so brief that a single blink could have hidden the moment He was away. His swift return to Earth was just enough for Him to see the writing on the wall and return to His office in Heaven, unseen by humans preoccupied with looking after the injured and dying. Sitting back in the chair behind His desk He realised that the saint was stood waiting for an explanation.

"Please sit down." He gestured to a large leather chair at the other side of His desk. "I have read the message."

"And…" The now seated saint leaning forward in anxious expectation of a single answer that would make everything clear.

"And…" It was God's turn to ponder and try and find an answer. "The words are in an old language. A writing that I have not seen for millennia, basic images unseen by any living human - not even the most industrious of archaeologists - and not recorded in any history books. I thought…I hoped… that I'd never see them again. Echoes of a dark time, a time when the world was young, and souls were more innocent than they are now - but just as destructive."

"What did it say?"

"Well, I understood the words, they were basic. But I do not understand the meaning." God ran his fingers absent mindedly through his neatly cropped hair. The gravitas of His words a contrast to His humble, childlike human form. "It said 'I am Ekeko, why have you forsaken me? Believe and be one again'."

Silence filled the room as the cryptic words were pondered by both of them. The answer raising yet more questions in the mind of St. Ignacius, but he hoped that God would elaborate without having to be asked. Luckily, he didn't have to wait too long.

Seeing the look on the saint's face God spoke. "Ekeko was… or more worryingly perhaps is once again, a god. Worshipped in the pre-Columbian days. One of the early Inca deities and a symbol of prosperity and fortune. I met him a couple of times and although he projected a jolly image, inside he was a twisted and sadistic sort of chap who would have murdered his own grandmother to get more power. Coming to think of it he did murder his grandmother for just that reason. He might have been unpredictable, but such pointless destruction wasn't his usual way of getting kicks. However, even then, like many gods in South America, he was insane and knew how to kill, or get others to do it for him, and it was on a scale that was hard to stomach. I felt certain that he was dead. I can't imagine anyone, or thing, taking his name in vain and doing this on his behalf. Besides, such destruction was not man made. If Satan is up to something, then I can't see what he hopes to achieve. But I will find out, I can promise you that Ignacius. But for now, I suggest you collect a few angels and return to the town. Assume the guise of some international rescue organisation and help the survivors in whatever ways you can. Meanwhile I will get some angels to find the culprit. Ekeko is a god who is out of his time, and this is not an act that I will tolerate. Oh, and one more thing, while you are down there, destroy the message. Some memos are best not read by the intended recipients. Humans are ingenious and I don't want to risk them finding a way to translate it."

St. Ignacius left God's office and began his mission. He knew that he'd easily be able to find more than enough willing and able angels to help him on Earth. Now his main enemy was time and the sooner he got back to the eponymous, if slightly misspelt, town the sooner he would be able to save lives.

As He stared at the now closed office door God pondered His options. How could He deal with a rogue god that He thought had died long ago? There were not always answers to questions, only more questions. Making a decision, He reached forward and pressed the button on His intercom. "Angelica, can you come into my office please?"

"Yes, my Lord?" she enquired when she had joined Him.

"I believe Dedan is still on one of his long-winded missions to Earth. No doubt he completed it a while ago but is dragging his feet about coming back." God knew that Dedan preferred to spend as much time as possible on Earth rather than being in Heaven. A strange choice but He understood that His chief angel had interesting tastes and specific peccadilloes. If sex were a sin, then Dedan would have booked his place in Hell long ago, but thankfully it wasn't as it was one of the preoccupations that God didn't judge, providing it was consensual. His trusted friend just took the invocation to 'Go forth and multiply' as a direct order, to be practiced for fun, rather than a human metaphor for telling someone to go away instead of swearing.

"Yes Sire. Last I heard he was in the Himalayas. But that was several months ago."

"The Himalayas? Interesting. But not to worry. Do you know where Roxy is?"

"Yes Sire, she keeps nipping down to Florence to smoke cigarettes, but I think she is currently having tea with Limbo again. They have become quite good friends." Angelica smiled at the thought of an angel having to creep down to Earth to enjoy a surreptitious smoke, like a school child sneaking behind a bike shed at lunch time. Cigarettes existed in Heaven but didn't give Roxy the kick that she craved. The need for her nicotine fixes often made her request missions to Earth; the closer they were to tobacconist shops the better. As the entrance to Purgatory, Limbo's domain, was in Florence that location gave her an excuse to kill two birds with one stone. Smoke a few packets of cigarettes then go have a civilised tea with scintillating, but unusual, company.

"With Limbo? That is even better. That is all; thank you Angelica." Then, before she could leave "There is one more thing, could you be an angel and make me one of your amazing cups of coffee?"

"Of course, Sir." Giving her master a genuinely happy smile as she went back into her office.

Opening a drawer to his desk, He removed a small white cell phone and dialled a number. "Oh, Hello there. This is God…"

3 – The Return to the Hall

The sound of the ringing phone caused Roxy to pause in mid-sentence. She had just been recounting a tale about one of her escapades as a human living in Germany. Limbo had been listening with a captivated look on his face. Or at least that is what his countenance could have been assumed to have taken. His flesh was blue flickering flame that rippled as he moved and changed hues to reflect his mental and emotional state. The darker the shade the more likely the unspoken message was saying 'Stay Clear'. But thanks to his liking of Roxy, and being enchanted by her presence, he was at his most relaxed state. The blue of his flaming but cold flesh was such a pale shade that he was almost white. The unwelcome and unexpected interruption made the tone turn slightly darker.

"I am sorry my dear." Giving Roxy an apologetic smile, he put his fine bone china cup of tea, and matching saucer, on to the coffee table that was between the two of them, reached down the side of his comfortable sofa chair and lifted up an old fashioned 1920's style candle stick type telephone. Holding one part to his ear he spoke into the mouthpiece, a quizzical look on his face. "Hello?"

Thanks to his job as the judge of souls, that didn't quite qualify for direct entrance to Heaven or Hell, he tended not to get friends ringing him up for a general chat to see how he was or invite him out for a beer or two. In fact, in the decades since the device had been installed, he had only ever had to answer it five times, with even one of those calls being a wrong number, a drunken man in Belgium insistently demanding, with slurring words, to speak to someone called Mavis and taking some persuading that she wasn't there.

Realising who was on the other end of the phone Limbo respectfully altered his posture in his chair, becoming more upright. Putting his hand over the mouthpiece he whispered to Roxy "It's God!" That simple sentence made Roxy give him a puzzled look. She mouthed silently back at him 'What does He want?' soliciting a shrug from Limbo, indicating that he didn't have an answer yet.

"Hello old Chap. How are you?... Oh, really?... But that is impossible. He is in the hall... I am almost positive. But okay, if you insist. And then what?... I hope it doesn't come to that... Are you sure it isn't one of Satan's little tricks? Yes, I know you are right. Of course, she is here now, of course I will ask her to investigate and then let you know. Yes, she certainly is. Tootle pip, old boy." Returning the earpiece to the main body of the phone he placed it back on the floor next to his chair and sat looking silently at Roxy. He was deep in thought, his calculating mind trying to make sense of what he had just been told.

The one-sided conversation, punctuated with silences as Limbo listened to God, that Roxy had just half heard, had her sitting on the edge of the large and elegantly designed sofa. She raised her eyebrows questioningly, in expectation of that simple action would initiate some answers to all the questions she hadn't asked but assumed Limbo would provide unprompted.

His silence was broken as he looked at Roxy with a fixed stare, as if he had momentarily forgotten that she was in the same room. "I am sorry Roxy." His voice had the capability of entering people's brains without having to be processed via the ears, but despite that it still managed to covey his uncertainty and discomfiture at what he had just been told. "That was God." The statement about the caller was redundant but he felt that he still needed to reiterate it. "There has been a disaster in Bolivia, it seems that a town has been devastated by an earthquake and lightning attack. I think the human expression is 'a double whammy'. An act of god, but not done by God. Apparently, St. Ignacius was there at the time and there was a message left written into what was left of a church wall. A calling card, in an archaic language, claiming to be Ekeko asking why he has been forsaken."

"Ekeko?" Roxy wasn't totally following Limbo or, if she was on the same path, then she was several steps behind him.

"Yes, a dead god, you passed his statue in the Hall when you first came to visit me with Dedan. All being well he is still there. If not..." he paused to gather his thoughts, unsure how to finish his sentence. "There could be a lot of problems and I have no idea how to fix them."

Roxy looked in his marble blue eyes, surrounded by, now cobalt coloured, blue flaming flesh. They had a distant look as if he was staring at something 1,000 yards, or several thousand years, away. His thoughts lost looking for sense in a foggy mind, trying to believe the impossible, or what previous experience had at least always proven to be impossible.

Eventually more words formed in his brain and found their way to his mouth where they took the opportunity to reluctantly escape. "God would like you to go into the hall again and see if his, or any other statues for that matter, are not there. Once you've checked you need to go and report to Him." He lifted his left hand and, out of nowhere, several sheets of A4 paper and a pencil appeared, the cold fire of his skin running across them but leaving the paper undamaged. He then passed them to Roxy. "Hopefully you will not need these but take them just in case you have to make a list. Oh, how I hope you do not need them!"

She took the proffered paper and pencil and stood up.

"I am sorry, Roxy, it looks like the rest of your wonderful and fascinating tale will have to wait for another day."

Her first visit to the Hall of Dead Gods had been several months ago, accompanying Dedan. Since then, she had walked through it many times on her frequent visits to take tea with Limbo. However, like many works of art that are seen frequently, she had begun to take all the statues for granted and stopped taking any notice of them. Originally, she'd been fascinated by all the deities that had lost all their believers and turned to marble images of themselves, as death struck, but the novelty had eventually worn off and she had started to walk through the hall as if they were no longer there or the magnificent objects were just passé. Having to take notice of them once more made her remember how beautiful they all were. No matter how evil or malevolent a particular god might have been, or unusual the pose they had adopted on death, she couldn't help but be impressed by the magnificence of the supernaturally made statues. Sculptures of similar sizes to Michelangelo's David and equal in their beauty.

Strolling along the hall, she could see the statues on their plinths towering over her. Men and women, young and old, of various shapes and sizes; some standing, others sat and even a few laid down. Like photos of all stages of life converted into three-dimensional stone. One was captured in the act of straining while sitting on a toilet. Another, with a long flowing beard, was stood drinking from a cup made from a cow horn. As she progressed along the hall Roxy had to supress a loud laugh as she discovered one extinct god stood with his trousers around his ankles and his penis in his hand in a pose that looked like he had found oblivion midway through rapid and intense masturbation. His strained expression indicating that he had not reached final satisfaction, going before he could even come, his look of squinted-eyed concentration caught for all eternity in the strange gallery of beings that no longer had followers. Apart from their gender, the physical attributes that went with them, and occasional choice of partially animal shaped bodies, there was an equally varied collection of postures. Roxy half expected to find one pleasuring itself with some ancient phallus shaped object, but fortunately she didn't see one in mid stroke as death's stony oblivion had struck.

After about 10 minutes of admiring the different gods and wondering who they were, where they came from and if they were good or bad, she came to a plinth that didn't have anyone on top of it. Briefly she checked behind it, to ensure that the rock monument hadn't simply toppled over and left a pile of rubble on the far side. Returning to the front of the unoccupied base she looked at the name engraved into the marble, but it was in an unfamiliar language. The symbols were just like squares with rounded corners, random dots and smaller squares inside them. Removing the paper from her trouser pocket she began to try and copy the words but, not being an artist, the first attempt bore little resemblance to what she was supposed to be copying. The pictograms ended up looking more like badly drawn kittens looking through windows than depictions of an ancient language. Discarding the piece of paper, she pulled out another sheet. This time acknowledging that copying was out of the question so, placing the paper against the cold white stone, she rubbed the end of the pencil firmly across the paper, the spaces where the letters were leaving lighter shades of grey amongst the black charcoal of the harder surfaces. Once finished she held the paper up to the light and compared the image with the real thing. Happy with the facsimile, she carefully folded it and placed it in her pocket and proceeded along the hallway towards the exit door in the distance. Seeing another empty plinth further down the hall, on the opposite side of the walkway, she repeated the process. Eventually, after zig zagging along the hall, she'd managed to reach the exit and found that there were only five gods unaccounted for. One of the plinths had been badly damaged but if she put some of the pieces together like a giant stone jigsaw the name was just legible. A couple more had names on the plinths which were written in the modern, or at least Latin, alphabet but to avoid any risk of errors the pencil and paper rubbing exercise was repeated for those as well.

Eventually she had completed her task and was about to head for the door leading to the Piazza Della Limbo, the square in Florence where the dimensional portal crossed from Purgatory to Earth, when she paused. For a while something had been nagging at her mind, but she couldn't quite put her finger on it. Not only was there was something about the name Ekeko but there was something else as well. Something that could be important, if only she could remember what it was. Roxy wanted to get back to Heaven and report but until the niggling half thoughts, which were spiralling around her brain, had been captured and resolved she knew that she couldn't simply go through the door; her brief appearance in Italy a precursor to opening another portal and being back in Paradise.

Then it came to her, the tiny thread of a memory dragged into her consciousness and the more she pulled at it the more it filled her mind with what she had been searching for. 'Ekeko, of course!'. Running back along the hall she finally reached the first empty plinth that she'd encountered. Even if the statue had been present, she still couldn't be certain that it was the former final resting place of that particular god, but the location seemed right.

On her first visit to Purgatory, she had paused by one of the dead gods and Dedan had spoken of Ekeko. Walking behind the plinth she swore under her breath. The crude scatological expletive a mixture of anger, frustration and despair as she realised that something was missing.

On her first visit she had been pursuing some demons and to avoid any risk of being judged incorrectly by Limbo, when she had first entered the hall, had left some weapons behind the plinth, and they were no longer there. Perhaps this was the wrong god, she half-heartedly hoped, even though she was convinced that it was the right one. She knew for certain that the weapons had been left on that side of the hall so, if she looked, she should theoretically be able to see them somewhere. But her heart sank as the more she looked the more she didn't see them; they were not there. She wasn't sure what an old, but pissed off, South American god would do with a couple of semi-automatic pistols but whatever it was she doubted it would be good. But if the angry deity could wipe out a whole town without them, then two guns might just be an insignificant issue. Or at least she hoped that they would be.

Returning to the exit door she checked her pockets to ensure that the papers, containing the absconders' names, were still in place. Assured that they were there, she gave the hall one last look, as if to acknowledge the existence of gods that had once been real and a few that had, somehow, returned to existence. Pushing against the seemingly solid door she passed through it, the atoms in her body mingling with those of the wood as she passed from one dimensional reality into that of Earth's. Standing in the empty, seemingly insignificant, and plain piazza she stood blinking in the bright sunlight, a stark contrast to the gentle soft blue light of the hall. The afternoon sun was about to move behind the roof opposite her, so the shadow cast was only reaching her feet.

She still clearly remembered the square from the first time she had been there. The decapitated human form of the demon, that she had helped to kill and send the spirit back to Hell, had long since been removed by the puzzled police. It had been high summer then and the city had been full of tourists. Now it was late spring and there were fewer visitors to be seen walking along the street that passed the tiny and seldom noticed square. Whereas, before, she had been left drenched in perspiration Roxy felt comfortable in her black designer jeans and t-shirt; the heat was also less oppressive. The air was cool and fresh and even if she hadn't already known it, she could have sensed that she was back in the country of her birth. Italy had its own vibrant feel, and it permeated her very essence. She sighed nostalgically, wishing that she'd been able to spend more time in the place while she'd been alive. But such regrets were immaterial now.

Then she considered a slight detour, a visit to a shop to buy a several packets of cigarettes, and then to smoke a few. Although she knew it wouldn't take up too much time, she reluctantly thought better of it. The names of the missing gods had to be handed to God. Hopefully He would know what to do with them and be able to return them to their previous rigid state. But as the whole subject and concept was new to her, she had no idea how that would happen. After all, how does one god destroy another seemingly invincible one? And if it was possible was there a risk that Ekeko could try and do the same thing to God? It was a philosophical question that she doubted any human philosopher had ever contemplated.

At will the inter-dimensional portal, leading back to Heaven, appeared just in front of the wall by her side, an almost invisible door, a tall rectangle of seemingly solidified air shimmering in the dwindling sunlight.

Taking a quick look around her, to ensure that she wasn't being observed, she stepped through the meeting of reality and unreality and disappeared. Then, as if it had never existed, the portal disappeared leaving the atoms in the air to return to their normal gaseous state. Light atoms of gas dancing above the tighter packed molecules of the ground.

4 – Hell, Oh I Must be Going

The torment chambers, located in all the numerous rings of Hell, were almost as varied in their forms of pain infliction as there were sins which caused the damned souls to be there in the first place. Every punishment fit for the moral, or immoral, crimes committed in life. If you tortured someone, then you would receive the same, only magnified and implemented in ways unimaginable to the limited human mind. Pain felt in Hell would be beyond tolerance of even the toughest and best trained Special Forces soldier or Secret Agent on Earth. No orifice having a 'No Entry' sign or out of bounds to a wide array of pointy, blunt or just cumbersome implements, most of which were never originally designed for such undignified insertions. And when it came to the use of these objects it wasn't just normally existing holes in the body which were probed or investigated. Agricultural machinery could be used for mutilation, mechanical tools could be utilised for more than removing bolts or formerly well attached metallic nuts, while plumber's equipment could cause more than just water leakages. As for the inventors of some of the more obscure cobbler's tools of the trade, they would have cried in sadness, and abject horror, to see the fruit of their genius corrupted in such perverse and unconventional ways. Suffice to say pain and suffering was what Hell was all about and the demons who were responsible for handing it out to the souls, that failed to qualify for entry into Heaven, had only one solid and true guarantee: for the rest of eternity the less than innocent victims would suffer. The demons knew that their prisoners would be there forever, providing them all with a career that would keep them busy until time came to an end.

Today was no exception to the monotonous rule of repeated, day to day routine of horrors issued by some and received by others. A Dolore Demon, in a chamber designed to replicate a medieval dungeon and torture chamber, was currently busying herself with the intricate, complex and delicate task of making some small but sturdy prickly pear cacti disappear into a part of the anatomy of a condemned soul's body which had never evolved to repeatedly receive such an unwanted gift. Impervious and blithely oblivious to the unending screams of agony, she carried out her task with a skill that only many centuries of repeated practice could ever provide, while her maniacal, sadistic and evil smile would not have been out of place on the face of any high school physical education teacher on Earth. If such punishments were allowed by education authorities, then gym classes would be even more terrifying and humiliating than they already were.

The demon was sat on a padded milking stool and had just completed the latest game of introducing a fruit into the unattractive fleshy bowel when she turned slightly so that she could retrieve another handful of the green and red objects, from a basket behind her, ready for their dispersal. When she returned to her upright seated position, she was shocked to see that the intended recipient had vanished. The shackles and chains, that had held his feet in their reluctant akimbo position were empty and just laid on the dirty and fruit juice-stained floor. The holes in the stocks that had restrained the damned soul's neck and wrists, were now just empty spaces.

The initial surprise was quickly replaced by consternation before worry finally won the emotional battle and filled her mind. Franticly looking around the demoness couldn't see any sign of her absconded victim. Thoughts of how he had managed to escape began to form. Speculation that, somehow, a fellow demon was playing some sort of complex practical joke on her came and quickly went. Could she expect the freed soul to pounce and start enacting revenge on her for the many centuries of pain she had inflicted on him?

She checked the basket and saw that it was still worryingly full and if used against her could seriously impede the fun activities that she had planned for her date, when she had finished her shift, with a particularly randy and well-endowed Komo Demon later that evening. When the demon had asked her out on the date, he had said that he'd like to suck on her fruit and eat her prickly pear, but she hadn't thought he was meaning that!

The Dolore Demon's final reaction was to pretend nothing had happened and act as if all was normal. One damned soul, more or less, was insignificant in Hell so why worry about an individual that might be hobbling around the corridors of the place, with a strange walk and fruit juice dripping from an unusual place? But she knew that, although they might be normal for demons, cover-ups and lies were all too often discovered with the perpetrators receiving far worse punishments than if they'd simply just told the appropriate authorities. The demons could easily swap places with the damned and that was not a situation that any of them wanted. In Hell, it was certainly better to give than receive.

Demonic hierarchies were quite simple but very rigid. In the dog-eat-dog world that made up the mentality that permeated Hell, going over someone's head could result in the guilty person quite literally briefly losing theirs before it was inserted into a place it was not meant to go. The levels of authority tended to be fairly simple, there were the demons that gave out the day-to-day punishments to the damned, and then there were the masters of all the chambers that ensured that the demons did their jobs with enthusiasm. There was Satan's second in command, there was his private secretary who tended to control the flow of information, and finally there was Satan himself. For lots of reasons, mostly involving the desire to avoid pain, the vast majority of demons preferred not to have face to face meetings with their supreme master. If he didn't like the news given to him, it was not unknown for him to punish the bearer of the bad tidings in ways that made even the vilest demon shudder and their blood run cold.

With dark thoughts filling her mind the walk to find her supervisor was slow and full of fear of impending recriminations and something more than a mere verbal assault. When she finally found him, he was in a good mood, or as good as a demon could get. He'd just vented his spleen, in a quite literal way, on a damned soul that he'd discovered hiding behind an iron maiden torture device. When she had finished explaining to him what had happened, he had started to lose his pleasant demeanour and had to struggle to refrain from using violence on her. However, despite him believing her story, he didn't understand how it could have happened and was concerned that the occurrence could have wider repercussions than just head scratching. He harboured the same initial reactions as his underling but was wise enough to know that he could always pass the buck if any metaphorical brown stuff were to hit rotating blades. Turning to walk towards the chamber's exit, he said one simple word to the worried looking demoness. "Come!"

Like condemned prisoners walking to the gallows, the journey was in silence. As they walked along the long and winding passages leading to Satan's inner sanctum and well-guarded domain, they had too much on their minds to indulge in small talk or general chatter. The minutes that it took seemed to last hours as images of possible punishments filled their minds.

The demon responsible for running the punishment area was also busily thinking of the right words to us so that he could ensure that all responsibility would land squarely on the shoulders of his subordinate. He had been an office manager when he had been alive on Earth, so such actions and tactics were second nature to him. Sacrifice others to ensure no finger of blame could ever point at him. If he'd been a frying pan, he'd have been non-stick.

Suddenly they were not alone; other chamber commanders and underlings joined them as they all strode silently in the same direction. Soon the corridors became crowded, and demons began to jostle with each other in attempts to ensure that they could get to the front of the line. Gentle shoving soon became more pronounced and direct. Elbows were less than accidentally swung into ribs of neighbouring demons. Feet were extended at unusual angles so that others could trip and fall to the ground and, once they were down there, would not be given the opportunity to get up. Demons saving energy and walking over prostrate backs, limbs and heads, rather than walking around and avoiding them. Any attempts to rise, and avoid the trampling, thwarted by malicious colleagues. It was fortunate that most demons have thick skulls otherwise more serious injuries would have been received.

On they went, like a marching army gathering even greater numbers as they got nearer to their destination. Eventually the narrow corridor became blocked as no demon was willing to give way to any other. Bodies wedged tightly against each other with their destination tantalisingly close, they could see the entrance just ahead guarded by four Marching Horde demons, members of Satan's own personal private bodyguard. They were eyeing up the approaching crowd with suspicion and had their AK47 assault rifles ready in their hands, warily pointed at the crowd in anticipation of trouble. Revolts by demons in Hell were not frequent but they were known to happen so the soldiers were taking no chances. Fingers hesitantly placed over triggers, they tried to make sense of the demon cork in the bottleneck with the ones in the front trying to move forward and the ones behind them trying to hold them back while the others, even further away, pulling on those ahead of them. If any were to simultaneously release their grips, then the whole mass of bodies could rush and overrun them before they even had time to fire off a single round.

Greggg, a Pompös Demon, who was the Marching Horde equivalent of a sergeant in charge of the guard, decided that his small detachment would be woefully inadequate if things were to get nasty; and in Hell nasty was not unusual and could be REALLY NASTY! Turning to face one of his troops standing behind him, he barked out an instruction in a way that only Sergeants seem to be able to do "You! Go get Satan's assistant and bring him down here to talk to this rabble. And find reinforcements, lots of them." Without pausing to allow the demon to move, or even acknowledge the instructions, he added the mandatory military admonishment, "Well? What are you waiting for? Get a move on!"

As with the rank in any human army he wasn't high up the military food chain but as far as Greggg was concerned he was more important than any general and, at least to his underlings, his word was law. The unfortunate soldier knew better than to dawdle, or at least not to do it within sight of his sergeant, so he quickly ran into the relative safety of Satan's private domain. Once there, and safely out of ear shot, he released an expletive in Ugaritic. However, thanks to that language being extinct for over 3,000 years, very few other people would have understood what it meant and, thanks to his accent, even if they had it would have been lost a lot in translation. The nearest a modern linguistic expert would have come to giving an explanation was that the demon would like to stick a primitive farming instrument, similar to an early plough, into his foe's armpit. So as pithy insults went it left a lot to be desired.

Despite the anger he felt, which wasn't a unique emotion for demons anyway, he carried out his instructions promptly. First, he found a small detachment of soldiers patrolling one of the inner corridors and instructed them to go and add force of numbers to the outer door. Then he proceeded to run up the stairway leading to Satan's assistant's office. On reaching the closed door he knocked, and without waiting for an invitation to enter, he opened it and walked in.

Sat at the desk, poring over some information in a giant red leather-bound ledger was Satan's latest assistant, Kran. He was just the latest in a long line of private secretaries that had been given the job after the predecessor had made some minor mistake or failed to please their dark master. Ever since Satan had sent Stuart, his long-standing clerk, on a mission to Earth the tenure of replacements had not been long. This precarious role had left Kran in a nervous state, that was bordering on paranoia, in case he accidentally said or did anything that resulted in him being sent to some deep and painful cave where he would suffer for his clerical errors. This perilous position made him less arrogant or supercilious than his power and authority would normally have permitted. Looking at the soldier Kran smiled nervously

"Hello, how can I help you?" the words and tone of voice far too polite to be released so close to Satan's office.

The soldier, taken aback by such civility, was momentarily left unprepared for the question. "Sir, there are a lot of demons just outside the inner sanctum. And they are…. Stuck."

"Stuck?" Kran understood the word and meaning but the context eluded him.

"Yes sir. There are so many of them that they are wedged against the walls and can't move. I've been sent to fetch you." The final simple expression would not have been tolerated by Stuart. Such words would have had him shouting and snarling at the presumptive soldier, but Kran was no Stuart. "I think it is best if you come and talk to them and see what they want. Ensure that they are not up to mischief before we open fire."

Nonplussed by the request Kran felt that he had no option but to agree and follow the member of the Marching Horde. "Alright, please lead the way."

Feeling that running would be inappropriate for someone of such authority, the soldier walked, adopting a fast pace so that they could get to the awaiting crowd as soon as possible without Kran having to exert himself too much. In the soldier's opinion the more powerful someone was they less they liked to physically exert themselves.

On arriving Kran felt more overwhelmed than a newly qualified proctologist on his first day at his office, with the blocked passage that he had to deal with looking menacing and liable to imminently release its contents in a messy way. With a phalanx of demon Marching Horde standing closely behind him, weapons cocked and at the ready, he felt that going forward or moving back were equally unpalatable options. Caught between the devil and well… the devil, his feeling of insecurity began to grow. Approaching the nearest demon in the compacted mass he saw that it was straining to move forward but was being held back by hands which were grabbing his shoulders.

"All right, you there. What do you want?"

"I need to speak to Satan." The request was then repeated by those behind him "No, I need to see Satan" which in turn was met with others shouting "No, I need to see him first!" The cries of demons desperate to see their dark master filling the already crowded corridor. Each extra voice adding to the din and making it impossible for anyone to clearly make out what anyone else was saying. The general cacophony having the opposite to the desired effect. Instead of Kran hearing the pleas and picking someone to go first all he got was an indistinguishable blur of sound. He shouted as loudly as he could but his demands for silence were lost in the noise being thrown at him. Frustrated he turned to Greggg with a resigned look on his face.

"If you'd be so good as to get their attention" and gesticulated to the waiting AK47 rifle and pointed to the ceiling. The signal was clear to the sergeant as he raised the barrel from the heads of the crowd and fired a volley of rounds into the stone ceiling of the narrow alleyway. Each round hitting the surface and sending chunks of rock, blackened from centuries of flame with hints of yellow from the brimstone, onto now terrified heads, the debris, and deafening noise, making them all fall into a frightened silence.

"Thank you. See? Isn't that better?" Kran shouted, this time his voice being heard by all. "I am going to speak to one person and one person alone. If it turns into some giant shouting match, and you all start making noises, then I will not hesitate to give the instruction to open fire and not take their fingers off of the triggers until the Marching Horde troops run out of bullets." Pointing to a demon at the front of the crowd, he barked, "You there, do you understand?" There was silence as the demon that had been randomly chosen looked around to ensure that he was the focus of the question. "Yes, I mean you!"

"Err, yes sir."

"Good, then you had better tell me what is going on and what you want!"

"Well sir, one of the damned souls in my chamber was in mid punishment when they just… disappeared. I need to tell Satan and get further instructions." Relieved that he had got to speak first he fell silent, convinced that now the message was passed on so was any responsibility or accusations of culpability.

Turning his attention to another demon, in the front row, he pointed to it and spoke again "And you there, what are you here for?"

"That happened to me as well, a prisoner in my chamber just disappeared. There one second and the next she was gone. No trace of him to be seen."

Kran repeated the same question to others and received similar information. It was soon apparent that all the demons, stuck in one giant cramped huddle, had the same thing happen within their chambers. The condemned disappearing with no trace or explanation. "Alright, you there" pointing to the nearest demon, "come with me. We'll go see Satan together. As for the rest of you wait here for further instructions."

The demon that had been selected for the visit to Satan began to regret his eagerness to be first in the crowd. The concept of safety in numbers was good but not so great when the number was simply one. When it was just him face to face with Satan then there was no safety at all. With Kran walking just ahead of him and with two members of the Marching Horde close behind he had an ominous feeling of impending pain and suffering. Each step felt as if his legs were made of lead as he forced himself onwards towards the private room of the master of Hell. Eventually, after what felt like an eternity to the demon, they reached first Kran's office and once there, he found himself in front of the large and imposing door leading to Satan's room. Kran gave it a firm and loud knock then stepped back.

"Come in, you pathetic turd. What do you want?" Satan's voice was booming and full of a burning rage that could have destroyed any forest.

Kran nodded, indicating that he should enter. The demon attempted to push the door open, but it only moved an inch, and that small shift was escorted by a scream-like wrenching noise as the door resisted any attempt to make it move. Undeterred the demon decided that he needed to use more force. Placing his shoulder against it he pushed even harder, and the recalcitrant door finally decided to give ground to the demon. The door had made its point; it might not be in charge but wasn't to be taken for granted and simply pushed about. Finally, allowed access, the demon walked into the office closely followed by Kran and the two heavily armed and armoured guards. Once inside, they saw Satan standing in front of his fireplace, staring intently at the flames. They stood silently waiting for him to acknowledge their presence, but he didn't move. He knew that they were there, it was hard to sneak into his room when he had such a loud and annoying door, but he had no desire to rush and turn away from the sight of the soothing flames. Gradually he turned to look at his guests, a sneer on his face revealing his contempt for what he saw. Whenever a demon came to see him, it usually meant bad news, so the suspicion he had of the cowering specimen, stood before him, was overwhelming.

"And...."

"Sir?" The demon was puzzled by the single unsupported word.

Sighing in exasperation Satan gave the unfortunate demon a stare that could have melted lead. "AND what do you want? You idiot." The question being as much a veiled threat as a request for information.

Hesitantly the demon began to recount his own experience of losing a damned soul, how the former human had been receiving an acid shower when he'd simply disappeared. In an attempt to ensure that no blame could be levelled at him no overly graphic detail was left out.

As he listened Satan was pacing the floor with his arms behind his back and with a distant look on his face as if he were simply talking a refreshing walk in the open air. He was taking it all in but wasn't revealing any emotions. The lack of reaction did nothing to calm the petrified demon. When the visitor had finished, he fell silent and the atmosphere in the room became oppressive.

Satan looked at him with calm eyes. "I see." Then, turning his gaze to Kran, he spoke with an impassive voice. "Have there been other instances of this happening?"

"It would appear so sir, there are quite a few demons just outside your gates recounting similar experiences."

"I see." There was a dark and heavy silence as Satan paused to contemplate on the appropriate course of action. His instincts said that mindless violence, and the infliction of pain, would be suitable and fun; however, he knew that it would achieve little. The lost souls would not be returned because of it and there would be fewer demons available to inflict punishments. "Take some details and then send them back to their punishment chambers and get them back to work. The damned won't punish themselves!"

"Very good Sire." And with that, Kran turned and began to pull the reluctant door open, the angry grinding noise getting the demon's attention and assuring him that it was time to leave as quickly as he could before Satan changed his mind and decided to redecorate his quarters in a delicate shade of demon brain. Bowing slightly, he rushed through the now open doorway, closely followed by the Marching Horde guards. Once he was alone Satan sat at his desk, his elbows resting on the dark oak surface, his hands steepled as he contemplated all that he had been told. He wasn't sure what had happened, but he had suspicions. And if he was right, it could work to his advantage. But for the moment all he could do was wait; wait and plan.

His wry smile soon evaporated as his renegade sound system took that moment to fill his room with Barry Manilow singing his cover version of 'We've got tonight'. The sound made Satan cringe. Ever since he'd had the machine installed, in a futile attempt to fill his private room with thrash metal, hard rock or punk music, the device had taken on a mind of its own and found its own evil gratification by taunting the evil master. In its own right, and if only played occasionally, there was nothing wrong with the music of Barry Manilow and Satan would have been able to put up with it if it had been tempered with a variety of other artists and genres. Even the occasional country and western song would have been tolerable if it had infused the sound with a modicum of variety. A smattering of George Jones or Hank Williams might seem like Hell, but if it gave some contrast to the easy listening crooner it would have been welcomed. Unfortunately, for Satan at least, the speakers adhered to their limited play list and even when demolished managed to reform themselves and continue playing. The irony wasn't lost on him that he was the master of Hell and could inflict punishment on any of its residents but he, in turn, was punished by his own music player. Sometimes life, or the afterlife, just wasn't fair.

5 – Spirits Having Flown

Although Heaven, by definition, was a place to be desired, a destination to be sought and not relinquished once found, there were the few that preferred to be elsewhere. Satan had chosen to be the master of Hell rather than a servant there and Dedan, God's chief demon hunter, often looked for excuses to go back to Earth as he missed the seemingly organised chaos, bustle and smells of the place. But on the whole souls, on arrival, tended to like Heaven so much that they had no desire to leave and therefore stayed where they were. However, now, things seemed to be changing ever so slightly in that regard. Whether they liked it or not the ripples caused by events were spreading.

Things change in Heaven. As new generations pass on their ideas, pleasures come with them as elements of their desires become real. For example, modern clean, sanitised and generic trendy coffee shops have become de rigueur on most high streets in the western world, often with many of them living next door to each other. The same overpriced and similar tasting cups of coffees could be bought in Paris, Rome, New York or Sydney. With the influx of good souls arriving in Heaven their idea of paradise included such shops, so they are now there. Obviously, as you'd expect, the coffee was not astronomically expensive, in fact it is free. There are not the long and slow lines as people waited to be served, there were always tables available and the brews actually tasted like perfection in a cup. The one exception to the taste rule was the liquids infused with pumpkin spice, but that was for the Americans who tended to lack any sense of taste when it came to coffee. These new locations had no need Wi-Fi either. The customers didn't have to sit staring into cell phone screens to try and socialise; they could sit there and talk to each other, face to face. Possibly a frightening concept on Earth, but when you die, and move on, the signal on people's phones dies with you and you have to resort to such antiquated but well proven methods of communication. After a while, the people get used to it and learn that the unusual experience was extremely enjoyable.

In one such coffee shop St. Andreas was sat drinking a coffee with Sandean, an angel from ancient Petra, discussing comparative experiences, whilst living on Earth, when suddenly the old and bearded angel disappeared. The saint had few faults but one of the biggest ones was his conversational skills or, to be precise, his lack of them. He had the ability, usually only honed by a few women, to take the simplest of pieces of information and string it out so that it seemed to last for a painful eternity, making a thirty second news flash become three hours of aural torture. After a few minutes of having to listen to him digress from a topic, and drone on about some insignificant matter, his companions often found excuses to leave and go and do some other critical thing that they had only just realised was critical and needed doing. Even if there was nothing to be done, they would gladly commit the minor sin of lying just to get away from the brain melting tedium that the saint induced just so that they no longer had to suffer his prattling on. Even men, that had lived long married lives and learnt the skill of switching off when their wives were talking at them lacked the skill to put up with his monotone and adenoidal voice.

Although other angels and saints often left his presence, he'd never experienced them simply vanishing into thin air before; that was just rude. He was left sitting on his own looking around the room trying to see his erstwhile companion but realised that he was nowhere to be seen amongst the other customers sitting around the place. He even checked underneath his own table to ensure that Sandean hadn't just fallen asleep and found sanctuary there. This was rare but had happened on a couple of occasions. These curious glances, and his apparent desire to talk to someone, were not unnoticed by those sat around him. Many had experienced his company before and had no desire to have it inflicted on them again. As a method of self-preservation, they quickly drank their drinks, ate their snacks and left the place. All intent on being somewhere else, or anywhere else for that matter, as quickly as they could manage. The location unimportant, just as long as it was out of ear shot of St. Andreas.

Finding himself alone he contemplated what could have happened to Sandean. He hadn't a clue and couldn't explain it, but he felt sure that he needed to talk to someone about it. There was no one close by, but he was sure that he could find somebody if he tried hard enough and caught them unawares. Whether they wanted to listen to him or would be able to survive the whole tale was a different matter.

Making a decision, he left his table and made his way to see Angelica. He felt that he really should report the occurrence to somebody, and he knew from experience that she was a good listener. Or at least he thought so, whereas I reality she often slid tiny earphones into her ears whenever he walked into her office and, as they were hidden by her hair, she could listen intently to music while she gave him the expressions that she thought he'd like, nodding sagely every now and then. Thus, she managed to save her brain from possibly melting and running out of her nose thanks to its inability to escape his voice and tiresome tales. Such a thing had never happened to an angel before but, as she saw it, there was a first time for everything, and she didn't want to take the risk.

By the time the saint arrived at the entrance to God's Personal Assistant's office, he found that he wasn't the only person wanting to talk at her. The doorway was blocked by several angels and the rest of her room was full of various saints and angels, of both genders, cramped together all trying to be the focus of her attention so that they could recount their experiences of vanishing angels. Voices were raised as they all spoke together in the assumption, or hope at least, that they would be the one that she heard. In response, Angelica was valiantly trying to keep calm, remain professional and avoid shouting at them, but her patience was wearing thin, and she was getting dangerously close to losing the battle where the released expletives would begin to escape her mouth and fill the room.

The combined din eventually made its way into God's room and necessitated His investigation. He opened His door and, thanks to the number of people squashing into the adjacent room, several bodies were forced against it. The sudden mix of additional space and gravity caused them to fall into His office, some landing on the floor and other's landing on the bodies that had already landed on the floor. Thankfully God's divine reflexes allowed Him to see the impending collapse and jump out of their way, otherwise He would have been buried under the avalanche of people. Helping the fallen to regain their footing, He assured the embarrassed and reluctant interlopers into His room that 'such things happen' and 'no harm had been done'. Once He was sure that they had injured nothing more than their pride, He turned his attention to the crowded and noisy antechamber. He was not averse to noise, as long as it was friendly, and people playing a strange game of sardines was no sin either, but there were standards and such disturbances right outside His room were unusual and should only be done if there was a valid reason.

Being the supreme being, He could quite easily have opted for a booming voice that would have grabbed everybody's attention, brought silence to the room and probably created cracks in the walls of any building within a mile of where he was. However, thankfully, there was more to His vocal repertoire than just shouting. It might be Satan's party trick, but God knew how to talk to people in a more civilised way. "Silence please!" The request was made with a polite voice that managed to carry gravitas and authority while, at the same time, sounding friendly and jocular. The words had their desired effect and the entire group fell respectfully silent. All were well aware that when they were told to quiet by God then they had better shut up and do it promptly. Enjoying the new-found silence, He smiled indulgently. "Right, to save a lot of time and to avoid everyone trying to speak all at once, I am just going to have a quick read of all your minds. I hope none of you object, but it is the best way for me to find out from you all off you what the problem is." His voice calm and full of reassuring tones. The words met by a gentle murmur of agreement.

Despite human dogma and expectations God wasn't omnipresent or omnipotent. The ability to watch everybody for every single second of the day would have been simply impossible and even if He could do it, the idea of witnessing people going to the toilet, picking their noses or masturbating was not something He was into, this in turn ensured that people could go about their business free from any Heavenly voyeurism. He could see into specific minds if He so chose to and could often find the specific person amongst the millions of minds on Earth but even that could be draining and hard to sustain for long periods. He found most humans far too complex or neurotic and seeing into their minds occasionally gave Him a headache. However, when required, He could look into to a few minds and briefly take a snapshot of their thoughts and then be able to look at them in the same way a human would look at a photograph.

On this occasion He had a willing audience, and their minds would be relatively free from all the mental turmoil that populated the living's psyches. Concentrating, He allowed the prominent concerns of them all to enter His mind. Then, within a millisecond, He was done. Briefly pausing, He analysed the data and realised that, despite the varied locations and circumstances they had all encountered the same thing. They were talking to angels one minute and then, in the blink of an eye, the other person had disappeared without a trace. A mystery, but He suspected that it could have some connection to the occurrence in Bolivia, but He'd need more information and hopefully Roxy would be back soon with more pieces for the mysterious jigsaw.

"Thank you, ladies and gentlemen, very interesting. If you could form an orderly line and give the details of the missing angels to Angelica that would be appreciated. Thank you." Then, allowing the fallen, or toppled over, angels to leave his room and join the line to speak to his assistant, He closed His door and returned to His desk to think. There was one theme on His mind and that could be summed up in a single word, 'Trouble'.

As it was Heaven the residents had turned the act of queuing into an art form that would have made the English, with their knack of patiently standing in line, look rambunctious, rowdy and bordering on anarchic. Without further words being spoken they all created a long and civilised line that snaked from the front of Angelica's desk along her office, out of her door and into the adjacent corridor. The angels and saints casually chatted with each other, mostly happy that they knew that they would be listened to and all they had to do was wait.

The one main exception was an unfortunate angel that was the penultimate one in the long line. He was stuck next to St. Andreas and had to listen to his inane, repetitive and vacuous recounting of Sandean's disappearance, but what should have been a simple tale had metamorphosed into a meandering recounting of how the saint had found a piece of wayward litter on Earth and how he had disposed of it. If the poor angel hadn't got such an important thing to report to Angelica, he'd have made his excuses and found a secluded room to hide in and beat his head against the brick wall so the pain could remove the numbness of St. Andreas's verbal equivalent of a colonic irrigation.

Roxy had rematerialized in Heaven via one of the portals and had decided to report directly to God rather than getting changed first. Entering the central area of Heaven, where God resided, she walked up the luxurious carpeted stairway with vast cream coloured marble columns on either side. The splendour of the place always took her breath away but, on this occasion, she could sense something in the air. She couldn't quite put her finger on what it was but there seemed to be a tension like an invisible coiled spring waiting to be released. As she walked higher, past numerous equally beautifully decorated floors, the feeling in her chest seemed to grow stronger, as if fear and confusion had become air and was forcefully filling her lungs; then she was at the top of the stairs.

The corridor, leading to God's office was a stark contrast to the opulence and elegance of the steps. Plainly decorated as if to deliberately avoid unnecessary ostentation and pretension, the simple and hardwearing beige carpet meeting magnolia painted walls. The only contrast to break up the simplicity were works of art placed in well planned spaces along the walls. Modern brightly coloured Salvador Dali's next to Monet's poppies and Turner's seascapes, all vibrant and created after the artists had died and entered Heaven. To Roxy, the magnificence of the art seemed out of place on such drab walls but considering the fact that the corridor led to God's office perhaps He was trying to make a statement, although she had no idea what it could be. As she walked along the corridor she glanced at a painting by Picasso, it had a small plaque underneath it simply saying 'God' however, even with turning her head at strange and uncomfortable angles, the likeness was not apparent. Even though He could change His form at will and was only limited by His own imagination Roxy had never seen Him adopt the shape depicted on the canvass. Whenever she'd seen him in person, He'd always had 2 eyes, so didn't have a third one on His right cheek; and His mouth was always horizontal not vertical with black and orange lips. Shuddering, she tried to rid the mental image of Him adopting that shape in the frame from her mind.

Continuing her journey, she turned a sharp corner and was met with the sight of a long line of people stood waiting to go into Angelica's office. Recognising St. Andreas, she hesitated in her steps. Although she had never had the dubious pleasure of his company, she'd seen him before and knew of his reputation for causing catatonic states in others. She could see that he was currently chatting to an angel whose eyes had glazed over and had a small amount of drool slowly running down his chin. It looked as if he was there in body, but his mind had retreated to

41

a safer, quieter, and far happier place well away from the dull saint. Resuming her walk she got close enough to hear that he was entertaining his unwilling audience with a tale about a mild drizzle he had once encountered while having a walk in a field one summer morning. Even that brief snippet of his tedious voice was enough to make her mind endeavour to switch off. Shaking her head violently, in an attempt to stay awake, she quickly walked past them, diligently avoiding eye contact, just in case he decided to turn his attention to her.

Roxy didn't like queue jumping but, as she understood it, her mission was of critical importance, so she casually walked along the side of the waiting angels and squeezed her way through the doorway into Angelica's office, repeatedly saying "Excuse me" as she went. Once inside the room she moved towards the busy manager's desk. Conscious of the angel who was currently speaking to her, Roxy caught Angelica's attention. Receiving a smile of acknowledgement, she was told that God was expecting her so she should just knock and go into His office. Once the instruction had been given, Angelica returned to her task of recording the details of the circumstances of all the disappearing occupants of Heaven. A role that she was beginning to find repetitive and tedious but performing her duty with a smile that didn't betray her true feelings.

Knocking on God's door Roxy politely waited to be invited in. On hearing a loud but friendly "Enter" she entered, closing the door behind her. "Oh, there you are Roxy. I'm pleased to see you. Take a seat and make yourself comfortable." As requested, she chose a large antique brown leather-bound chair nearest His desk and sat down. She returned His smile but didn't speak as she thought it best if she adopted the approach of only answering direct questions.

"I am sorry that I interrupted your quality time with Limbo but sometime the 'needs must', as the saying goes. Were there any statues missing?" His voice adopting a more solemn tone.

"Yes, Sire." Taking on an equally serious voice. "There were five statues missing. I couldn't translate some of the writing so did a bit of rubbing with pencil and paper. I hope these make sense to you." Removing the neatly folded pieces of paper from her pocket she unfolded them and placed them on God's desk.

"Thank you. Excellent work." He picked them up and silently studied them, His initially expressionless face changing first to confusion and then to ominous concern. Once He had finished reading and thinking about the information that had been given to Him, He refolded the papers and passed them back to Roxy. "I have another mission for you I'm afraid, I need you to find Dedan, give him those pieces of paper to read and explain the situation to him. Tell him that it looks like Ekeko is pissed off and has already laid waste to a town in Bolivia and he needs get back here as quickly as possible."

"Of course, my Lord, but where is he?"

"We haven't heard from him for a few months but the last thing we heard was that he was demon hunting in the Himalayas. As I said, that was a while ago, so he is probably living the life of luxury with his feet up by now. But, just in case, I suggest you go armed. With Dedan you never can tell. He doesn't always look for trouble, but it usually finds him."

Brief pleasantries were exchanged before Roxy excused herself and left His room. She'd never been to the Himalayas before but, in life, it had always been somewhere that she'd wanted to visit. She was deep in thought as she entered the corridor, on her journey to find a suitable firearm and get to the dimensional portal.

It was a good plan but, once in the passageway, her attention and mind was dragged back to her present location by St. Andreas gently touching her elbow and speaking directly to her. "Hello, it's Roxy, isn't it? I'm St. Andreas, so pleased to meet you. I'd love to get to know you. Are you free? We could talk while I wait in this queue."

Now that the unfortunate angel, that had been his previously captured audience, was no longer the focus of the mind numbingly boring saint's attention, he seemed to return to a state of relieved consciousness. His brain attempting to function properly again and rid itself of the echoes of what he had just had to listen to.

"Hello Andreas, I am terribly sorry, but I have, just this minute, been given a critical mission by God so I do not have time to chat. Maybe another time?" With that she quickly strode on before further conversation could develop. Her relief, at being able to dodge the saint, was not mirrored by the saint's previous victim. He realised that he was about to, once more, become the focus of the saint and his brain was already, metaphorically, battening down the hatches and closing portholes in anticipation of a long and tiresome verbal storm. A far from Heavenly situation for an angel to have to deal with.

6 – Indirect Line

Thanks to the all-pervading state of entropy that permeates throughout Hell even Satan's favourite chair was not immune to decay. The imposing high-backed red leather chair, strategically placed in front of the fireplace and its raging log fire, was worn and the material was cracked as if it had dried out long ago. No matter how well it was treated, the damage was inevitable and even if replaced, any new chair would soon end up in a similar state. But despite the condition of the piece of furniture it was still one of the few truly comfortable place in all of Hell and was Satan's most frequent and popular location for him to sit. Many a long hour had been passed just staring at the flames as he mused over all the problems that entailed running an organisation as large, seemingly disorganised, and bureaucratic as Hades. He continually needed to consider new methods of punishment for the damned and there were security concerns, as there was always paranoia over any possible hostile takeovers by demons. And of course, he was always scheming and making plans to usurp God and take over Heaven.

One of the perks of his job was that he could always get his hands on a plentiful supply of his favourite drink, single malt whisky. And even that had to be the finest, most aged, and rarest of stock. Today he was sat quietly sipping a glass of 40-year-old single malt whisky from a dirty and chipped crystal cut glass. As he savoured the taste and the sensation of warmth on his tongue, he wasn't thinking evil thoughts; he was simply musing over the news of the disappearance of so many demons and souls sent to him to suffer for all eternity. The numbers were large but seemed to have plateaued with no more disappearances having been reported in the last few hours. Unless they were to leave the dimension via a portal nobody should ever be able to escape from Hell. But then a thought stuck its small head around a dark corner in his mind. 'Unless...' No, it couldn't be possible. Surely not so many and not all at once. The thought was enough to have him worried. The only conceivable way that anyone could manage such a feat was if they were summoned. But, outside of horror films, those things seldom occurred. It required a great deal of time, energy and usually a fair amount of virgin's blood. Even when invoked, the obscure incantations were usually aimed at specific demons and couldn't drag such a wide variety of spirits back to Earth, or wherever they'd gone. The more he tried to explain it all away the more he came to dead ends full of impossible solutions. He continued to sip his whisky as he looked into the dancing and flickering flames. Neither gave him any new answers but it made the mess of the mystery more comfortable.

Lost in his own private thoughts, he seemed to be hearing a strange ringing noise. At first, he ignored it as its presence didn't make any sense and was probably a trick of his subconscious mind or some unrecognised introduction to a Barry Manilow song. But despite his determination to pay no attention to it, the noise continued, chipping into his consciousness like an insistent woodpecker attacking his skull. Dragging him away from his private world, and back to reality, the noise finally had its desired effect. Waking from the distant reverie, he stood up angrily looking around his room trying to work out where the noise was coming from. Focusing, he could tell that it was the muffled ringing of a telephone. The problem was that he didn't have a phone available in his office. Walking around, tensed up like a ninja, he followed the sound and walked to a painting of an upturned crucifix which was hanging on his wall. Taking the picture down, the noise became slightly louder, and he saw the locked safe. Realising that it must be the only phone in Hell, the direct line with God, he pulled futilely at the metal door. In the past it had invariably been him that had rung Heaven, so it was rare, and unexpected. "Kran" he bellowed, loud enough to make the flames of the fire, at the other side of the room, move with the force. "Kran, get in here and open the safe, NOW!"

He heard a mumbled and indistinguishable reply from the other side of his door. Then, slowly, and reluctantly the door began to open, releasing a sound like a large ferret suffering the pain of having its testicles squeezed. Rather than wasting time with trying to get the door fully open, the flustered assistant squeezed himself through the narrow gap and emerged red faced and breathing heavily from the exertion of trying to force the refractory object to move for him.

"I'm here, Sire". Outstretching his arm as he walked hurriedly towards Satan, ready to turn the combination lock on the safe. One of the perks of the job that he had taken advantage of when taking the post, was the privilege of changing the number of the safe's door. He had readily availed himself of this and had picked the most obvious number, but with a slight alteration so it wasn't so obvious. 669! However, he was not being very imaginative as virtually every predecessor had also chosen that number and any would be burglar or troublemaker managing to gain access to the safe, would have tried that number first or second.

"About time too." Satan snapped.

Once the safe was unlocked, Kran turned the small handle and opened it, and stepped aside to allow Satan to retrieve the noisy phone. Inside was an old-fashioned black Bakelite telephone with a round dial mechanism, that wouldn't have looked out of place in a black and white crime thriller movie, made in the 1930's. All that was missing was the cable, attached to a wall, to allow the message to be transmitted. Lacking any real link between Heaven and Hell the messages were communicated by a method that modern human scientists would not be able to explain and, even if they did see it, would have probably just put it down to magic anyway. Lifting the phone with one hand he picked up the receiver with his other and placed it to his face. As he did so he started to walk towards his desk.

"Hello? Who is it?" The irony was not lost on him that there could only really be one person on the other end of the phone. Angels were not known for sneaking into God's office and making crank calls.

"Hello, it's God here." God also realised that identifying Himself was a pointless exercise, but He still wanted to be polite as He knew such conventions annoyed His eternal adversary.

"Hi, what do you want?" The total lack of polite formalities was part of Satan's character, and he was always wary on the very rare occasions that God phoned him. It was hardly likely that God would ring him just for a social chat and the most probable reason was that one of his diabolical plans had been discovered and he was getting a warning call to tell him that he needed to stop what he was doing. However, although he had lots of schemes fermenting in his head, he currently didn't have any major ones in play. So, despite quickly trying to find one, there was no reason that he could think of to justify this intrusion into his private thoughts and disturbing his relative peace and quiet. He was so preoccupied that he didn't even use any insulting words or nicknames when he spoke into the device in his hand.

"Well, Satan, is that any sort of welcome for your God?" God's voice deliberately light and the words consciously chosen to anger the Prince of Darkness.

"You ain't my god. So don't expect any prayers from me that you can use to give you strength!" Satan's voice terse and wishing that God would get to the point. "After all, I doubt you'd answer any of *my* prayers."

"Very true my erstwhile friend, very true. Anyway, I will cut to the chase. Have any of your residents been disappearing for no apparent reason?" God had no vision of what happened in Hell and as a matter of course Satan made it a point of principle to lie to God wherever possible so that, no matter what the truth was, the answer might be filled with duplicitous words and unreliable information rather than simple facts. However, despite his best intentions, Satan's pause was enough to give God an answer to his basic closed question. He could tell that Satan was trying to work out whether he should tell the truth or try and find an advantage in playing mind games.

"Yes." Having finally decided that he'd give a straight, but laconic answer and hopefully, in return, get some slightly more detailed answers from God.

"Okay, thanks a lot. Chat later. Have a nice day!"

"Hang on, HANG ON!" Satan screamed down the phone. He didn't give God a straight answer for nothing. He wanted some information in return. "I presume that, because you are asking the question some of your goody-goody winged cupcakes have gone astray as well?"

There was no hesitancy on God's part. He had anticipated the question and had no problem with giving a straight answer. "Yes. A fairly large number of angels have vanished, and I have a good idea as to how it happened and where they have gone."

"And…" Satan decided to allow God to impart information and once he had some more facts he'd then decide if he wanted to share more details or just end the conversation.

"And… It seems that five formerly dead gods have become reanimated and left their plinths in the Hall of Dead Gods. One of them has also taken out his frustration at being stone for so long and he has managed to do some damage to a small town in Bolivia. By all accounts he made good work of it too. I doubt you could have done a worse job, or better job; depending on perspectives."

"Challenge accepted, but some other time." His bass voice sly and dripping in sarcasm. "Who are they and how did that happen?"

"Well, it seems that the main troublemaker is Ekeko. As for the others they are Hor'idey, Elsa, Sonja and Falacer. None of them were that great or powerful, even in their heyday, so hopefully they will not be too much trouble. As for the how, there is only one possible answer, somebody, or even a group of humans, have started worshipping them again and brought them back into existence."

Allowing the names to register in his memory Satan spoke slowly as if the words were struggling to form in his mouth. "But five at once? That sounds like the act of a cult; or some similar word beginning with a C. The various gods aren't exactly similar. If I remember them correctly one was, or is once again, South American, one Norse, another Hellenic, one was Roman and the last one was from the Middle East, or something like that. Eclectic and I can't even think of anything that connects them."

"Me neither, but I intend to find out."

"And then what?"

"Then?... At the moment, I have no idea Satan, I have absolutely no idea. After all this has never happened before." The genuine concern was evident in God's voice. "But leave your phone somewhere where you can readily answer it. I might be ringing you some time, sooner or later, to let you know what is happening and I might..." He paused, unwilling to use the words "…need your help."

Satan heard the last part but decided not to react, instead he stored the words in his mind so that he could use them to his own advantage at some later date. "Alright, I don't usually do as you tell me but, in this case, I will. Bye." Satan pensively put the receiver back on the phone's cradle and placed it on his desk, absent mindedly chewing on his bottom lip, staring at the machine with his mind instantly deep in thought. Even in the *good* old days, when he used to be in Heaven, there had been many gods being worshipped alongside God. They could be cruel or kind, and God tended to overlook their actions as people had to find their own way in life and if they chose to worship other deities then that was their prerogative. After all, he knew that any god that needed to apply force to maintain loyalty was not worth following. Goodness or evil actions didn't matter as each faith had its own versions of Heaven and Hell and, depending on their actions, the souls of believers went to those places. It was only after the gods died that their adherents transferred dimensional plains and ended up in either Heaven or Hell. Even today, there were numerous gods worshipped around the planet with their own versions of paradise and, on the whole, they didn't cause too much trouble. But the fact that there were some old gods returning worried Satan. They were an unknown quantity, and he didn't like what he didn't understand. But, on the other hand, they could make useful allies if they joined forces with him.

7 – Hiding

The relaxing and therapeutic effect that Roxy initially felt as she materialised on the barren rocky path was immediately nullified as she suffered the bitterly cold air biting into her exposed cheeks. The fresh air entered her nostrils, filling her lungs and making her gasp at the unexpected change in temperature. Even with her brightly coloured thick thermal clothing, she could feel the heat leaving her body. She was glad that there was little wind, or the chill factor would have made her mission even more uncomfortable. As it was, the slight breeze was blowing down the narrow valley, whistling hauntingly as if ghosts were dancing around her. Shivering, she patted her body energetically with her gloved hands as she tried to keep her blood circulating. One of the problems of taking human form, on Earth, was that bodies became susceptible to the same problems that everyone else suffered from, making hypothermia a genuine risk.

Looking around, she saw the same monotonous grey colour of the rocks all around her but further along the valley, in the distance, she spotted a small village with brightly coloured Buddhist prayer flags draped across the narrow street. The houses seemed to be clinging precariously to the side of a steep mountainous rocky outcrop. Beyond that, she saw a giant snow-capped mountain wearing a thick white cloud which was hiding its summit, as if it were a flowing crown. All she knew was that she was in Bhutan, the small country hidden along the Himalayan Mountain range. The transportation process had deposited her at the same location that it had sent Dedan to many months ago. Not knowing where he currently was, it was the only clue as to where to start the search, but in the time since his arrival he could have ended up anywhere. As he hadn't returned to Heaven, he was still on Earth but other than that there was little to help her with her quest.

Walking carefully along the stony path, she eventually reached the village. The cold seemed to be permeating her entire body and even the brief and insubstantial shelter, provided by the buildings, from the now increasingly unforgiving wind was welcomed. Despite the weather, she saw some children playing between two buildings, seemingly oblivious to the bitter coldness of the day. They were more interested in their games than the stranger, so when she approached, they took no notice of her.

"Hello," she said cheerfully, hoping, but not expecting them to speak English. They briefly looked at her with apathetic eyes, then returned to their games. "Parlez-vous Français? Sprechen Sie Deutsch? Parli Italiano?" The idea that they might speak French, German or Italian was as slim as the hope that they'd speak English, but it was worth a try. Then, stopping their game, one of the boys took pity on her; Roxy sensed that part of their games was to tease her.

Giving her a broad smile, he nodded and gestured for her to follow him. He ran along the village, and it took all her strength to keep up with him in the thin, high-altitude air. Finally, and much to her relief, he reached the weathered, bare wooden door of a brick-built hut a hundred yards away from the rest of the village. Knocking briskly on the door, the boy shouted something to the occupant in Dzongkha, the language of Bhutan. Eventually the door was opened from within to reveal a grey-haired old man wearing a dark red gho, the traditional robe of the country. On seeing the elder, the boy spoke then ran off to resume his game, leaving Roxy in the doorway.

Placing her hands together, as if in prayer, she bowed respectfully. "Hello, do you speak English?"

"Yes, I speak a soupçon. I went to University in Cambridge, in England. A beautiful and friendly country but it is so warm."

Taken aback at hearing anyone sincerely calling England friendly and complaining about it being too warm, Roxy suppressed a laugh. "Yes, I suppose it is warm compared to here. I am Roxy," she said, offering him her hand.

Shaking it politely, he bowed his head slightly. "Pleased to meet you, Roxy. I am Thinley. How can I help you?"

"I am looking for a friend of mine. A man in his early fifties, about so high." She used her hand to indicate Dedan's height. "Slightly thinning on top, often with bags under his eyes, and looks like he has eaten a few too many meals."

"You mean Dedan?" replied Thinley, raising his eyebrow in surprise.

"Yes, yes, Dedan."

"Well, why didn't you say that in the first place?" His soft and quiet voice was gentle with its reassuring accent. "He is staying in a cave about two miles up the path. If you follow it, you will come to a slight clearing and a smaller path, on your left, leading up to the entrance to a cave. That is where he is staying. I can take you there if you like."

"No, no thank you. It is very kind of you, but I think I should be able to find it from your directions. Besides, I want to surprise him on my own." Somehow Dedan managed to attract danger, trouble and unexpected problems so, if there were any demons lurking up there, she didn't want to expose any of the local inhabitants to unnecessary risks.

Saying her goodbyes, she began her trek along the narrow winding path. To her right, she could see down an ever-narrowing gorge that snaked along the valley. At the bottom was a rapidly flowing stream that appeared so insignificant in such an overpoweringly grand landscape. The path wound along the side of the mountain, and, in some places, it was so close to the edge that one foot on a loose rock would have sent her tumbling to her death. In other places it widened and took her between giant boulders towering above her. Eventually, just as the sun was beginning to set and cast the entire valley in an all-encompassing shadow, she reached the plateau that Thinley had described to her. There were deep patches of snow scattered amongst the rocks, last traces of the winter when the whole place would have been a thick sea of white.

From where she was standing, she could see the narrow path on her left but couldn't see any indication of there being a cave entrance. Slipping on the loose pebbles and fallen debris from the mountain stretching high above her, she managed to get closer to the seemingly solid rock face and then she saw it, a dark and uninviting crack in the rough and uneven rock wall. Walking through it, she found it to be lighter than expected, although she couldn't work out how it managed to be so bright. Taking a closer look, and running her fingers over the rough surface, she found it softer than anticipated and slightly damp. Picking up a piece of the light-giving material, she realised that it must be some bioluminescent algae; without its presence she would have been left in total darkness. Turning her attention to the way ahead, she saw that, at first, the cave was more like a narrow winding path with jagged outcrops, making her twist her body so that she could get past them. Then, eventually, the cave opened to expose a giant chamber with smooth walls and moraine covering the ground; dull remnants of a once strong flowing, underground river which had cut its way through the rock, creating a network of caves.

Then, at the far end of the natural hall, she saw him. There, sitting on a pile of stones laid out to look like a colossus's throne, was Dedan. He was deep in thought, and it wasn't until Roxy drew nearer and her feet disturbed some stones, making a dull rumbling noise, that he noticed her presence. Looking in Roxy's direction, he screwed up his eyes as he tried to make out who had come to see him, tensing his muscles slightly in anticipation of a possible hostile visitor. It was only when she was twenty yards away that he realised who it was and relaxed again, giving her a broad smile.

"Roxy? Is that you? It's been a long, long time. How are you? Welcome to Bhutan." His voice was croaky as if he hadn't spoken in a long time and he was re-learning a lost skill.

"Hello, Dedan. I'm good, thanks, but next time you decide to disappear on Earth and start a game of hide and seek, can you choose somewhere warmer? I'm bloody freezing." In the light, she could finally fully make out his face. His hair was unkempt, and he had an untidy brown beard with grey patches. He was wearing a dark blue gho that looked like it hadn't been washed in an exceptionally long time. Over his shoulders he had an immense white fur cloak filled with holes and decorated with small red patches that gave an overall appearance of it trying crush him. "Good grief, Dedan. You look like crap."

"Thanks, Roxy, it's good to see you as well. How's Heaven? I presume, from your presence, that I am needed back in the world of my peers or to go somewhere where there are more humans?" There was obvious and undisguised sadness in his voice, as if he were a small boy being called to come home by his mother after a fun afternoon playing in the sunshine.

Looking around her, Roxy saw the bleak grey walls. "Yes, I'm sorry, Dedan, but there is a problem and I need to drag you away from your warm, comfortable and luxurious palace of gold."

"Scoff all you like, my beautiful angel, but this is where I choose to be." There was a resigned look of despair in his tired brown eyes. "All right, please pull up a rock, sit down and tell me all about it."

Sitting on a large boulder just by the side of his ersatz throne, she made herself as comfortable as anyone could be when sitting on a cold and hard lump of stone. Once she was settled, Dedan added, "Sorry I can't offer you much in the way of hospitality. The facilities are a bit basic, but it is home to me."

On Earth the expression "That is on a need-to-know basis" is frequently used by enterprises, be they business, military or espionage. Sometimes it is said as a way of telling someone that some under informed person shouldn't have any knowledge of certain facts and if they were told, then somebody else would have to kill them. Usually, this threat is just a joke but in other, fortunately rarer, occasions, it isn't. However, in certain cases, the phrase is all too often used because the person saying it either forgot to tell another or because the details are just too long and complicated, and they can't be bothered to talk about it. But whatever the reasons for such secrecy, it is a cover-all term which ensures that ignorance, inefficiency, and confusion are forever maintained. The people in power are thus able to feel smug and superior because they know something that their underlings don't. So that, all too often it is only one small piece of knowledge that differentiates those in power from those out of it.

Although, in this instance, nobody had used the expression to Roxy, she felt that there was much that she was desperate to know. She well knew what, where and, when things had happened, but there were massive gaps in her knowledge base when it came to the how, who and why elements. But she felt sure that, once she had imparted her limited knowledge, Dedan would be able to fill in the empty spaces in her understanding. With that at the forefront of her mind, she told him as much of what had happened as she could, even if she didn't understand it all. She recounted the information about the attack on the Bolivian town, the Hall of Dead Gods, the missing statues, and the broken plinth.

With pride she told him about her pencil rubbings, to ensure that she'd got the names right, and how God had promptly instructed her to have a trip to the Himalayas.

Her soft accent and rapid Italian way of speaking ensured that she had his rapt attention. While she was talking Dedan remained silent, for once more interested in listening to what he was being told to him than trying to imagine the female speaker naked. Hidden from Roxy by his beard and dirty face, he scowled, grimaced, or frowned at the appropriate points in her story. He understood what he was being told better than Roxy did, and he was already racing ahead with possible scenarios, depending on which gods had been dragged back into existence. Eventually Roxy came to the point where she had told him all she knew so she fell silent, looking at Dedan with eyes expectant of some response and further information so that she could make sense of it all.

With a concerned scowl, chewing on the ends of his long moustache hair as he collected his thoughts. "I see." He finally said, his demeanour calm and enigmatic. "Can I see the papers with the names on them?"

"Oh, sorry, there you go." Roxy quickly unzipped her thick padded coat, removed the sheets of paper from an inner pocket, and passed them to him. He carefully unfolded them and studied each one in turn. Even though his facial hair made his face inscrutable, she could tell from his head movements and occasional releases of exasperated breaths that at least some of the names meant something to him. After he had finished looking at the fifth sheet, he carefully folded them again and laid them on his lap. Even though he had only stared at them for a few brief seconds, to Roxy the delay seemed like an interminable amount of time. When he did finally raise his head and look at Roxy, she could see sadness in his eyes as if the names had a personal connection to him. "So..." she said, the impatience clear in her tone.

"So?" There was a hint of an ironic laugh in his voice, as if he were remembering a joke told to him long ago. "There are five gods that somehow have managed to find favour with someone, somewhere, on Earth and have become 'real' again. I know..." He paused as he contemplated what he had just said. "I *knew*, a couple of them in their heyday, before they became petrified but, as far as I understand it, they were all just local gods with no international appeal, and there is nothing to connect them all together to make them into some cult or new belief system. I think that the first thing we need to do is go see one or two of them and try and find out more about their new-found followers. Perhaps they will remember me, and I am sure one definitely will, but despite that, might still be willing to talk. I suppose it is time for me to leave my adopted home and return to work. Heigh-ho, there might be no rest for the wicked, but the good don't get many chances to enjoy things either."

As he was getting up from his rocky seat, Roxy decided to take the opportunity to interrogate him on other matters. "Dedan, what are you doing here?"

He sighed and gave her an exasperated look. 'It's a long story' is another expression frequently used by people that can't be bothered to tell someone else something, and the phrase was about to leave his lips when Roxy guessed what he was going to say and made a pre-emptive verbal strike.

"Don't you dare try and give me any crap about it being *need to know* or *not wanting to talk about it*. When you try and put on the mysterious strong and silent personae it just comes across as being the annoying, pathetic and 'in need of a heavy slap' type. So, I suggest you just tell me." Despite the smile, there was a hardness in her voice, and fire in her eyes, that left little room for negotiations or compromises. Dedan knew better than to argue with an Italian, especially an Italian woman. He was well aware, from bitter experience, that if anyone tried, they would eventually realise that there were only two possible outcomes. They would be wrong, or they would be even more wrong. Either way, winning the disagreement with her was not on the list of options.

"It's simple." It wasn't simple but he had every intention of redacting his version of events as much as possible. "A rogue Yeti demon managed to escape from Hell and rather than winning hearts, minds and, more importantly, souls with subterfuge he decided to run around eating any goats, yaks or humans that he could get his clawed hands on. I was getting bored in Heaven, so I volunteered to be the one to return to Earth and track him down. I materialised at a spot a bit lower down the mountain and spent the next couple of weeks freezing my arse off as I traipsed around some picturesque bits of the Himalayas looking for it. I finally tracked him down and trapped him in this cave. Unfortunately, he had the ability to climb bare rock walls and, quite literally, got the drop on me. He almost flattened me and when I finally came to, I found myself hanging upside down from the ceiling by a type of rope that I suspect was made from his own pubic hairs. The Yeti had my pump action shotgun and decided to use me as a human Piñata. Luckily, he forgot to tie my hands, so I managed to block a lot of his blows, but even then, there were quite a few strikes that made contact with my head. This pummelling went on for about a week. I'd slip into unconsciousness and, when I came around again, he would repeat the process. He was, I suppose, just displaying his basic training in inflicting punishment for a long period of time. But thankfully the part of the rope nearest the ceiling must have been touching a jagged stone, so the pendulum motion eventually cut through it."

On hearing that part of the story, Roxy was tempted to interrupt and tell him that God had said that he'd be putting his feet up, but she thought better of it and allowed him to continue.

"Thanks to the combined elements of nothing to keep me up in the air and the power of gravity, it was my turn to get the drop on the Yeti. I fell and landed on his head. It only briefly stunned him, but it gave me enough time to free my gun from his grip and shoot him. He was a tough sod and I had to fire all the cartridges into him before his soul was returned to Hell. I think that if I'd had any fewer shells loaded into the rifle, it would have been me that would have ended up dead and found myself back in Heaven sooner than I wanted. I then managed to get out of the cave and staggered to the local village. Luckily Thinley, their village elder, found me, took me into his home, and looked after me until I had recovered. Ever since then I have been staying here in this cave. In thanks for killing the demon, the villagers bring me food. It isn't much, but they are poor, and it is enough to keep me alive. A pleasant enough existence, apart from all the enlightenment seekers."

"Enlightenment seekers! What do you mean?"

"Bloody tourists that have more money that brain cells and think that they can get all the answers for the problems of the world by walking around remote mountains carrying oversized backpacks. They find out that there is a hermit with a beard living in a cave and I become a damned tourist attraction. I should have charged them a fee and sold tickets. Mainly clueless Australians, rich, posh, and spoiled. Also, chinless Brits or pseudo hippies from California that dropped a bit too much acid or smoked too much grass and think they are modern versions of John Lennon or Janis Joplin. The worst ones are the Germans, 'VOT IZ ZEE MEANING OF ZEE LIFE?'" Dedan shouted the words in a loud and aggressive accent. "As if, once they found the secret, they'd use the knowledge to conquer the world."

Having lived in Germany as a human before her death, Roxy had to supress a laugh. "Well, Oh Great Hermit, what did you tell them?"

"Despite having known God for millennia and consider Him to be my closest friend, I still don't have any answers. His purpose is as much a mystery to me as it is to the dozy idealists travelling halfway around the world to ask stupid questions. Why ask me? I can't even use a cell phone properly. What I say to them depends on how much beer or food they have in their backpacks. If they keep me happy, I tell them some inspirational crap like, 'Look into your soul and find your own peace!'"

"Deep. And what does that mean?"

"How should I know? I think I once saw it on a cardboard beer mat in a New Orleans bar. However, there was one muscle bound Swede that was all arrogant ego and full of shit. I told him to go to Varanasi, in India, and drink from the river Ganges."

"Ganges? I know some see it as a holy river, but what good will that do for his soul?" she asked, giving Dedan an incredulous look as she tried to see the significance of the instruction.

"His soul? Probably nothing, but it will help stop him being so full of shit. Afterwards he'd probably spend a week just sitting on the toilet cursing me and he will hopefully stop bothering people in caves that just want to be left alone."

There was a brief pause as Roxy thought about what Dedan had said and then they both burst into raucous laughter. "Dedan," she said as she caught her breath, "how come you didn't return to Heaven?" Suddenly, as if he had been doused in icy water, he went silent, and his face went solemn as he averted his gaze from her and began to look intently at his feet. Seeing his discomfort, she decided to add some comforting words. "It's all right, Dedan. I'm here for you."

He looked up and gave her a weak and feeble smile. "Thank you." He paused again as he pondered how to tell his tale, allowing the uncomfortable silence to pervade the stony hall. "I went on a few dates with Angelica."

"I know. I heard; such things don't stay a secret for long in Heaven."

"Anyway, we went out and had a few laughs. But when it came to the crunch, she said that the chemistry wasn't quite right, but she did love me like a brother!"

"Awww, that is lovely and wonderful." Roxy said, her voice full of joy.

"Spoken like a true woman. To any man, that is like a kick in the groin from an irate gorilla. It's like giving someone our heart and then they promptly do an Irish jig on it. Any man would rather be told that they're a slime ball and to get lost than hear that."

The look on Roxy's face was one of disbelief. "Surely not. I think it's great. You have touched her heart and her life. She cares about you."

"Yes, I might have touched her heart and life, but that's all I'll ever get to touch. I truly thought we could be more. But oh well, such is life. Or life in Heaven anyway."

"So that's why you stayed here? I am sorry, Dedan. You are an angel in more ways than one." She got up and gently kissed him on his cheek, immediately regretting it as his foul body odour filled her nostrils. "But you are an idiot sometimes, and you can't stay hidden here forever. Heaven needs you. There is a job to do."

"I know. Unfortunately, you are right. It had to happen someday, and besides I was getting a little bored at being a wise guru. I suppose we had better get a move on. After all, God is waiting for me."

As he stood in readiness to walk out of the cave Roxy looked him up and down. "Ewww!" The disgust in her voice echoed around the cave. "Please, PLEASE tell me that you are not wearing the demon's fur?"

"Don't knock it, Roxy, it's warm and I knew that the Yeti didn't need it anymore. At least he was dead when I skinned him, which is not a nicety that many demons adhere to, or would have extended to me, if the situation were reversed."

To avoid walking out of the cave and getting cold again, Roxy made the dimensional portal back to Heaven materialise in front of a wall just to the left of Dedan's now vacant throne. It hung there, in thin air, an almost invisible translucent rectangle. The only indication that it was truly there was an incorporeal shimmer as if part of the observer's retina was smudged.

"After you, Dedan. Oh, by the way, which god do you plan to go visit first?"

"Thank you. I think Hor'idey will most definitely be the first one we should go and see. I am sure she will talk to us rather than fire a lightning bolt into our heads. Or at least I hope she will talk first."

"Why her?"

Dedan was about to step into the portal but stopped, turned to face Roxy, and gave her wide and cheeky smile that she completely failed to see due to his messy beard. "That is simple, my angel. She used to be my beloved wife." And before Roxy could overcome her surprise and ask for more details he was gone, having instantaneously, but reluctantly, taken his trip back to Heaven.

Shocked by the revelation, Roxy stared at the empty space that had just the second before contained her colleague. As she entered the portal, the last words of her mission were spoken but heard only by the soon to be totally empty cave. "Oh, shit!"

8 – Lockdown

Piero Uomoduro of the Polizia di Stato was feeling as if the whole world, that he thought he knew and fully understood, had suddenly turned into an ocean and the surface, where the good ship Reality floated, was way over his head. He had been in the Italian state police for over twenty years and had proven himself to be a talented and clever officer and been able to steadily rise to the rank of captain. In that time, he had seen many things and had, one way or another, always been able to deal with them. He understood that sometimes rules and laws were open to individual interpretation and could be gently bent without being completely broken. Protecting innocent people was more important to him than worrying about protecting the rights of hardened criminals. His methods were often violent and not officially condoned, but his supervisors tended to turn a blind eye and did little to condemn them either. Politicians' weak rhetoric was one thing, but the need to maintain the laws required strength and more integrity than any elected official possessed. The ability to be an iron fist in a velvet glove, or in his case, an iron fist in an iron glove, made him an ideal figurehead for his department and a respected leader to his subordinates. Even the criminals knew and avoided him wherever possible, as hard experience had shown them that his clenched hand could feel like a, sometimes fatal, steam hammer. He was an uncrowned king of the streets, there was little that went on that he didn't know about and, if he didn't like it, he would quickly put a stop to whatever was going on. But today, there was much that he couldn't explain and would find it difficult to put down on paper when he completed his reports.

No matter what time of year, Rome was always full of tourists eager to visit as many of the beautiful historical buildings as time and budgets would allow. Spring was no different, and today the sheer numbers and compacted mass of them in the narrow streets was not making his job any easier. He had been forced to cordon off the Piazza della Rotonda, but the police blocking the free access of visitors was not going down well with the sightseers, who were demanding that they be allowed to see the Pantheon and the fountain just by its entrance. The magnificence of the place was mostly lost on the visitors, as cameras took photos without their owners really appreciating anything greater than the fact that the building was old, and the fountain looked 'nice'.

Piero always thought of the tourists as philistines pretending to be cultured. And today, their inability to access the place was making them even more loud and obnoxious than they normally were. But no matter how much they complained, remonstrated, or argued with the police, all words were wasted as there was no way that they would be allowed past the barriers. Apart from the heavily armed police, the square was now empty, providing the world with an unusual sight, the fountain not obscured by tourists sitting on the edge of it while they ate their ice creams or snacks. There was a noise at one of the corners of the piazza when the unhappy crowd were further inconvenienced by having to move out of the way so that an army armoured car could get past them and be allowed into the square. Once it came to a stop, four soldiers appeared, sub-machine guns at the ready. Seeing the police captain, they approached him, weapons still raised, although they were uncertain what they were supposed to be aiming them at. All they knew was that there was an emergency and they had to get there as quickly as possible. A soldier adorned with the straight stripes of a *maresciallo ordinaro,* or sergeant major as they are known elsewhere, approached the captain and smartly saluted.

"Captain, what is the problem? We were told to report to you, but we have no idea what is wrong."

The befuddled captain rubbed his temples as he tried to work out how to start or even what to say. He was sure that whatever he said would sound crazy and not be believed. After all, he was struggling to believe it himself. "Thank you for getting here so promptly, Sergeant Major, I am not totally sure what is going on myself. The Pantheon over there…" He accompanied the words with an arm gesture pointing to the ancient building, in the unlikely event that the soldier had no idea which building he was referring to, "…has got some sort of force field surrounding it and nobody seems to be able to get in or get out."

On hearing the expression 'force field' the cynical soldier wanted to laugh. In his mind, such words were the works of science fiction and not concepts that had a place in the real world. He expected the next sentence to include aliens, teleportation devices and quite possibly anal probes. "Force field? Really?" If he had been attempting to hide any derision, he totally failed. If it was some elaborate practical joke, at his expense or the expense of the army, he was not impressed.

Ignoring the obvious tone of the soldier, Piero put his hand into his pocket and removed a small copper coloured five cent Euro coin. Holding it between thumb and forefinger so the sergeant major could see it, he instructed, "Watch closely". Pulling his arm back he threw the coin as hard as he could in the direction of the Pantheon. In a blur of dark brown, the projectile flew towards the building, then its natural arc was drastically changed. Despite there being nothing to see, the metal bounced off seemingly thin air ten yards from the entrance. There was a dull *bong* sound as if a bass drum had been struck and the coin then fell harmlessly to the ground. "And it seems to be covering the whole building. It is closer to the walls in some places, but we still haven't been able to get in there. We have no idea what is causing it or how many people, if any, are inside, but whatever it is, I don't like it and I want it gone."

Being slightly more frugal than the police officer, the soldier removed a hand full of one cent coins from his pocket and began to throw them at random places in front of the building. Each one suffered the same fate as the higher denomination coin. He lifted his Beretta ARX160 assault rifle, drew back the firing mechanism and put it against his shoulder in readiness to fire, adopting the natural military assumption that bullets were able to penetrate everything better than any coinage.

"Hang on, if you are planning to do that, can I at least get my men moved to somewhere safe? Soldiers might not have problems with friendly fire, or collateral damage, but I have no desire for you to kill anyone thanks to stray ricocheted bullets flying all over the piazza."

Pausing, the sergeant lowered his rifle and nodded in agreement. "I think you might be right. Excuse me a minute." He walked to the other three soldiers that were still standing by their vehicle and, from what the police captain could see, they became engaged in a heated discussion accompanied by wild gesticulations as arms swung around the air accompanying the words. The talking seemed to momentarily stop as they all looked from the captain to the Pantheon and then back to the captain before they resumed their private conference. Finally, after plenty of deliberation, he saw their meeting break up and the sergeant major resume his previous position next to the captain.

"I think we need more troops."

It was the captain's turn to deliberately avoid sarcasm. "You don't say?"

9 – Don't Unpack

Many angels enjoyed returning to Earth, even if it was just briefly, and then promptly returning to Heaven, just for the exhilaration they felt when they used the dimensional portal. It was like the most powerful opiate ever created by underground pharmacists if it were being taken in the middle of an orgasm. It had been known for the weaker willed angels to deliberately spend all their time just going backwards and forwards just for the hit. Eventually some of the more puritanical saints, and fun hating Born Again Christians, complained to God. He wasn't that interested in enforcing some arbitrary rule that restricted happiness for any occupant of Heaven, but upon careful consideration He had to admit that saints, or angels, suddenly appearing in populated areas of Earth with looks on their faces as if they were coming, and making appreciative groaning sounds to match, was probably not the best thing to have happening. In the wrong circumstances, they could end up getting arrested, especially if they materialised in a school playground or the anatomy section of a library. Much to the smug satisfaction of the dull, spoilsport saints and the far too prurient angels, He was, after a few minor tweaks of the process, able to tone down the effect so that it was still enjoyable, just not *that* enjoyable. No longer the greatest sexual encounter that anyone could have, even if they were on their own, it became more akin to the sensation of having a long relaxing soak in a warm herbal bath. Suffice to say, the use of the portal reduced drastically after that, but it was still a popular process.

Thanks to the changes, Dedan's return to Heaven, closely followed by Roxy, was enjoyable, albeit not comparable to the old days, much to his regret. However, they both felt better for the process. Roxy was finally warm again for the first time in hours and Dedan had been so long in his own self-imposed exile on Earth that he had forgotten what a relaxing and comforting process it could be.

On seeing his female companion appear, Dedan gave her a welcoming smile. "Hello again, my beautiful angel, I need to go get freshened up and changed before I go see God, and I am sure you will feel like doing the same. Shall I meet you at…" He paused, not wanting to use the name of the woman that had innocently used a gentle and friendly expression but still managed to break his heart. "Angelica's office?"

Roxy picked up on the brief silence and recognised it for what it was and gave him a comforting smile followed by a hug. "Yes, Dedan, I'll see you there. And I promise that it will be all right."

Silently he stepped back, nodded to her sagely, and walked out of the room containing the dimensional portal.

"Men!" Roxy whispered to herself and then left the room as well. After realising that she had come into such close proximity with the foul smelling, bloody, dirty and, quite possibly, flea infested hide of the Yeti demon, she decided that she needed a shower.

The process of cleaning himself up so that he looked presentable had taken longer than Dedan had anticipated. The quick and perfunctory washes in the icy water, obtained from the Himalayan mountain's glacial meltwater or streams, was far from sufficient to meet most modern standards of cleanliness, and it had taken a considerable amount of time in the shower to remove the accumulated grime, sweat and traces of demon blood from his skin and hair. During the first few minutes of his shower, the water making its way down the plug hole was similar in appearance to a muddy landslide after a tropical monsoon. Pollution wasn't a problem in Heaven, which was a good thing because, had it been on Earth, the hair infused slurry that he released would have been considered a serious health risk and may have been utilised by some tinpot dictator as a biological weapon of mass destruction.

Once he had reached a state where the true colour of his skin could be identified, he felt confident enough to tackle his beard. With the remnants of ancient meals and spilled Bhutan butter tea removed, he felt safe touching it. His first sweep was more in the style of an explorer in a jungle. He used a large and sharp bowie knife as if it were a machete. Fists full of tangled and matted hair were severed and carelessly dropped on the floor by his feet. Once the initial cut had been completed, he checked himself in his bathroom mirror. The remnant of his beard was an improvement and he no longer looked like he had just been rescued from a desert island, but it was still uneven and was far from neat. Eventually, he reluctantly decided that there was only one thing he could do, a full shave. Along with the obvious physical side of the growth, he had become quite emotionally attached to his rugged look. Taking the knife, he scraped it across his skin, releasing the last of his beard from his face. Upon finishing, he moved his face closer to the mirror and inspected his reflection. He looked tired and old, but sleep could soon solve one of those features. He could always adopt a different, younger, appearance but he liked the way he looked, as it made him feel like a normal human rather than some perfect example of what a living person could never achieve without plastic surgery and the lack of decent things to eat.

He knew that before he got to see God in His combined private apartment and office, he would have to bite the bullet and face Angelica. Dedan was no coward but, in this instance, he would happily have fought a dozen angry demons rather than see her. But, as he still had hope in his heart, he decided that choosing smarter attire than he would have normally worn would not do any harm. Selecting a dark grey two-piece collarless Neru style suit, he gave himself one last inspection in the mirror and set off to finally report back on his extended mission to kill a recalcitrant Yeti demon. He frequently extended his stays when he had completed his set tasks on Earth, so he knew that Angelica wouldn't ask him too many embarrassing questions relating to his absence.

When he reached the door to God's secretary's office he hesitated, hand raised in mid-air ready to knock. Plucking up inner courage, he knocked and immediately heard a cheerful voice inviting him in. On seeing Dedan enter, Angelica sprang to her feet, ran up to him and gave him a tight hug. "Dedan, where on Earth have you been? It has been months, I've missed you. You really need to stop skiving so much. Surely Earth doesn't have more attractions than Heaven? The Yeti demon duly despatched, I presume?"

Once the barrage of joyous chattering questions had ended, Dedan casually replied, "Hello my beautiful angel. Yes, all done and dusted. The demon has been sent back to Hell and I am sure Satan will exact some suitable punishment on it for its unsanctioned actions. As for my extended stay, I thought I'd have a bit of a holiday. And besides, I became something of a guru with trekkers looking for enlightenment."

The idea of her friend, and reluctantly honorary brother, being confused for a deep-thinking philosopher made her laugh out loud. "I'm sorry, Dedan, but I can't imagine you being some sort of Dalai Lama or

Maharishi Mahesh Yogi. Perhaps they thought you were a woolly llama?"

"Thanks for that. But I have many friends that used to be philosophers on Earth, and I managed to spout the same sort of claptrap that they did. So, I think I passed the test. Anyway, I need to report to the Big Boss. I presume He is in?"

"Of course, Roxy arrived about two minutes before you and is already in there. Just go straight in, He is waiting for you."

Once in God's office, he was invited to sit down and he had to admit that the leather chair he'd selected, next to Roxy's, was far more comfortable than the pile of rocks that he had grown accustomed to in his cave. Stones digging into buttocks was not a common design feature for popular furniture, not even some of the strange, over-priced, angular chairs that Scandinavians fooled the rest of the world into buying. They might be ergonomically designed to help with posture, but they were not suitable for the average person that enjoyed the simple act of sitting down.

He noticed that Roxy had got changed and the choice of attire was definitely a distinct improvement to the amorphous appearance that the warm padded thermal clothing had given her in Bhutan. Even when she was seated, he could clearly see that the figure-hugging navy-blue two-piece trouser suit was emphasising all the right parts. It looked like it was made by one of the top fashion designers in Heaven but, not being interested in such a subject, he neither knew nor cared which brand name it was. She had obviously had the same idea as Dedan and dressed for the occasion for the meeting with God. God Himself had no strict dress code, over the many centuries he had seen styles come and go and, as far as he was concerned, the only real dress code was that people were dressed. But even then, there were many that entered Heaven naked and, as He saw it, people couldn't get more natural, and as He had intended, than that. Dedan was of a similar opinion. He didn't mind nudity either, and wouldn't have had any problems if Roxy had chosen to turn up in her birthday suit. However, Roxy would have objected to such a suggestion and more than likely slapped his face for mentioning it.

"Hello, Dedan." God's voice was grave, its usual jaunty and ludic tone absent. "Roxy has told me that you have seen the list of names. Obviously, with Hor'idey on there, I thought you'd be the ideal choice to go see her."

Dedan shifted uncomfortably in his comfortable chair, as if the Himalayan rocks had suddenly re-appeared or had become a more desired option. "I am not sure *ideal* would be the word I'd choose. The last time I saw her, she was promising me a quick but painful death and was pretty much doing all she could to deliver on her promise. I know it was several thousand years ago, but some women can carry a grudge and find it hard to move on. I doubt that Satan, and his domain, could ever provide a greater fury!"

God took a slow sip of coffee as He thought about Dedan's words. "Yes, I suppose apostasy and the betrayal of a god can be hard to forgive and forget. I should know! At least you didn't try and steal her throne. Maybe a few millennia of being dead and a statue has calmed her down a bit? And if not, I am sure that your talent for charming ladies can be brought into play."

"I know I have a reputation that I have to work hard to live down to, but some formerly cold marble hearts might need a thermos-nuclear weapon to warm them up."

"You don't think your weapon is up to it?" chipped in Roxy, unable to supress a slight laugh at her mild double entendre.

Without pausing to think, Dedan looked her in the eyes and gave her a wry grin. "You'd be amazed at some of the troubles that have been averted thanks to my *peacekeeper*!"

"Yes, yes, yes, thank you children. If you can both leave your teenage smut for another day." God's words of chastisement were not delivered in a stern voice, but they got the message across, as both of His guests adopted looks of contrition and fell silent. "Dedan, I have managed to locate Hor'idey's dimension, and I want you to use the portal and go talk to her. Charm the pants off her, either metaphorically or literally, but persuade her to tell you where on Earth her newly found disciples are. Then, once you have the information, get back here straight away."

Then He turned his gaze to Roxy. "As for you, Roxy, I have had a message from the resident angel, posted in the Vatican City, that there is something unusual going on at the Pantheon in Rome and it has all the hallmarks of Falacer. He's an obscure god that might have taken the meaning of the building's name to mean that 'All Gods' as an invitation for him to take over the place and make it into his private version of the Elysium Fields. I need you to go there, talk to him, and point out that taking over buildings on Earth is no longer acceptable and it isn't his private domain. He needs to find his own dimension, or he will have a problem."

Roxy nodded as she processed the seemingly simple instructions. She'd never encountered another god before so wasn't sure what they were really like. She had read many myths and stories about ancient deities, but their reputations didn't fill her with optimism for reaching a positive outcome. Cruelty, vanity, and capriciousness seemed to be their main traits, so being told what to do by God might not work with their egos. The name of Falacer was unknown to her so she knew that, before she went back to Italy, she'd have to do a bit of research and find out more about the ancient Roman god.

"Angelica will provide you with a few pieces of equipment that will help you in Rome. Good luck, both of you." God maintained His serious expression and gave them a slight nod to emphasise His respect for the two emissaries. He knew they had difficult tasks but felt sure that they would be able to fulfil them.

10 – Knock Knock

The knowledge that Roxy had managed to acquire about Falacer, prior to being transported to Rome, had been scant and quite possibly completely inaccurate. As with many minor gods, academics had not bothered to spend a lot of time researching, or recording, details of his existence. Any information which existed was often contradictory and vague enough to be dangerous, if she took the so-called *facts* as gospel truth. All she had found out from the vast library in Heaven was that there was a town in Italy named after him and that he could be temperamental. So, with such minimal data, she felt that what she had found out was not much help when it came to planning a meeting.

On her arrival, she saw that she was at the Via della Rosetta. When she had been alive, she had lived for a few years in Rome and knew the area well and was pleased that the Piazza della Rotonda was just at the end of the street and, from where she was, she could see the crowds of tourists standing around impatiently wanting to be granted access to the cordoned off square.

Giving her jacket one last check, to ensure everything was where it had been placed prior to leaving Heaven, she was relieved to feel the fake Interpol badge in her pocket, the small Beretta M9 pistol still in its shoulder holster and was pleased that the weapon was compact enough not to spoil the elegant appearance of her clothing. She wasn't sure what good a pistol would be against a god, but it was comforting to have it, just in case, and it reinforced her role as a member of the international police force.

Pushing her way through the mass of compacted tourists, adopting an officious attitude, she ignored their indignant looks and rude comments and managed to reach the temporary plastic bollards and barriers which were there to prevent the crowds from getting in the way of the strange, but as yet unspecified, crime scene. Although the noise of the tourists around her was loud, she managed to attract the attention of a soldier on guard duty. She waved her badge in his face and succeeded in explaining to him that she needed to be allowed into the square. On seeing the emblem of Interpol, the planet Earth with a gold sword stuck in it as if it were its axis, he understood that he was not in any position to argue, so he gave her a smart salute and moved the barrier slightly so that she could get through without having to climb over it. He politely directed her in the direction of Captain Uomoduro, reclosed the gap in the cordoned off area, and resumed his duties.

Roxy, on finding the busy captain, attempted to get his attention but, on each try, he just glanced at her and said, "One moment" and carried on with trying to give orders to soldiers and police officers. There wasn't much for any of them to do, but it always looked good to any civilian on-lookers if people were rushing around and appearing to have set tasks to perform.

Finally, losing patience, she grabbed him by the shoulder, forcing him to spin around so that he could give her the respect and attention that she imagined a member of Interpol would expect. "Excuse me!" she said, raising her voice with an authoritative tone.

"YES? Who are you and what do you want? Can't you see I am busy?" Even if it was by a beautiful woman with impeccable taste in clothing, the captain wasn't used to being manhandled and today, of all days, was not the right time for someone to start doing it.

It was only at that point that Roxy realised that she hadn't checked the name on the badge. It could have said anything and if she incorrectly introduced herself, she could have ended the mission before it had even started. She decided to bluff it out and use her surname from when she had been a living human. "Rossana Doloreo, Interpol." She quickly flashed him her badge, giving him enough time to see the emblem but insufficient to read the name on the ID card in the opposing side of the badge holder. Her confident approach had its desired outcome, as the sight of the ID and the word 'Interpol' was enough to make him give her his full and undivided attention.

"Yes, Signora Doloreo, how can I be of assistance?" the sentence spoken much more calmly and politely than the previous one had been.

Relieved that her bluff had worked, she gave her badge a perfunctory glance as she folded it and replaced it in her jacket's inner pocket. Fortunately for Roxy, Angelica had not been tempted to create some elaborate alias or use the name of some existing human field agent. The name she saw was her own, so she needn't have been concerned if the captain had decided to scrutinise it.

"Please call me Roxy. You are Captain…?"

"Captain Uomoduro, Signora. At your service." He had not been sure who had jurisdiction here when the army officers had started to appear and thanks to the new arrival, he sensed his power slipping away. There was even talk of government scientists on their way as well, which was, in his mind, turning the whole thing into a circus. Everyone was treating it as a terrorist incident, but there had been no explosions, no guns, and no terror. All that he knew was that there was some inexplicable force field preventing anyone from entering the Pantheon. If, and when, they managed to get into the building, he had no idea what to expect so he had no problem with the soldiers being present, but as far as he was concerned, the Polizia di Stato were in control and, as their senior ranking representative, he was by default the boss. The sudden and unexpected appearance of Interpol was just another nuisance. But until the pretty agent started to get in his way, he would be happy to humour her.

"Thank you, Captain. For reasons I am not at liberty to divulge, I need to be allowed to try and gain access to the Pantheon, alone, and investigate whatever is inside it."

"Alone?" Even if she found a way in, the captain felt uncomfortable with the idea of allowing her to go into the building on her own. It was a mixture of chivalry, machismo, the desire to stay in charge, and plain curiosity. If there was something, or someone, in there then he needed to know about it and be the one to deal with it. He had no intention of allowing anyone, especially a woman, to usurp his authority. "Over my dead body. I am afraid that I can't allow that. If you do manage to get in there, then I insist that I come with you. Just to ensure your safety, of course."

"Of course. Thank you, Captain, but I assure you that I can look after myself. What is in there is not for your eyes, is classified and could be more dangerous than you could ever imagine. I can't guarantee that I could protect you if you tagged along."

Roxy's words did nothing to change his mind and he had no intention of standing in the middle of the piazza and arguing with her in front of his men, especially if there was a risk of him losing to a woman. He'd never had many dealings with Interpol, but he suspected that she could easily pull rank and speak to someone higher up, going over his head so that he was taken off the case altogether. So, with that unissued threat rolling around his mind, he was happy to step back, for now. "If you say so, *Roxy*." He gave her a salute that, to his colleagues viewing from a distance, looked like a respectful acknowledgement of her rank but, up close, was tinged with sarcastic contempt which wasn't lost on her.

Choosing to ignore the slight, Roxy sighed and whispered under her breath, "Men!" She had too much to do and had no time to argue with someone that, in her opinion, had his brain somewhere in his genitalia. "Stay here and keep your men back. What I am about to do might look strange, but trust me; once inside, things will probably get even stranger."

The captain swept his arm grandly in the direction of the ancient building. "Be my guest, signorina, do what you need to do," only just managing to keep his misogynistic contempt under control and refrain from making a comment that could have caused a complaint to be sent from the Interpol head office in Lyon to his superiors. Roxy was familiar with the outdated attitudes of many Italian men so, even if he had made a comment, she would have ignored it and not reinforced his prejudices by letting herself get upset.

Calmly but hesitantly walking forward, she reached out her hand as she approached the building and as soon as it made contact with the forcefield, she stopped. Her eyes and brain were telling her there was nothing there, but the sensation on her fingers felt strange and told her otherwise. It was a feeling of mild heat and a slight electrical tingle as if static were dancing invisibly in the air, with one single jolt of contact doing nothing to discharge it.

Captain Uomoduro watched her and began to follow. When she stopped, he followed suit, ensuring that he remained a few paces behind her. What she did next left him thinking that he should have inspected her badge a little more closely and perhaps verified her identity and presence with his office. There could have been a report of an escaped lunatic, and he'd have been able to return her to her special room with padded wallpaper and a suit with snug arm straps.

Conscious that the police and soldiers were watching her, and were a curious audience, she blithely ignored them. She knew that her actions would seem crazy to them, and if she'd been in their shoes, she'd have felt the same, but sometimes life can be inexplicable and still go on. Lowering herself down, she placed one knee on the hard ground, bowed her head and spread her arms wide in a gesture of supplication. "Oh mighty, powerful and wise Falacer, I humbly seek an audience and request the boon of being allowed to draw near and enter your temple."

On hearing the words, Captain Uomoduro raised his eyes to the cloudy sky and swore under his breath. He could see himself being the laughingstock of the Rome police department. In his mind, he could hear the jokes and sniggers aimed at the officer that allowed a lunatic to take over his investigation and turn the event into an occult festival. At least she wasn't dressed as a Vestal Virgin but, if she had been, he'd have been more wary and not allowed her within a mile of the building.

Then he began to see something that he wasn't expecting and couldn't explain. The air in front of Roxy began to shimmer, as if there was a heat induced mirage isolated into the confines of a rectangular door shape. Roxy tentatively put her hand against it and her fingers passed through the barrier, altering the image so that it looked as if it were bent like the rays of light in a bucket of water. Then, as she moved the rest of her body through the rippling illusion, she appeared to bend and then, once on the other side, appear normal again, as if nothing had happened. Not wanting to be left on the wrong side of the strange translucent curtain, the captain sprang forward and was through the doorway, just fast enough to get to the other side before it disappeared, leaving just them on one side and the rest of the bemused crowd on the other.

Seeing that she had been followed, Roxy glowered at the captain, eyebrows furrowed in anger and frustration. "You idiot, I told you to stay outside. You are not safe here."

"Relax, signorina, I know how to look after myself." He reinforced that statement by gently tapping the holster containing his pistol, which was attached to his belt. "I think I can handle anyone that wants to cause trouble."

"Really? I doubt it. Just stay outside," she instructed sternly, making it clear that she would brook no disagreement. Without waiting, or giving him any opportunity to speak, she walked up the steps and went between the two central columns just in front of the main entrance door. Before she could touch the doors, they swung inwards, allowing her to enter. Despite the light streaming through the large round oculus in the centre of the ceiling, she still had to briefly screw up her eyes so that they could acclimatise to the mix of focused bright light and the surrounding gloom. Then, just as the doors began to swing shut behind her, she heard Captain Uomoduro as he ran and shimmied through the dwindling gap. Turning around, she looked at him with pure rage filling her face.

Raising his hands, palms facing outwards, he shrugged. "What?"

Facing the inner chamber, she looked around. The concrete dome overhead with its indentations, like alcoves, had been adorned with lit candles, their flames gently swaying in the breeze emanating from the large round hole in the ceiling. The sixteen Corinthian columns supporting the vast porticos, hiding dark shadows behind them.

"Hello?" she said, her voice echoing in the vast hall.

There was a shuffling noise to her right, in the dimly lit alcove and chapel containing the remains and memorial of King Victor Emmanuel II. At first, she just saw a black movement as if the shadows were coming together and heading out of the gloom. Then it began to change its shape, adopting the form of a muscular dark-haired man. He was wearing a toga that was so brilliantly white that it made Roxy's eyes hurt from the glare and she feared that she might get snow blindness if she had to look at it for too long. The main difference in his appearance to any other human, other than the bright and archaic clothing, was that he was eight feet tall, as muscular as an ox on steroids and his skin seemed to be radiating a golden glow.

On seeing the strange figure suddenly appear, as if out of thin air, the startled policeman instinctively reached for his pistol. Turning, and seeing what he was doing, Roxy gave him a panicked look and shook her head slightly as an urgent signal to remain calm and to keep his weapon safely where it was. The last thing she needed was a policeman trying to negotiate with a gun in his hand; Falacer's interest in talking and, more importantly, listening would probably diminish if he were being shot at. The gunshots might not harm him but, just like most mortal humans, he probably wouldn't have appreciated bullets hitting him.

She had encountered men like the captain in the past. Before dying, and going to Heaven, she had been married to a lean and attractive German. He was her type, but the best way to fully describe her type would be to use the term *arseholes*. He was narcissistic, egotistical, and controlling, and saw women as the natural, silent and unquestioning servants to men. Even after they had divorced, he punished her by using their daughter as a tool to prevent her from moving out of the small Bavarian town where she lived. The captain gave her that same impression of a man full of the desire to control. A sexy body on the shallow, charming surface, but someone that viewed women as subservient and inferior.

Ancient Romans had a propensity to create gods for virtually every possible situation and function. Among many others there were deities to be worshipped if you had sick cattle, an impending battle, or a leaking roof. Roxy would have been displeased if it were Cloacina that had been resurrected. Being the goddess of sewers, it could have been unpleasant if she'd set up her domain among the underground pipes containing the excrement of the modern city.

The current god, standing before her, might be equally minor and unimportant, but she knew that his own self-image and ego may not see it that way. Therefore, turning her attention to the demigod, she carefully lowered herself down and prostrated herself on the ground, arms outstretched so that no offence could be interpreted from her actions. "Oh, mighty and wise Falacer, I am on a mission for God and need to talk with you."

"God? Which God? There are many, but alas, not as many as I remember." His voice was booming and seemed to fill the air with so much sound that it made it hard for the two humans to catch their breath and breathe properly.

"Falacer, it is *THE* God. He has many names but is the ultimate creator. The bringer of light, moulder of Earth and protector of humanity."

"Oh, Him!" Falacer was about to continue but his focus was taken from Roxy to the police captain, his face full of contempt for the lack of respect that he thought was due to him. "And you in the strange uniform, are you also an emissary from God? Do you not pay me homage?" The anger in his voice shook the walls, loosening dust from the domed ceiling and making it fall to the ground like a fine grey misty rain.

Feeling that his own personal authority was being challenged by a tall man in a white dress, the captain was in no mood to play any games at a terrorist fancy dress party. Seeing that Falacer was unarmed, he decided that his pistol gave him the upper hand. "I am Captain Piero Uomoduro of the Polizia di Stato of Rome and you, sir, are under arrest." To emphasise what he perceived to be his control of the situation, he removed his standard issue Beretta 92 pistol and pointed it at the god. "Just lower the force field and come with me, and I promise to put in a good word for you when you go to court. I am sure that the psychiatrist's report will also work in your favour."

Seeing the pistol pointed at him, Falacer gave the captain a sardonic smile. "You will have to excuse me, I have been away for a long time, but I have no idea what a psychiatrist is. Also, am I to assume that you are holding some sort of weapon and you are trying to display dominance by pointing it at me?"

Lifting her head so that she was no longer facing the cold and dirty white marble floor, Roxy could guess what had happened behind her. "Please, Falacer, excuse his ignorance. Your name has long been absent from people's hearts and minds. He is ignorant of who you truly are. He is a policeman; I mean a city guard. He is just doing his job and genuinely means no disrespect." Lifting herself up, she turned to the captain and hissed, "For God's sake, put the gun away and get on your knees."

"This man is under arrest, so I will not put my gun away. I'd rather die!" he bellowed; his voice full of angry sarcasm.

"That option is acceptable to me!" Falacer raised an arm and pointed his finger at the captain, and a single bolt of green energy was released from his forefinger. It flew through the air and across the hall, striking the officer directly in the chest. There was a bright flash, the sound of bones cracking, and a thick, sickening smell of burning flesh. Piero looked down at the ever-growing hole in his midriff and then collapsed. The burning continued to spread out until all that was left was a human shaped pile of black ashes and the pistol lying on the ground where it had been dropped.

There are people all over the world, in every walk of life, that are up for a challenge. Humanity is always reaching for the unreachable and proving other people wrong. Give them a mountain to conquer, and up they go and, once it has been climbed, others will go out of their way to find more difficult and seemingly impossible ways to plant their flag on the summit. Tell them that reaching the moon is hard, and they will spend billions and smile as they try and tell you how easily they made the journey.

This pig-headed approach to life is not limited to science or exploration. Give the right person, or more accurately the wrong person, a red flashing button with a sign next to it saying, "Do NOT press this," and they will shake and twitch like a tormented jelly in an earthquake until they finally give in and press it, only then spending the rest of their short lifespan realising it was a mistake. Give someone a pretty pink pill and tell them that if they eat it, it will be fun, but there is a good chance it will kill them, many will say, "Okay, can I have a glass of beer to wash it down?" Warning labels are all too often treated as instructions, helping to rid the world of people that would be too dangerous to swim in the gene pool without armbands. The captain was one of those people.

As if he had just swatted an annoying and insignificant fly that had been buzzing around his head, Falacer turned his attention back to Roxy. "There, that's better. Now, where were we? Oh yes, you have a message for me."

As Roxy stared briefly at what was left of the late Captain Piero Uomoduro, she realised that he was not suited to listening to wise advice, especially if delivered by a woman. Once he had a key role in society but now, he was only good for spreading over snow covered paths. She wasn't sad that he had been killed. She knew that if he was good, he'd go to Heaven, and if he was bad, then she wasn't unhappy for anyone that went to the other place either. Besides, being a loose cannon, he would have been a liability with the current situation. She'd have been trying to use sweet words to massage the ego of the god, while the captain would have been engaged in testosterone fuelled verbal battles with him. He was not one of life's natural calm negotiators and was even less so in death. Turning her attention back to Falacer, she tried to put the fate of Piero to the back of her mind. "Yes, mighty Falacer. He…"

Before she could continue, he interrupted her, raising his arms so that his hands were level with his shoulders. "Where are my manners? Please be seated." Then, out of nowhere, two ancient long Roman accubita couches appeared in the centre of the hall. She saw a small table next to them supporting bowls of grapes, a jug of wine and two gold goblets encrusted with rubies and emeralds. "There you go, that is better. More like home."

Roxy had seen the furniture before in movies, usually during scenes involving some cruel emperor languidly laid out eating rich foods, covered in fish sauce, as he talked of the downfall of a senator that had upset him, or some rich merchants having every wish fulfilled by semi naked obedient slaves. It might be like home to him but to Roxy, it was a world, and too many centuries, away from what she had grown up with as a child in a small town in the south of Italy. Seeing that Falacer had semi reclined on one of the accubita, she sat rigidly on the other, giving the impression that she was afraid that it would absorb her into the plush fabric if she made herself too comfortable.

"Thank you, Falacer, that is better. As I was saying…" Just then, she was interrupted once more as the god snapped his fingers majestically and three scantily clad women appeared. Without receiving any instruction, they automatically began to pour the wine and offer fruit to both of them. Roxy declined all silent entreaties from them to partake in the feast, but Falacer simply lay back as one concubine fed grapes into his mouth. "As I was saying," she continued, determined to speak without interruptions, "you have been dead for many centuries, but now you have a following and have returned. But Earth has changed and moved on. With all due respect, you just can't return and take over the whole of a national monument and claim it as your own."

"As my own? Is this not the Pantheon? The home for all gods, sacred ground even before this building existed. A place of worship and sanctuary for all immortals. Or at least, immortals right up to the point that they die. I have as much right to be here as your God and if He were to come and join me, He would be made most welcome. I have plenty of wine." His tone was matter of fact, as if he were talking to an insignificant slave.

Roxy looked around at the ornate building. "But that was long ago. The only residents here now are the vague memories and faint ghosts of lost religions. All the old gods long since left this place, leaving only the name and an outdated idea. Nobody comes here to worship any more. There are just tourists wanting to take photographs."

"I have no idea what the *photographs* are, but I can feel what you are saying. This place used to be full of wild parties and holy prayers warming the spirits of all that were worshipped. Now the cold empty desolation grips my soul with its icy fingers and fills my whole being with sadness."

"Then please go back to your dimensional plane. You have the souls of your followers there."

"Yes," he replied sadly, still thinking of the days of glory in Ancient Rome. "This world is no longer mine. There was a time I would have argued and fought your God for the right to stay here but I am so weak and so tired. I long for the comfort of oblivion again. An eternity of stone would be better than this hollow existence. Do you know how many believers I have?"

"No. How many?" Suddenly she was paying more attention, as she realised that his volunteering of information was saving her from having to sound like she was interrogating him.

"One. Can you believe it? Me, a Roman god. I used to have many thousands giving me strength with their supplications. Oh, so many homes with shrines where they laid out offerings to me along with their prayers, giving me power. But now? A weak and inattentive man in a land that I don't even know. I have seen into his soul and even his faith is feeble. Unsure, sceptical and more of a distraction from his lonely life than faith. I am a candle that barely illuminates a dark corner of his life. Belief should be a raging fire, not something that could be snuffed out by a mucus filled sneeze."

Roxy was taken aback by the dejected words. She had expected the god to be full of life and determined to make up for many years of lost hedonism. "So, Falacer, you do not want to be here? Why don't you just return to the Hall of Dead Gods?"

"Return? I wish I could, but the lone half-hearted disciple has me trapped. I am a prisoner seeking the freedom of non-existence. Oblivion is sweet compared to this bitter existence."

"If I promise to try and release you, so you can die again, will you return to your dimension?" Roxy wasn't sure who the worshipper was, where he lived or, if she found him, how she'd get him to stop believing but she knew that she had to try.

"You would do that?" Falacer's eyes were full of desperate hope. Many gods would lie as second nature, but she could see that he was genuine.

"I give you my solemn word!"

"In that case, I will go. But if you fail, I'll be back! Please don't let me down. I hate this modern life; it is confusing, and it is so full of anger and hatred. That used to be the job of gods so that all mortals had to do was fear and worship us for the protection we gave them! Oh, those were the good old days."

With that, he clicked his fingers and disappeared, taking with him the furniture. The absence of anything to sit on leaving Roxy momentarily sitting in mid-air before gravity noticed the anomaly and sprang into action. The fall was unexpected and uncomfortable, inducing an almost silent profanity as she lay inelegantly on the floor looking up at the large hole in the ceiling, with the once burning candles, that had provided extra illumination, now gone. The only two things in the hall that were unusual were Roxy and the grey police officer dust that wouldn't have looked out of place in a large ash tray. Returning to her feet, she rubbed her sore bottom and dusted off her clothing.

She decided that she had better open the dimensional portal inside the building rather than risk going outside. She had best return to Heaven as quickly as possible as the transformation of the captain from a large male to a small pile of powder would be difficult to explain to the soldiers and police waiting outside of the building. Once the portal obediently appeared just in front of the angel, she walked through it and was gone. Other than leaving a mystery and a feast of half-baked ideas for conspiracy theorists, there was nothing in the room to show that she had ever been there.

11 – Making up is Hard to do

Not all religions had the same ideas when it comes to what Heaven or even Hell should look like. Some themes tended to repeat themselves but that was not always guaranteed. Faiths founded in sweltering desert lands liked to create paradises that were verdant, cool and full of relaxing streams. Northern religions often went for places full of sunny and tropically sandy beaches. The only common thread was that their version of Heaven was better than where the believers had to exist and live their ordinary and dull lives while on Earth.

The dimensional plane belonging to the goddess Hor'idey wasn't what Dedan had expected. It was hard to be a living human husband of a god but in that time, he had tried to get what he thought would be a good impression of what her Heaven would be like. But, like many husbands and ex-husbands throughout history, he was totally wrong. Instead of a plush palace adorned with silk draped over every conceivable piece of furniture, and quite possibly the residents as well, the sight that filled his eyes was far from his simple preconceptions.

Although it was night, the whole place was lit by a giant full moon directly overhead, bathing everything in a pale blue light and casting dark but comforting shadows that made everywhere look like a scene from a romantic art era painting. There were pine trees on either side with a path leading downwards to a tranquil lake and, in the distance, he could see a tall cliff with a narrow waterfall. At the top of that was a plateau and, in the further distance, was a mist shrouded, snow-capped mountain. The air was cool and moist but not uncomfortably cold on his skin.

He couldn't understand where this version of her paradise came from, as it was as far from her historical reality as spaceships were to cavemen. When he had first worshipped, met, fallen in love with and finally married her, the home terrain they lived in was a bleak and desolate wasteland full of sand dotted with small towns and remote oases. In his time as a human, he'd never encountered such a landscape and, as far as he knew, neither had Hor'idey nor any of her followers. So how could either she, or they, have projected such an image into their version of the afterlife? Water he could understand, but the pine trees and almost alpine appearance were a paradox.

Taking his first step in the different version of the Promised Land, Dedan realised that there was an age-old question that was frequently asked with regards to the toilet habits of bears, but other animals were left to do their business without questioning. Feeling something soft underfoot, he groaned in suspicion of the cause of the accompanying squishing sound. Lifting his foot behind him and leaning back, so he could see the offending substance, he saw some brown and sticky goo that was unwelcome, especially if it was walked into the family carpet.

"Bloody dogs," he muttered, but he was quickly corrected when, in the moonlight shadows, he saw bright eyes glinting and then heard angry snarling. His next silent utterance could have either been him swearing or just describing what was on the underside of his shoe but, irrespective of the meaning, the "shit" was lost in the noise as half a dozen grey and white northern timber wolves came crashing into the clearing of the path. Branches and twigs broke underfoot as they ran towards him, the menacing growling becoming louder as they got closer to him. Then, when they were just five feet away, they stopped. Dedan could see that he was encircled and had nowhere to run but wasn't sure what the hungry animals were waiting for. He could see their teeth and knew that, even if he had chance to draw his pistol, he wouldn't be able to shoot them all and he'd be ripped to pieces if he made any sudden hostile movements. Raising his arms above his head as a sign of surrender, he looked at what he thought to be the alpha male in the eyes. "All right, doggies, you've got me!"

Then he heard laughter coming from amongst the dense forest to his right. "Not the best battle I have ever seen but a wise choice. The wolves have just two settings, win easily or rip the enemy to pieces and eat them in the process of winning." Straining to see into the gloom, Dedan saw a figure step forward. It was a man wearing a brown robe with a hood covering his head. What could be seen of his face was partially hidden behind a neatly trimmed black beard decorated with yellow beads. The stranger stepped into the light, but even that didn't help Dedan to get a better view. He released a shrill whistle which made the wolves look at him and then run back into the forest, the only noise they made being that of padded paws on the wooden and leafy detritus covering the ground. Once they had disappeared, the shrouded figure pulled his hood down, revealing the rest of his head. He was bald with tattoos depicting stars and flames decorating his scalp. "Hello, I am Bangledmuttocks, and you are?"

"I am Dedan, I am here to see…" His sentence was stopped as lightning began to strike the edge of the plateau and thunder rumbling as if it were a tidal wave of sound. The noise was so powerful that it hit him like a punch and nearly knocked him off his feet.

"Oh, dear." Bangledmuttocks suddenly became serious and stern. "It sounds like Her Highness knows you, but I am not sure if that is a good thing." Setting off along the path, he told Dedan, "You'd better come with me."

Seeing Bangledmuttocks begin his trek, Dedan began to follow him. "As I was saying, I am Dedan and…" At the further use of his name, there was a repeat of the thunder and lightning. The sound made the guide stop and turn to face Dedan; a perturbed expression partially hidden by his ornament encrusted beard.

"Yes, I got the name, and you are here to see the mighty Hor'idey. I get it, but can I ask you to refrain from saying your name out loud? It seems to solicit an unwelcome reaction. We are heading to the point where the lightning keeps meeting the ground and I have no desire to be struck by it. I have heard that, by all accounts, it can be an uncomfortable experience."

He'd never felt a direct lightning strike either, but Dedan had to admit that it probably wasn't much fun so decided to avoid saying his own name, for the moment at least.

As they walked, Dedan tried to make some sort of sense of all he was seeing. Sporadically, scattered on either side of the path, there were broad clearings full of buildings mainly resembling the flat roofed red brick type that he used to see every day in his own kingdom during his time as a ruler in the early Old Testament days. Vaguely familiar, there were old people sitting outside drinking and enjoying the moonlight, younger adults standing around chatting and laughing, and children were playing, totally oblivious to the fact that it was night-time. As he drew closer to the lake, the settlements became more frequent and larger and when he got to the water's edge, they were sprawling like a primitive city where waterfront properties were at a premium. On the lake were oniyoths, the ancient boats made from tall and hollow reeds tied tightly together into bundles, their broad sails open and full as they gently skimmed across the water. There was so much that was familiar to him, but the setting was completely wrong. For all this to be right, it should have been a dry and arid wasteland with a single wide river and the only trees should have been figs, dates and palms. But he had to admit that this was a definite improvement on the rather pathetic kingdom that he used to rule.

On reaching the shore, they walked onto a narrow wooden jetty extending out into the lake. There was a small boat waiting for them manned by a young boy in dirty brown rags who was busy eating a chunk of bread. Despite the apparent poverty of the child, he greeted them with a broad smile and words of welcome. Bangledmuttocks and Dedan climbed onboard and even before he could sit down, the boy set sail and they were on their way. The lake was placid and calm with the only sound being the gentle breeze in the sails and the water parting as the bow of the craft broke the surface.

As the boat reflected on the barely rippling waters, Dedan had to admit that it would have been a perfect setting for a romantic evening where he'd have ended up 'accidentally' losing an oar and having to 'entertain' his female companion until the morning and the inevitable rescue. Unfortunately, looking at his bald male guide, the fires of passion were far from ever being lit.

Dedan was full of questions but realised that, if he survived the first few minutes of his reunion with his ex-wife, he would be able to address them directly to Hor'idey. Bangledmuttocks seemed to be preoccupied with staring at Dedan without making it obvious that he was doing so, his furtive glances tinged with suspicion, unspoken questions, and distrust. Dedan couldn't think of any small talk to fill the silence so decided to go back to enjoying the view. Even though the distance covered was large, the boat reached the other side of the lake at a speed that, if it had been on Earth, would have thrown the passengers backwards and needed a high-powered outboard motor to achieve such velocity. But in this dimension, the ride was so smooth that Dedan felt like the primitive boat had drifted aimlessly the whole way.

Pulling up to the sandy shore, near the waterfall, they disembarked. There was a path that led along the edge of the lake and zigzagged up the cliff and both casually walked along it. As they went higher, Dedan was able to look across the lake and get a better view of where he'd just come from. The forest spread out into the distance, as far as he could see, and in the gaps in the canopy there were wispy smoke plumes rising to the sky indicating that there were extensive settlements. From the sheer number of them, he surmised that the population of this paradise was bigger than he'd expected. The number of inhabitants was clearly more than his world had ever held at any one single moment in time. Then he remembered that the dead souls in any paradise grew over the centuries as generation after generation of believers passed away. Despite it being early in civilised history, and being geographically remote and isolated, he was certainly impressed; his ex-wife had been a popular lady and had accumulated a large number of followers while she had lived in people's hearts and souls.

On reaching the wide plateau, Dedan had to do a double take. He rubbed his eyes in disbelief, as if he'd had some flashback or hallucination. But even that didn't change what he saw ahead of him. It was missing the big black imposing fence with spikes on top and the heavily armed security guards trying to look inconspicuous but, beyond the immaculately cut lawn and trees, was a fountain and behind that an exact replica of the northern facade of the White House, including the columned portico and the flagpole on the roof. However, the flag that was fluttering in the wind was not familiar to Dedan and it was hard to make out some of the finer details in the moonlight. Despite his disinclination to resort to small talk with Bangledmuttocks, he decided that the subject was large enough to initiate a conversation. He stopped in his tracks and grabbed hold of the sleeve of his companion's cloak. "But that's the White House! How can it be the White House?" he asked incredulously, his voice carrying further, in the darkness and silence, than he had intended.

Bangledmuttocks looked at Dedan with a puzzled expression, not fully understanding the question. "Yes, it is a white house. I would imagine that it is white because of the paint. But it isn't all white inside if that choice of colour offends you." Dedan got the impression that Bangledmuttocks had no knowledge of the building at 1600

Pennsylvania Avenue in Washington, D.C. And that assumption would have been totally correct.

Bangledmuttocks's version of Earth, and all that was in it, had been restricted to a life in a small valley in the Arabian Peninsula in what is now known as Yemen. He had died then gone to his paradise as a servant of his beloved goddess. When her earthly believers disappeared, so did she, and his soul was automatically transferred to Hell, where he had spent the intervening millennia being sand blasted in the daytime and then healing over in the night. His sudden, but very welcome, return to his version of paradise had been a shock but he wasn't complaining. Therefore, any architectural or historical references beyond 3023 BC were meaningless to him. Considering the black and white interpretation of what he was saying, Dedan decided not to try and explain so he simply reverted to silence.

Dedan had been in the real building on a couple of occasions. The first was when he had helped Theodore Roosevelt get a bill passed, despite several demons who were determined to block it, and the second time was when he had to rid the world of a cell of Boden demons that had tried to ensure that Richard Nixon's exploits were not made public. As he walked through the entrance, Bangledmuttocks bowed and took his leave, apparently eager to exit the large building, allowing Dedan to take in the full magnificence of the lobby. He was impressed to see that, despite a few changes in furniture and pictures on the wall, it was exactly as he remembered it.

The only anomaly was the people - instead of the dour and formal suits and smart haircuts, there was long and greasy hair with dull and dirty sackcloth robes that would have had the wearers arrested if they tried to gain access to the real building. A couple of men, adorned with gold moon shaped pendants attached to chains around their necks, approached him with hands held together, as if they were multi-tasking by combining walking with praying. "Greetings," their soft but oily voices speaking in unison.

"Hello I'm De…."

Before he could finish saying his name, both priests reached out their hands as a signal for him to stop talking. "Yes, we know who you are.

90

But please, there is no need to say it. You have damaged the roof of this palace enough as it is. Have you any idea how much destruction lightning can do to a building?" The rhetorical question was synchronised so that Dedan heard it in stereo. "You are *he who must never be named*, so please come with us, and we will take you to see Her Most Majestic Highness. The Mightiest of the Mighty. The Greatest Glory of the World."

The aggrandisement of his erstwhile wife made him want to laugh, but he thought better of it. No matter who they were, in what era, and who the deity was, the ability of priests to suck up to their respective gods was universal and only limited by their vocabulary and time available for them to talk. The expression 'My god's better than your god' was never uttered, but it wouldn't have been out of place in any temple when opposing clerics met. The flowery and stereotypical superlatives aimed at his former spouse were all the more out of place as he'd seen her dark side and numerous foibles and knew from bitter experience that she was far from majestic, mighty or even glorious; especially when she had been drunk or had a hangover. On such occasions, it had been best to run and take cover. But if they wanted to keep their jobs, most acolytes would overlook, or deny, such character flaws. Inebriation, nudity, lewd singing, projectile vomiting, flatulence and eventual falling over might be fun to witness but could result in prompt demotion if they admitted to seeing it. He remembered a spectacular drinking session where she had disappeared for three days and returned naked, apart from an inch-thick layer of mud covering her entire body, with just a vague memory involving wrestling a family of hippos. Happy days indeed, but that was so long ago.

As he walked behind the two solemn clergymen, he was tempted to say his name a few times just so that he could see their reactions and the chaos that his words could create, but he thought better of it. He knew that he must refrain from such frivolity at least until his meeting with Hor'idey. He might not need to say anything to get a bolt of lightning melting his skull and boiling his brain, so why tempt fate?

The corridor leading to the white panelled door of the oval office seemed to be longer than he remembered but, in a parallel dimension, architectural perspectives could vary from those on Earth. The slightly taller of the two priests knocked on the door, pulled it open and stood back slightly so that Dedan could enter. They gave him a deep bow and then, after he'd entered the epicentre of what would have been the American president's most sacred inner sanctum, they closed the door after him.

Straight away, two things caught his attention. The first was the goddess Hor'idey, but he didn't have much time to appreciate all her stunning physical attributes and appearance due to the second thing that caught his eye. A compact ball of bright yellow and red flame was heading from the direction of the goddess and, more worryingly, it was moving towards his head. Despite his frame being far from the tall, dark, and handsome athletic type, Dedan's reflexes were quick, so he was able to dive to the floor. The bulk of the projectile just missed him, but he felt the heat on the side of head, singing his hair in the process. Failing to hit its target, the missile struck the wall, sending a cascade of flames outwards like a beautiful, but deadly, chrysanthemum flower. Once the fire had burned out, the white wall was no longer so pristine, leaving a smoking, scorched and blackened circle as a record of a goddess's anger.

"Hello, Dedan. It's been a long time. Nice dive. How are you?"

Although, from his position on the floor, he couldn't see the speaker, he recognised the sweet and calm voice, the gentle tone a stark contrast to the violence of the fireball that he'd just had to dodge. He was also relieved to hear his name spoken without any thunder or lightening accompanying it.

"Oh, Dedan, you look ridiculous down there. Please get up, I promise not to try and cremate you again…well, for now at least."

Carefully Dedan got up, his muscles tensed just in case his host was only joking about any further attempts at immolation, ready to dive out of the way of the physical manifestation of furied Hell delivered by a scorned woman. He looked at Hor'idey and was relieved to see that there was no indication that she was making any attempt to create any sort of projectile with which to incinerate him. Moving his eyes away from her hands and arms, he was able to concentrate on the rest of her body. Although some details could slip from the mind, especially after several thousand years, as he looked his heart jolted as she seemed to be even more beautiful than he remembered. Her long hair, that seemed to flow over her bare shoulders like a river, was a gold colour that made him wish he had sunglasses to protect his eyes from the glare. Her skin was perfectly tanned, and her face seemed to fit the now standard artistic golden ratio for beauty. Every feature seemed to be just right and even the greatest painter in the world would have struggled to have truly captured the glow that radiated from her face when she smiled, or the sizzling playfulness of her piercing blue eyes. As for her clothing, she was wearing a tight silvery blue, off the shoulder, figure hugging dress that accentuated her slender figure and round bosom. The colour seemed deliberately chosen by her to emphasise and highlight the gold of her hair.

Staring at her, his mind went back to his days as a king, how they had met, and how he'd fallen so heavily in love with her. A wandering lay preacher had visited him and began to extol the virtues of a new goddess who was becoming popular with the people, each virtue and grace exalted as the stranger tried to introduce religion into Dedan's heart and soul. Being a devout agnostic, Dedan had been a polite and civil host but sent him away with the admonishment that if he wanted religion, he would look for it himself, not the other way round.

That night Hor'idey appeared in a vision and spoke to him, from that point he was hooked. The next day, he sent guards out into the city to find the preacher and bring him back to the royal palace. After that he built a temple and made Hor'ideyism the state religion; even making the money lenders close during her festival days. Other gods would be tolerated but she alone could claim to be 'by Royal appointment'. In return for his eager conversion and devout fealty, she began to adopt a tangible form and visit him in a more real sense than just nocturnal dreams. Her physical rewards ensured that he worshipped on a regular basis, sometimes prostrate and other times on his knees. Eventually the romantic trysts developed, and she began to share the same feeling for him as he had felt for her since he first set eyes on her. It was rare for a deity to marry a mortal, but neither of them was bothered with such prejudices and could easily have dealt with any gossip whether it was from humans or other gods.

It all came flooding back to him; if it wasn't as if it were yesterday, then at least it felt like only a week last Tuesday. The softness of her skin on his fingertips, the warmth of her gentle lips, the feel of her hair brushing against his face, or other parts of his body, and the sensation of ecstasy when their limbs were wrapped around each other like vines entwining a single tree. They had been the happiest days of his life, but like many of the rare human/divine marriages based on philosophy, sacred incantations and almost cripplingly acrobatic sex, cracks eventually began to appear in the relationship. Hor'idey began to spend more time on divine goddess duties and less time on, or even with, him. He began to feel like he was an inconvenient distraction and, despite having Highest Priest as part of his resume, he felt like he was no longer part of her existence. They grew further and further apart until he felt estranged, and his spirit was lost. It was not a case of him deserting a religion but of his faith seeing him only as an afterthought or an occasional companion when the goddess had some spare time.

Finally, during a low patch, God visited him in a vision and explained the benefits of what He had to offer and the place the now lonely king could take in the battle of good against evil. At first Dedan had resisted, but the loneliness and disillusionment drove him, reluctantly, into the arms of another religion. Feeling angry and betrayed by his perceived disloyalty and apostasy, Hor'idey left his kingdom and retreated back to her dimensional plane, swearing dire, painful and definitely fatal vengeance if she ever saw him again. Regrets had been there, a few but too few for him to mention to her. But ever since then, he'd been trying to find someone to fill the gap left in his soul; a search that didn't end even with his eventual death and entry into Heaven.

Now that he looked into her eyes, the rage that had filled them all those many centuries ago was gone, replaced with the joyous sparkle that had first drawn him to her. Perhaps the fireball had just been part of a game or the final piece of catharsis on her part, the release of a bitter piece of history so that forgiveness could take its place. His thoughts and uncertainty were soon dispelled with her next words.

"Come here, doll. You are looking good, despite the strange clothing." Without waiting for him to advance, she ran up to him and first gave him a tight hug with her cheek pressed against his; then she loosened her hold slightly, leaned back a little, and gave him a firm kiss. The feeling of her body next to his brought back memories of better times and he had to admit that it felt good. Eventually, and reluctantly on

Dedan's part, they freed themselves from the passionate clinch, the bulge in his trousers evidencing his joy at the reunion was obvious.

"Come, sit down and we can talk. How are you? Tell me all about the world since I went away. Being a statue meant that I am a bit behind the times."

Although he would have loved the excuse to spend a long time with her going over old times, he felt sure that recounting several thousand years of history, and complex technological innovations, would take too long and, for the moment at least, he had other priorities. Maybe they would have time once the mission was over, but he knew he had his duty to perform first.

"I am good, my beautiful angel," he began, then paused as he noticed the hurt expression on Hor'idey's face. Realising that he had just demoted his ex-wife, he decided to begin again. "I am good, my beautiful goddess. You look amazing and in all the long years since you left, I have never found anybody more beautiful than you."

"Thank you, Dedan, you always were a silver-tongued flatterer, and I must admit flattery wasn't all your tongue was good at." She laughed and the sound made him feel as if Heaven was embodied in one person. "Do you remember the poems you used to write for me? Each word able to melt my heart and make me go weak at the knees. And do you remember what happened when my knees went weak?"

The recollection of all those magical experiences made him return her smile and laughter. "Yes, they were amazing times. I'm also amazed that we didn't break more beds."

"BEDS? Are you joking? Do you remember the Rhinoceros position we once tried?"

At the mention of that experience, Dedan began to shake with pent up excitement. "Remember? How can I ever forget? You damned near killed me. I spent a week in the infirmary and, if I recollect correctly, you were walking strangely for a few days and had to cancel an important and very serious religious ceremony, all because you couldn't get a crazy grin off your face. Alas, as for poetry, I haven't written anything like that since you left me. When you walked out of the door,

I lost my muse." He sighed, releasing many lifetimes of remorse and 'what ifs' before continuing. "But regrettably, I don't think I have much time right now for reminiscing and catching up. God has sent me to talk with you."

"Oh, Him!" Her voice was suddenly full of bitter resentment, the unspoken buried hatred for a homewrecker and husband stealer.

Her reaction made Dedan feel uncomfortable, but he saw that she didn't make any sudden movements, as if she was going to send some flaming object towards him, so he remained where he was. After all, a fireball contacting with his head would have made him far more uncomfortable.

"I know, Honey, but He… I need your help. You were dead for a long time, and that was something that should never have happened in the first place, but you were brought back into existence, and I need to know who did it and where they are. I think they have also resurrected some far more angry and malevolent gods who are intent on causing trouble, and the modern world has moved on from such ancient violence." He wanted to admit that the human race hadn't moved on *that* far from the primitive and ancient habit of destroying each other, but he felt that nuclear bombs would take too much explaining.

Hor'idey gave Dedan a look of uncertainty. "All right, I haven't investigated any followers since you were part of my world but, as it is you, I will do as requested. Give me a few moments and I will visit them." Then she closed her eyes and disappeared.

In her absence, Dedan took the opportunity to take a proper look at the goddess's version of the Oval Office. There were the yellow curtains hanging by the windows directly behind the dark wooden presidential desk. Portraits of long dead High Priests hung on the walls and interspersed around the edges of the room were rigid and formal high-backed chairs and assorted cabinets. Then his gaze moved to the floor and saw the cream-coloured carpet with the great seal of the United States of America woven into it. As he focused on the image of the eagle with a ribbon in its beak and arrows and branch in its clenched claws, he saw a faint brown mark and, following it with his eyes, he traced it back to the door that he had used to enter the office. It was at that point that he realised what it was and regretted not wiping his feet as he came into the building. All he could do was hope that Hor'idey wouldn't see it or notice the smell of wolf crap until after he had gone.

He was just contemplating trying to find something to clean up the marks when he was prevented by the sudden re-appearance of Hor'idey. She was paler than when she left, shaking slightly and, as she looked into the distance, had a blank stare on her face that could have easily been taken as a shock after having seen something terrible. She took several deep breaths as she tried to regain her focus on the current reality. Slowly, she realised where she was and turned her stare to Dedan. Taking long blinks, the sight of her former husband seemed to help to calm her down.

"I visited him. I entered his mind." She stopped as she tried to sort all the information into some sort of order that would make sense to her. There was much of the modern world that she'd witnessed and didn't understand but, even when she had encountered the basic emotions that she knew about, she was still left feeling confused. "There is just one person. He is surrounded by friends, yet he is so alone in the world he has created for himself. In an attempt to fill some emotional void, he has started to worship gods that he doesn't know or understand. He is the one that brought me back to life, yet his faith is weak and uncertain. A belief that is fickle and possibly temporary. Dedan, please help me. If his faith dies, so do I. I don't want to go back to being a statue; it was cold and dull. Despite being a dead statue, I had consciousness, and in spite of all the other gods, I was lonely. After all statues are not the greatest conversationalists."

There was a brief silence as she collected more thoughts from around her brain. There was much she didn't want to confess, especially to Dedan, but she felt that that it would help him to understand and could be good for her soul.

"When you left me, I just returned to my paradise. A paradise that looked nothing like this, but it was mine and I was safe. I think this place is a manifestation of his idea of where I should live, and I can't change it. Anyway, I turned my back on earthly believers and concentrated on ensuring the souls that had joined me could be happy. But my neglect of the world was my downfall. With no visions or miracles, my followers slowly turned their backs on me or died. Eventually there was just one true believer left and by the time I realised that it was too late. I was too weak to do anything, and his prayers were desperate and lonely, as was I. When he eventually died, so did I. All the souls in my care, and under my protection, were left homeless and condemned to go to your God's Heaven or Hell."

Dedan had never seen his ex-wife so scared before. Thanks to powers that were only limited by the imagination of their followers, gods were usually full of a wild confidence that was backed up by vanity and ego. For a god to be frightened by a human was not normal, but he could understand her feelings. One casual believer was not enough to save a deity from inevitable and unavoidable oblivion. If Hor'idey was to be saved from a return to her lonely, rigid, and stationary eternity, she would need more people to feed her with their prayers. She had to be more than just a passing cult; she needed to be a proper religion again.

"Of course, my love. Who is he and where can I find him? I will go and see him." Dedan had no idea what he could do when he confronted the religionist, but that didn't matter. He felt sure that he would think of something and do all he could to help save his ex-wife. Although, when he had still been alive, they'd never obtained a legal divorce, so she was technically not so much an 'ex' as a present wife. But as both of them had died millennia ago, any contract was probably void by now.

Closing her eyes in an attempt to concentrate, Hor'idey took a deep breath. "He is called Gordoon Simpson, and he lives in a place called Boulder, in a country called Colorado in the empire of America. I think it is across a vast ocean. Have you ever heard of the place?"

"Yes, my love, I have been to Boulder in Colorado many times."

"He is a scholar at a university there, studying something called 'computer science.' I do not understand the term or the sorcery but, having seen his mind, I believe that he does."

"Great," Dedan sighed heavily. "That's all we need. A nerd!

12 – The Devil and the Detail

Captain Piero Uomoduro was confused. He was convinced that he was having some sort of strange dream and just wanted to wake up; that must be the simple answer, as there could be no other explanation for it. He was either asleep, had been knocked unconscious by someone in the Pantheon, or was in a deep coma in hospital and the drugs were having strange side effects. Or just maybe he'd just sprinkled too much parmesan onto his chicken cacciatore meal the previous evening and the whole day had been a surreal figment of his imagination.

First there were forcefields and eight-foot-tall fireball shooting giants dressed in togas, and now he was seemingly in some big, old and dingy decaying office with an ornate wooden desk and, sitting behind it, was a figure that he could best describe as his mental image of what Satan would look like. The red suit and matching skin, twisted horns and Van Dyke beard were a bit of a give-away to who it was. Then, to cap it all off, there was the endless stream of Barry Manilow songs playing loudly in the background. He wasn't a massive fan, and his English wasn't great either, but he knew enough to know that the singer was thanking Mandy for preventing him from shivering, or at least that was as good as his translational skills allowed.

The devil was asking him questions in a gruff and coarse voice, interrogating him on what had happened during his day. The recently deceased soul seemed oblivious to the simple fact that he was actually in Satan's private office and the music wasn't just some radio playing on a hospital ward where he was wired up to a monitor, much to his host's anger. The Lord of Hell was trying to find out what had happened, but all he was getting were strange answers that made him think that the former captain was struggling to grasp the concept that he'd died and was about to suffer for his sins. Eventually, his finite and very limited supply of patience ran out and he had to resort to more pointed ways of being taken seriously. In this instance, the point was that of a miniature ornamental axe that he was using as a paper weight. It flew, spinning blade over handle, before the top of the weapon hit Piero on his forehead, knocking him onto his back and leaving him with a cut that promptly started to gush out blood. The dazed Captain grabbed his head in pain and stared in disbelief at the devil.

"SEE?" Satan snarled. "If this is a dream, then it is a bloody painful one, isn't it? Now get up and shut up until I tell you to speak, and then only answer my direct questions."

Piero was about to speak but thought better of it, the realisation of his location finally sinking into his head just like the axe would have done if it had impacted slightly differently. His own indignant rage boiled inside of him, for although he often utilised such violent tactics, and frequently far worse methods, with criminals, he was not used to receiving them from others. If a crook on whom he was using *'unconventional questioning techniques'* decided to return aggression, rather than turning the other cheek, the criminal would have invariably found themself unable to walk, possibly because of losing either their kneecaps, testicles, or their lives, which one depended on Piero's mood at the time. During the course of normal duties, he'd received worse injuries, but the necessity to take it and not retaliate was never part of his nature. However, now that his soul had transferred to Hell, he would be soon entering a punishment chamber and have little choice but to suffer far more excruciating injuries and humiliations. His mouth once again opened and was about to speak, to acknowledging the instruction, then he recognised the trap that Satan had set for him. He had used that ploy as an excuse to *re-enforce* his authority as well, so decided that anything he said that was unsolicited could result in him being on the receiving end of some other desk ornament being thrown at him.

Seeing the open mouth and the obvious decision to remain quiet, Satan gave him a sly and devious grin. Obeying his orders to the letter was always good, but ignoring them was not a massive problem either, as it gave him an extra excuse for doling out overly and unnecessarily agonising punishments. But, being Hell, compliance was no assurance that a demon, or a soul due for eternal torment, would avoid being on the receiving end of some sharp, or blunted, reprimand.

"Very wise of you, I see that you are a quick learner and know how to play the game. I also see the anger in your eyes; perhaps someday I might have further uses for you. But at the moment, I just need some information. One of my ambassadors in the Vatican has informed me that something *unusual* has been going on at the Pantheon, and I believe that your last few moments on Earth as a living person were spent in the building. Also, as I understand it, whoever is in there is the one that generously gave you a free cremation and sent you to me. I want you to carefully tell me exactly what happened. Leave nothing out, no matter how insignificant you might think it is."

As far as Piero was concerned, the simple instruction was clear and concise, but the words 'ambassadors in the Vatican' had him confused. As far as he could work out, he had somehow ended up in Hell, and he intended to try and appeal against that ruling at some point, but the idea of the Vatican City having emissaries of Satan had made him begin to wonder if the dream had restarted again.

As with most humans, with perhaps the exception of the Ku Klux Klan who hate virtually everything that isn't American and therefore accuse the Pope of being the Anti-Christ, the presence of demons as staff in the city state was not an accepted fact. They didn't sit in designated offices with plaques on the doors announcing the fact that they were there, but they had been part of the infrastructure of the place even before the Borgias took up residence and started having 'cheese and poisoned wine' parties. Their exact identities and duties were often vague and could change over time, but they had become part of the place's structure. Among other tasks, they could on occasion work in the Vatican Bank and, perhaps, at other times be part of the Congregation for the Doctrine of the Faith, or Inquisition as it used to be known. If the opportunity arose, they would whisper in the ears of the Pope or a high-ranking cardinal in an attempt to steer policies or decision, but on the whole their primary function was to be spies. They would provide Hell with regular reports on anything that they found out about relating to ecclesiastical matters in Rome, Italy in general, or even the rest of the Catholic world. There were similar demons carrying out espionage in other religious centres around the world, but none were as useful as the ones based in Rome.

Thanks to years of police training and experience, Piero was able to describe in precise detail all the events that led up to him being made an ex-police officer but ensuring he got a hero's funeral, although his coffin would be very light, and its size wouldn't be such an issue. When it got to the part of the tale where Roxy appeared, Satan sat up and began to stroke his beard as the name resonated in his head. Along with Dedan, she had been part of an angelic Special Forces team that had foiled one of his plans to destroy God. That had made her a category 'A' target and he planned to exact his revenge on her at some point. But for now, he was more interested in other things that had ended up in the Pantheon. He allowed Piero to finish talking and, once there was silence, he decided to double check a fact that he needed to be sure of before he decided on his next move. "And you say his name was Falacer?"

"Yes, Roxy called him that, a young guy, perhaps in his thirties, and he was about eight feet and tall dressed in a white toga," Piero responded, repeating the description. "I'd certainly recognise him if I ever saw him in an identification parade." He had a smile on his face as he proudly provided the additional details. Unfortunately, he didn't gain any favour from Satan by this, as the appearances of gods could change at the whim of the deity. They could be a tall and muscular colossus of a man in one manifestation, but in other instances they could be an old beggar woman bent double trying to sell apples to passers-by, or even take the shape of kittens to see how they were treated by random strangers. But the confirmation of the name was useful. His recollection of the obscure, and mainly insignificant, ancient Roman god was not that great, but he was aware of him. As far as he remembered, Falacer was vain, as most gods throughout history were, but he was never that potent or creative when it came to seeking power so didn't pose any sort of threat to Satan or Hell. He felt that it was a pity that the police officer hadn't been able to behave himself for a few more minutes, so that he could have found out how Roxy dealt with the situation, but he knew from other sources that the force field surrounding the Pantheon had disappeared and there was no longer any trace of the minor god or major angel.

"Right, you can go." He pointed to the door leading out of his room. "My assistant will ensure that you are shown to your new accommodation. I might have a use for your skills at some point but until then, I know where to find you."

The definition of what might be seen as accommodation was not the same to both people. As Piero dragged the groaning and stiff door open and left the room, he envisioned a room with a basic bed and perhaps some furniture to make it a home away from home. Satan's real meaning of the word was far more draconian. It was a punishment chamber on the fifth ring of Hell specifically created for officials that wore uniforms and abused or misused their powers. The punishments were designed to fit the sinner's crimes, so all the confessions that were beaten out of suspects, each bribe taken to turn a blind eye, and every unofficial execution were repaid for all eternity. Once Piero unsuspectingly walked into the chamber, and the doors slammed shut behind him, he would experience the daily routine of angry demons kicking and beating him and finally issuing a coup de grâce with the aid of a bullet to the head. Then the next day, the whole process would start again. As in many human court systems, his right to appeal was there and, just like some legal processes of Earth, he had no hope of ever being listened to.

13 – Elsa

Bob liked going to Earth and carrying out missions, but he had to admit that he preferred to be warm, safe and comfortable in Heaven. The food was tastier, the alcohol was plentiful, the beds were comfortable, and there were almost countless beautiful women to keep him busy as he tried to seduce them. For the last few months, he'd been spending most of his time jamming with Jimi Hendrix, Miles Davis, John Bonham and Janis Joplin, so God's instruction for him to leave the wild musical party and join Him in His office was accepted but not particularly welcomed.

God's strongly worded orders had been specific and had left the angel intrigued. Instead of going to some random location on Earth, he had been told that he'd be visiting a parallel dimensional plane belonging to a goddess. The exact details about what she would look like, or what to expect when he got there, were so vague that he'd decided that he'd just take it as he found it and hopefully it would be comfortable and not have any demons trying to kill him, inflict torture, or find other ways to be a nuisance. A plentiful supply of free alcohol would also be a bonus.

His arrival, in Elsa's version of paradise, had resulted in him being filled with the usual euphoria that all angels received after the dimensional transportation process, with it taking him a few seconds to catch his breath and come down from the buzz. The next sensation, after the feelings of joy subsided, was that of chilly feet. Looking down, he saw that a thin and low fog was enveloping his ankles, obscuring most of his sturdy black boots, and was covering the surface of the place for as far as the eye could see. Scattered around the landscape were sprawling olive trees and occasional grassy mounds rising out of the mist, but their bases were lost to the low cloud. These mounds were occupied by people sitting around, with the men in the traditional chitons, tunics of ancient Greece, and the women in peploses, the matching female gowns. They seemed to be chatting merrily as they drank out of goblets and small urns. Bob hoped it was wine and was tempted to go and ask for a drink before accepting that he had better be sober for when he met whomever it was he was supposed to be talking to.

In the distance, he saw a larger hill and sitting on top of it, like a white marble crown, was a majestic building. The tall, grooved columns surrounding it reminded him of the Parthenon in Athens, only larger and far more intact. Between a few of the columns he could see that there were statues but from his current location, he couldn't make out what they were depicting.

As he walked towards the building, he looked longingly once more at the happy drinkers, wishing he could forget his orders and join the party. He knew the most severe punishment that God could issue was banishment to Hell, but he doubted a slight detour would result in that level of retribution, so a few minutes to enjoy one drink, two drinks or even a bottle full wouldn't be too much of an issue. As he casually chatted with the inhabitants of the sunny but foggy alternative paradise, Bob got the impression that it wasn't a bad place to be. The wine was called nectar but to him it didn't taste like flowers, so he couldn't quite identify the flavour. But whatever it was, it tasted divine. Everyone he spoke to assured him that Elsa, the goddess in charge of the place, was benevolent and kind and that he'd enjoy meeting her. The mention of her name dragged him out of his alcohol induced reverie and back to the facts of his mission. He wanted to carry on with the pleasant drinking party but knew that an angels got to do what an angels got to do and decided to bite the bullet and speak to the goddess.

As he walked up the gentle slope leading to the temple, he was finally able to make out the statues. He was no expert on classical Greek mythology, but he had seen enough cheap 'swords and sandals' movies to recognise a few features that gave him clues as to which ancient heroes some of them might be. One was standing with his arm raised with a lightning bolt in his hand, so Bob assumed that was Zeus. Another bearded figure had a trident so was probably named Poseidon. There was a woman in a battle helmet and carrying a spear, and Bob's memory went into overdrive to recollect her name, but eventually he came up with the name Athena. The last statue that he studied had him totally lost without any idea as to who she might be. It was a tall and well-proportioned woman clasping what, in Bob's limited world view, could best be described as a large dildo. Bob was impressed at the scale of it and thought that any goddess that could accommodate something so big would be insatiable and he'd most definitely like to meet her someday.

Proceeding up the pristine white steps, he entered the building through an ornately carved marbled archway and, once inside, he was met by the sight of a spacious hall that seemed to be larger on the inside than the outside. Benches and tables were strewn about the place and occupied by people dressed in similar attire to those outside. Once again, they were talking, laughing, and drinking. The more that he saw of the place, the more he liked it, and he wondered how he went about requesting a transfer or a post as ambassador. He saw at the far end of the room, a raised platform, similar to a stage, and on it was a cream-coloured marble throne. On seeing it, his first thought was that it must be cold and uncomfortable having to sit on that, but gods could have harder arses than mere mortals, however such subjects were never discussed in philosophical circles. There was a sudden silence with the background chatter and laughter abruptly stopping as he drew nearer and stopped, unsure of the correct protocols for getting too close to a goddess's furniture.

Looking to his right, he saw a female figure walking towards him. There was no possibility of misconstruing her gender, as she was completely naked. He was surprised at her lack of clothing but didn't mind. However, thanks to her appearance, he wasn't sure where it was polite to look. He could avert his eyes, stare awkwardly at his feet, or just solemnly look her in the face. However, being a male, that didn't like to look a gift horse in the mouth, he opted to stare, open mouthed, at her firm breasts and hope that he didn't start drooling in the process.

If Bob had chosen to take more time to appreciate all that was in front of him instead of looking at the main focal point of a man's mind, he would have seen how truly beautiful she was. Her tall and firm build was emphasised by her olive-coloured skin, dark eyes and wavy dark brown hair which covered her shoulders. If someone had to describe female Hellenic perfection, they would probably have created a photo-fit picture of her. They might have, out of polite respect or dull political correctness, drawn her with clothing on, but that was personal choice. Her look was a stark contrast to that of Bob. He was on the wrong side of middle age with a craggy face and stubbly beard, and under his poorly fitting suit was a tattooed body that once was muscular but had seen better days and had been allowed to go to pot.

"Greetings, stranger. My name is Elsa, goddess of this domain. How can I help you?" She moved to her throne and sat down, Bob all the while maintaining his gaze on her body while he kept his hands nonchalantly clasped in front of his groin as he tried to hide his obvious and rising pleasure at what he was looking at.

"Greetings, Elsa. I mean Your Highness; I mean Your Majesty. Ma'am." What blood was left in his head was moving to his cheeks and making him blush with embarrassment at his lack of knowledge as to the correct way to address an ancient, obscure but very naked Greek goddess. "My name is Frederic, but my friends call me Bob."

If his eyes were that way disposed, he'd have noticed that she gave him a sweet and understanding smile and was unperturbed by his vocal fumbling and the lack of eye contact. "It's all right, Bob. As I said, my name is Elsa, and my friends call me that. We are very informal here. How can I help you?" Her voice was sweet and low with a gentle Greek accent.

He mused over how cold and uncomfortable the throne must be on her bare flesh so was slow to reply and then, before he could speak, his stare was momentarily taken away from the bosoms as he saw something out of the corner of his eyes. Coming up the steps towards the goddess were three males. Tall, dark haired and built like full time body builders, they too were in the same natural state as Elsa and were carrying several pieces of crockery. One had a bowl of fruit, the next was carrying a silver goblet on a gold tray, and the last one was holding a large earthenware jug. Bowing as they drew near, they obediently took up position behind the throne and began to feed her grapes and pour her a generous glass of wine. After pausing to let them perform their duties, Bob returned his gaze back to their former target and allowed himself to separate his primary thoughts from what he needed to say. That way he could avoid using the word breasts or any variations thereof in his sentence. Freudian slips happened, but now was the wrong time and place for him to give her one.

"Elsa, I have been sent by God to try and find out how you managed to stop being a dead goddess and became a live one. He would also like to know your intentions. Will you be raining down death and destruction on humans or will you just be there in visions, dreams and that sort of thing?" The words spoken; he returned his attention back to the view.

There were two ways of seeing his actions. The first one was the most likely, that he was a typical male and if they saw a naked woman their brains would shut down and divert control to their penises; or the other, far less likely, option was that he'd never seen a pair of breasts before and was wondering what they were. And anyone that knew Bob would definitely have said that he'd seen and experienced them on a multitude of occasions in his previous life and in Heaven.

"I assure you, Bob, I am not aggressive, vengeful or vindictive. I left the violence to my more uptight and insecure siblings and godly relatives. I hope that I can continue being here in my Olympus looking after the souls that came to me and guiding those that worship me, just like I did in ancient times. Unfortunately, the return to my statuesque death might be sooner than I would have liked. When I was reborn, I investigated who had brought me back and all I found was one single and desolately lonely man. His faith is weak and that makes my life equally so. He lives across the furthest ocean. His name is Gordoon Simpson in a place called Boulder. I also looked around the world and I got confused."

"Confused?"

"Yes, it seems a little bit disorganised and chaotic. I couldn't understand any of it."

"Oh, that. It isn't just you. Try living there for any amount of time. You'll soon realise that it isn't a little bit disorganised and chaotic. It's totally disorganised and chaotic."

"I see." Elsa was uncertain as to whether Bob was joking or not. "If your God fears that I will be a danger then, even if I became bad tempered, I doubt my sole follower will believe for long. He seems precocious and unlikely to accept any peace in his heart that I could give him. His spirit is like a butterfly. Flitting from one flower to another sipping on the nectar but never settling. But I don't want to go back to being a statue. This is far more enjoyable."

Bob looked at the naked flesh before his eyes, not that he'd stopped looking for long, and thought of all the people happily drinking, and could see why this was a better choice than spending an eternity as a lump of marble, even if it was in the form of the stunningly beautiful goddess.

"I've been to Colorado before. There are herbal benefits that some parts of the rest of the country don't have. I'll request that God allows me to go and visit him. Perhaps I can reinforce his belief in you and persuade him to spread the word and get you more followers. I can't promise anything, but I will do my best."

"Thank you, Bob. I would be eternally grateful, and you would always be welcome here as my esteemed guest."

Bob liked the thought of returning to this dimensional plane and being esteemed. Even if he couldn't transfer, he could possibly holiday regularly or buy a time share.

14 – Respecting Talents

There are many words you couldn't apply to Satan. Alright, you could call him calm, patient, loving and kind, but you would be totally wrong. Evil was part of his DNA, was mixed with his blood, and filled his brain. Traits that would get a human into Heaven were not things that he tolerated, and there had been a few demons that had found themselves eviscerated or dismembered for simply smiling at him or saying good day before he'd had his first cup of coffee in the morning. Although they did happen, such occurrences were few and far between as word quickly got around Hell and the cautionary tales about not trying too hard to be overly obsequious and pleasant to Satan were quickly learnt. There is nothing like the suffering of a fellow demon to make the others acquire valuable survival skills.

Today the Lord of Darkness was the boiling casserole of all the usual negative emotions. Rage was whistling out of the pressure cooker spout of his psyche and that rage wanted to boil and splash itself on some of the damned in their respective punishment chambers. But that could all have been described as a routine day for him and wasn't out of the ordinary. Ulcers existed in Hell and were a small part of the punishment process for many a soul that had chosen a wayward path in life. Such was his rage that if they had taken up residence in Satan's stomach, the corrosive acid would have eaten them up as a light snack. But there was currently an extra ingredient that was making the whole mixture taste even worse, and that was suspicion. Not just mild conjecture that something wasn't right but a full-blown conviction that something was wrong, and he was being used.

Ever since he had received a phone call from God and been updated on the whole 'resurrected gods' situation, he'd had the feeling that he was being played like a chess piece. Not even a useful piece that could move backwards and forwards in interesting directions or jump over others to make a killing, but like a pawn only able to take tiny blind steps, moving forward slowly and unable to go back. It was times like this that made him remember why he ended up in Hell in the first place; at least chess pawns could become kings. He was not good at taking orders or following others' instructions, and even if God had done it subtly and politely, over the phone, he still felt manipulated. He might do as he was asked, but God saying it first made him want to do the complete opposite, just out of spite.

Nonetheless, he recognised the vague threat that obscure gods could pose to his power and authority. If their followers grew in number, then they would stop going to Heaven and Hell and end up in whatever dimensional reality the new deities created for their worshippers. He got his power from all the souls under his control and from humanity's fear of him and, if he lost that, then he could end up just another old and lost myth and possibly become some statue in a bleak and lonely hall.

Shaking such thoughts from his mind, for the moment at least, he returned his focus to the demon standing in front of his desk; although to use the word 'standing', or even any synonym relating to it, was far too generous. There were gibbons in remote Sumatran jungles with better posture, and they would have been offended by any comparison to Satan's visitor. Hellios had not been his name when he had been a human of Earth, but he had received it when he had died and entered Hell. The attributes that had ensured his place in Hades had quickly been recognised as an asset, and he had promptly been promoted from the massed ranks of souls being punished to that of a demon able to carry out important missions in the name of evil. After all, why let a proficient arsonist, murderer and liar go to waste?

In life, he could have gone into politics but didn't have the education, so he chose a more honest path and became a contract killer. His methods were far from discreet, as burning buildings and leaving blackened and charred remains inside tended to arouse the suspicions of the police but, despite that, he had been good at his job. If it hadn't been for a careless accident involving some spilled petrol, he could have had a far longer time on Earth. The play on words of Hell and the Greek god of the sun had been applied to him and stuck, and it was far better than the name of Ralph Jones with which he'd been christened.

The figure that took Satan's attention was hunched forward with arms hanging down and knuckles nearly touching the floor. His skin was a bright orange, and he resembled a shaved orangutan with a dead ginger cat pelt on his head. His eyes were screwed up like a constipated pig and were made even more severe by being mounted with a stern mono-brow that gave the impression that he was giving everyone a short-sighted contempt filled squint. The body that was holding it all together defied any comparisons to simians. If anyone had tried, the apes and monkeys, along with the gibbons, would have been complaining at the insult. His shoulders were built like a brick wall that had been run over by a tank, and his tattooed chest could have doubled as bullet proof toilet door. The overarching appearance was topped off by a dirty, singed, blood spattered and badly fitting light blue boiler suit.

When he had been called into Satan's presence, he'd been merrily following his hobby of torturing people. His sadistic tactic was to demand answers from damned souls while fully aware that they didn't know the answers. In many ways, and to many of the people, the pain and unanswerable questions were akin to a high school algebra exam, with the exception being that his questions had no answers. Despite his taste for infliction of suffering and his outward appearance, he had a keen and razor-like intellect. A request for him to attend a meeting with Satan meant that there would be a mission where his specialised skills and talents could be fully utilised. He enjoyed his work and always looked forward to being allowed to go to Earth and practice it.

Despite all his faults, Satan wasn't prejudiced. All demons and damned were equal in his eyes; they were all contemptible and were despised, so the appearance of Hellios didn't bother him, and there far were worse sights in Hell. As long as he could carry out his task, then all would be fine and if he failed, then he would pay in a nonmonetary way. He didn't trust anyone, but when despatching demons to carry out his instructions, he had to rely on them. This specific assignment required somebody that was strong and would stand their ground as they discussed the continued, or hopefully discontinued, existence of a bad-tempered, vindictive, and destructive Bolivian god.

He carefully explained the situation to the Hellios, all the while unsure, from the look in the demon's eyes, whether he was taking it all in and understanding it or just impatiently glaring at him and simply waiting for him to shut up. Even if eloquent words were not given, the grunts and growls of affirmation came at the right points, so there were signs that he was listening. As he issued his instructions, Satan left nothing out. He knew that the devil was in the detail, and he had those, with all contingencies assessed and planned for. Although, at first glance, the mission seemed simple, he knew that when it came to self-important gods, things were never guaranteed. They could be rude, vicious and contrary. Lies and anger packed into insignificant packages of power. He liked to think that he had the monopoly on them so he hated those attributes in others.

Eventually, Satan finished talking and paused so that Hellios could have the opportunity to speak and ask questions. A few seconds passed and no sound was made. All he got was the same scowling stare, like a myopic look of hatred. Finally, unable to put up with his underling's silence, Satan's brittle patience broke. "Well?" he snarled. "Have you any questions?"

"No, Sire. I understand everything. May I go now? I have a job to do." Hellios's voice was full of arrogance as if he was unaware of who he was speaking to or simply didn't care.

"Yes, get out and do NOT fail me." Satan would forgive, if not forget, the insult provided that the surly demon succeeded. If he came back a failure, then his attitude would be punished in some extended and painful way, possibly involving sharp and jagged spears as they could be long and exceedingly painful if shoved in the right places. With knuckles leaving thin finger trails on Satan's bloody and body fluid filled carpet as he walked, Hellios lurched towards the door, his entire body emanating contempt like an evil lighthouse inviting ships to join it on a storm-on-the-rocks hootenanny. His departure was stopped as Satan added one final instruction.

"Oh, and do not forget to take human form before you go to see him."

Without turning around, Hellios returned to his pre-simian progression. "This is my human form!"

15 – Jigsaw Pieces

Angelica's office was busy and emanating a stifled and uncomfortable atmosphere. Dedan was leaning against the far wall, adopting his usual stance with one foot on the floor and the other resting on the clean wall, attempting to appear nonchalant and cool while inside he could feel his guts churning, and just wanted to leave the room and hunt for a nice comfortable war zone on Earth where he could find some internal peace, or at least not have to think about his emotions. Not an easy task for most men, and even angelic ones could struggle with the process. If he'd had the option of staying there or chewing off his own arm to escape, he'd have grasped the latter with both hands. Or, realistically, one hand if it had been possible.

Being a woman, Angelica could sense the tension in the air. If nothing else, the static electricity was playing havoc with her hair conditioner. If she hadn't used the right shampoo that morning, her hair would have been standing on end as if she were sitting on a Van de Graaff generator with sparks flying into the ceiling tiles. However, even if she could feel the atmosphere, she couldn't understand what was causing it. She just assumed that something had happened on the mission and Dedan wasn't comfortable with it. Having access to most of the highly classified mission information, she understood he had just been to see his ex-wife and that their parting might not have been conducive to the greatest of reconciliations. Just because he came back in one piece and had managed to avoid being killed, it was no indication of things going well. The stony silence that Dedan was maintaining didn't help either. It was like a verbal wall, invisible but still bearing a sign with big red letters saying, 'KEEP OUT'. All attempts at casual banter had been met with polite but brief single word answers. Eventually, she had given up and returned to her normal office duties.

God had been informed that Bob and Roxy had also completed their respective missions and were on their way to His office, and He'd instructed Angelica to get Dedan to wait until they were there so that they could come into His room and make all their reports at the same time.

Although He was beginning to doubt the wisdom of it, He'd asked Satan to send one of his demons to speak to Ekeko, the rationale being that if any painful destruction of emissaries were to occur, it was better if demons suffered rather than angels. And from what He remembered of the minor god, he wasn't one to be receptive to polite conversation or forthcoming with any sort of requests for information, especially facts that were intended to be used to limit his power or preferably send him back to the Hall of Dead Gods.

As for the final god on the list that required visiting, He was still contemplating which angel would be best suited for speaking to Sonja. He remembered her from her previous time as a goddess and knew that she was, on the whole, good but was proud, impulsive and unpredictable, traits that could be worked with, but they needed a special set of skills. All three of his main angels possessed those qualities in one way or another, but He doubted that any of them had all of them.

Finally, and much to Dedan's relief, Roxy turned up, her presence in the office managing to dilute the tense air. Smiling, and oblivious of what she had walked into the middle of, she said hello to Dedan and was informed that they still needed to wait for Bob, so she began to chat amicably with Angelica, taking the focus of attention from Dedan and allowing him to relax. His thoughts were still making his brain wish it could switch off and delete memories of his date with God's secretary, but at least he didn't feel so isolated and awkward now that there was extra company. As the two women talked, Dedan was relieved of the sensation of feeling of being as useless as an indicator on a BMW, by the arrival of Bob. He now had someone to talk to and take his mind off memories of a date that didn't end well for him, even if the seemingly cataclysmic emotional effects didn't even register with Angelica.

"Hello, all. What's happening?" Bob was still full of thoughts of the naked goddess and felt nothing but joy and a rigidity in his groin that just didn't want to go away. He had found it hard, in more than one sense, walking through Heaven to get to God's office.

He was greeted with cheerful hellos from everyone before Angelica casually told them that they could all go right in and have the meeting with God.

"Dedan, you've been away for a hell of a long time. Didn't the date with Angelica go well?" enquired Bob with a sly lascivious grin on his face, hoping to hear some explicit details.

Roxy gave him a look that an assassin could have used as a new killing method, with Angelica giving him a shocked open-mouthed stare.

"Of course it went well. There's nothing wrong; we had a wonderful evening and then Dedan had to go on his mission the next day." Angelica volunteered, her voice as calm and casual as if she were describing a sunny day.

"Bob, apparently Angelica told Dedan that she loved him like a brother, isn't that wonderful?" Roxy had decided to add a bit more detail that she thought would reassure him that everything was all right.

On hearing that, Bob inhaled loudly through gritted teeth and gave Dedan a pained expression. "Ouch! Harsh, man! I am so sorry, bro. No wonder you disappeared for so long. Do you want me to kick you in the balls to help take away the pain?"

"No but thank you for the kind offer. I'll be all right; I've lived through worse." Dedan looked at Bob and gave him an unconvincingly cheerful smile. He might have lived through worse but was struggling to think of specific examples.

Angelica gave them a blank open-mouthed stare as she tried to comprehend what both men were talking about. In her eyes, and the eyes of probably most women, she'd let Dedan down gently and given him a true and loving compliment, but now she was being told that she had somehow hurt his feelings. "But, but, but…" She tried to formulate a sentence but was looking for the right polite and friendly expletive to use that would have likened him to the rear end of a donkey. She was totally failing and was left feeling like she'd somehow developed a goldfish's mouth.

Seeing Angelica's angst, Roxy decided to take control. "All right, boys, it's good that you are so in touch with your feelings, but we have work to do. Come on, we need to report to the Big Boss." Herding them like two bulky and wayward sheep, she first turned them around so that they were facing the door into God's room, and then gently pushed them forward. As they opened it and proceeded into God's office, Roxy gave Angelica one last look, reinforced with a conspiratorial smile. "Men!" was all she said as she raised her eyes to the ceiling and followed the two male angels into their meeting, closing the door behind her.

Still in his school child form, God sat quietly in His large leather office chair, His elbows resting on His desk with fingers steepled as His thumbs absent-mindedly rubbed His lower lip. He listened to all three reports while maintaining an inscrutably blank expression. As one spoke, the other two were watching God intently, in the hope that they could get some hint as to whether what He was being told was of use, but there was nothing to provide a clue as to what He thought.

Bob would have liked the opportunity to go back and see Elsa if more details were required. He'd have loved to have probed her in the line of duty, but there was no indication that he'd have an excuse to do that. The detail about a shortage of clothing was left out of his report as he wasn't sure if it would prejudice any future request to visit the goddess, and he felt sure that any apostasy towards God would send him to Hell rather than Elsa's domain. Besides, he only wanted to go there for an extended sight-seeing holiday and not move there permanently.

Once Bob had finished his slightly redacted report, it was Roxy's turn. Being far more methodical, she left nothing out. It ended up being more of a psychological profile of the god than a brief recounting of actions. Also, as she detailed the last moments of the captain, she made a mental note to check if he had arrived in Heaven. If he were there then seeing her again, as an angel of long standing, might make him less of a sexist pig. However, had she known that he had gone directly to Hell, no tears would have been shed over him. The first impression he had given her was pretty much accurate, and he had deserved his final destination.

Finally, as Roxy fell silent, Dedan's turn came to tell what had happened when he had seen Hor'idey. He left out large chunks relating to his ex-wife, as he didn't feel that they were relevant or anyone else's business, not even God's. Despite that, he ensured that all the pertinent parts were still there. Primarily, the common factor of there being only one believer and that he was the same one for all the gods. He also emphasised the point that she wanted to remain a deity and would behave herself if it happened.

When they had all finished, God frowned. There was still one god left for an emissary from Heaven to visit and the indications were that she would provide the same human name as the other gods, but one last trip to an alternative paradise shouldn't take long. There was a fairly simple solution, but there was also a massive blocker to carrying it out. Hor'idey and Elsa desire to remain minor deities was not a concern to him. They were not under his protection and, even if they were benevolent, their yearning to avoid turning to stone again was not His priority nor problem. All He needed to do was send a random, and fatal, act of God landing on Gordoon Simpson's head and all his belief would end along with the power that maintained the five gods. They would go back to the Hall of Dead Gods and all the problems would disappear. Unfortunately, there was one simple factor that prevented Him from taking such a direct action. Despite the strange choices of gods and all the problems he had caused, Gordoon was not an evil person. Being misguided, curious, or even foolish were not traits that, on their own, meant that someone would slip and slide into Hell, which was a good thing, as Heaven's population would be seriously depleted if they were.

After a few angry outbursts that were recorded in the Old Testament and blown out of all proportions, God had created a strict and unbreakable rule that no angel or saint could deliberately murder an innocent human who was good and not directly harming other humans with the protection generally extended to evil ones as well; natural deaths were His main rule. There was the occasional instance of collateral damage when someone walked into a gun battle between demons and angels but there were to be no deliberate assassinations. It was also complicated by the edict that if they thought an innocent human was the target of Satan's death squads, then Heaven had to intervene and do all in its power to protect the poor mortal. Even though, in his remote Colorado student accommodation he didn't know it, Gordoon was in the strange position where both Heaven and Hell wished him dead, but he had one side protecting him.

"All right." God's voice was calm and still and didn't reveal any emotion. "Even at her peak, Sonja never had a massive following and they were limited to a small geographical area. She believed in peace, harmony and freedom, ideas that didn't make her popular with the more traditional Norse gods. They preferred drunken wars and boozy discord mixed with sober slavery and didn't like her radical ideas. As a result, they banished her from Valhalla and then conspired to incite their human followers to have a religious putsch. This worked in a drunken and bloodthirsty way which resulted in all her believers being put to the sword and other assorted weapons. Then... no followers equalled no more existence."

"Well, that's good, if she is peaceful then the mission shouldn't be too difficult. I'm sure that I could go and..." Dedan's enthusiastic volunteering to leave Heaven once more was interrupted by God calmly raising his hand as a sign for Him to be allowed to finish.

"Not so fast Dedan, Sonja demanded monotheism from all her followers and would get 'tetchy' if they tried to hedge their bets and worship Odin or Thor. Her belief in peace was forgotten a few times and she caused a lot of damage when she emphasised her view. There are a few Norwegian fjords that were caused by her rage rather than glaciers. She might not like the idea of Gordoon sharing his affections, so that makes her unpredictable. I think, in this instance, that you should all go and see her. Let's just call it safety in numbers. I think Roxy has the right degree of empathy so she will be in charge."

None of them wanted to disagree with God, so they all agreed to go as a team. Neither Bob nor Dedan objected to Roxy being their leader, either. They had both been to Earth with her before and respected her skill; they had also both had lusty thoughts involving her in differing stages of undress, so they had no desire to play a game of egos and one-upmanship in case they ever won her heart, and she turned their primal male fantasies into realities.

Slowly they stood up and set off towards the door leading out of God's office. Their progress was not helped by Dedan's reluctance at seeing Angelica again. As they opened the door, God got their attention once more. "Oh, and don't forget to dress in warm clothing. Hopefully her heart won't be cold, but her paradise might be."

16 – Always Right

Nobody could ever accuse Hellios of modesty, false or otherwise. His self-confident arrogance was a constant comfort to his busy mind. When it came to wondering if he was ever wrong and someone else was right, he never let doubt inconvenience his train of thought. As far as he was concerned, when it came to any discussion, he was correct and the rest of the world wrong. Even when he was being deliberately mendacious, he would quickly persuade himself that his fictions were cast-iron truths. This deception didn't restrict itself to his own mind. Anyone, irrespective of who they were, that dared to contradict him was obviously a backbiter and would find themselves on the receiving end of a long tirade as he made it clear to anyone within ear shot that the other person was an idiot, fool, and liar. Although dishonesty is the default setting in Hell, most demons knew when to shut up and back down. Hellios could never be classified in the 'most demons' category. Some might have said that his mouth was his own worst enemy, but there were plenty of residents in Hell that could have vied for that accolade. This meant that there was a total lack of friendly votes in any possible Mr. Popularity or Demon of the Month contests and made him a prime target for attack by his colleagues. He couldn't understand why he was so unpopular, but if anyone had ever tried to educate him, they would have been insulted, so nobody ever tried to explain the concept and instead chose wise and diplomatic silence.

The number of unexpected attacks on his person had made it so that he enjoyed carrying out little tasks for Satan. Even the complete lack of opportunity to kill anyone or set fire to things didn't diminish his enthusiasm. He was being given a unique opportunity to educate a god and tell it what to do. Thanks to his ego, he could even see himself being thanked by Ekeko at the end of the meeting.

Like the vast majority of demons and angels, he had never visited a different god's domain but, so far, he was finding the whole experience disappointing. When it came to aesthetics, he might as well have been blind and deaf, so no matter how individual the architecture was, or stunningly beautiful the buildings, he would not notice anything over and above the functionality. Once the initial queasiness, involuntary bowel movement and nausea caused by the inter-dimensional portal jump had abated, he was able to focus and look around.

What he did notice, and find the most underwhelming, was the total uninflammable nature of all the structures. The terraced stone pyramids were too solid for his tastes. The barren dry ground running along the towering edifices was like a dusty avenue heading towards an imposing building in the distance, with perfectly matched blocks providing tiers with broad steps running up the middle of the structure that led to square buildings at the top. The typical Mesoamerican architecture was adorned with stone sculptures of crocodile heads sticking out of the walls and carvings of feathered serpents that seemed to be watching him as he walked.

There were people sitting on the terraces, drinking some sort of liquid out of pottery jugs and beakers. Some were wearing yellow capes with blue spots and green feather-plumed head dresses, others wore plain white robes, and the women had dull brown skirts and blouses. They were all happily cheering on what appeared to be a chaotic game of football. Men and boys were pushing, shoving, and punching each other as they fought to get hold of a ball and, once they got hold of it, they tried to throw it through round holes cut into stones protruding out of the walls. Once there was a goal, they would pick up the ball and begin to run in the opposite direction in an attempt to avoid being run over by hundreds of bare feet. As he walked through the game Hellios had to dive out of their way as they began to plough past him. As they went by, he realised that the ball they were using wasn't a basic pig's bladder filled with air; this one had bloodied eyes and a not so happy looking mouth that was stitched shut. The dirt was part of the camouflage, but it had seen better days, days when it had been attached to a human body. "I could get to like this place," he muttered under his breath, his tight grin looking more like a deranged snarl. He speculated on what sort of ball they would use if they ever played tennis or golf and made a mental note that, if opportunity arose, he would tell them all about those sports and let them take it from there. Dodging the players and ignoring the cheers and jeers of the baying crowd, he continued his lurch towards the towering building at the end of the road, his knuckles leaving eight lines in the dust as if thin snakes were escorting his footprints.

When he finally arrived at his destination, he was met by a phalanx of guards dressed in ceremonial loin cloths and long yellow capes with ornate head dresses that looked like flaccid rhino horns. To add to their authoritarian appearance, they were armed with the ancient macahuitl paddle shaped wooden swords with black obsidian blades wedged around the outer edges. Behind them, leaning against the walls, were a long line of tepoztopilli, highly decorated but lethal spears. The weapons might not have been a match against an angry demon with an AK 47 assault rifle, but in this dimensional plane they were effective and could still inflict quite a lot of fatal damage. On seeing him, and in unspoken unison, the guards took up defensive postures in a battle formation. Each had one arm outstretched towards him and the other holding a sword, raised overhead and ready to be brought down on his skull.

Unaffected and far from impressed by the show of force, he gave them a squinty eyed look of contempt. "Oh, grow up, you morons. Do I look like an army that is about to storm the temple?" he growled in the manner of an alpha male wolf whose authority had been challenged by a litter of hungry pups. "Do you see a sword? A spear, perhaps? Just take me to your leader so I can talk to someone that can hopefully spell the word brain and, even better, have one."

Unused to anyone simply walking up to them in the streets and throwing buckets full of sarcasm at them, the guards were unsure how to react. Such a conceited attitude usually indicated that the person speaking was high born and in a position of authority, but the figure standing, or what they assumed was standing, before them was hardly impressive or regal. Maintaining their stance, they hesitantly looked at each other and then finally one of them lowered his weapon. Although the suspicion remained, this was quickly copied by the rest of the detachment. They parted so that he could get past them and walk up the long stairway leading to the entrance at the top of the giant edifice.

Seeing the gap, he walked past them, giving them contemptuous glares as he went. To him, they were as insignificant as ants, and he would have gladly stomped on them in the same way if he needed to do so. As he went up the steps, four of the guards followed him, swords held tightly just in case they were needed. Like most people that had ever met him, they had all taken an instant dislike to Hellios and his surly attitude, so would have welcomed an excuse to see how far they could put the razor-

122

sharp obsidian blades into his head before they ran out of momentum and ground to a halt. Even if he had known about the instant loathing his undiplomatic personality had induced, he wouldn't have cared. They were just menials and hardly worth him wasting his words. He had encountered people like that on Earth and had usually ended up killing them, as it was far easier than trying to maintain a polite conversation with them; plus, murder gave him more pleasure.

On reaching the top of the pyramid, he was met by more guards who, on seeing him, adopted the same stance as the troops at the bottom of the building. Then, on seeing the escorts behind him, they relaxed and parted so that he could continue. He grunted at them dismissively. "Shit kickers," he mumbled, his voice quiet but deliberately just loud enough for them to hear. As he walked into the small square brick room, he blinked as his eyes adjusted to the relative darkness, a stark contrast to the bright sunshine of the outside. When his eyes had got used to the semi darkness, he saw more steps, this time going straight down a narrow passage.

His way was lit by burning torches and as he walked down, he saw glyphs on the walls, pictorial records of legends and histories that were lost on him. Occasionally images depicting decapitations or hearts being removed, during human sacrifices, would catch his eye and make him smile with glee, but the rest of the pictures were meaningless. However, even if he could read them, he wouldn't have cared about their significance; to him all images of big heads with squashed noses and oddly shaped animals were a stupid method of communication. If they wanted to send messages, or write about the past, why didn't they use letters like civilised people? Hellios's world view of multiculturalism was simple: his way was right, anything else was pointless barbarism.

The staircase was longer than expected and he surmised that, when he reached the bottom, he was below ground level. Once again, he was met by more soldiers guarding a large double door covered in gold with more glyphs depicting giant heads with wide eyes and seemingly damaged noses, all bordered with images of snakes and what looked like sloths. When the guards opened the doors for him, he saw the grand hall and inner temple. The walls were covered with gold and mosaics made from semi-precious crystals. In the centre of the room was a vast stone altar stained red with blood and furnished with an axe and knife, both with obsidian blades protruding from wooden handles.

Then, at the far end of the hall, he saw Ekeko sitting on a stone throne. Wedged into the corner of his mouth was a giant cigar, releasing a plume of grey smoke which made him look like he was surrounded by a cloud of smog. On his head there was a crown of feathers that spread out and draped over his ears, as if he had a proud pheasant nesting there, with his golden poncho hiding most of his body. At his feet lay two black panthers, their heads resting on their paws as they watched him with languid and apathetic eyes. On seeing his strange looking guest, the god gave him a jovial, toothy smile.

"Greetings, stranger. Welcome to my domain. I take it that you have come to pay homage to me and seek good fortune?"

"Hell, no!" Hellios responded, his voice full of contempt at the idea that he would ever kowtow to such an insignificant person. "I am Hellios, and I have been sent by the mighty Satan to see you and make sure that you behave."

Unaccustomed to, and taken aback by, such a disrespectful tone, Ekeko's smile leached away and was replaced by an angry scowl. He was used to fawning subservience and being spoken to in such a manner made him seethe with rage. "Moderate your tongue, demon, when you speak to me, or you might just lose it! Satan has no power here and I am the mighty Ekeko. I could cut out your heart and eat it, all done in front of your eyes so that you witness it before you return to Hell!"

"You are just a pathetic nonentity god. You will do as you are told. Leaving messages in an ancient language that nobody can read? You're a joke!" If such appeasement tactics were adopted in the United Nations General Assembly by despotic leaders, it would have taken about four minutes before World War III was declared.

His eyes wide with indignation and rage, Ekeko stood up and pointed at the demon. "GUARDS, KILL HIM!" he screamed coarsely, wide eyes now gleaming at the thought of the demon's imminent demise. "And bring me his heart, I feel like a light snack."

The guards moved fast, but despite his bulky size and unconventional shape, Hellios was faster. Diving, dodging and jumping, he was able to narrowly avoid the first assault of sweeping swords. As the soldiers drew their arms back to try again, he timed his counter strike perfectly, fists meeting faces and bare torsos and his steel toe capped boots proving that loin cloths alone did not make for great armour. The soldier on the receiving end of the kick instantly gave out an ear-splitting high-pitched scream, dropped his sword, and fell to his knees as he clutched his crushed genitals. Hellios lost no time in swooping down and picking up the sword from the floor. As he was bent low, a guard brought his sword down, intent on introducing obsidian stone into Hellios's skull and forcing its way downwards until the bone stopped its progress. But the would-be fatal strike was stopped as Hellios lifted his newly acquired weapon and blocking it, edge hitting edge, the obsidian of both blades chipping and sending splinters and shards onto Hellios's ginger hair. Pushing the ancient weapon to his side, he deflected the other's sword so that it followed its new trajectory, hitting the floor and sending more of the black glass like material across the ground.

Then it was Hellios's turn. He jabbed his blade forward, cutting the soldier's cape and goring into his unprotected arm, the laceration sending blood into the air before it landed on the ground. But even with two of Ekeko's personal bodyguard injured, Hellios knew that he was still outnumbered, vulnerable, and needed to find a position that was easier to defend. Darting between swords, which were narrowly missing him, he carefully began to fall back. He parried and counter moved as both sides tried to deliver killer blows.

Eventually he felt the stone altar pushing against his back, blocking him from retreating any more. Without looking or thinking, he arched his back and kicked his legs forward, throwing his whole body backwards. There wasn't enough energy in the movement to throw him completely over the blood-stained table, but it was enough to position him so that his stomach was on it with his legs hanging over the far end. Seeing the sacrificial axe just by the side of his head, he moved his arms upwards, grabbed hold of it and sent it spinning through the air. More by luck than any skill at aiming, it struck one of his attackers squarely in the chest, cutting through the sternum, piercing his heart, and sending him to the ground. As in all dimensions controlled by gods, souls were immortal so he was not dead, but he was incapacitated and would not be able to recover for a long time.

Pushing himself off the hard altar, Hellios now had the stone shrine between him and his foes. Seeing the sacrificial dagger, he reached out and grabbed it and sent it out towards another attacker. It made contact but this time only hit a shoulder, slowing down the target but not stopping him. The attackers moved around the obstruction, but the numerical advantage was lost due to Hellios's disproportionately long simian-like arms. He was able to swing his primitive blade and force them to keep their distance. Even though they were beginning to surround him, his stroke was fast enough to keep them all far enough away to ensure his safety.

Watching the standoff, Ekeko's thirst for blood, and raw heart, began to increase. His frustration at seeing his hand-picked, elite, and highly trained guard being kept at bay by a single impertinent demon was an insult to his pride and ego. Although modern folklore had mellowed his reputation to someone that was jovial and a god of good luck, abundance and prosperity, his true personality was one of quid pro quo, and the price he would invariably demand for his indulgences was human sacrifice. The more blood that was spilled in his name, the more generous and happier he was. Time might have softened the characteristics of his myth, but his true self remained as hard and sadistic as it ever was. The hunger for a new sacrifice was all consuming and the inability of his troops to feed him was making him shout with rage. "Kill him, kill him, KILL HIM!!! What are you waiting for, you fools? Get in there and kill him!"

Despite their eagerness to obey their beloved god, the soldiers had no desire to walk into the business end of a sword just because someone was blindly urging them on. Their hesitancy might have been tactical and practical, but Ekeko simply saw it as cowardice. As Hellios swung his sword once more, one of the guards saw an opportunity and took it. Lunging forward, he was able to thrust his weapon towards his foe. Thanks to Hellios's movement, the blow managed to miss his chest and any vital organs, but it caught his free arm. The sword might not have been made of some highly polished steel or modern alloy, but the obsidian was shaped to perfection and had a deadly edge. It cut through his sleeve, flesh and bone, amputating his limb just below the elbow.

Undeterred by the pain that filled his entire body, Hellios continued his defensive swinging motion. Only when his other arm had come to a standstill did he look at the arm that was now lying on the floor and the blood spewing stump. He looked up at the attacker with hate filled eyes. "You bastard!" he snarled. "That arm had my watch on it, and it was a bloody Rolex."

Whether it was his body's automatic reaction to the injury or the rage that was coursing through his system, the adrenalin increased and gave him renewed vigour and strength. Like a wild animal that happened to be proficient in one-armed combat, he swung his sword. With a single blow he decapitated the soldier that had removed his arm, sending the head rolling across the floor so that it came to rest at Ekeko's feet. Then he lunged at another soldier and head butted him, impacting with the guard's nose, and breaking it with a loud crunching sound. Dazed by the unexpected assault, the guard dropped his sword and put his hands over his face. Seeing his foe defenceless, Hellios rammed his weapon directly into the soldier's stomach, eviscerating him and causing his intestines to spill out like a sausage machine releasing its filling. Seeing that Hellios's attention was elsewhere, the soldiers at the opposite side of the defeated troops stepped forward, intent on forcing home their advantage and killing him while his back was turned, but they were too slow. Hellios swung around with his sword outstretched, the blade removing the top of one attacker's head and burying itself in the skull of another. Both collapsed, leaving just the injured demon and the enraged god standing.

"You fool. Now what? I am a god in my own paradise. Do you think you can kill me?" The pompous indignation making Ekeko's voice shrill. "As you are a demon I can't kill you either, but I can give you a painful sending off as you return to Hell!"

"Oh, you pathetic nobody. I know that. But perhaps I can drag you back to Hell with me and once you're there, Satan can entertain himself with you and put you in some dark little chamber where you can learn humility and modesty."

"Humility? Modesty? I am the most modest and humble god that ever existed. Nobody is better than me at those!" Ekeko's limited reserve of patience was quickly disappearing. The guest had outstayed his

127

welcome and it was time for him to be shown the door. "Enough! I am tired of these games."

Just as the god raised his arms, Hellios began to run towards him, but it was too little, too late. Electric sparks began to form around the god's fingers and then an orange energy bolt shot from his hands, hitting Hellios squarely in the chest and killing him instantly. The blunt impact lifting him into the air, sending his body flying across the vast hall like a limp tissue caught in a brisk autumnal breeze. With sword still clenched in his hand, he flew over the bodies of his defeated foes and over the stone altar, with his flight only stopping when he rammed against the doors through which he had so recently entered. There was a deep and hollow thud, the body fell to the floor, and then there was silence.

Drained by the exertion of creating the energy bolt, Ekeko staggered backwards and sat on his throne. He looked contemptuously at the still recumbent and disinterested panthers. "A fat lot of good you were!"

17 – No Such Thing as Evil Weather

Materialising into another god's dimensional plane, especially one never visited before, can be a risky business. There are no maps with big 'X's on them telling travellers where they should aim their transportation devices. There are plenty of atlases of Earth, so only the most badly planned trips ended before they began, with the angel or demon materialising in the middle of an active volcano, at the bottom of the Marianas Trench in the Pacific, or even worse, in the middle of an active volcano in the trench. Invariably, they would end up where they needed to be, or close enough to reach the location after a relatively short walk.

However, Sonja's version of Valhalla was unknown and uncharted territory. There was the risk that any first-time visitors might arrive at the furthest corner from the epicentre with no bus service to take them to their hotel, thus leaving the tourists to look forward to a time-consuming walk in whatever weather the god of that place deemed to be ideal for their home. The angels could easily have found themselves suddenly appearing high up a snow-capped mountain standing on a very narrow ice-covered ledge. Then one small slip later, they'd find that gravity works in the same way as everywhere else and they would end up at the bottom of the mountain doing a warm and steaming impression of strawberry jam in the snow, as blood and gore quickly cooled down and turned to messy ice lollies.

The trio of angelic travellers' arrival was disorientating and not helped by the arctic snowstorm that was trying its best to blow them off their feet. Visibility was reduced so that they could just see each other's bright orange thermal clothing but nothing else. It was like looking at a white wall through a cold shimmering lace curtain whilst being deafened by a howling wind. They turned to face each other, with hooded heads and faces hidden beneath thick red balaclavas and purple lensed snow masks.

Any attempt to talk would have been futile, with the shouted words caught in the air and dragged wildly and unceremoniously into the obscured distance, unheard by the intended audience. Roxy struggled as best as she could to resort to sign language, which wasn't easy to do or be understood. Thick padded sleeves and gloves that made her fingers as agile as salami sausages made signalling look more like an overweight clown trying to perform a mime act. With no map for guidance or landmarks to aim for, she pointed in a random direction that she hoped would lead to either some form of cover or whatever palace the goddess chose to lay her hat and call home. Bob and Dedan were just as lost as their leader, so they nodded in acceptance of her choice, but thanks to their head coverings the responses were lost. Realising the futility of their slight actions, they raised their arms in what they hoped would be understood to be a mix of 'Don't ask me, I'm lost too,' and 'Sure thing, you're the boss.'

On seeing the wild body language, Roxy understood, turned and began a slow and cautious trudge through the snow. She placed each of her steps warily in case there were any deep crevasses hidden just below the surface, a long ski pole stabbing the ground just in front of her, testing the monotone ground. The progress was slow, but there was no safe way of going any faster. Patience was the safest approach and they all understood that. Despite the sub-zero temperature surrounding them, the clothes that encased them were insulated and made them sweat due to the exertion. Each yard covered became more uncomfortable as the hot perspiration made the clothing which was touching their skin damp.

It was then that Bob began to wish that he had utilised the heavenly toilet facilities before he had set off. He had encountered relatively cold winters when he briefly lived in Washington State and spent time in the Rockies but had never experienced anything like this before and had no intention of getting frost bite on any part of his body, especially not somewhere that needed to be pulled out so that he could relieve himself. So that left only one option, and that was to add to the dampness that was already making his first impression of the dimensional plane a less than happy one. The added liquid ensured that his right leg and sock had an extra warm element that the two other angels didn't have, and he hoped that the insulated attire would prevent it from turning to yellow ice against his skin. He was just thankful that he didn't need to go to the toilet for the evacuation of more solid matter. It might have been warm, but it would not have been comfortable, and he didn't relish the idea of getting the adult version of nappy rash.

As the sun began to set, a contrast in the whiteness seemed to appear in the air to their right, a grey-peaked silhouette casting its vague shadow in the swirling snow. Seeing it, Roxy waved her arms and pointed toward the only difference in the view that they had seen since they'd arrived. The other two echoed her gesture and altered their course to follow as she changed direction. The encroaching evening darkness did little to change their already sedate pace. They were blind in the daylight, so the lack of light didn't drastically reduce their visibility. Stopping was not an option as the elements wouldn't have shown any mercy to their human bodies. They would have soon succumbed to hypothermia, collapsed, and been buried like comatose drunken snowmen. They would have returned to Heaven but that would have been little consolation for failing the mission.

On the three angels tramped, hour after long hour, until finally the wind began to die down. Despite the nocturnal bleakness, they were able to make out flickering lights in the distance. It gave them hope and an incentive to draw on their quickly depleting reserves of energy. Drawing closer, they saw that the light sources were flaming torches, their red and yellow flames valiantly dancing in the wind. "Burning torches," Dedan mumbled to himself, behind his balaclava, "why is it always burning torches? Why can't one of these gods do a bit of research on modern inventions and install arc lights and electric heaters?" He felt a foreboding that whatever accommodation they found would not be full of all the mod cons.

The flames illuminated their surroundings enough for them to realise, on looking up, that what they had initially thought was a mountain was actually a castle. Although, thanks to the weather, it looked more like a gothic fantasy version of one. The ice covering gave it the appearance of someone having doused it with a high-powered water cannon, with the liquid having frozen on impact ensuring that thick icicles hung from battlements like jagged teeth. The tall and imposing curtain walls of the main enceinte outer defences were covered with a layer of ice as smooth as cold glass that would have been impossible to climb. The only break in the sheen was where holes had been melted through it so that the arrow slots could, if needed, be used. The crenulations rising imperiously above the walls were like giant stone knights amongst the ranks of foot soldiers. Overhanging grey stone machicolations loomed threateningly ready for projectiles to be dropped on the heads of any attackers that decided that they really must conquer this domain. Although Roxy, seeing the lack of anything worth owning, couldn't imagine who would want such a place. The whole imposing building gave off an unwelcoming and cold appearance that had nothing to do with the weather. Any invaders would have to be desperate, and if this were preferable to their home then she didn't want to visit it.

Slowly they walked around the outer walls, seeing occasional dark and shadowy figures, high up, briefly glanced as they walked by crenel gaps along the tops of the parapet walks. But if the three brightly clothed visitors were noticed, then they were not challenged and were left unhindered to carry on with their nocturnal amble. Eventually they reached a narrow courtyard leading to a solid wooden door. Arrow slots along the walls made it clear that they were walking into a killing zone, which ensured that they would not stand much chance if they were seen to be an unwelcome enemy. They'd be dead by arrows or spears despatched from the slots or falling rocks and burning oil sent from murder holes before they could get anywhere near the gatehouse.

Suddenly Bob pulled down his balaclava and shouted to his two companions, "Hey, look at me!" He threw himself backwards into the snow and began to wave his arms and legs. "I'm a snow angel. Get it?"

Roxy and Dedan looked first at him, then at each other, and then back to Bob again. Dedan pulled down his balaclava so that he could be heard. "Bob, you really are a dickhead!" Then reluctantly he began to laugh. "I bet you've been waiting all day to make that joke. Get up, you idiot!"

It is hard to climb up from snow in heavy padded clothing, and it is even more difficult to do it so that is looks elegant, casual, and nonchalant - all of which Bob utterly failed to do. He looked more like a brightly coloured sack of potatoes coming to life. Once upright, he began to brush the snow from his clothing, the big chunks making a splatting noise as they fell to the ground. "That's better."

"Hang on, wait a minute, you missed a bit." Dedan aided his companion by gently slapping Bob's head, sending a small glob of snow to the ground. "There, that is definitely better."

"Thank you." Bob's happy face was hidden by his warm headgear and his fake fur lined hood. "I needed that."

"Men!" Roxy muttered; her voice muffled behind her balaclava. "It's too dark and cold for you two to turn into Laurel and Hardy. Come on, let's see if anyone is home." Walking up to the gate she looked up at the spiked portcullis high above her head, one last outer defensive device able to simultaneously impale and crush any would be assailant that made it through the deadly corridor. Despite the impediment of having thick padded gloves, she was about to attempt to knock on the wooden door but thankfully, before the soft material made impact with it, a small slot slid open revealing a dark brown eye that could barely be seen underneath a black bush of an eyebrow. Where the other eye should have been was a dull and weathered brown leather eyepatch.

"What?" The man's voice was gruff, with a thick Scottish accent. "If you are selling anything, then you should know that we are not interested, and you should get lost!"

Roxy wondered if castle-door-to-castle-door salesmen were major problems in this domain. With the climate, they'd certainly be cold callers. If they did exist, then they'd be a hardy bunch and would deserve to make a small sale just to reward their fortitude. Lowering her hood, removing her goggles, and pulling off her balaclava so that her face could be seen, she immediately felt the cold air attacking her lips, nose, and ears. She hoped that any conversation with the doorman would be brief. "Sir, we are emissaries from God and seek an audience with Sonja." As she spoke, her hot breath hit the frigid air and formed a cloud in front of her, eerily leaden grey in the semi darkness.

"Have you got an appointment?"

She looked incredulously at the single eye, trying to visualise the process of booking a visit to see the goddess. "No, we do not have an appointment. But we need to see her as a matter of urgency."

"All right, I'll go see if she's in." The slot slid shut with a snap and Roxy heard loud laughter from the other side of the door. Then it died down and was replaced by the noise of keys turning in locks that were in desperate need of oiling and heavy bolts being drawn back. Slowly the door opened, revealing a tall and bulky figure dressed from top to toe in a dirty brown fur coat. Behind him was a broad, snow-covered open forecourt and beyond that the inner bailey building. "Well? What are you waiting for? Come on. You're letting all the heat out."

Turning to look at Dedan and Bob, she shrugged her shoulders and gesticulated towards the opening. "Come on, you two. Don't forget to wipe your feet."

On hearing her joke, the one-eyed man laughed. "I was about to say that. I like your style, lassie. Come on in and make yourself at home. As long as your home is an ice-covered castle; if it isn't then you might be sorely disappointed." As she walked past him, he playfully slapped her on the bottom.

She turned and looked at him, delivering a stare that was as cold and hard as the castle walls. Using all her mental strength she had to restrain herself from punching the gatekeeper, but it was a close call.

"I bet you're a comely wench under all that padding," he said, his voice full of mirth. Then, turning his attention to the two men, he assured them, "It's all right, you're safe. I won't smack your arses. Not even if you say please."

Once they entered the courtyard, the vast door was closed behind them and, as they looked around, they saw people in furs walking around or standing and talking. There were stalls with various foods on display. Frozen fish hung from the canopies and suspicious looking chunks of grey meat were laid out on tables amongst more recognisable legs of beef and pigs' heads. Barrels were stacked up in triangular towers and they were being freely utilised by the population. Clay mugs and hollow cattle horns were filled and, almost as quickly, emptied again as the drinkers drank, drank some, more and got drunk. Indistinct conversations were punctuated by deep voiced hysterical laughter.

"I am Roxy; my fellow travellers are Bob and Dedan. What can we call you?"

"I am Aurumknob, but if most people want to talk to me, they just shout AU."

"Well. Aurum… I mean AU, we wish to see Sonja, but we have come far and would like to freshen up first. Maybe I could have a bath?"

On hearing the word *bath*, AU immediately gave her a leery look. "It is your Bathday? Congratulations." Looking around the square, he shouted to all within earshot, and with his booming voice that meant everyone, "Oi, lads, it's this here lassie's Bathday. Time for a paaaartyyyyy!"

Suspecting that baths were not a frequent occurrence and, when they did occur, they might just be a spectator sport where all the residents of the castle brought beer and snacks, she decided that she wasn't *that* dirty after all. "Errrr, no AU, I will give it a miss, I just remembered I've already had a bath this year. Perhaps if we could just have some warm water for washing and maybe borrow some clean clothing to change into before we see Her Highness?"

"'Ere, lads. This lassie here wants *clean* clothing!" AU was obviously enjoying himself at the expense of the guests. In such a cold climate, where keeping warm was paramount, such niceties as taking clothes off so that they, and the wearer, could be cleaned were apparently low down on the priority list.

"Oh, never mind! Please just see what you can do so we look presentable to Sonja." Roxy was barely able to keep her frustration out of her voice. "Men!" she muttered to herself.

The progress through the courtyard was slow, as AU insisted on stopping at every group of dwellers he encountered and introducing the visitors to them. Along with the introductions, he would take a drink and then move on to the next set of people. By the time they had reached the door leading into the inner castle building, AU had managed to drink enough beer to have downed even a sailor in the US navy but, despite that, he seemed to be totally unaffected. Once inside the building, they followed him along narrow corridors, dimly lit by more burning torches, up winding spiralling stairways, along more corridors, and down numerous spiral staircases. If they'd had to find the exit, via the direction that they had just come, they would have quite easily become lost. Eventually AU stopped outside three doors that looked identical to every other door that they had seen as they walked through the castle: plain dark brown wood with simple wooden latches.

"Here you are, your rooms. Make yourselves comfortable and I will return with clothing. And of course, *warm* water." AU said the word 'warm' as if he had been tasked with finding a virgin in a busy Parisian brothel. He watched them go into their rooms and then went off on his search, "Warm water? Clean clothes?" He laughed as if each item were a punchline to the funniest joke he had ever heard.

It was the same layout in each room. A large bed, covered with furs and animal skins, took up most of the available space. What was left was taken up by a small table situated against the wall and an equally small stool next to it. The decorations on the walls were assorted swords, spears and shields, items both decorative and practical if the inhabitant needed to defend the castle against attack. At the far end of the room was a small window ledge with a brown earthenware chamber pot resting on it, and behind that was a small rectangular window overlooking the outer castle wall.

Despite the lack of any glass windowpanes to keep out the elements, Roxy found her room to be quite comfortable and the single torch gave off enough light and heat to allow her to remove the outer layer of her thick winter clothing. She briefly sniffed at the armpits of her t-shirt and recoiled in disgust. The trapped perspiration had given her an odour akin to an athlete's jock strap that had been soaked in a bucket of sweat overnight and left to ferment for a week before it was finally used to carry rotting fish. However, she surmised that AU's reaction to the concept of hygiene was such that her condition would still make her smell like she was drenched in eau de cologne when compared to the local residents.

She was just absent mindedly staring out of her window, musing over the possible age of the castle, when her thoughts were dragged back to the present by a knock on the door. Without being invited in, AU entered and gave her a broad smile.

"Ah, lassie. See? I was right, you're a fine figure of a girl under all that padding." Roxy was about to try and correct his politically incorrect attitudes to women, but he continued before she had the chance to remonstrate. "Here you go lassie, clean clothing, or at least as clean as they can be. Laundry day isn't for another two months." He dropped them unceremoniously on the bed. "And here is some warm water." He placed a large bowl full of water on the table and gave her another smile. "If you want a hand with washing, I'm happy to help."

"No thank you, AU." Roxy's firm voice left him in no doubt that his less than subtle chat-up approach was never going to work. "That is all. And PLEASE, my name is Roxy."

"Aye, so you said, lassie. I'll come back in an hour and then take you to see Sonja. She knows you're here and is in the great hall." With that he left, closing the door behind him.

Relieved at the opportunity to finally get rid of offensive smelling clothing and lingering body odour, she stripped and plunged her hands into the bowl of water. Instantly, she regretted her brash actions as the cold liquid made her shudder and inhale sharply. She considered the temperature and concluded that the residents of this domain had a different view as to what warm water was. Any liquid that wasn't frozen must be warm and that was as good as it got. She thought that next time, she would ask for boiling hot water and then corrected herself by hoping that there would never be a next time. But, despite the chilly water, she cleaned herself as best she could and quickly got dressed. The clothes that she had been given were grey and white sealskin trousers with a caribou hide top. It was warm and comfortable and, compared to her own clothes, didn't have too bad of an odour. Just as she had finished dressing, there was another knock on her door and AU entered again.

"Hello, lassie. There, that's better." Pointing to her clothing, "You look like you belong here now, rather than some jester looking for work. If you come with me, I will take you to see Sonja."

Once in the corridor, she saw Bob and Dedan waiting for her. They had also managed to clean themselves as best they could. Much to Bob's relief, he'd been able to remove the traces of urine that had run down his leg, and they were both dressed in the same wild animal clothing as she was. They gave her a smile. "I feel like an Inuit," Dedan volunteered with a grin.

"You look like a complete Inuit," Roxy added with a laugh.

Then, before they had the chance to chat anymore, AU set off along the corridor, making the three angels momentarily run to catch up with him.

Without pausing, he led them along more narrow winding corridors before the passageway began to widen and they came to a large wooden double door, decorated with a vast and intricate engraving of the Yggdrasil, the Norse tree of life. In front of it were two guards. One of them was holding a spear and the other a curved bladed Viking axe. On seeing AU, they each took hold of a handle and pulled the doors open, allowing the visitors to walk through.

Once inside, they saw the great hall. It was rectangular with a single giant table in the centre and along all four sides of it were men and women in various states of consciousness and inebriation. Some were asleep face down in plates of food others were busily helping themselves to the mountains of meat and ale laid out before them. There were others talking loudly to each other, or else singing lewd songs about the best way to keep warm in the snow and odes about a troll that got frostbite where no man should ever get it. Set deep into the two side walls were fireplaces carved into the shape of giant bearded men's faces, with the raging log fires sending heat and occasional tongues of flame out of their mouths. In three of the corners were warriors drunkenly practicing their sword fighting skills. Weapons swung wildly, hitting walls and sending sparks into the air before the wielders fell clumsily to the floor, got up and repeated the whole thing again, much to the loud amusement of other equally drunken onlookers. Finally, at the far end of the hall, they saw a narrower table running diagonally from one side of the room to the other and sitting at the far side of it were a long line of similarly dressed and intoxicated men and women.

The only one that appeared to be sober was a woman taking pride of place in the centre of the row. Her chair was grander and appeared to be made of elk antlers and spears and, to add to the feeling of superiority, she had two heavily armed but drunk looking guards standing behind her. Seeing the three angels enter the room, she stood up and gestured for them to approach her. They weaved between staggering drunkards and stepped carefully over unconscious bodies spread-eagled on the floor until they were standing in front of the goddess. She turned her head to speak to the guards and they quickly ran to get some chairs and carried them to the other side of the table, placed them down, then promptly returned to their positions.

"Please be seated. I am Sonja, Goddess of this realm. It is so rare that we have visitors. How can I help you?" Her voice was soft and sweet, nothing like the harsh booming Nordic tone that Roxy expected.

It wasn't just the voice that surprised her, as it had the same effect on Dedan and Bob as well; it was her whole appearance. She had expected some buxom Valkyrie type maiden that would have been at home in an epic Wagnerian opera that took days to sit through and would leave most people wishing they were either deaf or dead. The sort of Aryan maiden that would have had Hitler drooling in his fantasy world full of tall female perfection, with flowing blonde hair and blue eyes. A mythical female resplendent in a winged helmet, an armoured short skirt, and a tight and angular battle corset made out of metal; perhaps not the most comfortable of clothing but it could deflect a bullet and frighten someone of a nervous disposition.

The lack of the stereotypical appearance had Bob severely disappointed, but he still liked what he saw. Sonja was the complete opposite to the Teutonic ideal and a total surprise to the angels' preconceptions. Roxy had to admit that she was beautiful, although her appearance wasn't obviously Nordic. From what they could see of her hands, her fingers were covered with diamond and ruby encrusted rings. Her shoulder length hair was black with delicate blue streaks and parted just off centre, revealing a pale and unblemished face with rich and pouting red lips and dark brown eyes that seemed to both sparkle and look sad at the same time. In Dedan's mind, her white face reminded him of a Japanese doll. Thanks to the way her massive brown fur coat surrounded her, it was hard to tell if she was wearing it or if it was trying to digest her. In poor lighting, she could have been mistaken for a bear and might have had her followers hunting her. Thanks to this covering, it was impossible for them to assess her build, but her neck was slender and didn't indicate the busty fräulein that could crush skulls with her muscular thighs.

Sensing the surprise of her guests, Sonja smiled at them. That look on its own had Bob, if not so much in love, then at least in lust. "From the looks on your faces, I suspect you were expecting someone a little more Norse looking. It's all right, I surprise a lot of people at first. It seems that the believers that created me were tired of seeing blonde hair and blue eyes and fancied something less daunting and slightly more exotic.

But there are plenty like that in Valhalla, where my drunken relatives live. But that is there and here I am."

With that, she unfastened her thick coat and opened it, revealing a slender body with a tight stomach and slim legs, and the only clothing she had was a gold bikini. "As you can see, my human followers had an erotic view of me. No matter what I do to change my clothes, Unless I wear equally sexy battle armour, I always end up looking like this. But at least they did allow me to maintain a little dignity; although not a lot of it. I can assure you a metal bra and panties are not ideal for a castle in a snow-covered domain where the idea of warmth is limited to remaining at a close proximity to an open log fire or having sex. If it weren't for my thick fur coat, I wouldn't need human prayer to make me solid again. I'd turn into an ice sculpture."

"It's all right, your Highness. I think you look fantastic," Bob added, with wide and greedy eyes that could have made a magpie's attraction to gold seem fleeting.

Casually closing her coat again, Sonja looked at him warily. "Yes, thank you. I am sure you do."

Sensing that there was a risk that Bob might drag the conversation below the neckline, where she would struggle to drag it back up, Roxy decided to take the initiative. "Please excuse my colleague. He is known as a dick and, like far too many men, he has only one thing on his mind and is easily distracted."

"Only one thing?" Sonja's voice was full of surprise. "Here the men have two topics that fill their consciousness... and unconsciousness. War and women. Three topics if you include drinking, which tends to stop them from doing the first two."

On hearing the last sentence, one of the formerly sleeping warriors at her table groggily lifted his body and raised his tankard. "WAR and WOMEN!" he shouted, in a drunken slur. Then he put the drink to his mouth, leaning backwards as he guzzled. The action made him fall back and collapse onto the floor unconscious once more as his spilt beer soaked into his beard, hair, and fur cloak.

Momentarily looking at the fallen warrior, she sighed. "Yes, as I was saying, they have fairly simple preoccupations and unfortunately have very little imagination when it comes to any of those. As it is my private domain, there are no enemies to attack us, so there is no war, which ensures that they spend their time drinking and eating. And, sadly, thanks to all the beer they consume, they are not much good with women either. Frustrating for me and all rather pathetic, but it keeps them quiet. Or fairly quiet, once you get used to the bawdy but unimaginative singing."

The image of gold against naked flesh made Bob want to gallantly offer his services, but he caught Roxy's stern glare and decided against it. He then glanced at Dedan, who looked like he was also reading Bob's mind, and was gently shaking his head as if to say, 'behave yourself'. Despite the unspoken chastisement, Bob suspected that Dedan's eyes had also caught gold fever and that he would have liked to have done some prospecting or ventured into a mine.

If Dedan had been willing to admit it, he would have probably expressed it in more respectful terms, but he had appreciated the beauty of Sonja's body and would have loved to get better acquainted with it.

"Please," Sonja added, realising that she was forgetting her manners, "eat and drink as much as you like. One of the benefits of this place is that there is an unending supply of beer and meat. I've heard of a concept called 'veganism,' but if you don't eat meat then you will go hungry here."

Roxy looked at the plates brimming with different selections of meat and jugs overflowing with frothy beer. "I take it there isn't much demand for greens or glasses of wine; just to break the monotony?"

The question made Sonja give the angel a kind but condescending look. "The only green food you'd see around here would be meat that has gone off and as for wine… we somehow got a barrel of the stuff once. My brave Viking warriors took one sip of it and decided that it would taste better if they mixed it with beer. If you're looking for a varied and sophisticated palate, then you have come to the wrong place. You two," signalling to Bob and Dedan, "please tuck in and help yourselves. Eat, drink and be merry, for tomorrow we repeat the whole thing. Forever and for all eternity!" Then, turning her attention back to Roxy, she said, "I am sure that us two can discuss things without the need for excess or overindulgence?"

Bob began to eat and drink with little finesse. It wasn't long before his chin was oily with the fat from the meat and, thanks to his rapid drinking, his front was saturated with beer. But irrespective of spillage, he was still able to consume far more than he wasted. Dedan had encountered similar medieval banquets before and knew that pacing himself was the only way to stay functional. There had been many occasions when he had not slept for a week as he ate and drank and at the end of one such celebration, he'd ended up convinced that he was a pixie called Ralph and that he could fly. Thankfully, during his hallucination, there had been a few revellers that were slightly less inebriated than he was, and they had been able to pin him down before he could climb a staircase and be proved wrong. Casually he nibbled on a roasted chicken breast and slowly sipped a mug of beer. Although he felt completely safe under the patronage of the goddess, he wasn't convinced that, thanks to his clothing, some drunken warrior wouldn't mistake him for a seal and then attempt to kill and skin him.

While the men were preoccupied with eating and drinking, the women were left to talk. Initially, Roxy explained about the sudden reanimation of the other gods, and the various reactions of them, and Sonja provided as much information about her sole living believer as she could, confirming his name and distant location. Once the formal elements of the visit were completed, they were then free to discuss less formal subjects. Despite the current army of seemingly useless occupants of her domain, Roxy was dumbfounded by the range of men and experiences in Sonja's past. It became apparent that her human followers were rewarded in ways that modern gods had abandoned. Although she had a typical Italian pride of her wild passion and lack of candour when it came to sex, Roxy was far from being able to match the goddess's prowess or athleticism, so she stuck to telling her about her useless and manipulative former husband. As the long night drew on, and the other angels continued with their gluttony, the two women bonded.

Bob found a comfortable semi-comatose position laid out on the table with his face pressed against a half-eaten joint of reindeer meat and began to feel a mixture of drunken boredom and all-consuming exhaustion. Dedan would have loved to have been excused and shown back to his room but wasn't sure of protocol. He was concerned that retiring before the goddess could be seen as a sign of weakness or a social faux pas. Much to his relief, Sonja stood up, stretched, and yawned loudly.

"Well, you three. It looks like you are all ready for bed. Some more than others," she added, pointing to Bob's comatose body, which was sprawled out across the table. "AU!" she shouted, and the manservant quickly appeared by her side. "Ah, there you are. Please help sleeping beauty there back to his room and show these two back to theirs. I'm sure that they would appreciate a good night's sleep before they return to Heaven. I doubt that God would be happy to be faced with drunkenness and blurry eyes."

Snorting derisively at the outsider's lack of stamina and inability to cope with such an insignificant amount of beer, Aurumknob lifted Bob up off the table, as if he were a roll of cloth, and then placed him over his shoulder. "Come on you two, this way." Without waiting, he set off, but this time he ensured that he was going just slowly enough for Dedan and Roxy to keep up and follow him. The last thing he wanted to do was waste valuable drinking time by having to search the castle looking for two lost angels. Winding along dimly lit and nondescript corridors, AU stopped by a door, opened it and less than casually threw Bob onto the bed. Pointing to the next two rooms, he guided Dedan and Roxy to their accommodation. "There you go. Goodnight, sleep well." His words were spoken brusquely and plainly insincere. Ignoring their good wishes, he was off lumbering back down the corridor, his mind already fixed on the idea of his next drink. It was thirsty work doing anything that didn't involve drinking.

In his room, Dedan had just undressed and was splashing cold water from his bowl over his face in an attempt to dispel the mild alcoholic fog that, despite the limited amount of beer consumed, had started to cloud up his brain. His harsh ablutions were interrupted by his door opening and Sonja entering. She looked him up and down and gave him a lascivious wink. "I see that you didn't get blind drunk and end up incapable. I like that in a man. It's been a long time since anyone has been capable enough to give me any attention and I can see that you are already standing to attention for me!" Keeping her face towards him she pushed the door closed with her foot then slid off her fur coat, letting it drop to the floor. "I hope you're still hungry!"

In the room next door, Roxy was just settling into her bed, and about to go to sleep, when she heard what sounded like some heavy metal objects falling to the floor with an unceremonious clang. "Men," she muttered. "Nothing like casual sex with a woman that they've only just met, and barely spoken to all night, to help them forget a broken heart."

The next morning, Roxy took great pleasure in loudly knocking on the doors of her colleagues so that they would wake up, be ready to go back to Heaven, and be able to report to God. As his companion had left him a few hours earlier, Dedan was the first to emerge. Despite his tired eyes having dark rings around them, he had the look akin to a cat that had fallen into a vat of cream and managed to eat his way out. Even though they could open a dimensional portal in the corridor and had no need to go back out into the snow, he had opted to wear the sealskin suit and was carrying his brightly coloured arctic clothing in a rolled-up bundle under his arm.

Eventually Bob emerged from his room, swaying unsteadily. Stuck to his chin and right cheek, there was a substance that looked suspiciously like dried vomit. He was also wearing his sealskin outfit, but that was only because he'd been in no state to undress when had been left on his bed. Squinting through blurred eyes, he looked first at Dedan and then Roxy and smacked his lips and gave them a bitter scowl that gave him the appearance of a pitbull dog chewing a wasp. "All right," he said, his voice croaky and deep. "Which of you two bastards shat in my mouth while I was asleep? From the feel of it you both have."

18 – The Naughty Step

Despite his painful death at the hands of Ekeko, it was nothing compared to the agony that the return to Hell caused Hellios. It was not designed to be a soft and gentle process; it was intended to be a deterrent to all demons that were on missions or participating in battles on earth. Succeed in the set task, or kill others in battle, then you would return unharmed, and it would be mildly uncomfortable, or mild for a demon; but if you fail, and end up getting killed, then it is not a time to expect leniency. The pain of the return to Hell was only the start and Hellios was certainly suffering from the process. His spine felt like someone had clamped a vice to it and was tightening it whilst someone else was utilising an electric drill to bore into the frontal lobes of his brain. The only way he could deal with it was to curl up in a tight ball on the floor, with his knees tucked into his chest and his remaining long ape-like arm wrapped around himself, until the effects wore off.

Eventually the worst of the torment subsided, allowing Hellios to first relax his tensed body and then stand up so that he could get his bearings and try and work out where in Hell he had rematerialized. The initial reaction was relief that he hadn't reappeared in the middle of a wall and been forced to spend the next century trying to dig his way out. But there was still the question of his location. From the vast size and smell of the place, he could tell that he was in a punishment chamber, but that didn't narrow it down; Hell was made up of such places and they could be difficult to get out of once inside. There was an eerie grey light filling the place and it was neither too hot nor too cold. Fire and brimstone were absent, and he couldn't see any other demons, which had him curious as they were usually needed to ensure that the damned souls could receive their punishments. After all, it was rare for the residents to inflict the punishments on themselves.

But even with the lack of evil guards, there seemed to be no shortage of souls. They were like a sea of bodies sitting upright on the floor, either clutching their knees in their arms or desperately clenching their hands to their faces. The usual tools or implements that filled most chambers with opportunities to carry out creative punishments were not visible, but despite that, the noise that filled his ears was deafening. The cries were not the usual sounds of torture being applied; instead, they were sounds of invisible torments within hearts and minds. He wandered between the bodies trying to get their attention, but when they looked up all he saw were empty unseeing eyes lost in their own worlds. He slapped the face of one, but it did nothing to break the trance. Selecting another, he tried harsher forms of violence. Slaps became punches, then punches became kicks, but nothing woke or dragged them into a state where they could even acknowledge his existence. Bodies were there, but minds were buried deep in other distant worlds.

It was then that he realised where he was. He had heard talk of the place but, as no demons guarded it, the details were often sketchy, vague, and subject to creative elaboration or exaggeration. It was the Chamber of Internal Sorrows, a place that even the demons were wary of entering in case they accidentally became the victims. It was Hell's equivalent of a child's naughty step, only for evil adults; a place where souls would be forced to sit and think about what they had done. Only it wasn't childish ponderings after scribbling on the wall with wax crayons or telling lies about not doing homework. Here the damned had to relive their sins from the perspective of their victims. Bullies had to live the terror filled lives of those they tormented, trying to find comfort and safety but finding only undeserved mental and physical punishments inflicted when they were least expected. Nazi or Stalin era German and Russian camp guards had to feel life through the hunger and daily terrors which they so readily dished out to innocent men, women, and children, with each emotion magnified and repeated inside their skulls for all eternity. Too late to make amends, and repentance was futile; all they had was the punishment in their minds. Laments could be released but could never free the sufferers from the figurative self-made demons inside their heads.

Hellios was relieved to realise that the punishment being inflicted on the damned souls had not automatically started in his mind. There had been much in his life that he had no desire to relive from the perspective of his victims. In Hell, empathy was not something to be desired. Even though he was not suffering like everyone else, he decided that it would be prudent for him to get out of the chamber as quickly as possible. Despite being less than a hundred percent successful in his mission, he needed to report to Satan as soon as possible and hope that his master's iron-like displeasure was tempered by the information that he had to impart. Sometimes the right details in a report could make the difference between remaining a punisher and becoming the punished. Thankfully, for him, the door to the chamber was neither locked nor guarded, the state of the inhabitants preventing them from ever being in a mental state where they could get up and leave. Exiting, he took one last look at the damned and had to fight the urge to feel pity for them. 'There but for the grace of Satan, go I.' he thought to himself. Then he closed the door and allowed any thoughts of the room to leave his mind. The damned souls were not to be seen as anything but objects of contempt and they simply got what they deserved. Looking at them in any other way was a shortcut to madness and punishments.

The long, dark, and narrow corridors leading towards the centre of Hell, and Satan's inner sanctum, were full of demons of all shapes and sizes, the sort of creatures that would have given horror writers nightmares and made them give up the genre and start writing fluffy romance novels. Some were talking in small groups, plotting the downfall of enemies, of which there were always plenty. Others were on their own watching the small groups, warily, in case there was a glimpse of a knife drawn ready to strike them. Being in Hell, they couldn't be killed, but they could be incapacitated in painful ways with it taking years for them to recover. One-upmanship could be a serious business in Hell. Ignoring them, he made his way to Satan's office. Occasionally he'd encounter a demon heading in the same direction but not moving fast enough and blocking his way. When that happened, he simply pushed them to one side or kicked them on the back of their knees and when they had fallen to the floor, he would walk over them, ensuring his steps were heavier than normal.

Having been allowed past the main entrance by Satan's guards he reached his destination and walked straight into the office of Satan's assistant. Kran was, as usual, bent over his desk busily writing in a thick, red leather-bound ledger. Despite the various permutations of grotesqueness of most demons, it was often hard to differentiate one from another. It didn't help when many of them had strange names that were almost impossible to spell, many with more letter Z's or K's than a Polish washing machine manual. But thanks to his semi-human appearance, Hellios was memorable and easily recognised, plus his name was short and easy to remember.

"Ah, Hellios. Satan has been waiting for your return," ventured Lucifer's minion. "Would you like me to announce you?"

Hellios gave him a contemptuous glare. "No, I think I know how to knock on a door and then open it!" he responded, his voice dripping with sarcasm and scorn heavy enough to sink a battleship. Walking to the door leading into the inner office, he raised his long ape-like arm and gave it a heavy and loud knock. The wood beneath his knuckles gave off a doom-laden thud and then left silence briefly in its place.

Then, in response, he heard a deep growling voice. "Yes? What is it, maggot? Whatever it is, it had better be important." The words, combined with the tone, would have been enough to send a lesser demon back into the labyrinth of Hell as they tried to find a hiding place. But not Hellios; he was confident and certain that he was important enough to warrant a respectful welcome. Such arrogance would frequently be beaten out of most demons, but Hellios kept hold of his like a medal of dishonour.

He attempted to push open the door, but the obstinate object resisted his efforts. Taken initially by surprise, it moved about an inch before it seized up and stopped as if it were locked in that position. Feeling the resistance, Hellios braced himself, pushed his armless shoulder against it, and used his full body weight to push it and create a gap large enough for him to get through. Suddenly the door gave up the struggle and decided to let the demon enter without any more trouble. The lack of any force to counter his assault meant that he fell forward and landed, face first, onto the thick red carpet covering the floor of Satan's office. The stench of blood, urine and other things that could be released by a body during torture and evisceration filled his nostrils as he scrambled to get up and regain his dignity. Not an easy thing to achieve by someone shaped like a one-armed primate suffering from back ache and haemorrhoids.

On seeing the mini battle between demon and door, Satan wanted to laugh, but he fought the urge as he knew that he had to maintain his stern and angry appearance. He opted instead for his default look. Glaring disdainfully at the demon, he remained silent, waiting for Hellios to get into position in front of his desk. Even the PA system seemed to be enjoying the floor show and stopped playing Barry

Manilow so that it could eavesdrop on the forthcoming conversation. Leaning back in his old weathered and cracked brown leather executive chair, Satan casually sipped a 25-year-old single malt whisky from a crystal cut tumbler. Finally, when he deemed the pause to have been sufficient to make Hellios feel uncomfortable, he placed the glass back on his desk and leaned forward, fiery red eyes fixed on the demon.

"Well, Hellios. What have you got to report? Will Ekeko behave himself?" he enquired, his voice no longer hard, having adopted more of a mild conversational tone. One look at the now one-armed creature made him assume the worst, but he wanted to hear it for himself. But Hellios knew enough not to read too much into any softness of tone. Satan's mood could quickly change, with a verbal light wind soon transforming into a wild and violent storm.

"Not quite, your Satanic Majesty." Hellios then proceeded to recount everything that he had seen, and done, in Ekeko's domain. As he talked, Satan sat quietly stroking his beard, listening intently, his face expressionless and giving nothing away with regards to his emotional state. Finally, the report came to an end and silence returned to the room.

Like an invisible sword of Damocles, Satan allowed the tension to mount up and fear to enter the mind of Hellios. He wasn't sure if the news was good or bad and was wondering if he could manipulate it to his own advantage before he swapped information over the phone with God. "All right, get out," he snapped. "That is all for now."

Hellios was surprised at the lack of even the mildest of admonishments, but he didn't want to push his luck, so he quickly headed for the door. Luckily it was still open, allowing him to leave without having to start another war as he attempted to persuade it to open for him. Once he was in the relative safety of Kran's office, he allowed himself to relax a little. He had half expected Satan to change his mind as he was leaving and send a ball of fire into the back of his head but was relieved to have found the Prince of Darkness in a good mood, or as good as his mood could be.

Once he was alone in his room, Satan picked up his phone and pushed the dial button. After a brief wait, it was answered. "Hello, God. I have some news...."

19 – The Angels That Came in From the Cold

As she sat in a comfortable chair sipping a cup of coffee while she waited for God to finish His telephone conversation, Roxy had time to look at Dedan and Bob. She was glad that there had been time for them all to get changed out of the sealskin suits, have warm showers, and get into more casual t-shirts and jeans. Thanks to the roaring log fire, His office would have been far too warm if they had stayed looking like they were on an arctic expedition or a polar bear hunt. Despite the lack of a full night's sleep, her two friends looked a lot better for the chance to freshen up and get into clean clothing. Bob was especially relieved that he'd had the opportunity to give his legs a more thorough wash and no longer give off the subtle and delicate hint of stale urine. Even Dedan looked comfortable and at peace. On his way into God's room, he had even stopped and been able to chat amicably with Angelica and apologise for his earlier stupid behaviour.

As the call came to an end, God put down the phone and turned His attention to the three guests. Instantly His expression turned from stern concentration to one of benign joy, ensuring that they were put at their ease. "I'm glad you all had a safe trip and made it back in one piece. Residents of Norse domains can be a little careless when it comes to playing with axes. I have heard that, thanks to all the beer, aiming is frequently wide of the mark and spectators can lose limbs or receive a hatchet lobotomy."

"No problem, Sire," began Roxy, returning his smile. "As far as the mission is concerned, the weather was cold, but the welcome was warm, and we were made comfortable. Of course, some were made more comfortable than others," she added, giving Dedan a quick glance and causing Bob to give her a curious look as, thanks to his unconsciousness, he suspected that he had missed something important. Roxy then gave Dedan a conspiratorial wink that made him even more confused. "I managed to have a long talk with Sonja," she continued, "and it seems that once again it is Gordoon Simpson who is responsible for her existence and that he is her only devotee. She genuinely wants to remain a living goddess and doesn't want to go back to being a lump of cold marble and, in addition to that, she also maintains that she has no intention, or desire, to cause any trouble for humans. I got the impression that she was being honest with me. She has lots of warriors that would love a good war, or even a bad war if that were all that was available, but their drinking habits seem to keep them sedated and in a blissful state."

God nodded sagely. "I see. That is good news. And Sonja, how was she as a god?"

Roxy hesitated, uncertain as to how much detail she needed to reveal to God. Although she strongly suspected that Dedan had been more than a pillar of strength to the goddess, she wasn't sure if now was the right time to bring it up. After all, Dedan had a reputation for being friendly with angels, humans, and even occasional demons of the opposite sex, and it had never been a problem before. Also, keeping Sonja on the side of goodness was important, so he could certainly have warmed her to the idea of fighting the good fight. However, she also knew that the act could rebound on him if Sonja got jealous when she realised that he didn't call or write. She could take the slight personally and decide to give Hell a lesson in fury at being scorned. Roxy decided that she would have a quiet word with God later and ensure that He was at least aware of the friendly relationship and, if any further precautions needed to be taken, He could implement them. So, for now, she decided to remain quiet on that side of the adventure and give a truncated character reference. "She was friendly and happy. Her subjects seem to spend too much time drunk so she might be a little bit frustrated when it comes to *filling her desires,* but other than that, she appears to be steady and reliable and shouldn't cause any trouble if she remains a goddess."

God laughed loudly and looked at Dedan. "Sounds like an ideal job for you. When it came to her desires, you could have filled her up!" God had known him for millennia and was well aware of his major weakness; He had no problem with it and enjoyed the opportunity to mildly wind up His trusted general. Despite many human believers trying to force a dour, serious, all-powerful, judgmental and stern persona onto their deity, as an excuse to look down their noses and feel superior to others, God didn't have a problem with anyone having consensual sex. As long it didn't hold up business meetings, He was happy for people to do what came naturally. Despite his age, experience and well-founded reputation, Dedan blushed slightly at the double entendre. But he was determined that any redness of his cheeks not be noticed by Bob or Roxy so he decided to join in with the joke. He might never be able to claim the moral high ground, but the immoral low ground could be more fun.

"And who said that I didn't keep her happy, several times? Just because Bob was unconscious, and Roxy was asleep, didn't mean that I wasn't standing up for all that is good and right!"

On hearing Dedan's claim, Bob's mouth dropped. The revelation struck him as he realised that he'd missed out on the opportunity of something more enjoyable than a few free beers, and he immediately regretted his choice of how he spent the evening. Roxy, on the other hand, displayed total sang froid and just maintained an apathetic look. She didn't want to pretend that she was surprised, but she didn't really want Dedan to know that she already knew about his actions. She was just thankful that they had kept the noise down and allowed her to eventually get to sleep. At least the confession relieved her of the need to go telling tales to God and, from the look on His face, He seemed to be unconcerned by Dedan having done the deed, several times.

"Okay, you three," He began, His voice taking on a serious quality, "it seems that, according to Satan, Ekeko is not going to play ball and will be genuine trouble. I doubt that any of you going to see him, and trying to appeal to his kind side, will work. He is one of those old school South American gods whose idea of fun is to rip out human hearts as sacrifices. Without blood to sate his hunger, he might get tetchy."

Dedan had to refrain from interrupting and adding a comment at that point. He found the word *tetchy* to be only the tip of the iceberg. He'd encountered gods that demanded blood sacrifices before. The fetish tended to be like a drug where they needed more and more human offerings for them to be satisfied and if they failed to get their hit, they turned out to be more than mildly irritable. He remembered one Asian god who'd sent a tidal wave to wipe out an entire island because they were struggling to kill enough people in his name. The ensuing destruction resulted in him wiping out every single believer that he had and suddenly finding himself turned into a statue in the Hall of Dead Gods, frozen for all eternity in the pose he was in when he'd realised what he'd just done, the face-palm he was giving himself captured for any rare visitor to see and ponder over. Unfortunately, his final exclamation of 'Ohhhhh, shit' was not recorded on his plinth. Succinct and to the point, but they were hardly the greatest of famous last words.

Oblivious of Dedan's thoughts, God continued. "I want you three to go pay a visit Mr. Simpson in Colorado and see what his intentions are. Perhaps educate him on the dangers of rampant pantheism, especially when he chooses obscure and long-lost gods to worship. He needs to be made aware of what his actions have done. He might be lost and looking for some light for his path, but sometimes there is only more darkness."

Pausing, He looked first at Roxy, then Bob, before settling His gaze on Dedan. There was the mutual realisation that what was being asked could lead to the destruction of his ex-wife, again. But there was a need to protect human lives and if needs be then Hor'idey must be sacrificed. The ties that bound might have been old, worn and frayed, but they were still there. However, sometimes ties had to be cut. Not something either God or Dedan wanted, but they both understood the rules and, from the look in his eyes, God could tell that Dedan reluctantly accepted it.

"Angelica has everything ready for you. Thank you." With those words, the trio of angels began to rise from their chairs. "Oh, and one more thing," God added, "please remember he is a human and, despite all he has done, he is not evil so is not to be treated as such!"

Roxy nodded sagely. "Yes, Sire, of course." She also understood the concept; innocent humans were not to be assassinated and had to be protected. A rule that she accepted but, in this case, she wished that they could bend it enough so that it broke. A convenient 'accident' would make all the problems simply disappear.

20 – Man of Constant Anger

Ravaillac, in life, had been a religious fanatic and, like so many that believed that their view of any god and how to worship them was the one and only way, anyone that contradicted such dogmatic views was seen as an enemy and worthy of death. This blind intolerance made him the perfect assassin and it was how he had lived and then died. He had been a zealous Catholic living in a time when the commandment about not killing people was taken as a vague suggestion rather than a rigid law and only applied to people that shared his own faith and religious fervour. Being a extremist, he saw anyone that didn't kneel the right way or speak Latin when they prayed as evil, and such sinners had to be murdered; a chore which he carried out with enthusiasm and aplomb. As he lived in the late sixteenth and early seventeenth century, he had plenty of opportunities to end the lives of innocent Huguenots, but eventually he tired of that boring day to day sport and decided to try a bit of regicide. Thanks to Satan putting on a soft voice and whispering in his ear, he opted to stab his king, an act which simply resulted in another king assuming the throne and the assassin being quickly caught, tortured, and then torn apart by horses - getting a free ticket to Hell in the process.

The blind hatred and basic lack of understanding of the value of life had made Ravaillac an ideal candidate for missions on Earth where Satan needed someone to be more pragmatic and thorough than subtle and discreet. He had carried out many missions and, with the spread of the internet and global communication, his exploits had been widely reported, even if they had been attributed to human terrorist groups. Quite a few political or religious organisations had even made it easy for him by claiming responsibility for his some of his handiwork, the irony being that many were the sort of religious groups whose members he would have gladly killed if he'd been a human. But as he now did the work of Satan, rather than the Lord, he no longer held such strict religious views, and his victims became far more diverse.

Notwithstanding the usual pain and discomfort caused by the transportation process from Hell to Boulder, he felt comfortable with his set task. The feeling inside his stomach was akin to his intestine being pulled through a mangle, but he ignored it and walked casually out of the empty, litter strewn alley. He briefly covered his face as the glare of the sun in a cloudless sky met his eyes, but he quickly adjusted and was able to take stock of his surroundings. Looking along the street, he could see the tall cream-coloured front of the Boulder Theatre, decorated with a strange art deco piece of art that looked, in his mind at least, like blue penises ejaculating golden cum. The sign below the artwork was advertising some obscure band; however, the massive words mentioning 'Boulder' in a cursive script reassured him that at least he was in the right place. It was not unknown for demons to materialise in the wrong city, time zone or even country. If he'd have told his required destination to a dimmer than average demon, in charge of the dimensional portal, he could easily have ended up in the middle of a large Australian rock. And that would have not made for a successful mission.

Despite his frequent visits to Earth, Ravaillac despised the modern era. To him, cars were nasty machines that had no dignity and should have been banned. That simple hatred alone made a large number of the human race legitimate targets in his eyes. But he allowed the rage and disgust to fester and mix with the pain in his stomach. He had a task with only a finite amount of ammunition, so he couldn't have an enjoyable shooting spree in the process. He was in America, so such things were normal, but he'd have to see how many bullets he had left after he'd met his target and completed his objective; perhaps he could have fun afterwards. Navigating his way across the street, ignoring the cars, and causing them to grind to screeching halts around him, horns blaring and drivers delivering loud expletives, he just stared at them with contempt and carried on his walk in the direction of the theatre. Reaching the sidewalk, he watched the cars carry on their journeys. To him, they were just human targets in tin cans. With the aid of a few bullets, he'd have enjoyed curing them of their road rage.

Entering the lobby of the theatre, he saw posters telling those who were curious about groups that were due to play there, but they were of no interest to him. Modern music was another thing that he hated and could be added to the ball of rage that pulsed through his system. Seeing a female cleaner busily vacuuming the floor, he approached the elderly lady. Thanks to an outdated iPod and earphones, she was totally oblivious to the stranger and was lost in her own world of soft rock ballads. It wasn't until she received a heavy tap on her shoulder that she was brought back to the dull realities of her simple job and the presence of someone else in the foyer.

"Oh, hello. How can I help you?" Her voice soft, with an almost imperceptible Spanish accent.

"Yes, madam, I have to find the son of a friend, but alas, all I know is that he is a student and lives somewhere in one of the university's halls of residence. Would you be able to point me in the right direction?" Struggling against his inner rage, he managed to accompany the simple question with a charming and disarming smile.

Fortunately, for the cleaner, she had no reason to suspect anything was untoward about the smartly dressed man in a dark red suit and was able to point him in the direction of the vast university campus. He didn't have far to walk in the sunshine but the sight of all the cars did nothing to help maintain his patience. As he reached the complex, he saw plenty of casually dressed students sitting on the grass talking, laughing, and enjoying the sunshine. He approached a few and attempted to strike up conversations, but thanks to his basic terse and abrupt manner, he was not immediately successful. Despite its far from conservative colour, the suit being worn in the warm sunshine immediately gave off a negative authoritarian message that made the young students instantly suspicious and cautious. There were too many things going on that the officials at the university didn't need to know about, and the students had no desire to inadvertently spoil someone's fun by accidentally sharing information.

Finding that his initial technique was just soliciting resistance, he decided to mellow his approach. He began to take on the role of a friend of the family having to deliver some bad news about a relative's bereavement. The tactic brought him a more receptive and sympathetic response but, thanks to the size of the student population, and having nothing more to go on than a name, he still got no more useful information. Eventually one attractive female student in a floppy yellow sun hat and tie dye Grateful Dead dress was able to point him in the direction of the admissions office.

At last, Ravaillac felt like he had a chance of finding the student and, arriving at the building, he went through the obligatory process when entering the centre for any bureaucracy: find one office and ask for help, then get passed on to another. This game of human pinball went on for almost an hour of impatient lining up and speaking to someone, only to be told that he had come to the wrong office and had to go elsewhere. Fortunately for the occupants, the building ran out of rooms to visit just before his self-restraint likewise disappeared and he was forced to start shooting random clerks.

The woman that he finally found gave him a broad and disarming smile, or if not disarming then at least a smile that made him less likely to reach for one of his guns. "Gordoon Simpson? Of course, sir. I know exactly who you're looking for." She told him the address and then removed a small, printed map from her drawer, circled the building in red, and gave him intricate and detailed directions.

"Thank you." Regardless of his status as a demon and his emotional state, which was automatically set on *rage*, Ravaillac was from a generation where manners were ingrained and instinctive, so the gratitude sounded sincere and warm. "Oh, one more thing," he added just as he was leaving the office, "surely there are thousands of students here?"

"Yes, sir, there are indeed, we pride ourselves in having…"

"So how did you know about Gordoon Simpson and where he was staying without having to look on your computer?" he interrupted her, maintaining his polite façade despite having no interest in listening to a long public relations speech on how good the university was and from how far and wide the students came to enjoy the numerous amenities.

"That's simple, it's the second time today that I have been asked about him. About an hour ago, two men and a lady asked me the same question. They were from the government, you know the type: official shiny badges, dark suits and glasses for the men, and the lady was very pretty. I loved her shoes."

Ravaillac's body tensed up and he clenched his fists so tightly that his fingernails began to dig into his palms. It was a struggle for him not to automatically reach for the pistol in his shoulder holster. "Really?" he said calmly, not betraying his inner desire to shoot someone, or something. "Other than shoes, what else was she wearing and what did she look like? I'd just like to keep an eye out for them and, if I see them, I'd like to say hello. I am sure it'll be a shock for them."

"Oh, silly me. Yes, me and shoes. She was about 5' 5", long dark hair, a Gucci clutch purse, and a grey patterned dress with black shoulders and sleeves. And the loveliest pearl necklace," she added, her observations proving that the woman's eye for fashion went beyond shoes and could provide the specifics he needed. The details were the devils that his boss would have appreciated.

"Thank you, my dear, you've been most helpful. I will definitely keep an eye out for them and try to surprise them."

Once he had left the office and was in the corridor, he casually reached inside his jacket and reassured himself that his pistols were still securely in place and then patted his pockets, feeling the spare clips full of bullets. Content that he was ready for action, he set off towards the appropriate building. He'd need to revise his plan, but that didn't bother him. He had the opportunity not only to kill a human but also have the pleasure of despatching three angels as well. Today was definitely looking up.

21 – Students are Not Dead, They Just Smell That Way

Despite protective parents and a Catholic upbringing, Roxy could not have been accused of living a sheltered life and knew that students were not always clean, and she also understood that, when they found their first bit of independence and freedom from parents, there was a tendency to have a wild time. The heavy, but sweetly scented fug that permeated the corridor of the hall of residence filled her nostrils and made her hungry for several large pizzas. Bob inhaled heavily and gave his two friends a knowing and satisfied smile, nodding slowly in appreciation of the herbal fumes. Dedan just shrugged his shoulders. He had no interest in what recreational substances were taken by humans and he knew that marijuana was hardly the most dangerous of drugs. The thing that was annoying most him was the thumping music that was escaping through the walls of one of the rooms and was filling the corridor with a dull indistinguishable thudding bass sound, punctuated with snarling singing that would have been incoherent even if there had not been the wall there to muffle the sound. They casually walked along the corridor, checking room numbers as they went. Despite the many signs of student occupation, the long passage was well lit and clean and, if it weren't for the noise and smell they could have been in any communal residence for fairly well-off people. Roxy arrived at a light brown door that was almost at the far end of the passageway. The plain brass numbers on it, telling anyone that cared to look that it was room 125.

"Here we are." Roxy's face showing that she was eager to knock and finally see the face that had launched a thousand ships full of troubles. "Ready?" She looked at first Bob and Dedan, who both gave her silent nods to signal their readiness. Then Bob stepped back to let Dedan and Roxy get closer to the door. This movement was accompanied by him letting out a squeal of pain as he grabbed his neck. Pulling out a long, thin and pointed wooden dart, there was a brief struggle to focus on the object before he inelegantly fell to the floor.

Turning to look at him Roxy saw two other darts that had embedded themselves into the walls which would have been in the same area as their necks if they hadn't just moved. Instinctively Dedan slipped his arm into his suit and removed a Glock 22 pistol. Its length doubled thanks to a silencer already having been fitted. Roxy had the extra step of having to open her handbag but was soon ready with her equally silent, but deadly, weapon. Quickly looking around Dedan saw a figure barely visible in the shadows of a slightly open fire exit door. Seeing a long hollow blow pipe aimed at him, he managed to duck just as another dart flew towards him, missing his head by inches. Once he was on one knee, he fired three rounds at the shape. The impact making the assailant fly back against the wall before falling to the floor. Roxy looked the opposite way along the hallway and saw three more figures in the open doorway of a student's room. Thanks to them being crowded into a narrow space they were not as quick with firing their next volley of darts, so they were just in the process of trying to reload when Roxy took aim and downed the first two with single rounds to each of their heads. The third one was kneeling so the weight of his fellow assassins falling on him made him less of a threat with a blow pipe but a harder target to hit with a bullet, so she had to fire three rounds into him before he finally died.

"Well, that was interesting." Muttered Dedan to himself.

"Oh Crap, am I gonna die bruh?" mumbled Bob looking up from the floor at Dedan. "I can't feel a thing and can't move!"

Dedan pulled out one of the darts from the wall and knelt next to his incapacitated friend. Studying the simple wooden projectile, he sniffed it and then gave it a brief lick before spitting. "No Bob, I think you are alright and won't die, again. From the bitter taste and smell I'd guess that it isn't curare. Probably just some drug that causes paralysis. You'll be even more useless than normal, for maybe an hour or so, but after that you should be back to normal. Or as normal as you get."

"More useless?" the words accompanied by a laugh. "Thanks man, you know how to cheer me up.

"I think they wanted us for living sacrifices so they wouldn't have used deadli poyzen." Dedan smacked his lips. "And I werly wissh I hadnnnnt likked tha dannned darr." His tongue lazily hanging out of the side of his mouth as the effects of the licked drug began to take effect.

"Oh great!" Exclaimed Roxy, frustration obvious in her voice. "Rip Van Winkle and a man that sounds like he has just left the dentist after having a filling. I suggest you stay sat out here" addressing the comment at Bob "and Dedan, when it comes to speaking to Mr. Simpson I think that you need to let me do all the talking."

"Ageeed" replied Dedan. "Gug igea. Arl murv dem innrr der starrwayyy" Hearing the noises emanating from his own mouth he decided that actions would speak far louder, and coherently, than any words he could say. "Nedder murnd!" He walked across the hall to the open door with the three dead bodies that were currently making an over efficient doorstop. He could see from their feathered head dresses, golden coloured skirts and blue painted faces and necks that they were not the average student that you'd find at an American University, not even the most progressive ones. From their weapons, light brown skins and facial features he surmised that they were agents sent by Ekeko. He presumed that they had come to protect their interests and ensure that Gordoon didn't stop believing and, perhaps they might have made anyone that tried to speak to him sacrifices. But they were in no state to answer his questions, even if his mouth would have allowed him to ask any. Looking into the room he saw a male student laid out on the floor with a wooden dart stuck into his forehead. Dedan strode over the body and checked the pulse in his neck. Relieved that the young man was still alive he removed the dart and put him into the recovery position. Returning his attention to the dead bodies he unceremoniously grabbed onto the ankles of the first would be assassin and dragged him to the stairwell of the fire escape. Repeating the process for the other two he laid them out on top of each other then closed the door so that they were no longer visible from the hallway.

Once he was back with Roxy and Bob, he used hand signals to tell Bob that he would be leaving him in the room across the hall.

"Okay man but leave the door slightly ajar and place me so that I can see through it. If I hear screams, I will come running."

Giving Bob a thumbs up, and a gormless grin, Dedan pulled Bob up and gave him a fireman's lift across the corridor. Seeing a bean bag chair on the floor of the study he kicked it so that it was positioned allowing anyone that sat on it to see Gordoon's door without being easily seen themselves. "Derr der ger!" he mumbled as he lowered Bob into it. Returning to Roxy he tried to give her a sophisticated smile, but such looks are difficult to achieve by someone with a mouth numbed by an obscure South American drug. The lolling tongue and drool escaping from the side of his mouth preventing any possible suave appearance he might have wanted to display. He reminded Roxy of a warm Spaniel trying to cool down.

"Classy Dedan, very classy." Roxy rubbed her chin and mouth in an attempt to stifle a laugh. "I think it might be prudent if you leave all the talking to me. You sound like you are either drunk, have had a stroke or both and if you do an impression of a drooling Hunch Back of Notre Dame then it might scare him."

Dedan wiped the saliva from the side of his face and nodded to Roxy. "Urr derr bosssh".

Roxy's firm knock on the door resulted in it being opened by a man that she assumed was possibly 19 or 20 and from his gaunt pale face she speculated that he didn't get out much either. He was bare footed and was wearing light blue jogging trousers and a red t-shirt with the slogan 'Nerds do it on Laptops'. "Mr. Gordoon Simpson?"

"Yessss." Gordoon saw the official looking visitors blocking his door and immediately began to rack his brains and think of what he could possibly be guilty of. There were the occasional visits to late night porn websites, and he'd played unlicensed copies of computer games with friends, but he felt sure that they weren't federal offenses requiring plain clothed officers to come knocking at his door.

Removing a small black wallet from her purse she opened it and briefly flashed a silver metallic badge at him. "I am agent Haurel of the NoYB, and this is agent Lardy. May we come in? We need to ask you some questions." Without waiting for an invitation, she walked in, closely followed by Dedan. Maintaining an impassive face, she looked around the room. The curtains were closed but thanks to the brilliant sunshine outside there was still light in the room. The main pieces of furniture were a fake leather-bound black computer chair that was in front of a desk supporting three computer keyboards and six monitors. There were empty pizza boxes scattered about the floor and, on a wall shelf, were cola bottles containing a pale-yellow transparent liquid that she felt sure wasn't soda and had no intention of drinking it to find out. She looked him in the eyes and gave him a happy and arousing smile. "Gordoon, I need to talk to you about some of your more unusual activities."

"But, but, but, I haven't done anything!" Thankfully the light that was soaking through the curtains was insufficient to fully display his blushing face, but the panic was obvious in his voice and expression.

"Mr. Simpson, please relax, to our knowledge you haven't broken any American laws but what you have done is causing lots of problems and we need to persuade you to change your mind about one or two things. Shall we call them...ill-advised life choices?"

As she spoke Dedan casually walked across the room and pushed open a door and stood looking into the adjoining room. Not wanting to speak he clicked his fingers to get Roxy's attention and pointed into the room. Roxy joined him and stared, open mouthed, at what she saw. There by the side of a bed, was a shrine with five small statuettes; making it look like Gordoon was an actor that had won various awards, while on the wall were a couple of posters. One a large image of the White House in all its glory and the other a moon lit scene of a forest. Seeing them Dedan began to realise how his ex-wife's version of paradise had been formed.

"Oh dear!" Roxy exclaimed. "Well, from the looks of it you are definitely the person we are looking for." Pointing at his computer chair "Gordoon sit down, I have something to tell you, but I am sure you will not believe it."

Gordoon watched Roxy intently from his chair as she talked and paced around his small room. Whenever she paused, he in turn stopped swivelling in his chair. When he thought that she wasn't looking he studied her legs and returned his gaze to her face when she turned to face him. His mind mesmerised as the delicate and rhythmic Italian accent filled his room. Apart from the time that his mother had dropped him off and delivered all the accoutrements of academic life at the start of his university life he'd never had a female in his room. However, if one had inadvertently gone in there by mistake, and not run out again screaming in disgust, then Roxy would have fitted his mental picture of a perfect guest. Perhaps he would have made her younger, slightly taller, more buxom, blonde haired and maybe facially different, but other than those minor points she was all he wanted in a woman - alive and in willingly his room.

Looks could be deceptive and Gordoon certainly didn't do himself any favours. Despite looking like a hippy that had decided to live rough, on the streets for a month, and allowing his flat to take on the appearance of an inner city slum he had a keen and sharp brain that would have put his lecturers to shame if he'd have had enough self-confidence to speak up and answer questions in their lectures. He had the sort of intellect where he could look at an equation on a blackboard and would find the solution without his brain having to move out of neutral gear. Often, in class, he would have the answer to a complex problem even before his tutor was halfway through writing out the question. Where many mathematicians could put long lines of letters and symbols on a board to help them get to the where they needed to be, he could have been given a can of alphabet soup and, immediately ladled out $E = MC^2$.

His brain wasn't just tuned to solving math's problems either. Give him a computer and he could, if he had the inclination to do so, have easily hacked into the Pentagon mainframe and started WWIII and there would have been nothing that anyone could have done about it. The one personality trait that he lacked, other than not actually having much of a personality, was his lack of creativity and imagination. If something couldn't be solved by mathematics or logic, then he needed to dismantle it and restructure the question so that it took the form of an algebraic equation or a computer algorithm. He had recognized the defect and thought that religion was a way of having imaginary friends that wouldn't complicate his life with illogical questions. That was the theory anyway, but now he was beginning to question his own seemingly unquestionable reasoning. There was currently an attractive, but slightly frightening woman in a stylish dress and carrying an imposing badge of a government agency, currently filling his ears with words that he understood as abstracts but, when they were put into structured sentences, they stopped making sense and that made his eye to begin to twitch nervously.

Talk of statues coming to life and becoming gods just didn't make sense or compute. Alright, burning a bit of incense and talking to small sculptures was his attempt at making friends in his mind was not logical either, but he didn't expect that he'd make deities in the process. The thought crossed his mind that perhaps one of his friends had set him up and sent them to his room as some sort of elaborate joke. But then he remembered that he didn't have any friends. The more Roxy's unofficial history lecture continued the less he was able to believe what he was being told. How could his prayer have caused so much destruction in a small Bolivian town that he had never even heard of? Where was the science? Where was the sense? Despite his internal struggles with philosophical acceptance of the facts he remained impassive. Details of naked goddesses ensured that his mind didn't wander too far from the subject but if he had to admit to his current mental state, and summarise it, it would have been one of confusion. Then there was the piece of information that they'd slipped in so subtly that it almost didn't register. The two people in his room were not bona fide government agents but were imposters with the magnitude of them being angels not totally lost on him. To Gordoon, secret agents were more real than secret angels. However, the veracity of the fact that they were from Heaven was not questioned by him. When taken in context, with the rest of what he was being told, it all made perfect sense. Or at least imperfect sense to someone of a less scientific mind.

When Roxy finished talking the noise disappeared leaving a pregnant pause that seemed to be wanting to give birth to more words, but Gordoon wasn't sure of the correct protocol when talking to angels. Lacking such frames of reference, he raised his hand so that he could get his new teacher's attention and obtain permission to speak.

"It's alright Gordoon, you don't need to put your hand up. You are not in class, and I am not a lecturer. I am sure that you have lots of questions so please just ask them."

"What does NoYB stand for?"

Roxy was taken aback by the question, and it was her turn to try and work out what was going on. "Sorry?"

"What do the initials NoYB mean?" Gordoon's face beginning to look frustrated at what he deemed to be an obvious and simple question. "On your badges it said you were from a government agency called NoYB."

"Oh that." Her voice relieved that the question bore some relationship to their presence and that Gordoon's mind hadn't gone off to another place and he was asking them the answer to an equation. "None of Your Business!"

"No need to be like that, I was only asking. Jeez, I thought you angels were supposed to be friendly!"

Behind Roxy, thanks to the condition of his tongue, Dedan released a laugh that sounded like an asthmatic piglet being tickled. With the noise making Roxy give him one of those expressions that only women can achieve. A look that didn't quite kill but could seriously injure and require an ambulance.

Unperturbed by the background noise and Roxy's expression Gordoon tilted his head slightly, as if the new angle would allow his muddled thoughts to make an easier exit from his mouth. "So...I created five gods?"

"Yes." Replied Roxy patiently.

"Three women, of which, one of them is very naked and another is almost naked, and two of them are men?"

"Yes." Unsure that she approved of his focus on the female's state of dress.

"So...they will do *whatever* I tell them to do?"

"No!" the unbridled alarm was obvious in her voice. "God's do not work like that. You can pray as much as you like but that doesn't mean that they will listen or, if they do, they probably will not answer you. It is only because you are the sole believer that they know that you even exist. If they had millions of followers, they wouldn't know your name, know you were there and wouldn't care if you lived or died."

Suddenly his attention was taken by Dedan, who was busily scribbling something onto a piece of paper. He watched as he then passed it to

Roxy who in turn read it. "My colleague has a question for you. Why on Earth did you pick those particular five gods?"

Finally, there was something that he could get his head around. A question that related to his reasoning and he could answer without any problems. "That is easy." With that he swivelled around on his chair and clicked some switches that made his computer screens come to life. He typed something into the keyboard and five of the six screens were filled with images of a separate god and a list of facts relating to each of them. Dedan and Roxy both stepped forward so that they could take a closer look and attempt to see a common thread. Each deity had different qualities mixed with strengths and weaknesses. They could all show kindness but could also be venal, cruel and jealous. Roxy was struggling to see anything that linked them and would make the lonely nerd select them out of the vast panoply of gods, be they dead or not. To her if there was a thread linking them it was invisible. On the other hand, Dedan had the sort of mind that could work out the strange puzzle and it was nothing to do with any skill at completing crosswords or intellectual quizzes. In life many people had called Roxy an intellectual and they had been right, thanks to her travels she was a polyglot, had been a successful businesswoman and a wise counsellor but when it came to finding Gordoon's wavelength she didn't even have a working radio. The reason that Dedan had the advantage was quite simple, he had a lascivious streak and looked for the hedonistic traits while he was searching for altruistic ones. As soon as the penny dropped, he released a laugh that sounded like a seal that was drowning in a bucket of trifle. His uncontrolled tongue releasing a wave of drool out of the side of his mouth; making him look like a lunatic. Concentrating he attempted to take back control of his wayward mouth. "I ath ith." A look of victory on his face. "You thily thod!" Pointing to the screen "Mar hi?"

Not fully understanding why Dedan was talking like he was, but understanding what the gist of Dedan was wanting, Gordoon stood up to allow the angel to sit down and use his keyboard. Even though he was several millennia old, Dedan had gone out of his way to try and keep up with modern technology so, despite not liking them, he knew and understood the basics of computers and was quickly filling the sixth screen with words. Waving at Roxy and Gordoon he pointed at the

168

screen proudly. Leaning over his shoulders they read what he had typed. 'I get it. It has nothing to do with good or bad. You want a party!'

"What are you on about?" Roxy demanded incredulously.

'Simple' he began typing again. 'Ekeko is a god of prosperity, luck and generosity. Falacer is the god of gifts and is similar to Bacchus in that he liked a drink. Elsa had a reputation for singing that would have put Ella and Sinatra to shame. Sonja was a wild party animal, especially after a few drinks. And Hor'idey… She was reputed to reward her followers.'

"Exactly Dedan. And let's not forget that the women were also hot and if they came to my party, I'd hope that they would let me…"

His recounting of his wild fantasy was interrupted by Dedan coughing loudly and frantically typing. Fingers hitting the keys quickly revealing words in bold block capitals letters.

Gordoon looked at them and stared at Dedan guiltily. "Wow, really? She was your wife? I am sorry if I had known…"

Dedan looked at him with stern eyes and nodded slowly.

Roxy decided that she needed to move the conversation away from orgies involving Gordoon and three goddesses and bring it back on course. "Alright Gordoon, I think we get the picture. You chose them because you thought they would bring something to your party. Be it presents, booze or good bodies. But I think you missed the point, Ekeko didn't just give away presents out of the goodness of his heart. He wanted something first and unfortunately, he had… has…a taste for human hearts. Preferably still warm and beating and the more he eats the happier he is. And for crying out loud Falacer was a Roman god. When it came to winning reputations for goodness and mercy they didn't even get past the starting line. Displease them in their respective versions of paradise and you would be a slave and quite possibly having sore orifices for all eternity as the gods lived out their perversion's. As for the women, surely you have heard of the Vikings and Alexander the Great? Not the best times in history for people that liked to keep their limbs. And Hor'idey…" She paused to look at Dedan. "I'm sorry Dedan but, by all accounts, she wasn't exactly a perfect wife and could be a high maintenance pain in the arse!"

Dedan gave her a pained look then relented and followed it with an accepting shrug. If he had to be honest and was able to talk without saliva wetting the carpet, he would have admitted that his erstwhile wife could be hard work and her precocious and changeable mood swings did make his life *interesting*.

"So now that you have made your choices what are you going to do about it? There is one homicidal god that doesn't want to exist anymore, three goddesses that seem to be harmless and would like to carry on existing and there is one downright psychopathic deity that, if he thought for one second that you were going to commit apostasy, would do all in his not insignificant power to ensure that he had one last feast on your heart before he turned back to stone. And probably, in the process, be immortalized holding the final morsel of your missing organ high in the air."

"Welllll...," Gordoon paused. His mind was not used to answering philosophical questions. "Couldn't I prey to them? As I understand it the believers give them their existences, but to a certain extent it also dictates their powers and actions. If I imbue them with good traits, then they will become good."

Roxy sadly shook her head. "Sorry but it doesn't work like that. They have already existed before and have all the characteristics that they had in those old days. You could prey for the rest of your life, and you wouldn't change them, and I think you might even annoy a few in the process. They'd probably see it as devotional nagging."

Lifting himself up from the chair Dedan walked across the small room and resumed his previous position at the back, allowing Gordoon to sit down and think about what he needed to do next. After all he was the university genius so this should be a simple conundrum for him to solve. Despite Gordoon's confidence Dedan suspected that the assignment, or even dissertation, on how to stop a god from existing was unlikely to be set even in theological degree courses. But then his thoughts and vague conjecture on course material was interrupted by the mild shock of something cold and hard being pushed firmly into the nape of his neck. An experience that he had encountered on numerous occasions, and he didn't need to turn around to know what it was. He might not know the make, model, or calibre but he could tell that he had a dangerous and unfriendly end of a pistol being pressed against his skin. Unprompted he raised his hands up into the air so that they were level with his shoulders, a reluctant public sign of capitulation.

Even though the weapon and person holding it was out of Gordoon's line of sight he saw the angel raise his arms and recognized the gesture, with shock and fear registered on his face. Roxy, who had her back to Dedan, saw his face and automatically swung around to look at the surrendering angel and see what the problem was. She wanted to retrieve her own pistol from her purse but doubted that whoever was behind Dedan would give her the opportunity to get to it and use it before they all ended up dead. From the darkness of the small hallway, leading to the entrance door, there came a calm voice with a rich French accent. "Very wise Madam. And if you would be so good as to remove whatever weapon is secreted about his person that would be greatly appreciated." Just as she began to step forward Ravaillac added his own extra caveat "And I would like you to do it nice and slowly with handle held between thumb and forefinger." Carefully she followed his instructions, removing the pistol from Dedan's jacket and held it up so that Ravaillac could see it. His eyes appeared bright and fiery red in the gloom of his hiding place. "Very good, now please drop it onto the floor and kick it towards me." The demon watched as it rapidly slid past his feet and came to a halt just behind him. "Very good, thank you, very wise indeed." He then pushed Dedan forwards into Roxy.

Just as they caught each other Roxy whispered in his ear "I'm sorry."

"Ith's aright." Dedan whispered and, as he stood back, he gave her a slight nod that was imperceptible to the demon assassin. He wasn't sure what he could do but he would be able to keep him talking while he looked for an opportunity to strike. His optimism might have been blind and unfounded, but it was all that he had. He knew that he couldn't move faster than a bullet, but his philosophy was one of where there is life there is always hope.

Stepping out of the shadows, Ravaillac casually waved his pistol, pointing it first at the student and then at the two angels. "I take it that you two are representatives of God, sent here to do your good deeds and protect this human no matter what." Maintain the code and avoid harming humans wherever possible. Your code of honour is far too predictable, and it makes you vulnerable." Then, without waiting for a response, he looked at Gordoon. "Maintain the code and avoid harming humans like him wherever possible. Your code of honour is far too predictable, and it makes you vulnerable. And you, mortal, you must be the one that has caused so much annoyance to Satan? Mr. Simpson I presume?" He looked Gordoon up and down with a look of complete and utter contempt. "I am sure you know why I am here; I have to kill you all. I could say that I am sorry, but I would be lying. Obviously, it will be a pleasure and I am looking forward to it." Then he paused and frowned at the two angels. "Where are my manners? I am François Ravaillac de Angoulême. You may have heard of me."

Roxy and Dedan gave each other puzzled looks. "No, never heard of you." A hint of taunting merriment in Roxy's voice.

"Never mind. But I think it is impolite to kill such esteemed people without knowing your names. So fair maiden, you are?" Pointing his pistol at Roxy.

"Yes. Because it is so very impolite to murder someone and not be properly introduced." If sarcasm were a syrup, it would have provided enough of the stuff to baste him. "My friends call me Roxy, but you can call me Rossana. And my tongue-tied friend there is Dedan."

"Very good, now time to die!" Pointing the pistol at Gordoon's head he smiled.

Before he could do anything Gordoon, seeing what was in store for him, decided to show one spark of defiance in his life before it ended. "Oi, Frenchie, turds say what!"

Taken back by the words the assassin stared at the student. "What?" Then was left bemused as his three prisoners all began to snigger. "Oh, never mind. Goodbye!"

There was an almost inaudible 'phsst' sound and Ravaillac's head jolted forward as his arm dropped limply to his side. A small stream of bright red blood began to trickle out of his nose and then, as if his body was in slow motion, he collapsed, at first to his knees, and then the rest of his body fell face first onto the floor, his body limp and lifeless. A small dark hole clearly visible at the base of his skull.

"See? I told you I'd come running!" Bob's voice was loud and full of glee which was a stark contrast to his shambolic appearance. Slowly he dragged his body out of the room's hallway and into the light of the room. "Gatecrasher! He wasn't on the list so he shouldn't have come in."

Roxy gave him a welcoming smile. "You took your time. I was beginning to think that you'd fallen asleep."

"You know me Roxy. I like to make a dramatic entrance." With a single sweeping gesture, he swung his arm upwards and sent Dedan's pistol flying up through the air to be caught by its owner. "Yours I believe. You might need it someday and may not have me around to save you."

"Thanx arthole!" replied Dedan with a grin, or the closest he could get to a grin with a mouth that was becoming slightly less numb. "I hadth him wight werr I wonkeyed him!"

"Now, now children." Interrupted Roxy with a hint of laughter in her voice. "Thank you, Bob. You did well and it is appreciated. As you seem to be slowly recovering, I think it is best if Dedan goes back to Heaven and reports on things while you and I stay here and guard Gordoon. I don't think that Satan will send any more assassins, but you never know."

It wasn't every day that he had angels coming into his room to tell him incredible stories, had Mesoamerican warriors killed outside his door and then, to top it all, a dead demon laid on his floor. The demon would have been getting blood on the carpet if his face hadn't landed on an already squashed and empty pizza box. Gordoon was struggling for words to express his confusion but sometimes silence was the best method of conveying feelings, and he was using that technique quite well. His eyes were transfixed on the body at his feet, his attention only changing when he sensed movement out of the corner of his eye. Looking up he saw a slight inconsistency of the air at the side of the room, as if a door shaped sheet of thin glass had suddenly appeared. He watched as Dedan gave him a conspiratorial wink, Bob a slovenly mock salute and was able to articulate a relatively clear and distinct 'Ciao bella' to Roxy and then he stepped through the almost invisible rectangle in the air and disappeared, as did the none hole in air.

173

"Right Gordoon," began Roxy as she went to help her colleague up off the floor, "have you got a kettle? I could kill a cup of coffee."

22 – Don't Go Breaking My Heart

Despite many existing prejudices and plenty of evidence to the contrary, there are occasionally honest and decent politicians. Admittedly there had not been many, and if God were to take them all on a tour of Heaven, he wouldn't have needed a very fleet of buses, but they do exist. A similar and opposite view could be taken of police officers, there are a few rotten apples but, overall, they are good people trying to maintain the law as best they can while sticking to the rules and having to cope with political correctness, a mountain of bureaucracy and enough red tape to wrap around the planet. And, of course, there is the clergy. Many have gone to Hell for the evil things they have done and for their avarice, but that brush shouldn't be used to tarnish everyone that decides to wear a dress, remains a virgin and then tells everyone else how terrible sex is.

One such person that had sworn off earthly pleasures and truly dedicated his life to helping others was Father Antonio. He had grown up in the abject poverty of rural Bolivia and thanks to help from his own local priest had been able to get an education and better himself. He'd chosen the cloth so that he could help those that needed it most and had started working in the small Bolivian town of Buen Jesus. He had stood fearlessly with the villagers as they had peacefully stopped loggers, miners and oil companies destroying their local habitat, undeterred by the government having ordered him not to do so, and he had ignored threats against his life to be there for his congregation. He was a simple man but had a fire in his soul and the courage of his convictions.

But at the moment, despite his outer appearance, he was afraid. With all the bad things he had seen and experienced in his life, he had never been as frightened as he now was. He could feel the rough ropes tight on his wrists, keeping his arms outstretched and taut. With his feet tied tightly, his body was sore and aching and he was unable to escape. The sensation in his shoulders and ankles had long since gone from being an acute burning pain to just a constant numbness from the discomfort and awkward position. As he was lying on his back with his vestments ripped, revealing his bare chest, he could see the cloudless sky overhead, the sun hurting his eyes, and feel a slight cooling breeze on his stomach. The stone that he was lying on was cold, rough, and hard on his back.

Although he had a restricted view, he knew exactly where he was. The strangely clothed abductors hadn't blindfolded him or made any attempts to prevent him from knowing where he was being taken. He had been manhandled and resisted being dragged through the dense jungle, but when he had arrived at the final destination, he had recognized it. The ancient pyramid had no official name and was too far off the regular paths to be visited frequently by tourists or cleared fully by archaeologists. The locals called it Coranoa, and legend said that it was as old as time, holding many secrets, and that the scent of death hung forever around the peak. He had visited it once, out of curiosity, but the experience had left his soul feeling colder than the grey stones of the building that was covered in rich green plants. But now he was back and was tied to the altar at the top of it.

He tried to settle his mind by silently praying in Latin, Spanish and even the indigenous Quechua language to offer up a message to God in a hope that He would intervene. But the calming and comforting words also allowed him to go over the recent events. He had been in his church sweeping the floor when the visitors had turned up. They were dressed in costumes that he had only seen in museums, with leopard skin capes, plain brown loin cloths, and blue and red body paint; and their faces were also painted red on one side and blue on the other. He'd encountered tribes that occasionally came out of the Amazon jungle to trade furs for metal tools, but they had never been dressed like that.

At first, when they grabbed him, he was indignant that the sanctity of the church had been broken, but as he was dragged deeper and deeper into the jungle, anger turned to bewilderment and then fear. The further he was taken, the worse it got. He'd tried to remonstrate with them, but their total silence made him wonder if they even understood what he was saying. If it was some assassination by some shady corporation then this was not the usual method. Killings were public messages to the community, telling those left alive that they should stop protesting or face a similar fate. Trips into the jungle and being tied to stones at the top of remote pyramids would hardly send out an instant message to his parish.

Then his thoughts and prayers were interrupted by a shadow being cast across his face. Opening his eyes, he saw a thick grey and blue fog hovering just over his head; then gently, as if it were being sculpted by the wind, it began to adopt a more solid and discernible shape. Father Antonio had no idea who or what it was, but he knew that people didn't normally possess the ability to transmogrify like that. Such qualities were usually part of myths and stories, yet here he was witnessing it, and in his world of devout religion, he felt sure that the apparition was malevolent. The now fully formed face of Ekeko loomed over the priest's head, his mouth a sneering grin with a thick cigar tightly packed into the corner of it. On his head was a dirty brown homburg, with the brim curled tightly downward, that looked like it had been lost in the mud by a jungle explorer and simply picked up by the god. His eyes carefully studied the Father, with a quizzical look like that of an ape on the rock of Gibraltar that had just stolen a top-of-the-range cell phone and was trying to work out what it was before attempting to make free calls to the Pentagon.

"I can see terror in your eyes, *priest.*" Ekeko said the job title with utter contempt and hatred. "I would like to tell you that you have nothing to fear, but unless you are totally relaxed about a slow and agonizing death then I would be lying. After all, such an end to life is not something people usually look forward to and I can assure you that yours will be exquisitely painful."

"You do not frighten me; my faith is strong and pure, and I know that I will enter Heaven and be with God."

Ekeko laughed a sinister laugh that did nothing to make Father Antonio feel any better about his current position. "That is good; in fact, I can assure you that I am counting on it. If not, then I have been wasting both of our time."

With that, the Father began to recite a prayer as if it would simply make the god disappear.

"How very rude, I was talking." Ekeko reached forward and grabbed Antonio's mouth. "Shut up and listen, I have an important message and you *really do* need to be giving me your full attention." His voice sent cigar smoke into his reluctant audience's mouth and eyes, but it had the desired effect and silenced the frantic praying. "There, that's better, isn't it? I can talk without you spouting mumbo jumbo. After all, do you think I'd have gone to all this trouble to get you here if I wanted to hear you pray? I have an important message that I need you to deliver to your God and it needs to be word for word, so please pay attention. I am Ekeko, once mighty but now forgotten and forsaken. In three days, I will have an army assembled at the Salar de Uyuni. I will have exactly 250,000 warriors and I invite Him to appear and engage in battle with me. The loser must step back and withdraw from any actions or interactions with humans. The winner will be free to carry on and do as they wish. But there are rules. There must be equal numbers. If there are more than 250,000 warriors facing me, then all deals are off and I will devastate the world so that all will know my name and curse your God for not stopping me. And there must be no thunder sticks!"

Father Antonio gave the god a confused look. He understood the challenge, but he had a question. "Thunder sticks?"

"Yes, your Spanish invaders had them, but they seem to have changed since then." He pulled out two pistols from the top of his trousers and waved them in front of his captive's eyes. "War should be fought with honour, skill and courage where the opponent's eyes can be seen as they kill or are killed. These are for weak cowards. Do you understand?"

"Yes, I understand, but why?"

"Because people have forgotten how truly great gods are and all they can do. Humans do not give their hearts yet expect everything to be handed to them. They need to relearn that life and happiness demand sacrifices." As he allowed his words to sink in, he stepped back, turned to one of his brightly painted warriors and gave him a slight nod. The sign was barely noticeable but enough to be seen and recognized as the signal to begin. Turning back to the priest, he said coldly, "Goodbye. They say that everyone has a purpose in life, and yours is to die!"

The scream that followed seemed to flow like a gushing source of a river escaping from the top of a mountain. It ran down the sides of the pyramid and once it hit the dense undergrowth of the jungle, it was absorbed by the verdant foliage. Several birds flew wildly into the air, disturbed by the haunting and unfamiliar noise, and then there was silence again.

Fortunately for the flora, fauna and, more importantly, the priest, the howl was short lived, as was the priest himself. The warrior responsible for his demise had a skill that had been honed by years of repetition. In ancient times, there had been tens of thousands of people lined up around the pyramid waiting like cattle to be slaughtered. Forget cars or even beef abattoirs; sacrifices created the first production line process as organs were removed and blood was efficiently drained via channels cut into the stone floor, ensuring that it ran like a red river away from the holy men and didn't cause a slip hazard. Even then, health and safety were considerations to be taken into account. They didn't want anyone getting injured, or at least nobody of any importance. Imagine the paperwork, especially when the paper took the form of stone tablets needing chisels and a hammer.

Regardless of the absence of face masks or rubber gloves, the demise of Father Antonio was clinical and efficient. Using a gold sacrificial blade, his chest was cut with the incision ending just after his sternum. Another Y-shaped tool was inserted in the small gap, and with a ninety-degree turn and a sound of cracking bone, the cavity was opened wide enough so that hands, and blade, could be inserted and the operation could continue. Finally, with dexterous and deft fingers, the still beating heart was pulled out so that the last thing the priest saw before life left him and his eyes faded, was his own heart fleetingly waved before his face.

Finally, the morsel was passed to Ekeko so that he could tuck into his warm and fresh lunch. Without cling film or refrigeration, it was an ideal way of ensuring that food didn't spoil. His appetite sated and his mouth, chin and front of his chest coated in a thick layer of warm haemoglobin, Ekeko gave the late father one last look, his eyes cold and unbothered by the destruction he had caused. The body in front of him was of no more significance to him than a tree that had been cut down to provide firewood. Then, with his mission completed, the god's body began to lose its form. The cloud reappeared, dense at first but rapidly becoming more translucent before it finally disappeared, leaving nothing but a bloody puddle on the floor as evidence of his presence. Once their god had gone, the warriors copied his trick, clouds turning into emptiness, leaving nothing but a grotesque cadaver to attract flies in the sunshine. The body would be eventually discovered, but for now the soulless corpse was food for the wild jungle animals.

23 - Dying to Meet You

Father Antonio hated to admit it, but his rapid and unexpected demise had been far more painful than he had imagined it would be. He had envisaged his end as being one met when he was at a great age, surrounded by loving parishioners whose prayers would have escorted him on his journey to Heaven. But much to his relief, there was a paradise and he had reached it. Full of excitement, he couldn't wait to meet as many saints and characters from the Bible as he could and ask them countless theological questions. Then, of course, he wanted to sit at the right-hand side of God; however, considering the waiting list, that opportunity had been put on hold for all new guests and was more of a metaphor for being allowed to stay in Heaven. If everyone were to sit on His right-hand side, the dinner table would have to be massive and God would be stuck on the left, pushed against the side wall as he waited for someone to pass Him the salt or garlic bread. But such confusions relating to the seating plans were lost, because not only was he standing in God's private office, but he was also in the presence of the Holiest of Holies. For someone as devout as he was, life, or even the afterlife, could not get any better than this.

The former Father had to concede that God didn't quite meet his preconceptions as to His divine appearance. Instead of the towering figure with a long white beard, flowing robes and a voice that would have made Charlton Heston sound like a high-pitched camp drag queen who had just been kicked in the groin, he was met by a figure that was more akin to a twelve-year-old, white, middle-class schoolboy. The short haircut and simple glasses did nothing to provide Him with an aura of gravitas. If God's secretary hadn't done the introductions and assured him, hand on heart, that this was in fact the God of his faith, then he would have not believed it and would have offered to find the boy some sweets to eat. Just like the body, the voice was far from the kind of tone that could have on its own flattened mountains or laid waste to armies. It was appropriate to that of a twelve-year-old boy waiting for puberty to strike and allow him to change His place in the Heavenly choir and to occupy His nights doing what boys tended to do at every opportunity when their bodies began to change.

God had listened intently to Ekeko's message and the barbaric method of delivering it. Behind the glasses, His eyes were sad but showed a keen intensity as He took in every detail.

"I am sorry that you had such a terrible death." God's voice was high-pitched, but even that made the priest feel at ease and relaxed as if he were being blessed. "There are far better ways to die, but I hope that you are happy to be in Heaven."

"Of course, my Lord. I have lived my life in the hope that I would be worthy of being here. But my only worry is my congregation. They are my flock and are vulnerable. I fear for their safety." God nodded slowly. He understood the sentiment and found it endearing that such concerns were not forgotten on entrance to paradise. Bliss didn't mean walking away from those left behind.

"Also," Father Antonio continued, "with Ekeko on the loose, I worry that he'll look for more sacrifices."

"Your concern for your flock does you credit, and you certainly deserve your place here." God gave him a placatory look. "I will send some guardian angels to your village, and they will do all they can to protect your community and ensure that no wayward god takes advantage." He paused, knowing that if Ekeko decided to hunt for fresh snacks and power giving sacrifices in the late priest's village, then a few angels, irrespective of how well armed they were, would be unlikely to be able to stop a god.

The best He could do was hope that the vengeful deity would be too busy readying his army for the imminent war. He had fought many battles before, but there had always been tactical or technical advantage that filled him with confidence. This time, however, He would have to fight on a level playing field against an unknown foe. Level in more ways than one, as the god had chosen the stunningly beautiful, but remote, Bolivian Salt Flats as the location of the battle. With there being equal numbers and similar weapons, He would need to ensure that He picked troops that were adept with anachronistic swords, spears, and arrows rather than pistols, rifles and machine guns.

Eventually the awestruck priest left the office and began the first part of his eternity in Heaven. He'd only been in the place for an hour and had already met God, so as days go, it had started off badly and dramatically improved. His leaving enabled Dedan to take the priest's place in God's office and report on the situation with regards to Gordoon Simpson. Thanks to time, and the healing transference process back to Heaven, his tongue no longer had the same muscle control as a soaking wet carpet. He broke off his conversation, and sidelong lustful glances, that he was busily engaged in with Angelica and sat in the comfortable chair in front of God's desk.

He was used to the Supreme Being adopting random human forms, so the presence of a pre-teen child didn't faze him, especially since God had taken this form before. In his millennia in Heaven, as one of God's closest aides, Dedan had encountered stranger choices. God's decision to adopt the form of a two-day old baby had been uncomfortable, as it made all the visitors automatically want to pick Him up and hug the child. In most people's books, that was an awkward thing to do to their God. Although the choice of an old and extremely flatulent female Scottish car factory worker did test angelic tolerance, especially as the form suffered from Tourette's as well. God's ways might have been mysterious, but they did sometimes make Dedan wonder what was going on.

As soon as God had told him about the priest and Dedan had finished his recounting of the exploits in Boulder, the angel fell silent as God absent-mindedly removed His glasses and wiped them on His shirttails. "I see. It seems that Mr. Simpson is popular in his own special way. One group wants to ensure he remains faithful to one of his chosen gods, Satan wants to go for the simple solution and murder him, and we have the fair Roxy and the less than active Bob to guard him. But there still doesn't seem to be a simple solution to the problem." His childlike voice failed to convey the true seriousness of what was being said.

"Exactly, Sire. We can hardly just turn our backs while some random demon does his business. Gordoon has started something, but I'm not sure he fully realises all that he has done. But at least we have a chance to fight them in, hopefully, a fair fight."

"Yes, fair! I somehow doubt that, and I'm not sure that our forces are fully up to the task of mustering a quarter of a million of the right sorts of skilled master swordsmen, or even women for that matter, in what could turn out to be a dirty war. For centuries we have been training our armies to fight with ever more modern weapons so a lot of the ancient and traditional skills will be rusty, if not lost completely. But fear not, I have a plan." Reaching forward, He pressed a button on the intercom that was on His desk. "Angelica, get me St. Michael."

"At once, my Lord."

On hearing her response, God's attention returned to Dedan. "Thank you, Dedan, I think that will be all for now, I think you might need to go home, dig up a sword, and get practicing. But before you do that, I need to take a slight detour…"

24 - Strange Bedfellows

As the delicate strains of Barry Manilow began to regain a footing in Satan's consciousness, he replaced the receiver on his phone and turned his attention to Ravaillac. The failed assassin had returned to Hell and managed to avoid rematerializing in a wall or landing feet first in an acid bath punishment chamber. The fact that he had appeared in a quiet corridor could have been seen by many as a lucky escape; however, considering Satan's intolerance of failure and current burning rage, a couple of decades stuck in a wall trying to dig his way out with only his fingernails might just have been the easiest and most pleasant option. The stare he was receiving from Satan was cold, hard and, even for someone that was already technically dead, definitely deadly. Despite the rhythmic background music, the atmosphere was corrosive to Ravaillac's sense of well-being and not helped by the noise of Satan drumming his fingers on his desk while he considered the bad news that the demon had given him, and the interesting information and subsequent unusual request that he'd just received from God.

"What shall I do with you, you pathetic maggot? You feeble, weak and shambolic failure!" Satan seldom made any attempt to hide the contempt he held for his underlings, and this was no exception. He saw no reason to show anything but hatred for the demon standing before him.

Ravaillac was taken aback by the question. He knew it was rhetorical, but he would have loved to have had the opportunity to choose his own method of punishment rather than leave it to the creative imagination of his dark master. He would have selected an eternity of eating fine cheeses and drinking the best French wine but, somehow, he doubted that such punishment chambers existed and even if there were any such locations, they would be full of Francophobes or lactose intolerant teetotallers and Satan wouldn't have allowed him to go there. He strongly suspected that his punishment might involve his throat and stomach, but pleasant food and drink would not be involved. His penalty would likely be of the burning, sharp and jagged type and if orifices were involved, it would be his mouth would be the last on the list of entry points!

But currently, Satan seemed to be preoccupied and silence was probably his best defence. It might be unlikely, but he might just have the chance to talk his way out of the whole infinity of pain that was stretching out ahead of him. The lack of talking from Satan weighed on him; if his silence had been a noise, it would have been deafening. The music and constant sound of fingers hitting the desk was beginning to get on his nerves and he was struggling to maintain his composure. Eventually Satan relented with the long finger drum solo that would have made a progressive rock band jealous of its length, leaned back in his chair and placed his hands behind his head. "How are you with a sword?"

Ravaillac had gone through a few possible scenarios in his head and had a plenty of potential answers ready to justify or excuse his failure to kill a simple college nerd, but he had not expected the conversation to have anything to do with his fencing skills. "My Lord, I am a champion and won many duels during my time on Earth. I am a master of the Schiavona, Katzbalger, Rapier and Swiss Sabre. In fact—"

The joyous boasting of his skill with various swords was brusquely interrupted by Satan, his voice impatient and terse. "Yes, yes, I get it, you know how to handle a blade. And although you failed me on your last mission, I think I can live with it. I tend to see a pattern whenever I hear the name Dedan or Roxy, so there might be a way for you to redeem yourself and quite literally save your skin. But be warned, if you fail me a second time, I can promise you that you will get familiar with swords in a way that you have never done before and you will NOT appreciate the experience." The words did much to fill Ravaillac's mind with images that he didn't want, or even need. From his occupation on Earth, and since going to Hell, he knew what damage a sharp and long blade could do and had no desire to experience Satan's creative utilisation of one or, more likely, lots of swords. "I have a task for you. I want you to put a little team together for me and provide a bit of basic training."

As Ravaillac walked along the dark and sulphurous smelling corridor away from Satan's central inner sanctum, he kept pausing and turning his head back in the direction that he'd just come, his mouth doing an uncanny impression of a goldfish that had got hold of some chewing gum. Although he was relieved that he had been given the opportunity to avoid punishment, he wasn't convinced that the task that he had

185

accepted was achievable and knew that failure would give him a greater punishment than if he'd turned down the offer. But now it was too late; he had picked up the metaphorical gauntlet. How in Hell was he going to be able to assemble 125,000 demons that were reasonably skilled with ancient weapons, arm and then train them, and all within three days? He had been given carte blanche to recruit or press gang anyone in Hell, be they demon or damned, but he would have to work hard and carry out some careful selection for delegation if he had any chance of being ready on time. Having worked with demons in the past, he already had a good idea of a few that would make ideal officers; however, knowing whom he needed to speak to was one thing, but finding them in Hell was a totally different matter. He sighed as he considered the search. Finding snowballs in the place would have been easier.

For the living, there are plenty of occupations that do not automatically send you to Hell. Jobs are jobs and, on their own, they make you neither good nor bad. Soldiers can do their duty and it doesn't make them evil, but if they go too far then it probably would. Children's television presenters might be annoying, even to children, but that doesn't make them bad people. There can even be good and honest used car salesmen, but they tend not to be too successful.

However, given the job description alone, there were plenty of hired killers in Hell. Being cold blooded murderers tended to preclude people from getting into Heaven, no matter how much they prayed or repented. As the skills were transferable, the hitmen and women often avoided instant entry into punishment chambers and were automatically promoted to demons and eventually sent back to work on Earth. They could just carry on the bad work that they had done while they were alive but this time in the name of Satan. There also would always be humans that had signed away their souls and, once the contract had expired and it was time to pay up, they decided that they would rather remain alive. That was when a professional liquidator really came into their own. They could find the missing person and send them on their way in any manner they saw fit. The *liquid* part of the word could occasionally be more literal than figurative and, as many of the demons were sadistic, the methods were not quick or pain free.

It was through this colleague network that Ravaillac was able to get things properly started. Many of his fellow assassins were on Earth, busily and enthusiastically carrying out their set missions, but there was still plenty left in Hell. Once he had found the first couple of volunteers, he was able to send them out and get others to meet up with him. Eventually, like a demonic game of hide and seek, or an evil hue and cry, he had accumulated enough of them for him to issue instructions and send them out to find what human generals call "cannon fodder."

*****

For the muster point and training ground, he had found a large punishment chamber that had been emptied and was in the middle of refurbishment. Sharp walls had become blunt and needed repointing, rough floors had become blood coated and smooth, and the general ambience had lost much of its oppressive feel. While the place was being made dangerous and dirty again, it was free to be utilised for a few days of ancient weapons practice.

Within hours, a strange mix of characters began to filter into the seemingly endless room. A contingent of Horch demons were the first to arrive. They had heard about the impending battle and didn't want to miss out on a chance to inflict some friendly carnage on others. They were arrogant, bad-tempered and not very bright, but they were fast. Although their jagged sword-like hands made eating difficult, it made them ideal weapons for battle, with their shark-like teeth also useful in close quarter combat. Next to arrive were 15,000 bedraggled and thin damned souls, closely followed by Achillas, an ancient Egyptian killer, who had recruited them with promises of a few days away from their punishment and possible jobs as demons if they proved themselves and excelled in battle, an offer that they found hard to refuse and for which they volunteered willingly. Away from the repetitive punishments, their bodies quickly began to regain their strength and they would soon be ready for battle. By the evening, or what could be taken to be the evening in Hell, the chamber had filled up and he had enough demons and damned souls to exceed his quota, 125,000 plus several thousand spares in case any failed to meet expectations during training.

There were several tense minutes after weapons were first issued as demons stood ready for the damned to try and take instant revenge and, in return, the damned souls held their weapons as if they were about to rain retribution onto their former tormentors. Eventually the standoff situation calmed down and both sides realised that infighting would benefit neither side, so weapons were cautiously and reluctantly lowered, and all eyes began to focus on the leader.

He was ready and waiting, standing on a pile of rocks at the right height to see and be seen. With a self-satisfied smile he looked across the sea of expectant faces, relief filling his mind, happy that he had been able to fulfil the first part of his set task. He dared to start to accept the distant possibility that his remit was actually possible. There was one blocker of which he was painfully aware, though. Thanks to a strange rule agreed upon millennia ago by God and Satan. As he had only recently been killed on Earth by Bob's delivery of an unexpected bullet to the back of the head, he couldn't return directly to the planet and wouldn't be able to lead his own army into battle. That annoying technicality meant that the choice of a general to take charge of things would be critical. But thankfully he had plenty of former soldiers, dictators and despots to choose from.

His speech to his troops was succinct and to the point, simply consisting of an outline of the mission and a description of what they might expect to come up against. At the mention of wooden swords inlaid with sharp stones, many of the audience began to laugh and make derisive comments, but Ravaillac quickly warned them against complacency and reminded them that once on Earth, they would have human form and a sharp pointed stone hitting them in the right place could do just as much damage as something made of metal. Once he had finished the speech, he gave them one last instruction and then fell silent.

The order to practice was followed willingly and with violent gusto by all. Long forgotten skills and talents were recreated as swords were energetically swung, jabbed, lunged and parried, with each practice stroke carrying the same force and intent as it would have had if it were aimed at a real enemy. Within the first half hour, he was beginning to think that he would need more soldiers, as the bloody practice wounds received were incapacitating a large proportion of his army. He loudly called a halt to proceedings and had to issue an additional clause to his original instruction. "This is practicing time! Fight but don't go for the kill, or even try to maim anyone." As a precaution, he also sent out a dozen members of the Marching Horde to round up an extra 50,000 spare troops as backup.

Once practice resumed, the number of casualties began to reduce. The swords were swung with slightly less vigour, but they could still inflict damage if the sparring partner didn't have quick reflexes or allowed their attention to wander. For instance, a four-headed Benza demon lost one of his heads as he was busy staring at a she-devil that was attired in far too much tight leather to be comfortable. Unfortunately, despite having three heads left, the one he lost was the one containing the brain responsible for coordination, so he spent the rest of the training session falling over tiny rocks on the floor or walking into walls.

Giant Pazzo demons, who were not proficient with swords but were deadly with battle axes and clubs, were standing around the edges of the chamber and instead of aiming their hits at others, they were simply swinging their weapons and hitting the walls and nearby stalagmites as hard as they could, each blow sending stony shrapnel flying in all directions. Overhead, arrows flew wildly as archers practiced and attempted to detach stalactites from the ceiling so that they would land on unsuspecting demons below. Then, at the far end of the room were troopers with a vast assortment of spears from various historical periods. Although their uses and purposes were very similar, the designs and styles were vastly different. Former Roman legionnaires tried to send their hasta spears further than ancient Greeks with their dories, but each weapon was just as deadly as the next if you happened to be on the receiving end of one.

Although they could handle their weapons, after the first day of training the vast army was still a disorganised and undisciplined rabble. Many of them were exhausted and could hardly hold their chosen weapon anymore, but they had started to make Ravaillac feel that he was beginning to meld together a formidable force. He still kept them training, though; after all, they could rest when the war was over. Guns might not be part of his arsenal, but the army that he had would have been a threat to any modern force on Earth and would certainly fight well against an equal number of Mesoamerican natives. It might not be an easy victory and there would be heavy casualties but, to him, all losses were acceptable as long as the demon army was on the winning side. A callous philosophy, but he knew Satan had the same view.

Suddenly the noise of metal clanging against metal seemed to leach away, projectiles stopped whizzing through the air, and the general roar of exhausted aggression disappeared, replaced by a disorganised chanting. Like children congregating around a playground fight, the trainees formed a densely packed throng circling around a central point and, like the black hole in the centre of a galaxy, the gravitational force causing the compaction of the massed people was out of sight to Ravaillac and his attendant officers. But whatever the cause, it was generating enough concern in the army for them to lose interest in everything else. Despite his instructions to get back to the intense training, his angry and raised voice was ignored. Deciding that the cause of the problem needed investigating, he began to push his way through the crowd, his progress closely followed by his subordinates. Even though the outer layers of engrossed troops were unable to see anything, they all seemed to be focusing on a central point, like a fleshy compass, so the frustrated leader was able to follow their gaze and head in the direction of the problem.

Pushing onwards, he got to the edge of a packed ring surrounding two demons. Seeing them, he realised what was disrupting his intense training regime. At one side was a Buio demon, a tall and slender red skinned creature dressed all in black. His face was full of rage and the two short and pointed horns on his forehead dripped with bright frothy purple blood. He held a sword tightly in his hand, drawn back level with his stomach and pointed in the direction of his opponent. Facing him was a naked Sbattere demon, a yellow creature that was more like a cross between a wild boar and a bear than any humanoid shape. He had two round puncture wounds in his stomach that were slowly releasing more of the liquid that was on the other demon's horns. Through a snarling tusked mouth, he was screaming ancient demonic obscenities, and his sword was raised just over his shoulder ready to be swung down.

Assessing the situation, Ravaillac concluded that somehow, in the heat of mock battle, the Buio demon had somehow managed to stab the other and things had gone downhill from there. Whether it was deliberate, or accidental was unimportant. Demons were not well known for apologising or backing down, so there could only be one outcome: one of them would need to be the obvious winner and the other must lose.

Taking control, he raised his hand and took a deep breath before he spoke. "Hang on!" His words were loud enough to cause everyone to fall silent and the two combatants to reluctantly take their eyes from each other and face their leader. "Come on, everyone, back up! We need a bigger circle so that more people can see what's going on."

The instruction took many of the onlookers by surprise. They expected him to try and put a stop to proceedings and get them to return to their repetitive training. But he had come to a different conclusion. His army had trained hard and now it was time for a bit of hard playing. They could let off steam by watching a gladiatorial battle between two demons. Yes, he might lose a skilled fighter, but there was still plenty left to replace the loser. As the inner battle circle grew so did the audience, but despite that not all were capable of seeing the spectacle. Some that couldn't see anything sought out raised vantage points or climbed on the backs of taller demons. There were still many without a line of sight, but those that could see something could give them a running commentary.

Once he was satisfied that the ring was large enough, Ravaillac gave the two waiting demons a brief nod and with that, the now sanctioned battle officially recommenced. With a cheer from the watching crowds, the two swords were raised. Muscles taut, the demons began to move around the battle area, slowly circling each other and looking for a weakness, waiting for an opportunity to strike. Each watched the other's eyes closely, searching for an indication that the enemy was about to attack.

As they prepared, the crowd watched, and the air seemed to fill with expectant electricity. Nobody really cared who won; as long as there was a battle, there was no rush. They wanted to savour every movement, they wanted blood and plenty of it. The two demons moved slowly, each leg carefully shifted into position before their bodies would be trusted to follow and move the centre of gravity. Like a macabre ballet, they seemed to be dancing at a distance from each other. Steadily, the Sbattere demon carefully advanced, his sword at waist height, swaying gently from side to side. Seeing the gap between them begin to close, the Buio demon raised his weapon above his head, just over his horns, pointed towards his foe and ready to be thrust forwards should the opportunity arise. Sensing that the battle was about to begin in earnest, the crowd fell silent as if just over a hundred thousand creatures of various shapes and sizes were simultaneously holding their breath.

Suddenly, as if by some invisible sign, it started. Perhaps there was a look in one of the demons' eyes or it was pure coincidence, but they advanced at the same time, swords poised, ready to strike. The Buio demon was slightly faster, so he sent his weapon forward first, making the other use his sword to block the blow.

The metallic clanging of the clash made the crowd release a cheer of excitement and sadistic glee. Whenever a fight started in Hell, an audience usually appeared quite quickly, but in this case the audience had amassed first, and they were looking forward to being entertained.

Back and forth, up and down, the deadly weapons moved like silver blurs, with strikes blocked and parried to be followed by counter strikes, none of which were able to find their targets and inflict any damage. Bodies swerved, ducked and occasionally leapt high into the air to avoid a sweeping razor-sharp tip or edge. If either of them failed with their rapid reflexes then they would suffer instant evisceration, amputation or death. This was no gentleman's duel where first blood would indicate who was the winner and both could walk away with honour having been satisfied. No energy was saved for later; it was all or nothing, and each blow carried as much power as the wielder could muster.

One strike released by the Sbattere demon would have bisected his foe had it not been stopped just inches from the Buio demon's head. Seeing that his combatant's attention was on delivering a possible death blow, the Buio demon lifted his leg and, pushing it forward, kicked his foe squarely in the stomach, the impact sending the recipient backwards. He managed to remain on his feet but was winded and had to retreat until he could catch his breath. As he maintained his defensive pose, the Buio demon slowly began to advance, knowing that a blind charge might not be the wisest of options. Despite that anger and red rage flashed in both demons' eyes.

To Ravaillac, it was like a rabid dog and a taunted bear in a pit, spurred on by a bloodthirsty audience. As the Buio demon closed in, the Sbattere demon swung his sword, making the other duck, but the movement wasn't quite sufficient to prevent contact. The swerving sword impacted with a horn, cutting cleanly through it at an angle and sending it flying into the crowd where, much to the amusement of the blood crazed audience, it impacted with the forehead of a Schlau demon, penetrating his skull and knocking him unconscious. Seeing the battle trophy, the trooper next to him swiftly swooped down, grabbed hold of it, and held it tightly against his chest as if it were a puck sent into the crowd at an ice hockey game. He had his souvenir, and nobody was going to relieve him of it.

Although he felt no pain from the loss of his horn, the Buio demon still felt the indignation and humiliation, and it increased the already high level of adrenalin in his body. Incensed, he began to swing wildly, giving the Sbattere demon no time to plan any further strikes, as each counter movement was just sufficient to stop repeated hits. Blow after blow was delivered as if the Buio demon were a lumberjack with an axe trying to hack down a tree. Wildly delivered, but still no victory could be found.

Then, once that blistering assault had run its course, it was the Sbattere's turn to advance, with his sword trying to find an advantage and force the other demon back. One sideward blow was enough to send the sword flying out of the Buio's hand, coming to rest in the stomach of one of the crowd. With the exception of the unfortunate recipient, this added spectacle was met with laughter and cheers from the audience. They were certainly getting more than they had anticipated and were enjoying the show. Finding himself defenceless, the Buio was forced to rapidly retreat, or run away if one preferred that phrase. Getting to the edge of the circle, he saw a demon standing there watching with his spear held casually in front of him. Grabbing it, he was able to turn around fast enough to lift it up horizontally, with both hands, blocking a blow that was aimed for his head. The two demons were face to face, so close that each could feel the hot air from the breath of the other. Pushing the Sbattere back, the Buio lowered his newly acquired spear and readied to thrust it at his antagonist. As he pushed it outwards, thanks to a rapid body swerve, the point missed its target leaving the wooden shaft exposed. An agile swipe from the sword and the long and practical weapon was turned into two less useful pieces of wood, one metal tipped and lying on the floor with the other blunt and ineffective part still in his hands. Throwing it down, he looked around, frantically searching for something else that he could acquire and continue the battle.

Soon his eyes caught sight of a demon kneeling at the edge of the ring, leaning on a Francisca axe. It was just what he needed. Its design was such that it was ideal for throwing and if he could just get to it without being cut down, he would have a chance to release it and claim victory. Dodging a blow from the foe's sword, he ran across the battle arena, focused on obtaining the weapon. Reaching the demon, he grabbed the long curve-bladed axe, pulling it from its owner and causing him to lose his balance and fall forward into the circle. The Buio was turning and raising the axe in one fluid movement, but he was not fast enough. The Sbattere demon had seen his opportunity and thrown his sword at the exposed and undefended back of his enemy. Spinning like a rotor blade that had been dislodged from a crashing helicopter, it flew through the air and hit its target perfectly. The point dug deep into the back of the Buio demon, with the impact and pain causing him to tense up as if he were being briefly electrocuted. As the life drained from his eyes, he fell to his knees, arms hanging limply down by his side with the now redundant axe lying next to him. Being a creature in Hell, he would eventually heal and be fit for demon duties, but for now, and to all intents and purposes, he was as good as dead and would be useless in the imminent war.

Seeing victory, the crowd released a cheer that filled the vast chamber and the echo seemed to make a living feedback loop, amplifying the sound so that it became deafening. Busy with the excitement of having witnessed a great contest, the crowd remained transfixed where they were, none of them moving forward to celebrate with the victor, nor moving away to return to training.

Noticing the uncertainty, Ravaillac decided that it was time to regain control. Stepping forward, into the centre of the impromptu arena, he raised his arms as a gesture for silence. Eventually the noise reduced, starting at the front rows, and working its way out, the inverse sound wave making the air feel like it was some sort of vacuum. Only when the quiet was complete, and he felt sure that he had everybody's undivided attention, did he even consider speaking. They were too full of euphoria and forcing them back to the hard realities of Hell would have negated all the positive effects of their brief break.

Taking a deep breath, he finally spoke, his words full of power and authority. "Right demons, damned and…" He paused, briefly looking at a creature that seemed to be more slime than flesh. "Errr…everyone else. You have seen how to fight, seen how to win, and you know what happens to you if you are not the victor. Now get back to the practicing and know that when you go into battle, it will be them or you."

The words could have easily been met by typical demonic anger, hatred and resentment, but the brief interlude had the desired effect and made them more focused on what was required and had to be done. Weapons of all shapes and sizes were made ready and the training recommenced. This time there was a focus that was not there before. Whoever was being sparred with was no longer a target for blind swings aimed with the sole purpose of removing a limb or two. Instead, there was now a tacit respect for the creature before them and although each blow, if unchecked, could easily have been deadly, the concentration given and received ensured that injuries were significantly reduced. Even when not aimed at other demons, the weapons, in the minds of the wielders, were no longer just hitting bare and defenceless walls and lumps of stone but ancient Mesoamerican warriors. They now imagined movements that forced them to do more than just strike in the same old way. Inanimate stone became an enemy to be dodged, and not just with relish but a side order of fries as well. Ravaillac watched the new method of training and felt the change in the atmosphere. He allowed himself a brief smile of self-satisfaction, brought on by the confidence that the war would be easily won and any punishment from Satan would be forgotten.

25 – Repeat Then Repeat Again

St. Michael could be, and had been, called many things in the past. Arrogant, egotistical, pedantic and supercilious were just a few words that sprang readily to mind. And those were the kind ones that were used by those that might be considered his closest friends. The troops in his vast army had a wider and far more vulgar vocabulary, which they used quite freely when he was out of earshot. No matter what the language they used, ancient, modern or even long since dead and unspoken on Earth for centuries, the insults tended to translate into the same few categories, words relating to certain parts of the female anatomy or the sexual act that was coarsely carried out by sailors whilst in a hurry. Although there was the odd exception to this rule - in the long extinct Scythian language, for instance, the obscenest insult involved wishing that someone would trip over an ant hill and sprain their ankle. Admittedly, it lost a lot in translation, but it made Scythians laugh like hyenas on acid every time they aimed it at the saint.

Ever since St. Michael had been requested to train up a vast army to meet Ekeko's challenge, he had returned from his self-imposed exile with renewed vigour and a newly discovered level of blind enthusiasm not usually seen outside of dogs that have smelled a bitch in heat behind a locked house door.

In rich and upper crust houses, the master occasionally had a manservant to help with complicated things like putting toothpaste onto toothbrushes, selecting which watch to wear, or the trickiest thing of all - tying shoelaces. But, as he was a military man, St. Michael renounced such obviously bourgeois trappings. For public opinion purposes, he wouldn't even countenance having a manservant. However, as an officer, he had a batman whose name was Matt. That type of assistant was far more appropriate and, in the saint's eyes, far less elitist and more egalitarian. The poor person was not only given the dubious honour of carrying out all the duties of a human manservant but, as he was a batman, he wore a uniform and had to salute.

Due to a clerical error, Matt should have gone to Hell but ended up in Heaven. St. Peter was planning to rectify the mistake but realised that there was a position that nobody else in Heaven wanted and working for St. Michael would probably be a far worse punishment than anything that Satan could think up. This meant Matt was quickly given his new role and told to shut up and get on with his work. Thinking he had been let off lightly, and thinking that he was lucky, he quickly accepted the offer of work. At first, he was happy, but he soon learned to regret his decision and long for the exquisite pains and torments of Hell. However, eventually he had become so browbeaten that he came to accept his role. He wouldn't have minded being a batman if his uniform were black and included a mask and cape, but unfortunately for him it was just a khaki army uniform.

While he had been in relative isolation with his superior officer, his duties had been mundane, repetitive and mind numbingly dull but, on the whole, fairly easy. Cleaning shoes and pressing trousers so that they had a crease that could cut through a telephone directory were hardly the most onerous of chores. However, ever since the return to the relative civilisation of central Heaven and the requirements of military appearances, his workload had increased exponentially. Not only did black boots need to be immaculate and have a glossy shine bright enough to blind anyone stupid enough to look at them but he had received extra work.

The most intricate and time consuming of tasks was the polishing of St. Michael's favourite suit of armour, which was the ultimate victory of style over content and practicality. A mixture of gold-plated steel and silver, it was decorated with images of demons and grotesque monsters being slain by the saint, a macabre and vain tribute to his own past glories, both real and fictional. Thanks to all the decorative art, which wouldn't have been out of place in a museum dedicated to tacky ornaments, the mass of metal held together by thick leather straps was so heavy that it restricted the wearer to limited movements. Arms could be raised to shoulder height and the torso could twist a few degrees, but walking required strength and power usually only found in an aroused bull elephant. The lack of mobility and the ability of the armour to shine on even the cloudiest of days made St. Michael an obvious target for any soldier, enemy or otherwise, that wished to eliminate the commander at the start of the battle. Matt had spent several hours trying to get the right shine on the metal but each time he had said that the task was done the Saint would spend several minutes scrutinising the work and always find some minor and almost invisible fault, then demand that the put-upon lackey redo the whole polishing process again.

Eventually time had run out and his army had mustered on a vast field outside his impromptu command tent, so he had petulantly scolded Matt for not providing a satisfactory shine before making the batman strap him into his metal casing. A task that Matt carried out with a certain element of quiet glee as it involved violently pulling straps extra tight so that bits of precious metal didn't come loose or fall off. Finally, the saint was fastened in and ready to meet his troops. The first sight of their leader that met the assembled, and eager, army was what looked like a decorative robot from a 1950's sci-fi movie, only with mobility issues. The walk was not so much like an alien creature imposing its authority as that of a metal coated Sumo wrestler suffering from a serious case of haemorrhoids. The light reflecting off his chest plate made an entire regiment shade their eyes so that they could no longer look directly at their titular superior.

At last, reaching the top of a small hillock, he halted and looked out across a sea of expectantly eager warrior faces. When living on Earth many would have been historical adversaries, but in Heaven all past enmities were forgotten. Spanish conquistadors rubbed shoulders with Dutch freedom fighters. American cowboys stood beside Native American Indians and, as they seemed to have had wars with most nations, British troops blithely stood next to anybody that they thought might have beers which would, at some point, be shared with them.

Raising his arms as high as his restrictive suit would allow, St. Michael lifted the visor on his helmet. "Soldiers," he began, his voice loud and imperious. "We are…" The rest of his sentence was lost to his audience as the headpiece, with its well-oiled hinges, gave way to its own weight and slammed the heavy visor back down into its natural position in front of his face, leaving the frustrated saint with only a limited view of his troops. Trying again, he raised the visor. "My wonderful arm…." Once more his voice was lost and, even to the soldiers closest to him, all that could be heard were muffled utterances that sounded as if someone were ordering a pizza on a cell phone, with a faulty battery, while going through a railway tunnel. Frustratedly and with sotto voce mumbled oaths, he lifted the helmet off his head and passed it to the nearest officer that was standing politely behind him. The saint was embarrassed and angry at his wardrobe malfunction and made a mental note to find some menial chore to punish Matt for overdoing the work on the visor.

Free of the heavy encumbrance, St. Michael was now able to see his army and be heard when he spoke. Whether his army wanted to hear him was a different matter. Many of them had been in battles where he had been in charge, so they knew how dull, high-maintenance and obtuse he could be. They had also heard all about the forthcoming war so there was little that listening to an uninspiring speech would do other than wasting precious time that could be better spent with practicing their rusty battle skills.

If Winston Churchill had been amongst the massed crowd, he would have been flattered by the compliment as St. Michael took a deep breath and began to speak in the measured and collected jowly tones of the former British Prime Minister. "Never have we, the massed army of God, had such a challenge." The impersonation he was affecting, in an attempt to add some gravitas to his words had the opposite effect. Eyes rolled and heads were nodded in disbelief. Some laughed and began to repeat the word 'Never' in a Churchillian tone and this in turn caused more sniggering. Eventually the noise from the unexpected gaiety was drowning out St. Michael's words. Increasingly frustrated as his hoped-for fire-inspiring speech was extinguished by the general cacophony, he fell silent, then aggravatedly turned to speak to one of his officers. "What is going on? What's the matter?"

Unwilling to jeopardise his rank and risk instant demotion, the officer chose the option familiar to most politicians and opted for a creative version of the truth, or what is more commonly known to non-politicians as *lying*. "They are just inspired by your words, sir, and are simply chomping at the bit. They now want to get on with practicing so that they'll be ready for battle. After all, sir, what with modern weaponry, it's been a while since any of them have been into combat with such old-fashioned implements."

Considering the words, the saint nodded with a sage-like look on his face, as if he'd just been told the ultimate secret of the universe. "A very valid point. Have the men..." He paused as he noticed a large contingent of scantily clad Spartan women in the crowd. "Tell the men and women to fall out and get on with their practicing. The sooner they have got that done, the sooner they will be able to ensure boots are clean, uniforms are immaculate, and weapons are gleaming!"

Fortunately, the officer at the right of the saint was just to his rear, so that his reaction on hearing the last part of the instructions was not seen. "WHAT THE F…" He had to hold himself back from completing the muttered oath. The saint was notorious for his love of spick and span soldiers, but the lack of priorities made the bemused officer wonder how St. Michael had managed to stay in charge of anything more dangerous than a Salvation Army band. Undeterred by his instructions, the officer marched up to the front of the assembled army, raised his arms, and began to shout, telling them to quieten down. Gradually, he got silence and was able to pass on the first part of the order. He deliberately redacted the last part as he knew that would crush any high spirits and remove the ebullient mood.

The crowd quickly dispersed and took up positions in the vast and verdant sunlit area. Sword masters were matched up with suitable sparring partners; archers and spear throwers were allocated areas where they could launch projectiles and skin piercing weaponry without any risk of collateral damage, or injuries from 'friendly fire'; and those with axes or blunt instruments merrily began beating other people's shields into odd and mangled shapes. Soon the air was once more filled with an even louder noise, this time the sharp sound of metal hitting metal and the whizzing of deadly arrows being released by tensed bows and crossbows. The sound was like music to St. Michael's ears. Admittedly, he preferred the rhythms of brisk shoe polishing, but this came a close second.

After several hours of the same moves and actions, the soldiers began to tire and get bored. For those that hadn't held a sword for centuries, the skills soon returned and even if they were building up stamina and muscle repetition, there were only a certain number of times the same finite number of moves could be repeated in one day before the whole thing began to be a dull chore. This increasing ennui was not just felt by those wielding handheld, close quarters weapons. The spear throwers had practiced enough so that they could hit their targets and, despite having plenty of projectiles, they still had to keep walking across the firing range to retrieve all the spears they had just thrown and, thanks to that, were beginning to tire. The archers were in a similar emotional and physical state. They had the added tedium of hitting a series of red concentric rings on static targets. Although they might not have been up against Mesoamerican warriors before, they felt certain that they didn't paint such obvious targets on their chests and keep still while the enemy casually fired arrows at them.

Time dragged on until St. Michael decided that there had been enough of the same repetition for the day, and he instructed his officers to tell everyone to rest. Even though, thanks to its positive energy, it was difficult to become physically tired in Heaven, the dull routine had left the entire army emotionally drained and exhausted. Weapons were left on the ground as angels took the opportunity to take a break. Sitting or standing around, they began to genially talk with their colleagues, conversations ranging from what they planned to do later in the evening, the forthcoming battle, or what a pompous dick St. Michael was. However, the not very popular saint's next instruction was that they should get on with polishing footwear and buffing weapons, including arrows, to ensure that they all had a shine on them. This message changed the tone of discussions so that the sole topic of conversation was relating to the Field Marshall's parentage and how he had a penis for a brain. Those in Heaven that were from armies that didn't wear shoes or wore fur skins managed to escape the saint's chore, as some dull pig iron clubs, coshes or kanabō would never achieve even a slight gleam, no matter how much elbow grease was put into the process. After much polish and a lot of resentment, mixed with venomous spit, the army was ready to take on the enemy with their clean footwear. Also, if the weapons didn't kill them, then at least they might have a good chance of blinding the opposition if the sun reflected off the boots at the wrong angle. Tasks done, St. Michael decided that he was satisfied with the appearance and dismissed his army, with the caveat that they should return at 06:00 hours the following morning and be ready for more of the same. These words were met with a dull, but still clearly audible, groan that the Saint chose to ignore, telling himself that it was just a sigh of exhausted relief released in unison.

*****

The long-standing enmity, and outright animosity, between Dedan and St. Michael was perhaps one of the worst kept secrets in Heaven. Throughout history, they had been to Earth on several missions together and on a few occasions had stood at the gates of Heaven repulsing attacks from armies of demons. But right from the very start, their personalities had refused to gel, and they had not got along. They had occasionally tried to patch up their differences, shake hands and be friends, but the truce and false bonhomie quickly evaporated, and they went back to the state of mutual contempt. St. Michael found Dedan to be undisciplined, slovenly, reckless and insubordinate, while those were the qualities of which Dedan was most proud of. And on the flip side of the coin, Dedan found St. Michael to be pompous, self-important and arrogant, and had said that to his face on many occasions. Admittedly not always in those terms, and the supercilious saint often took offence to being called a 'dickhead' or worse. On the last mission where they had been together, Dedan had pricked his precious and preening ego and on his return to Heaven, the saint had gone off to sulk. If it hadn't been for the recall to prepare for the forthcoming war, he would still be in relative isolation in a remote part of Heaven, spending his time resenting Dedan and issuing endless and pointless instructions to his put-upon batman.

On his prompt return from his additional mission for God, Dedan had decided that he had no desire to suffer the inevitable dull routine of St. Michael's training methods. He knew how to clean boots and had no inclination to spend his precious time rubbing polish into them, especially as he knew that the enemy wouldn't be starting a shiny shoe competition against the combined army of angels and demons. He had more important things to do before the battle began.

Despite having lived in a time where there were no such things as guns, bombs, napalm and all the other things that made war 'civilised' and having fought many battles throughout the millennia with swords, he was now out of practice. Ever since he had picked up a musket in the English civil war and gone demon hunting, Dedan had increasingly had to rely on guns. He despised them and could still handle a knife, but when it came to swinging a sword effectively his skill needed refreshing. In order to avoid the saint, he had decided to practice in the comfort of his own back garden and had recruited one of his most trusted friends to help him.

Paul had been an actor during his time on Earth. However, despite being amazingly talented, he had the main problem of many of the best members in that profession; he was far from being blessed with the chiselled male model looks of all the most famous actors. He was not ugly, but his big nose and sad eyes were hardly Hollywood 'A-list' material. This curse left him filling small roles on TV and being satisfied with bit parts in movies while people that couldn't act their way out of paper bags took the lead roles. But despite that, he didn't mind since he loved what he did and, for those that have the luxury of enjoying their jobs, it was a way of finding Heaven on Earth.

His untimely death was all down to a stagehand that was just learning the ropes in a theatre. Unfortunately, for Paul, he was not learning them fast enough and instead of releasing a rope that raised a stage curtain, he pulled a cord that allowed a sandbag to score a direct hit on the actor's head. The unexpected and extra death in a West End production took the audience by complete surprise, but not as much as it did Paul. The term 'corpsing' on stage usually referred to uncontrolled laughing but, in that instance, it was far more literal. The audience loved the special effect, thinking that the *fake* blood and hint of grey brain matter were very realistic but a bit over the top. It ensured record ticket sales for subsequent performances, but it reinforced Macbeth's reputation as an unlucky play.

In Heaven he had bumped into Dedan by accident, and they had become firm friends so that when the demon hunter wasn't on missions, they hung out drinking, joking and being generally immature and loud. Thanks to his theatrical training, he was adept at sword play and became the first choice as sparring partner for Dedan. They were currently covered from head to foot in the Japanese kendōgu, the practice armour for the martial art of Kendo. With the long bamboo Shinai swords held tightly in hand, they were preparing to try and hit the other as hard as they possibly could. There would be no mercy or leniency with the blows and, thanks to the bond that only true friends can have, both of them were looking forward to hitting the other as hard as they could. The thick black padded suits and helmets would provide protection, but each blow would be felt and probably leave large bruises.

Then, as if someone had blown an inaudible whistle, they started. With the identical garb, it was impossible to tell which was which. Repeated strikes were delivered with lightning-like speed and blocked with the same quick reflexes, each hit of bamboo against bamboo making a loud and hollow 'thwack' noise. Each time a limb or head was hit they would pause, step back, and begin the whole process again. When contact was made, the pain made Dedan realise that he'd have to do better in the real battle, as there would be no second chances and if he were hit then it'd be game over for him.

As they began to get into the rhythm of the practice session, the two different sword fighting styles began to become obvious. Dedan had fought for his life many times and to him, the sword was just a tool that was only as good as the user. Win at any cost or die. Style, finesse or elegance were not qualities that were required. However, during his time in a London drama school, Paul had been taught that a sword was a prop and it needed flair and skill to wield. Audiences had to be entertained, so the more dramatic the swoops and flamboyant the leaps, the better. Thanks to the dull thud of wood hitting cloth and the body parts underneath, the brutal and less theatrical approach was the most successful and Dedan's rusty skills were getting oiled and becoming more fluid. Paul was able to account for himself and make occasional contact with his opponent but if it had been a real battle, he would have lost his limbs one by one and died long ago.

After one particularly brutal direct hit to the top of his helmet, Paul was forced to step back and raise his spare hand to request quarter and be allowed to rest. Both took the opportunity to remove head gear, revealing sweat drenched hair and red flushed faces. Sitting at a picnic bench, Dedan reached into a cooler box, removed a couple of cans of beer and passed one of them to his friend. Draining them in one thankful gulp, they both released the universal sign of male satisfaction at a drink. "Arrrrrrr!" Unless they were the type to shout, "Geronimo!" or "He shoots and he scores," then it was a noise that was not dissimilar to the noise made after getting satisfaction from an orgasm. If a man could drink a beer while having sex, he'd be in his element and anyone listening would hear it and think, "And there is a happy man!"

Wiping the sweat from his forehead with his thick cloth sleeve, Paul looked at Dedan, his face adopting a look of earnestness. "Dedan, I know I'm not an angel that usually goes into battles but this time I want to go with you."

Dedan's expression also changed to match his friend's serious look. "That might not be possible."

"But…" The sentence halted as Dedan raised his hand, demanding silence.

"Trust me, I do not say that to protect you. I could think of very few that I'd like to fight shoulder to shoulder with and you're one of them. With the demons of Satan to the left of me and St. Michael on the right, the more people I have around me that I can trust not to cut off their own head, or mine, once they have a sword in their hands the better. But I have a far more important mission for you. I want you to…"

26 - A Quarter of a Million, Nothing More, Nothing Less

As per his own challenge, Ekeko had stipulated that there should be no more than 250,000 combatants on each side, and he had no desire to accidentally send in too many troops and lose the war by default. Despite being bloodthirsty and callous, he was a god and that demanded a certain degree of integrity, with his word being sacrosanct. Although he didn't believe that he would lose, the thought of reneging on his deal if he should lose was not something he could even countenance. It might take a normal human a long time to count to 250,000 but for a god, it was a skill that came naturally and allowed him to ensure that he had the right number of soldiers. Even so, he had to concentrate and de-select some as he had more volunteers than he had places.

Over the centuries, before his death, he had acquired a lot of souls. Many had been believers and others had been not so willing converts. Losing their hearts to the god was the last thing they ever wanted to do, but that was quite literally the last thing they did. When their figurehead had turned to stone, their souls had either gone to Heaven or to Hell, and while many now welcomed the pace of Ekeko's domain, there were others who missed Heaven but accepted that there was little that they could do about it.

However, with the aid of copious amounts of psychoactive and recreational drugs obtained from plants, snakes and frogs, the army was beginning to enter a higher plain of semi-consciousness. Many were seeing demons that were not there and were in such a state that they were ready to fight furniture, statues and small hamsters if they had not been held in check by their lack of weapons. They were being given one last narcotic high with the knowledge that they would be sharp and focused once they came down. The lost and mostly forgotten language of the indigenous people became even less understood as stoned natives began to try and describe the colour of all the noises they were hearing, the smell of the number nine, and what they thought when they looked at a small pet rodent that was transmogrifying before their very eyes and turning into a ten-foot-tall, three headed, bright orange and pink monster. None of them knew who Jefferson Airplane or the Grateful Dead were, but if they had then that music would have been an ideal accompaniment to their experiences. Ekeko was beginning to worry about his spare supplies of food as so many mouths began to get the munchies. Lacking pizzas, the stock of roast sheep, llamas and barbecued hamsters were quickly disappearing.

In the end, the state of the transcendental high went past consciousness, and the god was met by the sight of an entire army lying down on the ground as they rapidly fell asleep. Heads and limbs were placed haphazardly on top, beside and in some cases, inside various body parts of other people. They all seemed oblivious to the accumulated stench of the sweat of a quarter of a million soldiers that had spent all day swinging swords and lifting shields, before relinquishing them to get wasted on ancient narcotics. Getting high and then falling asleep was not the only effect of the strange and obscure concoction of drugs; it also had an adverse consequence on their bowels. The air was now infused with flatulent gases and could have been classified as a weapon of mass destruction if released on Earth. It was almost thick enough to chew and was making even the god's eyes water. Fortunately, thanks to it being daylight and the cooking fires having been extinguished, there were no naked flames available; otherwise, the army could have been cooked, if not in its own juices, then at least in its own by-product.

Coughing and spluttering, with arms waving frantically in a futile attempt to sweep some fresh air up his nostrils, Ekeko decided to retire to the safety of his own pyramid. The height should, he hoped, be sufficient to place him above the manmade smog that would have made the rush hour air in Beijing smell appealing. Climbing up the steps, flanked by his ever-present bodyguards, he reached the top and looked down on the light brown, grey and green tinted mist that hung like a pall over the slumbering bodies. As far as the eye could see, every open space was taken up by people in a drug induced coma, a sea of reclined figures with chemically altered minds contentedly creating dream images full of brightly coloured creatures.

Ekeko allowed himself a sly smile. He knew from long experience that the mixture that they had willingly consumed was his own private magic and, when it came to battles, it was his ace card. When taken, it made people euphoric and happy, taking them to a world where it might be strange but where there was peace and contentment. It made them eat a lot and then sent them to sleep, giving them solid slumbers that couldn't be broken until bodies were ready to return to consciousness. But, when they woke up, the instant withdrawal symptoms would leave them angry, aggressive and blindly violent. The food they had consumed also gave them plenty of energy, so the combination made them formidable opponents in any conflict. The energetic fury could be channelled against any opposition, and the only way to slow down or stop them was to either let the manic energy dissipate over time or simply kill them.

Suddenly his expression changed, as if a storm cloud had covered the joy in his mind. He looked pensive as he slid his hands under his long cloak and reached behind his back. Bringing them back in front of him, he looked at the two pistols, his disgust at the weapons obvious to his guards. Turning them slightly, he carefully studied them. Roxy had left them behind his plinth on her first visit to see Limbo, when he had been just a statue. On his unusual transubstantiation, he had found them and, despite his contempt, decided to keep the weapons. To him, they represented all he hated, but they might have their uses as a reminder of why he hated the modern world.

Long ago, Spanish conquistadors had invaded his lands, bringing religion, guns and diseases. All of them meant slavery, destruction and death. Guns were used to enforce a strange and alien religion and then smallpox and measles wiped out millions of people that had never encountered such illnesses and had no immunity to them. Deaths were slow and painful as the new masters took advantage of the situation and stole the gold. A nice-looking metal but, in his world, chocolate was of greater value.

The pistols may have been different to sixteenth century European muskets, but the basic shape hadn't changed that much and when he first saw them, he'd recognised them for what they were: evil and dark magic from another land. Studying them, to his untrained eye, the pistols were not dissimilar. The SIG Pro 9mm semi-automatic and the Smith and Wesson M&P9C were the same matte gun-metal colour and had similar weights. To him, they had no honour and were tools to be used by cowards.

He remembered, with longing, the old days when a child could step into manhood by walking into the jungle armed only with a basic stone knife and kill an animal, then return to the village to feed people and earn respect. Some even aimed high and tried to kill a jaguar or black panther. Those people almost invariably ended up being unsuccessful and found themselves in Ekeko's domain, but if they were cunning or lucky, they'd reappear adorned in a slightly bloodied, but fashionable, animal skin and be admired as brave heroes. In battle with handheld weapons, it was warrior against warrior, face to face, where you could look into the enemy's eyes as they died, smell their fear, and feel their blood splash into your eyes. Win, and their courage became part of your soul.

But guns were remote and needed no more skill than an apathetic attitude towards the prey, the ability to point the thing in the right direction and then pull the trigger. After that, it was a tiny explosion and a loud noise accompanied by grey smoke, and the target was dead. No honour to be gained and no courage required. He was tempted to just throw them as far as he could down the pyramid so that they smashed against the unforgiving stones but decided to return them to the back of his tight loin cloth. Not comfortable, but a constant reminder of why he was right and had to win. After the battle, he would be free to punish his human people, the ones on Earth whose ancestors had renounced him, and remind them that they should believe in him and forget the false impostors. With his flock growing, he would no longer have a fragile and almost untenable grip on existence, having to rely on a fickle youth in a strange land surrounded by technology that he did understand and had no desire to do so.

Raising his arms above his head, he conjured up a warm breeze. The soft wind was just enough to push the noxious smog below him away from his still slumbering army. If he were to go back and walk amongst his troops, he wanted to be able to breathe; although, oblivious to the improved air, the army slept on. No longer muffled by the dense gases, the sound of far from pleasant snoring could now be heard echoing amongst the pyramids. A far from rhythmic noise, it was like a large herd of wild boars revving motorbikes with misfiring cylinders, while they simultaneously brandished spinning chain saws. The increase in background noise doing nothing to encourage them to wake up. Even from his vantage point, high on top of his pyramid, Ekeko could hear them and smiled indulgently like a benevolent parent caring for his wayward, but still loved children.

Looking down, he strained to see a figure in the distance. Her movement looked out of place and made her stand out as she leapt over bodies carelessly strewn all around her. Agile as a gazelle playfully jumping across the grasslands, the visitor managed to avoid making contact with any and all body parts, her feet finding tiny patches of earth to land on before springing onto the next free space. The unquiet slumbers of the sleepers unbroken and left unmindful to her presence. As she drew closer to the pyramid, and the watching god, he was able to make out more details. Even far away, her clothing made it obvious that she was not from his domain, with the pristine white robe flowing behind her like a sail caught in the wind and with her smooth ebony skin and long jet-black hair making it apparent that she was not an ancient South American. As she strode forward, he saw the light brown sandals with straps wrapped around her muscular calves. Her dark eyes were fixed on him like a hunter selecting its prey. From the look of determination, he could tell that she had only one thing on her mind and that was to get to him as quickly as possible.

Instinctively his bodyguards stepped forward, swords and spears raised in readiness. What they expected was unclear. After all, if she were there as some sort of assassin, she was the least subtle one in the history of the profession. Additionally, the apparent lack of any form of weapon would have made that task even harder. Reaching the base of the imposing pyramid, she placed her left foot on the first step and, spreading her arms wide in a gesture of supplication, bowed while keeping her gaze on the god. The guards, unsure of how to react, tightened the grip on their weapons and moved down a couple of steps. They were still far higher than the visitor and their swords were useless at such a distance, but their intentions were obvious.

"Take it easy, men!" Ekeko's voice was calm and casual, as he deemed the woman to be less of a threat than his guards did. He didn't blame them as they were only doing their job, but all too often, be it on Earth or in other dimensions, common sense was a commodity that was rare amongst people chosen for their brawn rather than their brain. Their single task was to protect their god, at all costs, so a high IQ wasn't a prerequisite. "Lower your weapons and allow our beautiful guest to approach. Come closer, child. And tell me what brings you here?"

They maintained eye contact as she gracefully climbed up the steps. He had seen such dark skins before; the conquistadors had brought slaves with them on their later expeditions. More compliant, less susceptible to fatal diseases, and more obedient than his followers that were press ganged into servitude, but he had admired the courage, spirit and strength of the imported slaves. Once she was two steps below the still cautious and suspicious phalanx of guards, she stopped and repeated the elaborate bowing gesture.

"Oh mighty, powerful and magnificent Ekeko, I have been sent by my god with a request and to make you an offer…"

27 – There's Never a Speech Writer Available When You Need One

The basic time spacing in Heaven didn't follow that of Earth. It couldn't, in theory at least, go backwards or freeze but the nanoseconds that made up seconds, minutes, hours and all the other standard measurements, used to make a day go by, could be flexible in their quantity and durations. This was nothing to do with relativity, or how fast a person was going, and was more down to how happy a person was. The old aphorism that time flies when you're enjoying yourself was not a hard and fast rule, but a contended soul could spend what would be a lifetime on Earth just embracing a loved one and never have to play the game of waiting to see who breaks the clinch first to go get pizza, release the other person for a toilet break or to swing their arms about to get circulation going again. Plus, thanks to all the various time zones on Earth, telling the time on Heaven was not an exact science and, on the whole, meaningless. It was thanks to this disparity in temporal mechanics that the large round clock hanging prominently on the wall above the fireplace in God's office was more for show and artistic effect than any practical reasons. Its second hand smoothly moved around its face, but the minute and hour hands were permanently stuck on the symmetrical time of 10:10. The lack of an accurate, reliable and relevant timepiece didn't stop God from being aware of the passing of time. He created it and could reliably and instinctively tell anyone what the date and time was on any place on Earth without having to rely on any external chronographical devices. And currently He was well aware that the metaphorical clock was ticking, and it would soon be time to despatch His troop to the proposed battlefield in a remote and isolated part of Bolivia. He wasn't totally convinced that sharing the responsibility of winning the war with Satan was the greatest of ideas, but He also knew that trying to exclude him from the fight would have been difficult and could have resulted in the devil army just appearing and fighting both Ekeko's troops and His own. Or, even worse, waiting for God to have a large proportion of His fighting force incapacitated and unable to fight and then attacking the gates of Heaven. As it was God wasn't sure that they wouldn't turn on His army at some point. A risk but he knew from bitter experience that demons could fight well so, for now, they could be a useful asset. Strange and unreliable allies but hopefully not for too long. Trust and faith might be wonderful things in Heaven but on Earth, when fighting side by side with demons, it could be a distinct liability. Considering the short time left, God had come to a decision. He needed someone to deliver a good old-fashioned pre-battle speech to His eager troops. One of the traditional orations that would leave them inspired and full of the knowledge that they were on the side of good. There were many individuals making up His army but when joined together they were a single unit and would win, so they needed a speech of such power that they felt invincible. Even if modern politicians made it into Heaven their words tended to be aimed at the lowest common denominators and couldn't inspire someone, with a modicum of intelligence, to flush the toilet after using it never mind lay down their lives for a greater good. He needed someone different, someone that could put fire into an audience's hearts and make them go into battle feeling impervious to any swords, arrows and spears. Leaning forward, over His large desk, He pressed the intercom button and spoke, His voice childlike but still full of authority. "Angelica, can you get in touch with Pericles and ask him to come and see me?" God had admired the ancient Athenian leader's oration skills and knew that he'd be ideal as a guest speaker.

"I am sorry my Lord, he disappeared at the same time as the others. It is suspected that he has gone to Elsa's domain." Angelica's voice was sad and apologetic. She hated to let God down or bring Him bad news but sometimes it had to be done.

On hearing the news God paused and contemplated his options. There were so many great speakers that it wasn't a simple task to choose the right person for the job. Churchill was an obvious option, but He was reticent about utilising the WWII leader. Winston was a pleasant enough man but could be sarcastic and whenever he was in God's office, Churchill often gave the impression that he thought that he should be allowed to take charge for a while, plus he was a complete snob and believed that there should be a two-tier system in Heaven. One for the well-bred souls and the other for ones from a lower background. Running over the list in His mind He came up with a couple of names and mulled over both of their pros and cons. It was a tough decision and neither of them stood out as the over-all winner and the appropriate one to compose and deliver the ultimate motivational speech.

"Alright Angelica, can you invite Patrick Henry and Golda Meir to join me? I'd like to chat with them."

"Of course, Sire!" Angelica's voice instantly cheering up as she knew that the request was easy to complete.

Returning to His relaxed position on his plush office chair He tilted backwards and stared absent mindedly at the ceiling as He pondered over the two contenders He'd selected. Patrick Henry's 'Give me liberty or give me death' speech in Richmond, Virginia, just before the American war of independence, had always impressed God. At the time the rousing words had the power to motivate a dubious and cautious group of men to take up arms and fight for independence. His words went on to be echoed by revolutionaries ever since. On the other hand, there was Golda, the Ukrainian born Jew that went on to become the Prime Minister of Israel. During that country's independence the fledgling state had been left isolated and alone with the rest of the world unknowing if it would stand or fall against the combined forces of the all the Arab neighbours. Travelling to the USA she had delivered an impassioned speech where she had pleaded for donations so that they would have a fighting chance of survival. Her 'If we have arms to fight with' speech had the desired effect and raised millions of dollars enabling the fledgling state to fight the war that was forced upon it on its first day of its existence. For a brief second, He had considered General George S. Patton but his gung-ho attitude, as powerful as it was, would more than likely have prompted the angel troops to make the first strike a pre-emptive one against the demons in the belief that they could defeat Satan's forces and still have enough soldiers left to take on, and be victorious, against Ekeko's entire army. It was hard for immortal souls to commit suicide but following his tactic was a sure-fire way of losing the battle and the war. After mulling it over He reassured himself that His two choices were the right candidates.

As He waited God decided to go stand in front of his imposing fireplace and watch the flames. The fire was totally decorative giving a comforting dancing light which added a soft ambience to His office but, as none was required, no heat was given off. Unlike Hell you could have put your unprotected hands deep into the roaring blaze and not feel anything more than perhaps a pleasant tickling sensation as the red, orange and blue flames danced around your skin. In Heaven fire couldn't do any harm. It could be used at barbecues if an angel had a party and fancied cooking sausages and burgers in the open air, or a blacksmith, who refused to let his skills die, could practice their talent but no matter what accident happened they couldn't burn themselves or set fire to the buildings. His eyes looked to be lost in a distant place as He thought out a battle plan that was suitable for the flat, and occasionally buried under 6" of water, terrain. It might be fluid, but it prevented movements from troops that needed to be agile and react quickly. For the fighters it would be like a surreal dream where everyone was trying to run in thick syrup, possibly getting thicker as the blood began to flow. At least St. Michael would be kept happy as his soldier's boots would be kept clean, or just out of sight.

Just then there was a knock on the door leading to Angelica's office. Without waiting to be invited in it opened and Golda Meir entered, grey hair tied tightly behind her head. Her gentle face cragged and wrinkled but with eyes alert and showing a steely intelligence that couldn't be camouflaged by her stooped and elderly appearance. The heavy brown wooden beaded necklace, white blouse and beige tweed dress suit did nothing to make her look young. Looking around the room, in an attempt to see where God was her eyes finally rested on the form of a fair-haired schoolboy with glasses dressed in a t-shirt, and slightly muddy trousers.

"Hello young man. Are you waiting to see God as well?" Her soft eastern European accent comforting, safe and warm. Without waiting for God to enlighten her with regards to her misconception as to His true identity she strode purposefully across the room with steps longer and faster than her tiny frame would have achieved during the twilight years of her life on Earth. Suddenly she lifted her hand and was pinching what she thought was the cheek of a slim child. "Oh, my little bubala, look at you. So skinny, barely flesh and bones. Haven't you been eating properly? When I have finished here, you come with me, and I'll fix you a lovely meal. How about some chicken soup, nice chopped liver and then some delicious ingberlach? You'll love those. I'll soon build you up." Then she began to rummage in her purse as she looked for some sweets to give to the youth.

As tempted as He was to play along and not enlighten the former leader God knew that such a thing would be cruel and would only compound the eventual embarrassment once she was told about her mistake. "But Golda it's…"

Before He could continue, she gave His cheek another friendly tweak and reinforced the gesture with a warm smile and a caring twinkle in her eyes. "No buts my little man. You'll come with me and we can break bread together."

God knew the pain his guest would feel when she found out her mistake so decided to stay in character for just a little longer. "Thank you, Ma'am. That is lovely and kind. I would love to, but I know God does need to talk with you. I was just passing through so if you excuse me I will have to leave. But I promise that I will dine with you later. I am sure it will be delicious." With that he quickly walked to a door at the side of His office, opened it and walked out of the room closing the door behind Him. The room, He'd gone into, was His toilet and washroom but being God he never had to use it. He looked at himself in the bathroom mirror, gave Himself one last pre-pubescent schoolboy smile and then blinked. In the split second that His eyes were closed He had transmogrified from a boy to a more traditional and recognisable form of God; tall, stocky and aged with a short and neatly trimmed grey beard and wearing a loose-fitting white robe. Briefly checking His appearance, He turned and re-opened the door and returned to His room. Once there he was met by Golda.

"Hello Sire. I came as soon as I got your message. I was just chatting with a lovely young man. So polite and handsome."

God could tell that Golda would be happy to chat all day but knew that there was too much to do, and He needed to maintain control of the conversation. "Hello Golda, yes James is a wonderful boy." He had no desire to shatter her kindly illusion so chose a name at random for His young alter ego. "I am sure that you will see him again soon but first I might need your services. I am just waiting for Patrick Henry to get here and then I will elaborate."

Golda had heard the news about the imminent battle and noticed that a lot of her friends had disappeared, presumably to practice their sword skills; she assumed the meeting had something to do with that, but she couldn't understand what it had to do with her. As far as she was concerned, she was far from the perfect warrior build and her skill with any weapon other than a pistol, rifle or machine gun was non-existent. Give her a sword and she'd probably end up taking a swing with it, losing her grip and sending it flying into the nearest person, be they friend or foe. "Of course, Your Highness." She vaguely recognised the name of the absent guest but was struggling to place it. She was tempted to ask who Patrick Henry was but decided not to reveal her ignorance. She felt sure that all would soon be revealed.

Moving to His office chair God pointed to one of the plush leather armchairs placed conveniently in front of His desk. "Please Golda, take a seat. I am sure Patrick won't be too long."

As they waited, they chatted amiably about Heaven, the condition of her beloved State of Israel and the pending war until they were interrupted by a knock on the door and the appearance of the former attorney and politician. Despite the availability of far more modern and comfortable clothing he had deliberately chosen to maintain the style that had been popular when he was alive. His gaunt and sallow face was topped with an uncomfortable and obvious brown curly wig. His clothes wouldn't have been out of place on a Virginian plantation in the 1770's. A tight cravat wrapped around his neck, big red coat covering a pale-yellow waistcoat tightly buttoned up and brown breeches and pristine white stockings. Even God thought that such attire could not be comfortable, but He respected everyone's choices so ignored the formal garb.

"Ah, Patrick, thank you for coming at short notice. Please take a seat." Pointing to the other spare chair. "But you needn't have got dressed up so formally just to see me."

"Formally?" His pompous voice full of confusion and a hint of indignation. "I came here as soon as I got your message. This is how I normally dress."

Ignoring the awkwardness that had suddenly taken up residence in the air, like a belch from someone that had eaten too much garlic, God responded. "I see. Well, you look immaculate Patrick."

"Thank you Sire, one has to keep up standards. People in Heaven these days dress like savages and have no respect. In my day men knew about style and etiquette. If I were in charge I would..."

Before he could continue God raised His hand and smiled indulgently. The interruption made the former Attorney pause. "I am sorry Patrick, but I just realised something. Your genius for oratory is legendary but it needs the right kind of intellectual audience. I believe that your fine and eloquent words would be lost on the massed army. Thank you Mr. Henry, that will be all."

It is hard to mix contradictory emotions and fully convey both in an expression, but the angel managed it with a certain degree of style that most others couldn't copy, even if they spent a thousand years stood practicing in front of a mirror. The dual look of both pained crestfallen disappointment and smug self-satisfaction would have made anybody else look like they were chewing a mouth full of week-old dog turd that had been coated in honey, but Patrick made it all appear so simple. Before turning to leave he gave God a bow full of supercilious bravado and, turning to Golda, he gave her a slight nod decorated with a look in his eyes that was screaming smug victory. On reaching the door he turned to face God giving him another slight bow. "My Lord, I am as always, your humble servant." The words saying one thing but the tone making it sound the complete opposite. And then he was gone.

Once the door was closed God waited a few seconds, let out a long sigh of relief and turned His attention back to his remaining guest. "Thank Go…, I mean Me that he's gone. I should have known better, but I just lived in hope that for once he wouldn't get on my nerves. It was people like him in the Old Testament that wound me up and caused the great flood. They made me invent anger management courses, just so I could go on one." He gave Golda a placatory smile. "Do you know the difference between Patrick Henry and me?"

Golda paused. She could think of a great many differences and knew that listing them would take too long. She also knew that God was not expecting a detailed list as an answer from her. "No mighty one, I don't."

"I don't go around Heaven thinking I am Patrick Henry!" His face rigid and blank, as He said it, leaving her uncertain how to react. The silence was soon broken by loud and bellicose laughter at his own joke. Relieved Golda joined in, unsure as to whether there was a germ of truth in the casual quip.

Like the jokes of all powerful people, it is always hard to gauge when to stop laughing and to adopt a more serious face. With God it was even more difficult as, no matter how corny or old they were, it could be seen as the ultimate faux pas to stop laughing too soon or to continue laughing like a hyena, on gas and air, long after God had regained his serious face. Timing was everything and could be tricky. There would be no punishments dished out but the feeling of having made a fool of themselves was enough to keep people focused. Fortunately, Golda's mix of genuine mirth and wise diplomacy was perfectly timed. A split second after God came to the end of His own laugh so did she.

Then, abruptly, He stood up and gave her a knowing smile. "So, do you think you are up to the task?"

"Task?" She was puzzled as to what exactly was required of her.

"Yes, my dear lady, I would like you to come with Me and give a spontaneous and impromptu spirit raising speech to 120,000 troops. They need to have a righteous fire lit in their hearts and souls so that they can go into battle with courage and strength and ensure that each one of them fights with the prowess of ten demons or twenty followers of Ekeko. A passion that will let them go into battle as angels and come out the other side as heroes."

"Oh. Is that all?" Keeping a look of calm apathy on her face. "So, no pressure then? Alright, lead the way."

Despite who He was, and the location, He gave her what could only be best described as a devilish grin as if the challenge itself was all part of a game which He knew Golda would readily accept. Being not only able to meet all the specifications without having to think about it but also exceeding expectations as well. "Good. I knew you'd like it."

As they walked towards the hall full of angels and saints Golda remained quiet, deep in thought as she tried to come up with a powerful speech that sounded spontaneous and unplanned which, thanks to God's late brief, would almost be that anyway. Usually, like all the best orators, before any such speech was required, she liked to spend long hours that ran late into the night contemplating the objective and allowing the words to flow into her mind. Like a poet she would reach for an image she wanted to create, select a theme and then carefully select the words that had a rhythm and metre which worked best when they were put together. She knew from experience that when the composition was done correctly it could inspire an outnumbered, frightened and demoralised army to fight like gods and beat seemingly insurmountable odds but get it wrong and defeat was more than likely. With time she could have created something that would persuaded a dozen angels to take on all of the enemy forces and end up standing on a mountain of lifeless corpses with little more than blooded swords and only a few minor scratches that stung slightly. However, in this instance, the one critical part of the process was definitely missing. With the time available she could probably come up with a funny rude Hebrew limerick involving a young boy called Hymie and the inability of the Rabbi to grasp his foreskin or even a not very memorable quatrain poem, but a speech to send souls into battle? That was something that she was not sure she could put together in just a few minutes. The more she thought of the task the less she concentrated on the actual speech and the more she got into a wild panic. It wasn't until God sensed her distress, and placed a calming hand on her shoulder, did she calm down and begin to breathe normally again. His touch deliberately intended to take away her fears and reservations. He couldn't put the words into her mind, but He could at least clear it so that her own words could gain access. Sensing what He had done Golda gave him a relieved smile and went back to trying to think of at least a few opening words that would grab her audience's attention. Her mind now more like a calm lake rather than a sea full of angry waves crashing against a fragile boat.

Although God often took long hikes around Heaven, just to take in the beauty of the place and ensure that people were happy, He seldom did it in any form that might resemble His true identity. He usually adopted some human guise that could walk around unnoticed and not encounter a second glance. The flowing white robes, fading beard and blindingly bright halo tended to draw unrequired attention to Himself resulting in Him being mobbed by fans and autograph hunters. Such attention was usually unrequired but tolerable however now it was a total hindrance. Angels had seen Him, many for the first time, and wanted to make some sort of contact. Shaking hands was acceptable but like a superhuman rock star He also attracted people that were beginning to act like teenage fans of a pop idol. They madly ran up to Him and once they were within reach they were left with no idea as to what should be done. Some just stood in-front of him, speechless, others fainted with excitement and one person lost all sense of propriety and rubbed the top of the hair on His head before the inappropriate fan ran off shouting "Nice Heaven, God. Well done!" Once the adrenaline and euphoria had disappeared the offending angel would look upon his actions with dread and eternal shame but, for now, he was high on the excitement of meeting his God. Such rough handling was the last straw for God. He decided that there was only one course of action left open to Him. There was no giant arm gesture or incantation in an ancient tongue, instead he just let His mind make it happen. One second He was looking majestic and all-powerful the next he was invisible and all the fans had suddenly contracted mass amnesia. They were left standing in the middle of the Heavenly street looking at some empty space just in-front of them. Blinking rapidly, they were left with the feeling that they had to do something *really important* if only they could remember what it was. Under the cover of the mental fog God was able to carry on with His journey un-harassed by adoring fans. Golda was so busy thinking about the speech that she didn't even notice the crowds or the sudden disappearance of her companion. To avoid any unexpected collisions with unsuspecting angels, once they had turned a corner, God decided that some visible form would be advisable and opted for the form of tall and slim African Maasai warrior in full tribal dress and spear. His reasoning being that such a fighter would not be out of place in the great hall, hidden amongst all the other various fighters getting ready for battle. Under the new guise He bent down so that He could gently whisper into Golda's ear and warn her of His change of form. The new shape didn't bother her; she acknowledged the words but was so engrossed in her own thoughts that she didn't even look at Him.

"Alright God, whatever You say." Her words there but her mind still elsewhere.

Their rest of the now quiet, but steady, walk was soon interrupted when Dedan joined them on their journey to the hall containing St. Michael and his well trained and clean booted troops. He was dressed in tight fitting khaki fatigues with brown leather straps running diagonally across his chest. They ran behind him and supported four full scabbards containing broadswords. The swords' basket hilted handles visible as they protruded over his shoulders, their intricate bright metal glinting in the Heavenly sunshine. He looked a strange combination of modern and 17th century soldier. In belligerent anticipation of meeting St. Michael Dedan had gone out of his way to put on the dirtiest and most scuffed pair of boots he could find. An action that he knew would rile the supercilious leader. Recognising Golda, he greeted her with a broad smile. "Hello Golda, you are looking good. As you always do."

"Thank you Dedan, what a sweet boy." Coming out of her deep thought, happy that she had finally found the first fine thread of a speech. "But you can save your silver tongue charm. I am far too old to be turned by your flattery."

Putting his hands against his chest he gave her a look of mock hurt and indignation. "Golda, my beautiful angel. You hurt me with such a low appraisal. I see beauty and I appreciate it."

The words made Golda laugh. "I have heard it said many times about you, from many women, and I must agree with it. You are full of shit."

With those words it was Dedan's turn to laugh. "Yes, that has been said to me on numerous occasions and I suppose it is true, but I am sure you wouldn't have me any other way."

Noticing the African warrior, he smiled. "I see that you are leaving it as late as possible to join St. Michael. Very wise, I am doing the same thing myself. I have better things to do than listen to that bombastic and anal-retentive tosser as he prattles on, demoralizing everyone before he gets them to spend an eternity cleaning their footwear." He glanced down at the figure's bare feet "at least that would be one chore you could ignore but I am sure that that prick would find some other pointless and menial task to keep you from getting ready for the battle. Oh, I am sorry, where are my manners? I don't think we have met before. Apart from a few words that Golda and others might use when talking about me they call me Dedan."

"Hello Dedan. I know you by name and reputation. They also use lots of names when they talk about Me, but you can call Me God!"

Realising his possible faux pas he gave Golda a quick glance and saw her unsuppressed smirk confirming that the character was who He claimed to be. "So, God, going to see my good friend, and most competent of leaders, St. Michael I presume?" Mentally cursing himself for failing to recognise his Boss.

God gave him a smile and loud laugh that revealed bright white teeth, accentuated by the adopted dark face. "Relax Dedan, the high esteem you hold for Michael is well known, as is his equally wonderful view of you. I am looking forward to seeing you both fighting shoulder to shoulder and see which one of you 'accidentally' decapitates the other first in the heat of battle. After all accidents do happen."

"Yes." Returning the smile "accidents do indeed happen and in the middle of close quarter fights I can occasionally get clumsy! I'm sure that all his troops would be terribly upset if he was sent back to Heaven early on in the battle. Who can forget the time he took human form and led a battalion of British troops at the Somme in WWI? Not a single survivor. Or how, for some reason I could never quite fathom, he led an Italian army cavalry charge against well-armed Soviet forces in WWII. Drawn sabres against machine guns and mortars, how on Earth did he manage to lose?"

"True, very true, I must admit that he struggles to fully grasp the simple concept that machine guns and modern weapons have an advantage against bare steel so his tactics tend to be one dimensional but, in this instance, he should be in his element. When it comes to old fashioned ways of killing others in battle, he knows his stuff. Just remember that when it comes to fighting demons, he has a 100% track record."

Despite his strong doubts and reservations Dedan decided to keep them to himself. He knew better than to argue with God, He might not have been as omnipotent as Humans thought He was, but God did tend to know exactly what he was on about. "OK, You're the Boss! I will try not to lop of his head in battle, either accidentally or on purpose."

"Thank you Dedan, your faith in his leadership is underwhelming." God knew that Dedan wouldn't kill his own General although he wasn't sure about the other 119,998 strong force that had to put up with the annoying Saint. Also, if He wanted to be totally honest, He found it difficult to like St. Michael and He enjoyed it when Dedan went out of his way to needle him. Michael might have been the leader of all the angelic troops, but he could also be a total pain in the arse.

As they grew closer to the giant drill hall they were met with an ever-increasing noise. A strange cacophony of sounds, a mixture of swishing and metallic clanging with a faint background sound of frantic brushing as soldiers either got in a bit of last-minute practicing or did their best to get their boots clean, spit added to the polish as they imagined that the toe caps were the face of St. Michael. Both exercises were taking their toll on already tired and exhausted muscles and depleted patience. After the last few days of putting up with their leader a wild and frantic blood bath, hacking away at an enemy, would have been a welcome diversion.

As they walked through the imposing doorway, leading into the vast chamber, St. Michael saw them straight away and, on seeing Dedan, his face adopted a look which could only be described as being akin to a rabid bull having its testicles chewed by a hungry ferret. If cartoon steam could have escaped his ears and nostrils it would have done. His clenched teeth might not have been strong enough to bite through steel, but they would have certainly dented it, while the hatred in his eyes wouldn't have been out of place in Hell. His mind a mixture of desires, part of him wanting to maintain his authority, composure and discipline in front of his vast army and the rest of his brain just wishing that he could snatch an axe, that was laid next to a soldier preoccupied with cleaning duties, and lodge it so deep into his nemesis's skull that it wouldn't stop until it was embedded in the ground and there were two halves of Dedan laid on either side of the blood-soaked blade. His imagination toyed with the image and brought him a lot of sadistic, and far from saintly, joy but he managed to maintain his poise and avoid any grasping of weapons; voluntary or otherwise. Stepping down from his raised viewing platform he strode purposefully towards the visitors.

Ignoring Golda and the African tribesman he planted himself directly in front of Dedan, his face mere inches from the angel's. Breathing heavily, like a marathon runner trying to catch their breath the tension in his jaw was lowered, so that he could speak, but the tightening of sinews just moved to his hands as his immaculately manicured fingernails began to dig into his palms.

"What are *you* doing here?" the words accompanied by spittle as he barked out the question. "I am in charge here and you are not needed. We can win this battle without your slovenly indiscipline. You can just go home!"

Despite the unwelcome warm liquid that landed on his face Dedan stood his ground, placed his hands in his pockets as a sign of disinterest and gave the outraged saint a condescending smile. A delicate hint of devilment in his eyes. "Why Hello St. Michael, how lovely to see you again. It's been a while. How was the outer region of Heaven, peaceful enough for you?"

Dedan's calm and mocking voice did nothing to take away the red mist fogging up St. Michael's brain. The lack of antagonism was like petrol on a fire making his fingernails draw blood as they dug deeper into his sweating palms. "Get out of my sight you imbecile, just leave and never come back. I'd rather fight with Satan by my side that with you." Stepping back slightly he quickly looked him up and down. The sneer of disgust obvious to Dedan and his two companions. "Just look at you. Your boots, good God man, how can you expect to go into battle with such dirt on them? It looks like you've never once polished them. And good grief, have you slept in that uniform? I will not have you in my army!"

Dedan paused slightly allowing the silence, and refusal to get angry, to work its way into the General's psyche and annoy him even more. "Boots..." looking up at the ceiling as if he was trying to remember something important. "errr, I think you are absolutely right, I don't recollect ever cleaning them. And as for my uniform you are spot on. Not my best set of pyjamas but still comfortable enough for a quick forty winks. However, with regards to it being your army, I think you might be mistaken."

The indolence and relaxed lack of respect made the metaphorical rage barometer in the Saint's head begin to rattle as its inner liquid boiled. Such a blatant challenge to his authority could not be ignored. "And who's army is it? YOURS?" His voice rising two octaves as if his underwear had suddenly, and inexplicably, spontaneously shrunk.

Despite the calm and impassive face that He'd maintained throughout the verbal exchange God had enjoyed it and struggled to avoid laughing at his pompous and self-important General. Breaking His self-imposed silence, He spoke "No, it's not Dedan's it is Mine."

The Saint's fiery gaze was dragged away from Dedan as he turned to look at the spear wielding warrior. "And who the hell are you, the comedian's sidekick?" He squeaked as his voice rose even higher. Running the risk of becoming audible only to dogs.

"I don't think I am. I am God so I think that outranks you."

Suddenly, on hearing those words the burning rage, that seemed to be consuming St. Michael, disappeared and was replaced by an icy feeling as if he had slipped naked off an ice shelf into the arctic ocean. The look of terror evident on his face. He looked first at Dedan and then at Golda and they both nodded silently. The simple gestures, and slight smirks, confirming the information that God had just given him. With sinking heart, he began to struggle to find the right words with which to deliver his apology. If it had been anyone else, he would have tried to bluff his way out of the situation. Adopt a false joking attitude and claim that he had seen through the disguise all along but with God he knew that any such attempt to hide his mistake would be pointless and simply compound his already, quite possibly, dire situation. After what felt like an eternity, he looked God in the face. There was no expression to give him any clue as to what He was thinking so Michael lowered his head to look intently at his feet, as if one of them had disappeared and he had only just noticed and needed to search for it. "I am so very sorry Sire." He swallowed deeply and looked up again to face God. "I was overtaken by the..." He paused and pondered how to end the sentence, but nothing seemed to be obvious. He could have been totally honest and just told God how he simply hated Dedan and thought that he was a 'slang name for a certain part of a woman's body' but he doubted that would help his case. "... I was just overtaken by the surprise of seeing

Dedan. His just turning up and not being ready for training, I found it disrespectful and unprofessional."

Up until that point God had been enjoying the uncomfortable reaction that he had induced in his senior commander, but the end of the sentence had left him feeling slightly cross. "Yes, disrespectful and unprofessional. I can see how that sort of thing would make someone angry. I think that after the battle you and I need to have a very long talk!"

"Yes Sire," he mumbled as he returned to the metaphorical missing foot search. "I am sorry Sire!"

"Oh well. Changing the mood a little, I have brought Golda here so that she can address the troops and put them in the right spirit to go into battle and win. After all this is the most important fight that we've had in centuries." Giving Golda a broad smile he gestured towards the raised platform and a lectern that He'd just made appear out of thin air. "After you Ms Meir. If you would be so kind as to light fires in the souls of *my* troops."

28 – Talking the Talk

Relieved to have been given the order to stand at ease the vast assortment of angels and saints gladly stopped their polishing of footwear, and repetitious military manoeuvres, as they all positioned themselves so that they were casually stood facing the diminutive former Israeli leader. Despite her size the raised platform was high enough and the lectern was sufficiently low so that she could be seen over it; with even those stood at the back able to see her. Although many had no idea who she was, irrespective of race, gender, religion or historical period they were from, the entire crowd respectfully fell silent. Somehow her tiny figure, slightly stooped posture, grey hair and cragged, but maternal smiling face, made them all think of their own mothers, or grandmothers. If any of them had dared to not pay her full attention, or had the temerity of talking over her, they would have received a swift elbow in their ribs from one or more of their neighbours reminding them to behave. Whether respect was given just because she was an elder, or because there was a simple air about her that demanded it, nobody was sure which, but there was a sense of awe that was rare even in Heaven.

So that she could settle the fear and turmoil in her stomach Golda took her time to look at the massed assembly of warriors. Like a Radar picking up a giant school of fish they all seemed to be just one giant, multi-headed creature with bodies lost in one cleaned booted mass of military uniforms and protruding weaponry. Occasionally she would pause and be able to focus on a particular face and each one she saw had the same expression of rapt expectations. Once she'd finished her perfunctory inspection of her audience she turned, faced God and raised an eyebrow that was a black contrast to her grey hair "No pressure?"

God returned the question with a calm and reassuring smile accompanied by a conspiratorial wink "No, no pressure at all Golda!"

There were many things in her past that should have made her treat such a situation as second nature and allowed her to feel confident. She had acquired the nickname of the Iron Lady long before any British Prime Minister. She had been a teacher, but her class sizes had been far smaller than this. Plus, in her older years, she had been a moral, military and diplomatic focal point for a whole nation during the Six Day and the Yom Kippur Wars but, despite that, all of her experiences in life were nothing compared to this. Before she had helped to save a still young and unsteady nation, now she was expected to help inspire an army that would save Heaven. No pressure indeed! Slowly, and hesitantly at first, she began to speak. Her gentle voice quiet but, thanks to a little bit of divine intervention provided by the pseudo Maasai tribesman, the acoustics were perfect. Each word reached every ear and could be understood irrespective of whether they would have normally spoke English or not. One of the benefit of everyone being in Heaven, and Hell for that matter, speaking in tongues, a sort of universal interpretation service, ensured nothing was lost in translation. As she spoke her words seemed to enter heads, envelope their brains and then make their gentle way into the body and engulf hearts. Entranced they followed her as she made them proud of all they were, what they were fighting for and what they would achieve by victory. Passion was delivered and gladly received, words to send people to war treated as if they were secret passions from one eager lover to another. Finally, silence filled the training ground as her rousing speech came to its climax and left everyone in the vast hall wanting a cigarette while they bathed in the emotional afterglow. Giving such oral satisfaction to well over 100,000 people, all at the same time, was not an easy task but she'd managed to do it without even losing her breath or needing to clear her throat.

Seeing the relaxed stance of his troop St. Michael stepped forwards coughed authoritatively and took a deep breath in preparation to speak. Even though it would soon be time for them to march out of the hall, and make their way to the transportation chambers, he felt that there was an opportunity to get a little more practice or polishing done. However, despite his enthusiasm, his order to carry on was stopped before it could escape his mouth. God placed a hand gently on his shoulder and when the Saint turned to face Him, the African tribesman gave him a slight nod to indicate that he should keep silent and not break the gentle magic spell that had been created.

"Can I have a quiet word?" As St. Michael was not going to refuse to talk to God the question was rhetorical, but He still asked it. Manners were important and even more so for the supreme Deity.

Moving back slightly God began to quietly talk to the Saint. Even though the gathered crowd couldn't make out what He was saying Michael's body language was screaming in agony. His arms were at first placed behind his back but eventually they began to fidget, tense up and finally become a shrugged shouldered mess. It was obvious that the new instructions, from God, were not going down well. St. Michael attempted to speak but was hushed by God's raised forefinger encouraging him to remain silent, listen to what he was being told and to accept it. As floor shows went it was a different form of entertainment to Golda's rousing words but, for comedic value, it was a mix of gold, which had been layered with platinum and encrusted with diamonds. After the arduous dual ordeals of his relentless version of army routine and muscle aching training, the discomfiture of their leader was justice for all he had inflicted. Then, suddenly, the conversation came to an end. St. Michael smartly clicked his heels together, came to attention and gave God a crisp and professional salute. God returned the gesture with a casual smile which made the Saints frustration even more apparent. He expected salutes to be returned no matter who they were given to and not receiving one from God was unforgivable. Turning he marched back towards his troops and came to a halt next to Dedan.

"A'right Mick?" Dedan's voice full of glee at the Saints stern expression. "Good news?"

Closing his eyes St. Michael sighed heavily, determined to ignore the disrespectful nickname, the tone of voice and the sarcastic question. "Not really good news" in his mind he thought he was sounding calm but to Golda and Dedan he sounded as shrill as a kettle which was just beginning to boil. "It would appear that, despite my wise advice, God has instructed me to dismiss 20,000 troops. They will be surplus to requirements on Earth!" He looked at Dedan with a wounded expression. "What am I to do? I have a full army and don't have time to just go around and deselect so many people."

"Simple. Just choose a random group. You are the chief and God has given the order. They will accept it, I'm sure." Dedan deliberately spoke in a restrained voice. Despite all the animosity, he had some sympathy for the Saint and wouldn't have liked to be in his shoes, even if they were much cleaner than his.

"Yes, yes, you are right. I know. Get rid of all the women. So Simple."

"Excuse me?" Golda had been emotionally drained and quiet since she had finished her speech, but the Saint's idea made her mind snap back to the present. "And I thought Dedan was a sexist pig. He might see women as sex objects but at least he has respect and isn't a misogynist. In his way he is a gentleman. You should be ashamed of yourself."

Despite the attitudes prevalent in the time period that he had lived in as a human, it had to be granted that Golda's summary of Dedan was accurate. He saw women as his equals, and in many cases his betters, and knew that the presence of balls didn't make someone a better warrior. In fact, he knew that they were often a liability in close quarter hand to hand combat. A carefully placed knee or foot could leave even the strongest of men stunned for enough time to allow the opponent to place a dagger in the chest, neck or head. "Thank you, Golda, none taken!" The words escorted by a smile. "And as for sex objects you are right. I want sex and women usually object."

St. Michael was bewildered by the concept of political correctness. To him women were delicate and needed protecting by strong men, there might have been a few female soldier saints but, on the whole, their purposes in Heaven was to look beautiful and make the place prettier simply by their presence. An ideology that would have got him slapped frequently on Earth but in Heaven such thoughts were tolerated with pitying looks or just ignored. But either way he was the oldest of old fashioned and was not going to change his views. "What? Oh, the women thing." Using the word 'thing' as if it were a rather sticky and messy social disease. "Alright, what do you suggest?"

Sensing that Golda's suggestion, as to what she could tell the Saint to do, might not be diplomatic, or even physically possible, Dedan decided he had best step in before the diminutive female Jewish leader put the large and well armoured officer into hospital before the war had even started. "Michael, let me make a humble suggestion. The more experienced and skilled troops are the ones that have been here for a while, certainly before war became industrialised, mechanical and remote. Why don't you dismiss the more modern troops? To them swords, spears and arrows are not their natural weapons of choice so let them go. You can always use them another time. Start with those that entered Heaven post 1939, that should do it."

St. Michael paused and nodded his head wisely. "I suppose that will work just as well."

Before Golda could continue the debate Dedan gently got hold of her arm and swung her around so that she was facing God, who was still stood where He had been when He'd given His Field Marshal the new instructions. "Come of Golda, let's leave the boy to play with his toys. We can have a chat with God. I am sure that will be far more interesting and enlightening."

Golda gave the back of St Michael's head one last hard stare before turning away and walking by the side of Dedan. On reaching God they all stood quietly, as if by mutual consent, and watched St. Michael begin the simple process of filtering out surplus soldiers. Even though the trio were too far away to hear what was being said they could guess what was happening from his arm movements and the bewildered and confused looks on the faces of his troops. Seeing the problem, that his superior was having Matt, his less that adoring batman, decided to provide some far from divine intervention. Moving to the side of the saint the distant audience saw him raise his arms and listened as he began to talk to the crowd. After his brief initial outline of requirements, the entire army stuck up their arms, expectant smiles on their faces. He then gestured for them all to lower their arms and he began to speak again. This time, whatever he said caused the crowd to release a groan that, despite the distance, was audible to the three of them. Then Matt continued his talk with broad sweeping swings of his arms. There was a slight pause and then a smaller number of people quickly raised their arms. Where visible Dedan, Golda and God could see that they had smiles on their faces and the rest of the army had less joyous expressions. After one last unheard instruction those that had raised their hands began to leave the crowd and move to the far side of the hall so that they were separate from the rest of the gathered army. Several figures began to move around them. Once they had finished, they spoke to Matt who in turn reported to St. Michael. He nodded, and then issued a further instruction that was passed down the line. Eventually after a brief shuffling of reluctant looking troops, from the smaller gathering to the larger one, Matt turned to the Saint, saluted smartly, turned in full military fashion and then once he'd marched a few steps and was out of the saint's line of sight, began to walk in a more casual and civilian way. His intention was to walk past the trio of bemused witnesses and stand near the main entrance, but his stroll was stopped by Dedan whose curiosity was piqued by what he had just seen. "Excuse me. Can I ask you a few questions?"

After being spoken to, for so long, in an abrupt and arrogant manner by a demanding Saint, Matt was taken aback by being addressed in a polite and civil way. Stopping he gave the three expectant figures a surprised look. "Sure, no problem. What's up?"

"Well, what was all that about? We could see but couldn't hear. It looked fascinating though."

"Oh, that is simple I saw that Major Mess It Up over there was…"

"Excuse me," Dedan interrupted with a look of mock shock "respect the rank not the person."

"Yes sir, sorry sir. I mean Field Marshal Mess It Up over there."

"That's better." Nodding in approval at the identification of the correct military rank. The comment causing God to give Dedan an accusatory stare, but he remained silent.

"Anyway, he was having difficulty getting his message across and to be honest I got the impression that he didn't want to obey the order. Either way the troops were confused so I thought it would be quicker, and easier, if I stepped in and offered to help."

"And? All the raising of hands was…?" It was Golda's turn to speak, her voice full of puzzlement.

"That was simple, I knew that he needed to lose a few thousand troops for some reason so I thought I'd try a quick and simple question that might make the selection process quicker."

"And that was?" Golda was fascinated by the whole process.

"I just asked them all if any of them didn't want to go into battle with St. Michael as the leader."

"But everyone put up their hands." Although Dedan's statement was directed at Matt the raised eyebrow, and look of smug satisfaction, was for the benefit of the fake African tribesman stood next to him.

"Yes, I suppose you could say that my idea failed abysmally but did annoy Michael, so it wasn't all bad. Next, I decided to run with the original instructions but worded it so that the troops could understand. All those that had entered Heaven after the start of the Second World War were identified, separated and then numbers counted. There were slightly too many escaping their active service, so they were returned to the larger contingent. And Bob's yer uncle. Several thousand happier troops."

"Right, thank you err…"

"Matt, Sir. I'm St. Michael's batman."

"Oh, I am sorry Matt. Thank you for all you did. Carry on." Dedan was tempted to give the soldier a salute but resisted the urge in case it was a steep and slippery path and he ended up being a military type like the Saint.

Dedan looked at God and was about to speak but the bemused Deity beat him to it. "Don't say a word Dedan. Not one single word! St. Michael to the left of me, Satan to the right and I am stuck in the middle with you. I have the feeling that something isn't right!"

29 – So Many Batters, So Few Balls

Satan's method of motivating his troops was more psychological and required far less subtlety than God. They were demons and their default emotions were judgemental anger, hatred and rage. If they had been alive, on Earth, they would have made perfect born-again Christians. Any words spoken, in an attempt to make them go into battle and be determined to mutilate the enemy, would have been wasted. A single instruction had been issued but there were doubts in Ravaillac's mind that it would be followed. The simple order 'Do not attack the angels' went against the Demon's instincts. He simply hoped that the desire to avoid some extreme punishment chamber would be enough to ensure that weapons were kept pointed at Ekeko's army. There might be some collateral damage, as such things happened in the heat of battle, but he didn't want any *accidents* to be *too* obvious or prevalent.

Skills honed, weapons ready and the anger level at maximum he marshalled them and began the slow process of marching, or as close to marching as demons could manage, to the dimensional portal. 120,000 demons of various colours, shapes and sizes forced to travel through narrow winding dark passages was not the simplest of exercises. All the pent-up rage made it an uncomfortable process, especially for the smaller creatures. Demons were pushed and shoved against the hard and jagged walls or compacted between burly and muscular compatriots. Sympathy, consideration, or even compassion, were not concepts easily understood in Hell. It was like a London tube station during rush hour, only without the odours of sweat, curry or take-out coffee. The illogical desire to get to the front of the line did nothing to ease the smooth flow of soldiers. The combined pushing and shoving just accelerated the disorganised flow so it was more akin to a living form of volcanic pyroclastic flow being forced through a sulphurous lava tube. Despite the various routes chosen the effects were similar in each tunnel, a demonic bottleneck. This was exacerbated as the different paths got closer to the portal and began to converge. Even when it came to being positioned in a line, where it was it wasn't important who got there first, precedence was considered a matter of pride. Eventually all the demonic tributaries merged into one far wider estuary of evil. But without instructions, telling them to do so, the front ranks suddenly stopped, forcing those behind them to be squashed by both those at the front of them and those behind.

Right at the back Satan was casually walking behind his troops, unheeding their petty actions. His mind preoccupied in its own dark world full of violent images of him mutilating the South American god and then getting the opportunity to turn his sword on God before anyone else could jump to His defence. Blind to the sudden cessation of movement ahead of him he walked into the back of an aggravated Crab Demon. The creature was not the most ideally built for using a sword or spear but the hard exoskeleton, and pincer hands, made it ideal for claw to hand combat. It turned ready to swipe whoever had run into him but, on seeing who it was, he refrained from striking out at Satan. His brain wasn't that large, but he knew enough to know that it wouldn't have been a wise career move. Despite that the look that Satan was giving him was enough to make him think that his punishment might involve being dressed and served with a salad and seafood sauce. Having a blocked passage was not fun for anyone but when it was caused by so many heavily armed troops it was even worse for Satan. He could see no cause or cure so he decided to get through as best he could. He briefly considered his options then changed his form into a large bright red lizard complete with fiery eyes, long sweeping tail and a long-forked tongue that flicked out to taste the air. An automatic action for a reptile in its natural habitat but an act that Satan instantly regretted. The atmosphere in Hell was not one where tasting it was something to be savoured. No nature documentary had ever witnessed a lizard gagging from having encountered a noxious taste but Satan, in his adopted form, was proof that they could retch. Clawed hands made the futile attempt to wipe the taste from his tongue a futile gesture. Realising that he was wasting his time, he decided to focus on his main objective. With a cumbersome waddle associated with creatures that shared his adopted form he ran to the side wall of the tunnel and, with sharp claws, climbed it and rose up to the ceiling. Despite being upside down he managed to maintain his grip and run faster than any Earthly version ever could. Twisting and swerving he manoeuvred over the uneven sulphur coated surface, avoiding the jagged stalactites his eyes were concentrating on where he was going and was oblivious to the demonic mass of hate, rage and anger positioned just below him. If he'd had time, and the inclination, he would have defecated on a few of them as he ran but he didn't have time for such fun. Despite running fast, the length of tunnel, taken up by compacted demons, was considerable and it took him a while to get to the front of the line and see the cause of the obstruction. Passing the front section of devils, he released his grip on the roof and as he fell, twisting his body so that he could land feet first and change back into the more recognisable form of Satan. Landing crouched down, as if there was one last vestige of the lizard still within him, he quickly stood upright. His sudden appearance making those that saw him instinctively tense up from fear and a latent expectation of some form of painful punishment. Resisting his initial, and instinctive, urge to start shouting and releasing fire bolts he paused and turned slightly to take see the cause of the delay. Carsten!

Having been killed during a mission to Earth Carsten was a demon who had rematerialized back in Hell and, thanks to the haphazard nature of demonic returns after being killed, he'd been unfortunate enough to be bent forward when he died. This position had been maintained on arrival in Hell but, thanks to the proximity of a nearby wall he'd managed to have his front half stuck into solid stone with his rear end left protruding like a fleshy, and extremely vulnerable, bicycle stand. With demon nature such that any excuse for sadistic and violent fun would be grasped with both hands the posterior was quickly relieved of pants and exposed buttocks were enjoyed in many ways that the orifice wasn't originally designed for. Eventually the pleasure of such debasement became routine and tiresome to the perpetrators so a different way of dealing with them quickly evolved. As often happens with a joke it turned into a superstition and then it became a cast iron tradition where the breaking of it would bring at best bad luck and at worst utter doom. This was the case for Carsten's rear end. It was now seen as bad luck if anyone were to use the dimensional portal and not hit the tender parts of flesh with a cricket bat that had been placed by his legs. Each demon was therefore lining up waiting for their turn so that they could be handed the piece of sports equipment and deliver the swing and hit the arse 'for six'. Thanks to the sheer numbers of sticklers for tradition Carsten was in for a rough time and the process of getting all the demons to Bolivia would take several months rather than hours. With such a logistical nightmare Satan decided to take an executive decision that was uncharacteristically lenient. He had no objections to any sadistic actions, and he had no sympathy for Carsten's position, either physically or for the receiving of pain, but in this instance the mission had to come first.

"Stop it and stop it now!" His voice deep, loud and sinister. On hearing the words everyone fell silent while the next batter stopped in mid swing. Guilty glances were exchanged in an attempt to work out what was wrong and if any blame could be apportioned elsewhere. Seeing nothing evident they returned their gaze to their evil master. "Just leave Carsten's backside alone. Just get to the portal and down to Earth. NOW!" The tall and muscular green Krand Demon that was holding the bat in a mid-air looked from bat to buttocks and back again, disappointment written all over his face. He had psyched himself up for the hit and was now losing one last bit of fun before going to South America. He looked at Satan, the request unspoken but there in his eyes.

"All right." bellowed Satan. "Go on then. But then I want you to leave the cricket bat next to him and everyone needs to get down to Earth. Those that are not killed in battle, and return via the portal, will be allowed to use the bat. And they can take their time doing it."

With the dispensation the demon delivered a blow which made a sound that only buttocks being hit by a wooden object can make. More than a simple slap but not as hard as a cracking sound. Bare flesh was left red and bruised with the tenderness releasing heat that was several degrees hotter than the rest of the body. If the cricket bat hadn't been specially reinforced it would have surrendered on impact and shattered but, thanks to its extra strength, it survived to be used again. Leaning the unusual weapon against the wall next to Carsten's exposed body the demon gave Satan a respectful nod of gratitude and proceeded into the dimensional portal room, quickly followed by the rest of the troops, carefully moving around Satan so that they didn't accidentally jostle him. With forward movement renewed the crowd's progress was slow but steady and groups of demons were able to go through the portal and rematerialized on the Bolivian plane. Feet wet thanks to the combination of annual floods, violent liquid nausea and bowel releases, caused by the transportation process from Hell. Eventually the numbers of demons on earth began to increase and they were forced to spread out, their appearance from those in Hell changed so that they resembled humans, or at least what could be loosely called human. Despite some having claws for hands or unusually sharp teeth they had one head each, the right number of limbs and, in the right light, they could easily take up residence in some of the more bizarre areas of New York or maybe Louisiana; although that 'right light' might have to be very dim and subdued. Then, as the sun began to rise over the edge of the surrounding mountains in the distance, the entire army was in position with Satan being the last resident of Hell to appear on the field of battle. He looked along his waiting troops and nodded approvingly. If any human had happened to have been there, they would have seen a nightmare sight of tens of thousands of oddly shaped people in various costumes and brandishing a wide selection of old-fashioned weapons from various periods in history. They would probably have thought it was the cast of some medium budget movie that had skimped on coherent and consistent characters and run out of money when it came to buying cameras or any other equipment used in the making of a would-be blockbuster. However, despite the miss matched appearances, Satan liked what he saw; demons were ready, willing and able to fight. God help the enemy, he thought, but then thought again and doubted that even God would be of any assistance to Ekeko. It would be one minor South American god versus a lot of evil demons and just as many less evil angels with nothing more in common but a shared desire for destruction. A commonality of purpose that was all too often shared on a battlefield but had never before been aimed at a mutual enemy.

30 - Better Without Doubt

Despite the choice of enforced leader, the angelic army were still glowing from Golda Meir's motivational speech so their casual march to the dimensional portal, that would take them all down to Earth, was a happy and congenial affair. Discipline was not so strict that they were not allowed to talk. Irrespective of race, creed, colour or original language, soldiers conversed with those that were around them. Jokes were made at the expense of any enemy that was unfortunate enough to get in-front of their deadly weaponry and spirits were definitely high. Not far behind them God was nonchalantly strolling as he chatted amiably with Dedan and Golda, who was tagging along so that she could see them off. Small talk was not something God particularly enjoyed, after all the weather in Heaven was not something that people could ever complain about, and an angel's day tended to be good. However, His insights into the enemy god were useful and freely gave Dedan a few ideas for tactics if St. Michael should happen to accidentally fall, or be tripped, in battle. As far as the troops were concerned the African warrior was seen as just another soldier that turned up late for practice drill. If they'd have known the soldier's true identity, they would have been more conscious of their language and avoided any insults that they were making about their Field Marshal.

Of the entire procession the only one who wasn't in a happy mood was St. Michael. Like a petulant child, who had just been told off by a teacher, he was walking at the back, well away from everyone else. Instead of his usual regimental gait, that he maintained even when he went for a solitary stroll or even when he walked to the toilet, he was shuffling along. If there had been pockets in his suit of armour his hands would have been slovenly stuck in them, instead he held his baton of office in one hand which he absent-mindedly tapped it in the palm of the other. Impervious to all around him he was deep in thought; and what thoughts he was having. Even the most arrogant, conceited or self-confident of people occasionally have doubts and uncertainties. The small insect of self-doubt that sometimes gets into a brain and starts to feast on the confidence that is there. But such an emotion was new to St. Michael. Previously he had gone through life, and his subsequent time in Heaven, with 100% cast iron conviction that he was right and anyone else that disagreed or contradicted him must be wrong or simply misinformed. Not even the occasional face to face arguments and embarrassingly public shouting matches with Dedan had managed to change the view of himself and his moral invulnerability, but now that cast iron was starting to rust. Strange questions, aimed at himself, were beginning to take shape in his mind and were sinking like a heavy stone in fresh blancmange. They didn't cause ripples but left holes in what had previously been a perfectly smooth surface. What if he was mistaken? What if he wasn't perfect military leader? Could his tactics be wrong? Were clean shoes really an important factor for winning battles? Could he really be unpopular with his troops? These thoughts were not the best things to have just before a critical battle, especially if the person having them was in charge of tens of thousands of lives and the future of the Human race. Despite everything that was wrong with his personality he wasn't an inept tactician or strategist, he just had no personal skills that allowed him to be an inspirational, respected or loved leader, so any uncertainty in the heat of battle could prove to be disastrous. Hesitation or pauses, when giving instructions, might steal defeat from the jaws of victory. Yet such unhelpful thoughts persisted, and he didn't know how to deal with them. Then it came to him, there it was - the solutions. So simple and obvious and he was amazed that he hadn't thought of them sooner. The answers to all his inner unspoken questions answered in the right order were - Not Likely, Not Possible, Simply Impossible, Definitely Yes and Stupid Question. And with that the dark thoughts were gone like a handful of dust thrown up into the air during a strong gale. Free to be forgotten about as they blew into someone else's eyes, with that normal service resumed in the rigid brain of St. Michael with the picture now in ultra-high definition. He was back and confidence was returned, just as strong and unflinching as before. All the things he had seen and heard filed and locked away in a filing cabinet, in a long-lost room in his mind and promptly forgotten about. Perhaps it had all been someone's idea of a joke, which he just didn't get, or a breakdown in communication. Either way he would maintain discipline his own way. With the new, happier thought, filling his mind he regained his posture and picked up his pace.

Overtaking God, Golda and Dedan, he caught up with the stragglers in his army and began to bark orders at them ensuring that they picked up their feet, began marching smartly and stopped talking in the ranks. Despite the sudden and unexpected return to over-the-top discipline the soldiers still maintained their enthusiasm and good spirits. Golda's words had been so strong that not even St. Michael, in full bluster mode, could destroy that.

Thanks to there being far more dimensional portals in Heaven, compared to Hell, there were fewer bottlenecks with the transformational process down to Earth. The army split off and lined up patiently as they waited for their turn to be sent to the battlefield. As the spaces before them became empty they simply moved forwards and filled them, ensuring a smoother transition than could ever be anticipated in Hell. Gradually the entire army was gone, quickly followed by the Field Marshal with his re-found, but still misplaced confidence. Leaving just Dedan and God to be the last to head for Bolivia. Once they had disappeared that left only the elderly former Israeli leader to return to her home, contemplating the battle that would soon be raging and wishing that she could have been there. Even if she couldn't take part, she would have appreciated the opportunity to witness it. A war that will probably be quicker than her own six day one but far more spectacular. Such was life, or the afterlife, war was not a spectator sport, and she wasn't on the guest list. Maybe, she mused, the young boy she'd met earlier, could be found and she could chat with him? She still had plenty of treats in her handbag and, after all, what young child didn't like sweets!

31 – The Powder Keg and a Box of Matches

The steady arrival of well-armed angels suddenly appearing amongst the demons didn't have the effect that it would normally have had under any other circumstances. A handful of demons instinctively reached for their swords but quickly remembered their primary instructions and, just as promptly, sheaved them again without any injuries occurring and a civil war starting in the ranks even before the true enemy could arrive. Soon the balance of power was equalised as the numbers of angels increased and tried to find area that were separate from the demons. Not always easy as the newly enforced *friends* had scattered themselves across the northern end of the plain and hadn't left much space for God's army to be an independent entity. They could have stood in-front of the demons, but they suspected that such a tactic would be suicidal as they would have had a foe behind and another facing them. And, even if the demons didn't misaim and hit them, they could easily just rest while Ekeko's troops and the angels annihilated each other leaving the demons as victors by default. Seeing a small gap in the left flank the higher-ranking angels began to direct their forces towards it. The swelling number of soldiers soon forced the demons to make way and allow them space. However, despite the demonic presence, St. Michael's arrival caused more consternation amongst the angels. The demons, on the other hand, had nothing but bemusement and contemptuous laughter for the military legend. His armour was woefully inappropriate and unsuitable for the terrain that the battle would be fought on. The consistent 6" of water that covered the flat plain made his free and easy movement difficult and the weight also caused him to sink a further 2" into the softened salt encrusted ground. The necessary energy required for moving him, and his metal clothing was excessive, and the leg motion, with knees having to be raised high, enhanced the appearance of a cheap 1950's 'B' movie robot. There was also an extra discomfort that he hadn't accounted for although if forewarned would certainly have reconsidered his choice of battle wear. Although the transference process for the angels, from Heaven to Earth, was a smooth and totally pleasurable experience the physical side effect that the demons suffered had been many-fold and quite a few were quite messy, sticky and smelly. The resultant substances forcibly evacuated from every orifice either floated, sank or mixed into the temporary lake making the now multi-coloured liquid currently filling the saint's, leather lined shiny metal, sabaton shoes to fill up and surround his feet with a slightly lumpy soup. It was edible but only if you wanted it to be your last meal before a painful death from toxic poisoning. Lumps of material with the appearance and texture of tomato skins and diced carrots began to stick to his skin and wedge between his toes. Plus, out of sight and not noticed, his ankles were being stained an orangey brown colour. The type of shade that would indicate that a normal human was suffering from exposure to too much radiation, or they had used far too much fake tan. Feeling the detritus swimming around his feet, and making his movement even more difficult, he swore under his breath. The words, if they had been audible to others, were trapped inside his heavy helmet. The lowered visor making the sound bounce around his ears like a fading echoed expletive. The k – k – k – k – k ending of the final word gently disappearing into silent oblivion. His attempts to turn and see through the thin and narrow slot was like viewing the world through a small letter box.

Finally, God and Dedan, the last contingent of the holy army, arrived. The African warrior form didn't solicit any extra animosity filled glances from the demons. To them it was just another angel carrying a spear, but Satan immediately recognised his former master and erstwhile friend. No disguise could ever hide God's divine radiance from him. He had also met Dedan before, and he recognised the perpetual thorn in his side. Satan had plans for him, these involved capture and a long and slow tortuous death; a dark reward and heavy reminder of the price of foiling Hell's numerous expansion plans, but today would not be the day for such revenge. There might be an accidental blow from a sword, but Satan had more important targets to focus on. He might not be able to destroy God, but he could destroy a god.

Satan's choice of human form was less sophisticated than God's. He had no desire to blend in so that he would look just like any other soldier in the field of battle. The tall and muscular body was enveloped in tight fitting burgundy red battle fatigues highlighting his toned frame. Wrapped around his middle was a simple sword scabbard with the ornate filigree handle guard glinting in the dawn sunlight. On his feet were black leather riding boots, high enough to prevent the industrial slurry, that the nauseous demons had created, from making contact with his flesh. His whole appearance would have made him stand out in any battlefield but, proudly standing there, he left little doubt as to who he was. Even his absent horns wouldn't have made him stand out more. Stepping forward he approached God with hand firmly holding the handle of his sword. Getting closer he saw that Dedan had spotted him and had tensed up in expectation of some sort of pre-emptive strike on his leader. Dedan's hand gripped tightly on his sword but refrained from adopting an offensive or even defensive posture. Satan saw the almost imperceptible movement and recognised the distrust in the angel's eyes but ignored it. Thanks to thousands of years of manipulating humans he knew exactly how to react so that things wouldn't escalate but, in the process, still feel uncomfortable for Dedan. He simply gave the angel a slight smile and a gallant nod of his head.

"Dedan, we meet again. You can relax, you and your *warrior* friend might be my eternal enemies but today we have to join forces and fight shoulder to shoulder, rather than face to face. I am sure that at some point in the future we can meet under different circumstances. In fact, Dedan, I intend to make sure that you experience your own form of Hell. But that is not today."

"You are welcome to give it your best shot; I am used to your failures and look forward to seeing more." Slightly loosening his grip on his sword but still ready to swing it into action if required.

The slight was heard but didn't get a reaction. Instead, Satan continued heading towards God. "Hello, what an interesting choice of appearance but if my geography is correct the warrior is on the wrong continent."

"Hello Satan. Unlike you I decided not to stand out. I might be a little incongruous, but in an army of so many who would give me a second glance? And what enemy would decide to make me a special target to aim at? Nice choice of red uniform by the way very subtle and inconspicuous." God's voice was booming but with no trace of an African accent that a true Maasai tribesman would have had.

"Let them come. I will fight and they will die, I do not need to hide, or blend in, like some coward. Besides, I am sure that my sword can do more damage than your pathetic little toothpick of a spear." A contempt filling his face as he surveyed his former God.

"Perhaps but one single sword, or spear, doesn't win a battle. After so many wars I'd have thought you'd have learnt that simple but valuable lesson. But perhaps it is beneficial to me if you never learn."

Taking a deep breath Satan struggled not to change the parameters of the conflict and turn on the angels. A bloody and violent war with them would have been a pleasure and, in his mind, a great form of emotional catharsis. "Someday, and I hope that it will be soon, I will get a chance to show you all that I have learnt."

"Maybe Satan, maybe. But that time is not now. If you will excuse Me, I have to get into position and be ready for a battle. I am sure that I will see you after the war is over."

"Oh, you can count on it God." With that Satan abruptly turned and strode purposefully back towards his own forces. As he arrived his troops fearfully parted to allow him to go past and get to his rightful position at the rear of his army. He might look an easy target, but his vantage point was far enough away from the front line to afford him a great deal of protection.

God, on the other hand, had no desire to usurp His appointed leader's authority or position. As far as the vast majority of Heaven's troops were concerned, He was just another soldier taking his place in the front ranks of the awaiting army. A brother in arms willing to fight, and possibly die, for a just cause. Unspeaking, but giving out nods of recognition to several soldiers, Dedan took his position next to God, his sword drawn and ready for the arrival of the as yet absent enemy.

32 – Berserkers

What Dedan saw next was not what he expected and left him momentarily confused. Out of nowhere, as if the air itself was coalescing to create solid shapes, there appeared first a single man, or at least it had the bearded face of a man, but anyone could easily have been forgiven for thinking the rest of his body was that of a rather dirty and unkempt bear. He was the same size and shape as one and the matted fur that covered his body was the same colour as a brown bear that had decided to give up on basic hygiene. Apart from the facial variances the only other things that differentiated him from any ursine creature was the dome shaped metal helmet on his head, a giant axe, with a plain curved blade in one hand, and, in the other, a round wooden shield decorated with a red and black serpent. On fully materialising he raised both his arms in triumph releasing a loud "Aaaaargh!"

Not expecting anything like that to appear, and unsure if the cry was one of satisfaction or of threat, the combined armies of good and bad readied their weapons in anticipation. Although it was unlikely that a single warrior could have caused that much damage, unless it was to nostrils, in which case his stench could have hospitalised a few of the more sensitive angels.

Behind the surprise guest more shapes began to join him, as if out of nowhere. They were of a similar shape and size to the first warrior with the only variations being the designs on the shields and the choice of weapons. Many had axes, others spears while the rest had swords. Finally, once the initial influx of Vikings had stopped, there appeared one last form. This time the fur cloak was cleaner and instead of a long beard there was a beautiful female face which didn't need a shave and, perched on her head there was a gold crown resting on long blue streaked black hair. Moving to the front of her awaiting troops Sonja scanned the casually uncertain and tensed up combined armies of God and Satan. On seeing Dedan, she smiled and began to walk towards him closely followed by her own private army. Having fought many times in rivers and streams, that had quickly turned blood red, she was oblivious to the foul water that was splashing around her as she walked. On reaching Dedan she embraced the confused angel and gave him a firm kiss on the lips.

"Hello lover boy. Surprise! Missed me?"

"It certainly is a surprise. What are you doing here?" Dedan was unsure as how to react to the arrival of the only recently reactivated goddess. She could easily have decided to side with Ekeko and fight with him, but if she had done that, she had a strange way of attacking him. And, if it was it was a declaration of war, he liked it and would have welcomed the opportunity to come up against her again, one on one.

"At ease Dedan. It is alright," God placed a placatory hand on his shoulder. "Sonja would like to give some of her followers the opportunity to get away from their usual routine of drinking then falling over and get a bit of intense exercise. It was agreed that she could bring 10,000 of her bravest, or most berserk, warriors and join us, hence the shortfall in Hell's and Heaven's numbers. After all I think it is better that they fight with, rather than against, us. Don't you agree?"

Scanning the newly arrived army Dedan had to admit that he'd have hated to be forced to fight against them as they looked a formidable force. "I agree." Then giving Sonja an overly and undisguised salacious look "Sonja is agile, strong and definitely has stamina. I am glad she is on my, I mean our, side."

"Excellent, excellent." Exclaimed God, jubilantly. "I thought you'd say something like that. Sonja, welcome and please feel free to have your men and women join our ranks."

Once her troops had pushed and shoved their way into the front lines, and were ready for battle, Sonja took her place at the opposite side of God to Dedan. With a devilish twinkle in her eye she gave the angel a lascivious grin. "Phewwwwww, is it just me or is it hot?" And with that she leant her sword and shield against her legs and slipped off her thick bearskin coat and allowed it to fall into the foul water at her feet. What was revealed made Dedan, and every male soldier that could see the goddess, give her lustful stares. The golden metal that met their eyes was not so much defensive armour as a tantalisingly placed battle bikini. Neither totally suited for war or a day on the beach but she looked good and knew it. There was no danger of her being unnoticed in any conflict but, unlike Satan's chosen appearance, being such an obvious sight was not detrimental. Any male fighter that saw her would see a sexy woman first and that would, more than likely, make them pause just enough to allow her, or the forces close to her, to deliver the killer blow first.

With appreciative eyes Dedan looked her up and down and then repeated the exercise just for good measure, in case he had missed something the first time. He wasn't sure what defence the costume would be against arrows, but he had to admire the aesthetics of her uniform and he also had to agree that it was her that was *hot*. "What can I say Sonja? I have my weapon at the ready and it is at your service!"

"That'll do Dedan." Said God, releasing a weary sigh. "I hope that once the enemy do arrive, you'll be able to drag your eyes away from our companion and be able to focus on them."

"Yes Sire, sorry." Dedan's voice was contrite as his cheeks blushed slightly at the mild chastisement. However, seeing his reaction, Sonja laughed at his discomfort.

Having divested herself of her warm and heavy clothing she bent over and picked up her weapons again. The movement inviting, and receiving, many further lusty glances. Taking up a fighting stance she stood ready for battle. Her newly found admirers might have other things on their minds, but she was a true Shieldmaiden of old Norse sagas and all that she wanted, at that moment, was for the enemy to appear so that she could fight. Despite looking like something from a soft porn movie, she had a bear's heart. But, in this instance, she'd chosen to leave it at home on one of the giant and ornate fireplaces.

33 – Ekeko and Co.

Sonja didn't have long to wait for a glimpse of the adversaries. When Ekeko's troops began to appear, they did it quickly. Like a dark but primitively armed avalanche they emerged out of nowhere on the south side of the flat and featureless Bolivian plane. Without needing any instructions, they took up their places facing their enemies. Thanks to the effects of their narcotic cocktail fuelling their inner rage and making them ready for the command to attack; bloodshot eyes were glazed, and teeth clenched. Their numbers increased until they formed an almost solid wall of flesh several hundred yards away from the opposing side. The now polluted and churned up water between them still glinting in the early morning sun and reflecting the few clouds that dotted the sky. If it wasn't for so many people intent on killing and recent impurities, that had been added to the saline liquid, it could have normally been considered a sight bordering on perfection.

The armies of Ekeko could see the indistinct assorted shapes, sizes and attire of the mixed opponents framed against the background of the Tunupa volcano rising high in the distance whilst the southerly view, for the armies of God and Satan, was less spectacular thanks to the far edge of the salt flats being obscured by the living military anachronisms that were heavily armed with archaic, but still deadly, stone encrusted weapons. The last to arrive at the rear of his troops was Ekeko resplendent in his gold crown topped with red bird feathers and a cloak made from a Jaguar's fur. Not the clothing of an animal rights activist but such considerations were of no concern to him. From where he was, he couldn't see his enemy but knew they were there, so he began to issue instructions to his army who quickly responded to them. Even before the war had been arranged, they had been practicing and knew where they needed to be, in relation to their colleagues, and exactly what they needed to do. The lines at the rear of the formation withdrew arrows from animal skin quivers and placed them in bows, raising in readiness for the final order. Just a brief word of instruction and they could begin. They didn't have to wait long as, on seeing that his archers were ready, Ekeko gave out a single cry of 'Fire!' With that word ears were filled with a tumultuous whooshing sound and the air was momentarily darkened by a rapid moving cloud of death bringing arrows. They were not accurate, but they were powerful and numerous enough to bring indiscriminate carnage to those in the opposing army without shield cover and unluckily close enough to be on the receiving end of one of the sharp projectiles. Cries of those dying or injured replaced the sound of the arrows. The already polluted water accepting the bodies and blood of the fallen.

Then it was the turn of the combined army of the strange alliance. Quick orders were barked out and the archers returned fire sending their own metal tipped death cloud towards Ekeko's forces. Expectant shields were raised in anticipation of the rain of death and many arrows were made harmless by the protective canopy of stretched hides over wooden frames but plenty of arrows found gaps or flaws in the protective covering and, in turn, filling the other part of the shallow lake with injured and dead warriors. Volley after volley were released by both sides as the long-distance battle continued with each assault reducing the numbers in the opposing forces. Those still standing protecting themselves, and those around them, with shields that were rapidly becoming heavier thanks to the number of arrows sticking out of them. Eventually that method of attack seemed to lose all its benefits. Each subsequent black cloud inflicting fewer and fewer casualties until eventually only one or two were being hit. Finally, as if by some unspoken mutual consent, both sides stopped the aerial barrage. To many of the soldiers, of both forces, the tense silence seemed just as terrible as the sound of the arrows whizzing through the air and hitting the flesh of their comrades. Each side had suffered but neither had achieved a military advantage.

Ekeko surveyed his army. Thanks to their drug induced condition none of them were showing signs of fatigue and still appeared eager to engage in close quarters conflict. He then turned his attention to the sun in the east. It had risen above the horizon but was still several hours from being fully overhead. Without needing to think about it in too much detail he decided that there was no time like the present and shouted out the next order 'Attack!' This was met by a roar from his troops, like a vocal Mexican wave, that spread outwards to either end of the army as each soldier cheered and began to run towards their foes, shields, spears and swords raised ready for the imminent clash.

Seeing the approaching force both Satan and St. Michael began to issue orders. Although, thanks to his helmet, the Saint's instructions were, at best, indistinct and at worst totally inaudible. His heavily armoured arm, waving in the general direction of Ekeko, giving the only noticeable but vague indication of his desire for his troops to advance. But despite that they got the message without having to discuss it amongst themselves; they had seen too many of their friends fall to arrows for them to hesitate. Angels, demons and Vikings ran forwards with their weapons ready for the inevitable impact of two seemingly unstoppable forces. The battle cries from each side filling the air with an inarticulate cacophony as each soldier released their own traditional battle cry that was used in their specific historical period. The languages, words and sounds might have been varied but the messages were all the same and could be easily understood. *Kill and keep killing until the battle was over or be killed!*

St. Michael had the desire to be at the front of his men but thanks to his heavy and impractical armour, and water-logged footwear, he had been impervious to the onslaught of arrows but was now unable to proceed at any speed greater than that of a decrepit and arthritic tortoise. More of an obstacle than a leader as soldiers had to manoeuvre around him so that they could advance and engage in the imminent clash of armies. Giving up on the image that he seemed to think the armour afforded him he frustratedly lifted off his metal helmet and threw it to the ground like a petulant child. Now, free of the encumbrance, he was able to belatedly issue the now redundant order. "Forward!" His battle cry lost amongst the din of the army that was preoccupied in rushing past him. Ignoring him as they considered his presence insignificant and unimportant. Legs lifting like slow drawbridges his progress towards the enemy was like a tank that had run out of ammunition and had lost one of its caterpillar tracks. Ideal for people to hide behind to avoid getting shot but, other than that, unable to contribute to the actual battle.

Satan and his battalions of the damned weren't hesitant to advance either. Their lust for blood and destruction was even stronger than their enforced allies. Just because their immortal souls couldn't be destroyed and any 'death' in battle would just remove them from action sending them back to Hell, didn't mean that they were less passionate or viewed the battle as something to be taken lightly. Each one of the combatants wanted to be there at the end of the war and be waving their weapons victoriously in the air as they stood on a mountain of corpses. The charge was just as noisy and uncoordinated as the angels with the same objective, only bloodier.

On seeing St. Michael's plight, a demon ran past him and cheekily gave the metal skirting, protecting his buttocks, a firm smack with his sword, the impact releasing a clear *clang*. "Come on Tinman, you'll miss all the action." he taunted as he ran on and disappeared amongst the rapidly advancing throng.

Not to be out done the Viking hordes, having been at the front of the vast formation when the charge had begun, were making the most of having pole position and were maintaining their lead in the race to be the first to engage with Ekeko's army. It had not taken them long to reach a state of blind rage so that, like fur clad racing cars, they'd have gone from calm to full speed berserker in 3 seconds. Weapons and shields raised and ready for the inevitable and imminent clash. Even if the enemy avoided being impaled, or having chunks cut from the more vulnerable parts of their bodies, they still ran the serious risk of simply being run over and trampled to death by the heavily built Norsemen. The repetitive cry of *'Drepe!'* making it clear, to even the non-Norse speakers, that they wanted to do just one thing, kill. Ground shaking and shallow water being thrown up into the air as they made their bloodthirsty charge.

Soon they had reached their objective, weapons impacting with other weapons, shields or flesh. Conventional wisdom would have thought that the ancient wood and stone tools would have been no match for the more modern metal implements, but this fight was far from conventional and in the heat of battle wisdom was seldom to be found. For both sides the only tactical advantages were obtained from the agility and skill of the person wielding their respective weapons. The Vikings met the Mesoamericans first and the combined opposing momentum was such that some were simply knocked over by the force of the impact. The rest, that remained standing, had little room to move their arms efficiently but they made the most of the space available. Thanks to the relatively small Viking contingent they were quickly enveloped as the South American force, not directly involved in fighting them, swept past on their way to meet up with the far larger main contingent of angels and demons. This was soon achieved with the real onslaught starting. Swords and axes making contact, blocked or deflected by shields. Instinctively spears were jabbed forwards in an attempt to pierce flesh as yet more swords were swung wildly. Thanks to the clothing, opponents could be easily recognised but that was no guarantee that there wouldn't be collateral damage as the *red mist* filled eyes acted as blinkers with no time to pause, hesitate or select a target mid blow. As yet more bodies began to litter the floor the water began to, once again, change colour. Even where it hadn't been contaminated by the involuntary bowel and stomach evacuations of the demons the azure blue was replaced by the crimson red of blood. But despite all the carnage and death there were still plenty of fighters left to carry on the battle. Muscles tired but the fatigue ignored as the death toll continued to rise.

34 – Such a Dirty Word

Although it could receive several descriptions, be it God's reception, God's antechamber or even God's secretary's office, thanks to Angela's ever present friendly welcome, which she gave to most people that visited the place, it had acquired the simple sobriquet of *'The Room'*. Although it did occasionally cause a modicum of confusion and embarrassment to the newly deceased that were still learning the terminology. Irrespective of where in Heaven you were, be it a palace or verdant field, if someone said that they needed to go *The Room* then other angels and Saints would know that they were not using a euphemism for going to the toilet.

Currently Angelica was in *The Room* keeping herself busy with the vast amount of paperwork that a battle on Earth generated. Wars had to be planned, recorded and the correct forms completed ensuring that nothing went wrong, with all heavenly souls were accounted for. Then, once the carnage was over, clean up teams had to be sent to clear up the mess, remove bodies, return the place back to the state it was prior to the fighting and finally alter the memories of any human that might witnessed something strange or persuade them that what they might have seen was not real. Humans love a conspiracy theory and never believe the evidence before their eyes. Thanks to this an angel could tell them that they hadn't really seen a genuine vicious conflict between half a million soldiers carrying swords and that they'd, in reality, just witnessed a complex scene from a movie. A more credible reality so the witnesses would believe them. The total absence of camera's, film crews or catering trucks wouldn't even be noticed or commented on. The importance of filing the forms once tasks had been actioned and completed was a complete mystery to everyone including Angelica and God but, being an office, paperwork procedures had to be adhered to because things had always been done that way and, if they worked, why change them? Just like Hell bureaucracy existed, only it was less of an onerous chore when done by the right person, and Angelica had a skill for it that bordered on passion.

Being diligent the ever-efficient secretary, and office manager, was currently stood at a filing cabinet that had the mysterious capacity to accept as much paperwork as Angelica could feed into it. All this was done without it ever becoming full and jamming every time she tried to open or close it or topple over and land on top of her whenever she opened the top drawer. Even though the entrance of Roxy, Bob, Paul and Gordoon was noticed her focus remained on what she was doing and didn't turn to look at them. "Hello Roxy, had a good mission?"

Roxy wondered how she knew it was them without looking up but decided that now wasn't the time to discuss the special powers that many Personal Assistants had of knowing people were there without seemingly taking their eyes off the job in hand. "It went well thanks, no more would be assassins or kidnappers turned up. But we now need your help. We didn't get back in time to enlist in the army so we'd like you just to approve the use of a dimensional portal so we can go down to Bolivia and fight the good fight."

On hearing the request Angelica pushed the cabinet drawer shut and turned to face her guests. Looking at Gordoon her smile disappeared. "Are you Gordoon? I am sorry that you got killed but welcome to Heaven." Then she paused and looked from Roxy to Bob then Gordoon and finally back to Roxy again. "Hang on, no more assassins? If he died why haven't the gods lost their only believer and returned back to the Hall of Dead Gods? No Roxy, please tell me that you haven't brought a human to Heaven while he is still alive!"

Roxy pursed her lips and gave Angelica a guilty look. "I know it is unusual and goes against protocols, but he just might be the ace up our sleeve, and he could be useful to have on the battlefield. It is just that normal human transport methods would have been too slow, so this was the quickest and most efficient way of getting him there."

"Unusual?" Consternation in her voice. "Try unprecedented! Such things shouldn't even be possible. I don't know how you did it and I'm not sure that I even want to. Have you any idea how much paperwork you will need to fill out to clear up the mess you've made? And as for St. Peter, he will go ape shit when he finds out."

"I know and I am sorry but can you just sort it so we can get back down to Earth? Then we'll be out of your hair."

"Not so fast" Angelica's voice taking on a mellower tone. "I can do it but on one condition. You have to take me with you."

"But you are not field trained or approved for battle. Such a thing would be unprecedented."

"If you can break rules then so can I." A sly grin on her face. "I'd say it is extremely unusual, but I have never been in a battle and want to join in the fun for once. After all what is the worst that could happen? I get killed and return to Heaven? That is my single condition. Take me or nobody goes until the correct forms are filled out, and...."

"Who knows how long that would take? -That is blackmail!" Roxy was already sensing that further arguments would be futile but felt that she should at least try to stand her ground. Being Italian she was not one to shy away from a good argument but didn't want to waste any more time. "Wouldn't you coming along just generate even more paperwork for us and delay things even more?"

"Blackmail? That is such a negative word, I like to think of it as contract negotiations and a fair exchange of talents so that we are all happy and get what we want. Besides don't you know that I am the Paperwork Fairy? I can make things like that disappear if people go out of their way to help me."

"Alright" replied Roxy with a resigned sigh. "After all what is the worst that could happen? Besides, being stabbed by a sword is just like a paper cut, only much deeper and far more painful!"

"Exactly, those damned paper cuts can be nasty" Angelica gave them a smile and began to walk to a plain door at the other end of the room. Opening it, and leaning into the darkness, she dragged out a large cardboard box. "There you go, I think you'll find that these will fit you all perfectly." Opening it she began to remove folded army uniforms with polished boots resting on top of them. "I'm sorry Roxy but they are not the designer labels that you are so fond of, but you can't have everything. If we all get dressed up for the occasion, we can be on our merry way."

The three angel guests looked at her with surprised expressions and Gordoon just remained silent as he tried to understand what was going on. He was unsure what to have expected to find in Heaven, but he was sure that this wasn't it.

"How the f…" began Bob but decided that the rest of the question was self-evident.

"How did I know?" Angelica gave Bob a conspiratorial smile. "I know it might seem like it, but I do not spend *all* of my time with my head stuck in a filing cabinet or ensuring God has a constant supply of coffee, made just the way he likes it. If an angel goes to Earth, or returns, then I will know about it, even ones that bring an extra guest. So just accept the fact that I am too marvellous for words." Reaching back behind the door she removed an armful of swords that looked like they had been made for knights going on the crusades in the 11th century. "I think that these might come in handy as well." Giving the visitors an expectant look. "Well? What are you waiting for?"

35 – The Maleficent Seven

The only people that didn't seem to be in any sort of insane rush to engage in battle were Dedan, his African companion, Satan and an assorted contingent of more seasoned and experienced soldiers. They knew all too well that running madly into awaiting swords, or pointy spears, gave them a 50-50 chance of being the one ending up being killed. Allowing the first wave to tire themselves out, and deplete the oncoming foe, was beneficial and allowed them to fight and still have full reserves of energy. Casually they walked towards the on-going battle giving the appearance that they were on a pleasant morning stroll to the local shop to buy a newspaper; only carrying more weaponry than the average shopper. As they walked five figures suddenly materialised in front of the slowly advancing contingent of the demon and angel army. Indistinct at first their unexpected appearance causing swords and shields to be raised in defensive postures. No matter how skilled they were, a quintet of possible attackers wouldn't have posed much of a threat, but nobody was taking any chances. Eventually, as if eyes were focusing on an object after being closed for a long time, the figures became discernible. Weapons were first lowered by angels and then the demons unquestioningly lowered theirs as well at the sight of Roxy, Bob, Angelica, Paul and Gordoon. They were all dressed in matching US army universal camouflage pattern fatigues, all that was missing were the helmets and instead of standard issue assault rifles they all carried swords and rectangular Perspex riot shields. Each of the quintet had relieved looks on their faces as they realised that they had appeared before friends, or *friendly* demons, rather than blood thirsty foes.

"Roxy how are you? Bob, it looks like you have regained your mobility and well-done Paul. Good to see you again and thanks for doing as I asked." Dedan's voice happy at the sight of his friends. "And you Angelica, my beautiful angel, what can I say? Always wonderful to see you but I never expected you to join us here."

"I'm good thanks" replied Roxy casually "it was just a pity that the drug didn't effect Bob's mouth so that he could shut up while the rest of his body recovered."

The comment made Bob give her a mock pained look. "Why Roxy, I don't know how you could say such a thing. All I did was suggest a few things that we could do once the mission was over. What's wrong with a candle lit dinner?"

"The dinner would have been lovely and romantic, with perhaps anyone but you" her eyes glaring contemptuously at him, "it was the use you wanted to put the candles to which pushed the conversation so far down-hill that it rolled into the gutter at the bottom of the mountain!" The sentence losing much of its chastising veritas as she began to give him a smile. "And besides I think you shocked young Gordoon here. I'm sure he never expected such language from angels." She turned her gaze to the human who was avoiding any eye contact by intently staring at his feet while he blushed. Despite being a nerd who had access to as much on-line porn as he liked it had not prepared him for such common hard-core smutty banter between two friends.

In an attempt to save Gordoon from a terminal case of embarrassment Angelica took the opportunity to return Dedan's greeting. "You think I just type and file things? I decided it was high time that I had a nice holiday back on Earth and, in the process, see some action. Then, when these four turned up, looking for a change of clothes and some swords, I thought I'd join them. They didn't want to let me at first but then I told them about all the rules they had broken by bringing a human to Heaven before he'd died, and all the paperwork they'd have to fill in, that was enough to ensure that they acquiesced. So, viola, her I am."

"A living human in Heaven, Paul, why did you stop them?" Dedan raised his eyebrows in mock surprise. "Okay. And who am I to argue with such determination? But one slight thing," pointing forwards "the war is that way!"

As they turned Gordoon saw the battle and involuntarily released an "Oh shit!" which was an adequate summary of the sight that met his eyes. There were other expressions he could have used but none would have been so succinct in summing up the vision of half a million people, armed with handheld anachronistic weapons, all intent on putting holes into, or hacking bits off, other people while wading in what could best be described as an open sewer.

On hearing the exclamation Bob laughed and patted Gordoon firmly on the back. "Don't worry brah, stick with us, we'll make sure that you are kept safe."

The slowly moving part of the army, plus the additional contingent, resumed their steady walk into battle. As they advanced an awestruck Gordoon took the opportunity to have a look around at those by his side and, looking through a gap, he grabbed Dedan's shoulder excitedly. "Dedan, Dedan, Dedan, you have Cyborgs in Heaven?"

"Cyborgs?" Confused Dedan turned and stretched his neck so that he could look in the general direction that Gordoon was indicating. "Oh that." He added with mild glee in his voice. "That is no cyborg. That my friend is something far more robotic and with less flexible programming, that is St. Michael. Don't worry about him, he'll catch up with us eventually. Admittedly it might be nightfall and the battle could be over, but it is probably safer for all of us that way." Rushing to catch up with God, at the front of the line, Dedan heard something that made his blood freeze.

"Hello lover boy, long time no see!" The voice was shrill and heavy with a London '*Cockney*' accent. Despite not having heard it in a long time he recognised it straight away and had no doubt about its ownership. "Fancy meeting you 'ere. Yer don't write, yer don't call. Anyone'd think yer didn't love me anymore!" To him each word was like fingernails being dragged across a blackboard and made him abruptly stop his walk towards the battle. Turning around he was met by the sight of a stocky woman with wild and tussled dark hair dressed in a skin-tight black leather cat-suit. "Ey up cocker, ow's ya doin?" The greeting delivered with a sly smile.

Despite being taken aback by the appearance of the woman Dedan was determined to appear cool and nonchalant. "Hello KK. What a wonderful surprise. How the She-devil are you?" Then he noticed her companions and his heart sank even further as any attempt at maintaining a fake joyful demeanour evaporated and his face dropped. Behind her were six other similarly attired women all carrying extremely sharp and lethal looking samurai swords. Then, behind them, were seven similarly dressed men in heavily placed gaudy make up. "Hello ladies." His voice struggling to maintain composure. "I'd like to say what a pleasure it is to see you all, but I would be lying. Would it be impolite of me to wish you all rapid deaths and even faster and painful returns to Hell?"

KK was pushed out of the way and her place, in front of Dedan, was replaced by one of the other cat-suited women. This time her shoulder length hair was auburn and had a centre parting. "I've been waiting centuries to see you again." Her face sneering and full of contempt. "This miserable sewer is the right place for a shit like you."

"Oh, hello Lisa, it is lovely to see you again as well. Good to see that you are just as cheerful as always." Looking along the line of women, he bowed slightly. "Ladies, if you will excuse me, I am sure there is a lot of reminiscing to be done but I have better things to do and, besides, I don't want to." With that he turned once more and resumed his walk towards the enemy.

Just then Lisa, with a look of unbridled rage, swiftly raised her sword and drew it back over her head intent on bringing it down on Dedan's undefended skull. It began its journey but before it could impact with the vulnerable target and give him a splitting headache in the most literal of senses, an arm reached out of the surrounding crowd and grabbed hold of her forearm with a grip that would have made a Nile crocodile's bite feel like a toothless suck. With a mixture of indignation and frustration she turned to look at the owner of the arm which had foiled her assassination attempt. On seeing the face of Satan her demeanour instantly mellowed, leaving only the burning rage visible in her eye.

"Lisa," Satan snapped as he loosened his fingers but continued to hold the now relaxed arm in the air "this is neither the *time* nor the *place* for this!" Each word was precise and enunciated so that it left no doubt in her mind that the sword should only be used to kill Ekeko's warriors.

"Yes! Alright, alright!" Petulantly snapping her arm out of his grip and lowering the sword. The enraged look in her eyes along with the resentful posture making it clear that she had someone else that the weapon could be used on. But she knew that any attempts, whether successful or not, to kill Satan would have been an unwise career move and resulted in her spending a very long time in an exceedingly nasty and painful punishment chamber.

Seeing that his life had just been unexpectedly saved by Satan Dedan gave him a brief nod of gratitude. He had been expecting a demon to make an attempt to kill him, and the fact that it was Lisa was not a surprise either but having the master of Hell intercede and prevent it was more of a shock. But just because one person had been prevented from treating his head like a ripe melon, before getting into the fight, didn't mean that someone else might not try and do a similar thing during the heat of battle. He knew that he'd have to watch his back as well as his front. Not an easy task for anyone but a Pullmay demon that had an extra eye in the back of its head. Having seen what had just happened but being too far away to have come to his aid Roxy sidled up to him and began to speak to him in what she hoped was a level that would be quiet enough for him to hear but nobody else. An almost impossible task in the middle of a battalion of troops sloshing through polluted water on their way to a battle. "Dedan, from the looks of it you know those leather clad sirens. The fact that one of them tried to kill you also makes me think that they know you as well and you have upset them. Who are they?"

"Those seven parcels of death and destruction are Satan's daughters. They are seldom allowed on Earth as they tend to be a little bit too indiscriminate with their destructive tendencies. Rather than tempting people and winning souls, or simply killing the evil and sending them to Hell, they are like little tornadoes of destruction murdering anyone that gets their attention. They are a bit like the Ebola Virus in human form, only with less charm. On their own they are trouble, but this is the first time that I've ever known them all to be on Earth in the same place at the same time. Ekeko and his army might need reinforcements if he's going up against them."

"And the strange looking men behind them?"

Dedan glanced at them and curled up his face in contempt. "Those my dear are their camp followers. KK has a strange sense of irony and humour so just don't ask!"

"So, knowing your reputation," being Italian Roxy had no qualms about asking a direct question, even if it was disguised as a euphemism "did you ever *come* face to face with any of Satan's daughters?"

"Roxy! I am shocked. A Gentleman never discusses such things."

"Since when did you become a gentleman?" A smile on her face as she prodded him playfully in the ribs.

"Thanks for that vote of confidence Rox. Over the centuries I have had occasions when I've been forced to get to grips with them all. KK or Kelly Kelly, to use her proper name, is the eldest sister and quite possibly the least insane but that, in itself, is relative and no recommendation. Her mother came from London and her evil offspring learnt to drink from a very early age. In fact she can drink anyone under the table, and she once did that to me, but that is another story. When she isn't being evil, she is wonderful company but she was responsible for several strange and very fatal incidents in some German towns in the middle ages involving mouldy bread and hallucinations and you do *not* want to get in her way when she gets angry."

"And the one with the desire to give you a severe centre parting?"

"Oh, her. That complaining bundle of misery is Lisa. The last time we clashed horns was in the Renaissance. I ended up cutting her head off and I think she took offence at that. What can I say? Some people bear grudges. Forgive and forget is not part of her nature."

Before Dedan had the opportunity to elaborate on the other five sisters his attention was taken up by an almost imperceptible quivering of the air in the no man's land just to his right with two white horses appearing, as if they were running through an invisible barn door. Attached to them, appeared a gold and white chariot that followed them through the dimensional portal. There were long metal spikes sticking out of the wheel axle hubs and, stood in the carriage, wielding a curved bladed sword in one hand and holding the reins in the other was Hor'idey in a white dress and a cape that was flowing in the air as she sped towards the surprised collection of Angels and Demons. But the surprise was nothing compared to that of an angel who had managed to advance slightly quicker than his comrades in arms. The last thing he saw before being unceremoniously sent back to Heaven was the flank of a horse that was attempting to occupy the same space as he was. And in the battle of simple physics the horse, its hooves, and closely following chariot, won leaving a squashed, bloodied and broken corpse in its wake. The remains were further desecrated as, quickly appearing behind her, and running like a river, was her army. Clad in drab brown skirts and armoured chest plates they were not the same grand spectacle as their goddess, but they still looked like they meant business. It was obvious from their direction of travel, and drawn swords, that their intention was not to join in the existing battle and attack Ekeko's forces. The front line of demon's, closest to Hor'idey, were taken by surprise and there was little they could do to defend themselves against the onslaught of the horses crashing over them or the knee level spikes that jaggedly cut through flesh, bones and cartilage. Those that were not killed were left to lie on the floor, unable to fight or defend themselves from the swords of the rest of her force as they swept behind her and joined in the massacre. The first wave caught the defenders unprepared, so that they were barely had time to raise their shields to prevent injuries. This soon changed as the ever-increasing number of attackers spewed into existence and drove deeper into the heart of the angel and demon rear guard force. Engaging in battle just as the defender's weapons were fully raised. Swords met swords and the surprise attacker's advance was, if not stopped then at least slowed down. Hor'idey's numerical advantage soon began to take effect and the defenders were left wondering what to do next. Angels and demons falling; united in death in a way that would have been considered impossible on any other day. Bodies destroyed but souls despatched back to either Heaven or Hell, where they had originally come from.

Both sides mingling so that, if it weren't for the uniforms, friend or foe would have been indistinguishable. The only obvious individual was Hor'idey. Standing high in her chariot she'd ground to a halt but was vigorously slashing away with her sword at those that tried to reach her, leaving them either decapitated or badly wounded. On seeing the proximity of the new battle, the seven daughters of Satan saw the chance for some bloody action and instantly raised their swords, gave of a shrill battle cry and rushed madly into the thick of the fight. Being far from careful or discriminate with their blows random and unwary demons and angels became collateral damage as members of Hor'iday's army began to fall to the excited blood thirsty rage of the evil septet.

"Dedan?" Roxy asked as she prepared her sword, ready to join the fray. "Is that Hor'idey?"

"I'm afraid so!" Dedan's voice nonplussed at not only seeing his ex-wife unexpectedly join a war but also joining it on the wrong side.

"Your ex-wife?"

"I'm afraid so!"

"I thought you said that she was going to behave and be on our side?" Roxy was underlining the question with a stern look.

"I did, but I might have forgotten to mention a few minor things."

"And they are?"

"Well, some might call her endearingly fickle and changeable. Others might call her…" He paused as he swung his sword to down one of his ex-wife's soldiers that had got within range. "…a psychotic, untrustworthy and dangerous bitch. I learnt long ago not to trust her or believe a word she said. Even when I was her husband, I found her egotistical and narcissistic. Hard to live with and equally hard to keep on living after choosing to be without her."

"A few minor things? I think it would have been safe for you to divulge those minor details before now!" Roxy continued to speak as she despatched a couple of soldiers that had seen her as an easy target and foolishly chosen to take her on. Her aim faultless as her sword sliced through the neck of one and, in the same elegant movement, swung it so that the arcing trajectory sent it plunging through the chest of the other, making the armour look like had been made of cardboard.

Dedan looked from the impaled warrior to Roxy and shrugged. "Sorry!" Then he moved forward, keeping in line with Roxy, Bob and Paul. The group forming a small but impenetrable wall that repulsed wave after wave of attackers. Then God joined them and added His spear wielding skills to the team so that despite its unwieldiness in close quarter combat, He was able to kill His fair share of foes. He could easily have used His divine powers but knew that such a precedent would have been unwise as there were two enemy gods, and Satan, who could have utilised their own special powers and that might have turned the table against Him. Additionally, he wasn't sure that using celestial intervention in that way was allowed as part of the rules of engagement.

Ekeku hadn't used his powers so, until then, He had no intention of making thunderbolts appear or to cause earthquakes.

Looking up, to briefly assess the situation, Roxy noticed that there was something wrong but couldn't quite put her finger on what it was. Then it came to her, Hor'idey was no longer visible on her raised vantage point. Not convinced that a goddess would have become a casualty so easily she began to frantically look around to see if she could find her in the swarming mass of bodies and swinging weaponry but, no matter how hard she looked, there was no trace of the goddess.

"Queen Bee-tch has disappeared so keep an eye out for her as she might want to issue a decree absolute divorce on Dedan!" Her voice now shrill, shouting as loudly as she could, to ensure it could be heard over the general din of battle.

In between defensive and offensive strikes they all tried to catch sight of Hor'idey but couldn't see her. Wherever she was, she was probably busily occupying herself with killing people, but they knew that when she did reappear there would be trouble. God could have used his powers to locate her but, as he was preoccupied with preventing Himself from prematurely being sent back to His home, He didn't have the time to get distracted by the search process. All around them there was a constant ebb and flow of fighters as one side found a brief tactical advantage only to lose it and be pushed back by the other. All the time numbers diminished as bodies fell to the ground and were trampled over by those taking their places in the front of the action. Amongst the crowds Dedan kept getting occasional glimpses of Satan's daughters as severed heads flew into the air thanks to them merrily hacking away at their enemies. Although he might have seen them, he had no desire to get too close to them and risk becoming one of their victims. Seeing their blood splattered appearance, he realised that the black leather wasn't solely for sex appeal and to distract any horny male attacker. The clothing was also ideally suited for getting clean, with one wipe of a damp cloth the gore was gone. The pieces of intestine, brains and coating of blood could easily be wiped clean and, knowing them as he did, they could have a light snack with the gory bits later. Then, reluctantly and dangerously, his attention was drawn to KK. She was in a full berserker mode, that would have made the Vikings look static and calm, but that wasn't the main thing that caught his eye. Not only was she utilising her sword to despatch anyone unfortunate enough to get in her way, but her feet became a vicious part of her arsenal. The soldiers quickly realising that body armour might be one thing, but battle skirts were scant protection as high velocity booted demon feet met all too human and delicate groins. Not fatal but damaging enough to make them stop caring about the battle for long enough for KK to follow through with sword strikes to more vital parts of their bodies. But that was not what he was waiting to see, Dedan had seen her fight before and even had to face her in mortal combat. There was her unique demon party trick that he found mesmerising and was glad that he was not going to be on the receiving end of it. Then it happened, her thick and messy black hair began to join together forming thick strands, turning a dark grey they transformed into long and slimy eels. Writhing they began to strike at any heads that got too close. The opponent's faces might not have deliberately moved towards them, but her additional tactic of head butting made the creatures hard to avoid. Needle sharp teeth biting hungrily at exposed flesh, jaws tight and refusing to relinquish their grip until they had freed skin and could swallow their little meals. The sight reminded him of a time when he'd experienced it first-hand. Although it was long ago, and he'd been healed in Heaven, the indescribable pain still lingered in his mind. His grasping at them as he tried to break free, but their skin was coated in an oozy substance that made gripping them impossible. It was not an experience that he ever wanted to repeat.

Angelica, who'd manoeuvred herself so that she was able to stand next to Dedan, managed to break the spell of the strange Medusa like demon, "Dedan, you okay?" Her concerned voice was soft and managed to have the effect similar to gently waking someone from a deep dream. Shaking his head groggily he turned and looked at her.

"I'm good thanks Angelica. Enjoying your holiday away from the office?"

"Yes thanks, it's good to get some fresh air, see the sights and find out what you and Roxy really get up to on your missions." Her conversation was momentarily halted as she blocked the blow from an attacker with her cumbersome shield and then swung around and planted her sword into the attacker's face.

Seeing the manoeuvre Dedan nodded approvingly. "Well Angelica, you know how it is, not all my missions are as dull as this one." Smiling as he admired her unexpected skill in battle. Not something that is required on a resume when applying for office jobs, but it was nonetheless impressive. He wondered if there were many humans that were office workers but, in their hearts, were dreaming of being warriors. All they needed were the right weaponry and the opportunity to rescue some trapped damsel or peasant. Noble and Quixotic dreams of glory to make up for dull career choices.

"I must admit I could get used to this. And Dedan, are you *alright?* You know about the…"

He saw the look in her eyes and knew exactly what she meant. "Yes, thank you my beautiful angel." He lifted his sword as both of the angel's simultaneously struck the same attacker. "I am a lot better and no longer a self-pitying wuss." The words accompanied by a consolatory wink to the former object of his desires and love. He would have also included a placatory shrug, but it was hard to do that while wielding a sword and striking out at troops attacking him. "We still good?"

"Of course we are Dedan. Always! Now if you'll excuse me, I think someone needs my help." With that she sped off towards the seven leather clad demons. Dedan watched her as she approached four of Hor'idey's soldiers, who were gingerly approaching the back of Lisa. Angelica managed to spoil their deadly plans by deftly decapitating one of them and, before they had time to realise what was happening, ram her sword through the armour and chest of another. The remaining two fighters turned to face her and, seeing that she was struggling to free her sword from flesh and metal, decided that she was an easier target. Raising their curved khopesh, sickle like swords, they prepared to sink them into her skull. Just then she heard a loud cry of 'Oi, Angel!' Looking up she saw Lisa swooping down to relieve a corpse of its sword, then, in one fluid movement, sent it flying handle first towards Angelica. Instinctively she let go of her own weapon and caught the projectile and swinging it, as if it were second nature, she blocked the downward blows from her attackers and swept it into the neck of one of her foes. As she did that the final soldier seemed to tense up, his face a mixture of anger and surprise. Falling to his knees Angelica saw the reason for his sudden change of posture and demeanour. There behind him was Lisa, an outstretched arm holding a sword that was still stuck in his back. As Angelica looked into the demon's face, she saw an expression of sadistic glee that made her blood run cold. Removing the blade Lisa briefly looked at Angelica. Her face suddenly changed and seemed to adopt a look of bitter resentment, but then there was an almost imperceptible nod of acknowledgement as she turned and disappeared back into the fighting crowd. Angelica looked first at the sword in her hand then at the four bodies at her feet, gave a shrug as if everything was going exactly as she'd planned it and ran into the same fighting mass that Lisa had just entered. Dedan watched her disappear out of sight and smiled. Happy that he still had such a friend and that she was fighting on his side.

There was a loud clang just behind his head and turning was met by the sight of two swords right in front of his eyes. One straining to become better acquainted with his scalp and the other determined to stop it. Briefly looking to one side he saw Roxy, both hands struggling to keep the weapons in their position and then, looking the other way, he saw a Hor'ideyian disciple with a look of intense concentration as he attempted to win the battle of strength. Sweeping his sword around and upwards Dedan rammed it into the most vulnerable spot of the enemy that he could reach. The point of his blade entering the armpit at an angle and continuing through the body of the attacker until it reappeared through his neck, just above the body armour. "Thanks." Seeing the look of relief on Roxy's face as the enemy fell to the ground.

"Don't mention it, but I am worried about his goddess though. She is trouble."

"Tell me about it. You should try living with her. Out of sight but still in mind. When you can't see what she is up to is when she is at her most dangerous."

As if in answer to their mutual concerns there seemed to be a silent explosion in the middle of the brawling mass as bodies, as angels and demon limbs flew up into the air and fell back down onto the heads of those around them. It was then that Roxy and Dedan saw her but wished they hadn't. With sword swinging above her head Hor'idey came running out of the crowd, headed towards them.

"Oh shit!" Exclaimed Dedan as he bent down and pried a spear from the ribs of a nearby corpse. Drawing it back he threw it, with all his might, at the newly re-appeared goddess. The aim was perfect flying straight, releasing a whooshing noise as it went, but just before it could make contact with her white gown, in the proximity of her heart, she swerved. Deprived of its primary target it went past her and embedded itself into one of the loyal adherents that was following her.

"Hello." A sarcastic glint in her eyes *"I'm back*! Miss me?" Her voice loud and taunting.

"Yes, but if I find another spear, I am sure I won't next time!" Dedan readied his sword and gestured, with his free hand, for her to come closer. The universally recognised gesture to *give it your best shot!*

Smiling she screamed something in a pre-Sumerian language, that hadn't been heard on Earth for several millennia. Having been a king in that period Dedan had been a fluent speaker and understood the words, as did her troops. The order 'With me followers' made him tense up in anticipation of what was to follow.

God also understood the words and had His spear raised in expectation of the oncoming onslaught. But the rest of Dedan's comrades in arms needed a brief warning.

"Get ready, I think things are about to turn nasty." Although their state of alertness couldn't have been much higher, they all heeded Dedan's words and focused their attention on Hor'idey and the troops that were leaving their own individual skirmishes and forming ranks behind her. All attacker's weapons were pointed at the small force stood in front of Gordoon and this made Dedan, Roxy, and the rest of the party feel vulnerable and exposed. They knew they had to protect the sole human that was embroiled in the war but defend him from what? Killing him would be a truly pyrrhic victory as Hor'idey would lose her only believer and return to being a cold and forgotten statue. All they could do was kidnap him but that would have been a futile exercise too as they would only have been able to hold him for his relatively short life span and then she'd be left with no followers. If there was any danger of his death then that would have realistically come from the demons, but they were far too busy enjoying themselves to care about what the human currently believed, or didn't believe in. But such speculation was academic as her forces began to advance. A well organised rapid march as those around the edges of the formation fought off blows from the demons and angels that were left to swarm on them like enraged wasps striking the thick hide of an elephant that was apathetic to their presence. Seeing her chance to gain a decisive and instant victory Roxy raised her shield and stepped forwards determined to meet the oncoming goddess head on. Hor'idey's sword swept horizontally, at chest height, and sliced cleanly through Roxy's shield as if it were made of tissue paper. The top half falling to the floor leaving the useless bottom half still attached to Roxy's arm.

"Out of the way girl, I have business to do." Hor'idey's voice full of contempt for her opponent. Unceremoniously raising her foot, she gave the remaining section of shield a vicious kick sending Roxy off balance and causing her to step back, tripping over a body, laid by her feet, and fall to the ground. The deity ignored the prone figure and carried on her advance. With the tip of her spear, she gestured to a contingent of her army that were following her and not currently occupied in their own little fights. They recognised the gesture and followed her instructions. Silently, or as silently as a battle could be, they began to run towards Dedan, Paul, Bob and God. Out-numbered God and His angels began to frantically defend themselves as best they could against the superior numbers. Speed and skill were enough to keep them alive, for the moment, but they all knew that it was only a matter of time before the attackers managed to get some lucky blows and the defenders ranks began to dwindle and fall. Left with no enemies to obstruct her Hor'idey stepped up to Gordoon. Trembling he held his sword in front of his face with both hands, a petrified expression on his face as he stared at the approaching goddess. Casually she raised her sword and gently gave his weapon a firm tap sending it flying out of his hands. "Hello Gordoon, I am Hor'idey the woman of your dreams. It's nice to formally meet you at last. I think it would be best if you came with me while you come to realise the true benefits of worshipping me. I will..." Her speech was cut short as the blade of a blood washed sword appeared next to her neck, pushing against her windpipe.

"Not so fast *bitch* and I'm not just *some girl!*" Hor'idey looked to her side and saw the stern expression on Roxy's face. "Back away while you still can."

"It's alright Roxy, I've got this." Gordoon's voice was trying to sound calm and collected but was failing abysmally. "Hor'idey, I denounce you!"

Turning her gaze to the human Hor'idey's face was confused. "What?"

"I denounce you!" He repeated, only louder.

Paul, who had managed to sneak into the battle, was close to him, and holding off the blow from an attacking sword, just above his head, decided to assist in the conversation. "It's *renounce* dumbass, *renounce* not 'denounce'." In such instances diplomacy and tact were hard to muster, and come spontaneously, so the frustration was obvious in his voice.

"Oh, yes. That's what I meant." Being a computer nerd didn't mean he had a perfect grasp of languages, especially ecclesiastical ones. "Hor'idey, I renounce you!"

Hor'idey looked confusedly from Paul, to Gordoon and then Roxy before her eyes widened and her skin began to exude an aqua-marine flickering light. She released a blood curdling scream as her flesh began to turn to dust followed by organs and bones which were somehow blown away in the breezeless air, leaving her clothing to fall freely into the red and brown liquid that now covered the entire battlefield.

On her disappearance the second front, which Hor'idey's appearance with all her forces had created, seemed to take on the appearance of a delicately and intricately carved three-dimensional stone reliefs. Bodies froze in mid action with Demon and Angels left uncertain as to how they should react to their enemies who were suddenly stuck in rigid poses. Expressions showing rage captured and weaponry left in mid-air, defending or attacking but not moving. Even the evillest spirit seemed reticent about simply taking advantage of the situation and stabbing the static attackers. But such confusion was short lived as the rigid followers suffered the same fate as their goddess. An eerie glow lighting up the area, making it look radioactive, followed by heatless cremations as dust was blown into the faces and mouths of those still standing. Coughing

273

and spluttering the troops were left with a drab soot covering them, leaving them with the appearance of being a totally grey and slightly more politically correct versions of the black and white minstrels, only without the banjos and trite songs.

Seeing what had happened Roxy gave Gordoon an incredulous look. "You did it!" Then turning to look at God. "It was that simple? All he had to do was renounce her and it was dust in the wind time?" Although she'd not been formally introduced to God in His current incarnation, she seemed to instinctively know it was Him.

God raised his hands, palms upwards and gave her a shrug as if to say, '*What can I say?*' Then, seeing the continued consternation on her face, He decided to elaborate "Yes, yes, it is. That is all that is required but the apostasy has to be genuine. It had to be felt in the heart and soul. I had looked into his soul and saw Gordoon's doubts and uncertainties, so if he'd simply said the words from the safety and comfort of his little flat in Colorado, he would not have totally believed his own words and they wouldn't have worked. Especially if he'd just tried to *denounce* Hor'idey. He is basically a good person despite his random tastes in deities, but he needed more than you forcefully telling him about his mistakes. He needed to see it all first-hand, so your bringing him here was fortuitous. The ramifications of worshipping god's that enjoy wars, destruction and blood spilt in their honour witnessed first-hand. I think his experience here has taught him a valuable lesson." Pausing God looked across the plane to where the first battle was still being fought. He then saw the dust covered angels and demons, that were no longer engaged in fighting Hor'idey's forces, running as fast as they could to join in the giant melee. They were all determined not to miss out on the action, or to allow the Vikings to get the bragging rights for their small contribution. Even Satan looked intent on washing the dust off of him with the aid of enemy blood. Turning His attention to Gordoon God looked into his eyes and it was a glance that did more than see the student's face, it also saw into his soul. "I think you have seen enough and know what you have done and what Ekeko is capable of so…" He left the sentence unfinished so that Gordoon could come to his own conclusions.

His heart filled with sadness and disgust Gordoon guiltily scanned the ground around him and although he grasped the concept that the mutilated bodies that littered the place were just empty vessels, and the souls had either returned to either Heaven or Hell, the sight still sickened him. His previous experience of war had been restricted to films and overly graphically violent computer games but, no matter how gory or gruesome they were they'd always seemed distant and unreal. The reality of war was not what he'd expected, and it was not something he ever wanted to encounter again. Giving God a nod he looked in the general direction of the ongoing fight and raised his arms. "Ekeko, I Renounce you and all you stand for!" This gesture was redundant and pointless, but Gordoon thought it gave his words more power and looked cool. He'd seen a film where Moses had made the same gesture, so he thought it was appropriate. Once uttered the words flew through the air like an ever-widening sonic boom compressing the air before it as it grew, making the empty space visibly ripple. The surface of the shallow dirty red lake below it was picked up and carried along making it glisten in the sun and adopt the appearance of a wall of fine mist trapped in a vertical wave. Then it began to hit the armies of both sides leaving those it hit first soaked in the fine mizzle as the wave passed unchanged through their bodies. As it struck each person the jolt made them sway involuntarily but was not of sufficient force to make them fall over or even lose focus on the destruction at hand. It moved deeper and deeper into the battle until it finally found Ekeko. The god was preoccupied in attempting to throttle an angel, that had lost his weapon, in one hand and to fend off the assault of Viking with the other. As the wave hit, he instinctively knew what it meant. Relinquishing his grip on the angel he released a loud 'Noooooooooooooo'. It was powerful and seemed to sum up, and convey, all the despair and desolation that being banished back to the Hall of Dead Gods entailed. Even the hardened and most evil of demons within earshot were taken aback by the sound released by a god that was doomed and knew it. Briefly jerking, as if electrocuted, he started to radiate the same bright glow that Hor'idey had given off and began the rapid desiccation process as flesh and bones turned to dust. Then, once his transformation had been completed, the sonic boom effect disappeared and was replaced by horizontal wave, akin to a nuclear blast, radiating outwards from the spot that Ekeko had only recently vacated. The impact leaving Angels, Demons and Vikings unaffected while the god's followers were stripped of their corporeal form and blown away in the blast, leaving just grey dust, clothing and weapons in the polluted water or on top of bodies whose souls had already left the field of battle.

The absence of targets, with which to fight, left the remaining soldiers looking confused and bewildered and this state wasn't helped by the arrival of the troops running to join the fray after their own war with Hor'idey had drawn to a conclusive, if unsatisfactory, end. Finding no enemy to engage with in battle the troops forgot their natural distrust and animosity for their enforced allies and lowered their weapons and stood waiting for further instructions. Eventually the silence became unbearable amongst the carnage, that laid at their feet, and they began to break the first rule that was in place to ensure peace could be avoided in any war. Fraternisation appeared as they began to forget their differences and talk to each other. Fortunately for the Angels their Field Marshall was still stuck in the mud several hundred yards away and was unable to intercede in the situation. If he'd been there St. Michael would have ensured discipline was maintained by having them stand with weapons ready or, failing that, have them march away to a safe area where they could clean the blood off their boots. But his presence was neither missed nor noticed. He had tripped over a corpse at the beginning of Hor'idey's assault and spent the rest of the time doing a convincing artistic impression of a turtle that had been placed on its back. However, St. Michael was far bigger, metal coated and less of a pleasant conversationalist than your average hard-shelled reptile, so the comparison was perhaps unfair to the harmless animals. Thanks to his position the bottom half of his suit of armour had filled up with foul water and he'd been forced to suffer the indignity of having friend and foe alike walking all over him as they carried on the fight, totally oblivious to his predicament and not missing his participation. It would have been virtually impossible for him to get up-right on his own and, even with the assistance of his batman, difficult for him to get out of the horizontal position. Thanks to the added weight of the polluted liquid, he would have needed a hoist and at least a dozen burly Angels to pull him to his feet. Neither of which was available for now so there he remained.

Realising what must have happened Satan allowed himself the sort of self-satisfied grin that he wouldn't have tolerated from any soul that was in his care in Hell. Even though he had been fighting alongside God, rather than against Him, the taste of victory was just as sweet. Looking around, in the distance, he caught sight of God, His retinue of faithful angels, and Gordoon all sat down. Adopting a nonchalant walk he meandered casually across to them, determined to savour every minute of the bloodshed that surrounded him before he had to return to his domain. Getting closer he saw that they were sat casually on top of corpses as if they were just grassy knolls. "God, I am shocked. Such disrespect from You. Treating bodies in such a cavalier manner." Dedan had been sat with his back to Satan but, on hearing his voice, began to get to his feet and raise his sword in readiness for any possible first strike but God simply gestured for him to remain seated.

"Calm down Satan. The souls have gone so they are just empty shells and, besides, if you look carefully, you'll notice that we are all sitting on dead demons. And I must admit that they are more comfortable than I thought they'd be. Pull up a corpse and join us, we are just relaxing and enjoying the newly found peace."

Satan gave the angels a bemused look as he scanned the seating arrangements and their choice of furniture. "What the Hell. Why not?" He deliberately walked to the nearest angel body, which was laid in the water, grabbed hold of an arm and a leg with the intention of carrying it to the circle of angels but the corpse was less than willing to go with him as the arm had been severed and just fallen next to its deceased owner. Determined not to give the angels any excuse to laugh at the situation he adjusted his position and grabbed the other leg and dragged the one-armed cadaver to a position on the left-hand side of God. "There you go," a broad grin on his face as he stretched his legs out and crossed them "just like old times."

There was a mixture of emotions in the circle of resting warriors. God and Satan were relaxed about the situation and, despite his history and dark nature, Satan, at that moment at least, felt no urge nor compunction to raise his sword and attempt to send God back to Heaven via the quick method. Roxy, Angelica, Bob, Paul and Dedan were wary and on edge as they were cagey about discussing too much in front of their immortal foe and it was hard to relax when they were sat bolt upright with hands at the ready, resting on sword handles, just in case weapons were needed to defend God. Then there was Gordoon, the sole living human. He was still trying to take in all that he'd encountered over the last day. In that time he'd found out that he'd inadvertently created a set of gods, had a demon assassin try and kill him, Mesoamerican warriors, looking like they were going to an early Halloween party, trying to abduct him and then had angels save his life. As if that wasn't enough, and to top it all off, he had visited Heaven and participated in a holy war. As days went it had been a strange one and he doubted that he'd ever have another one like it. Now he was sat in the presence of God and Satan listening to them casually chat about *'the good old days.'* He no longer felt sure how he should react but what he did know was that none of his relatives or fellow students would ever believe him.

Seeing his expression and sensing the emotional turmoil God gave him a placatory smile and gently patted him on his knee. "It's alright Gordoon. You'll be okay." The words, and simple gesture, enough to fill his soul with complete and utter peace. He had no idea what the future would hold but he knew everything would work out fine.

Eventually Satan began to remember the armies that he'd left merrily chatting to each other. Giving God a serious look he spoke, his voice earnest and deep "God, I know that we came here to fight a rogue god and ended up with more of them, on both sides, than we anticipated, but it still feels like there is a lot of unspent energy over there. What do you say to letting them play for a bit longer? Those that want to can lop bits off each other and the last ones standing can call themselves the winners."

God looked at the gathered troops in the distance and smiled. "Why not? I am sure that Sonja, and her Viking horde, will be amenable to the suggestion and be happy to carry on the war, although from the way they have been fighting I am not sure if they will choose a side or just kill any non-Viking that gets in their way."

"With those rabid berserkers I doubt that being another Viking would be any protection either." Standing Satan gave God a slight bow. "If you'll excuse me, I'll go and give the good news to those that feel like having a good healthy work out, or perhaps wipe out."

Jumping to her feet Angelica stood excitedly in front of God. "Please Sire, can I join in? As I am having a break from the office, I want to make the most of it."

God gave her a resigned look. He didn't fully approve and was a little surprised, but He could think of no valid reason to refuse. After all, fighting demons was part of an angel's job and being His secretary didn't exempt her from that. "Of course, my dear, but just know that being killed in battle can be a painful experience. Go with my blessing and I will see you when you get back to Heaven."

Turning her gaze to Roxy, "Do you want to come with me? Kill a few demons. It'll be fun."

"No thank you Angelica" enthusiasm lacking from Roxy's voice as she remained seated, leaning forward, with her elbows resting on her knees "to me war, even against demons, is not fun and it isn't a game. I am tired and just want to go back to Heaven, get out of these clothes and have a nice long soak in the bath."

"Do you need…" Dedan's voice eager.

"Don't even say it Dedan. No, I do not need a lifeguard or someone to scrub my back. And yes, it might be my loss, but I will survive." Roxy's dark eyes sparkled coquettishly as she laughingly chastised Dedan. She knew him well enough to know what to expect from his far from appropriate or politically correct sense of humour. She did like him but not in any sexual way and was far from willing to take him up on any such offers that he made.

With appreciative eyes Dedan, Rob and Paul watched Angelica walk away. There weren't many heterosexual male angels in Heaven that didn't find her attractive and enjoy finding excuses to visit her in *the office*. Her normal attire was a tight black pencil skirt and even tighter pristine white blouse but even in off the peg army fatigues she still managed to exude an air of natural sex appeal. An appeal that the three men would gladly have donated to. Then, once God's vacationing secretary had reached the waiting army they saw Satan walk into the thick of them and begin to issue instructions. Both the Master of Hell and Angelica were then lost from sight as the battle resumed, this time angels fought demons. The natural order of things returned, with the added ingredient of Vikings who didn't seem to mind who they were killing, as long as they got to kill. Sonja was hoping that when they eventually returned to her version of Valhalla, they would have plenty of wild untamed energy in reserve, and fires in their groins, that weren't quickly extinguished by beer.

"God?" Gordoon ventured hesitantly "what should I do about Sonja over there? And come to think of it what about Falacer and Elsa, should I denou... I mean renounce them as well?"

With his mind quickly filled with images of Elsa, and her lack of wardrobe, Bob quickly butted in before God had the chance to answer. "Gordoon, don't be too hasty. Elsa has not harmed anyone, and I can definitely vouch for her wonderful assets."

If ever there was a look that expressed the word '*really?*' so succinctly then God's face had it and was aimed right at Bob. Without taking his eyes from Bob He spoke, His voice calm, relaxed and aimed at Gordoon. "I can sense doubts in your soul and that would make renouncing any of them difficult. Any hesitance or uncertainties make the simple speaking of the word useless. If it isn't spoken from the heart, then it is just another word." He paused to allow his words to sink in and for Gordoon to think about them. "When it comes to worshipping other gods, I am not as jealous as some people might think. There are just far too many to get 'Old Testament' about them all and, besides, some of them are my good friends and throw some great parties. Odin definitely knows how to have a good time and who am I to object to that? But all I can really say to you is to be true to yourself and follow your feelings. Even if her army's focus has become a little bit blurred right now, and they are happily hacking chunks out of Angel and demon alike, Sonja showed up and fought on the right side. Her followers might seem like barbaric animals at times, but they appear to Me to be more like barbaric party animals." His gaze was now fully on Gordoon. "Also, as Bob so eloquently put it, Elsa appears to be benevolent and is probably more interested in spreading her... love and understanding." He gave Bob a quick glance to encourage him to remain silent. "However, from what I have heard your sudden re-animation of Falacer has proven to be painful to him and definitely fatal to an unfortunate police officer. He has told Roxy that he wants to be freed from your worshipping. An unusual situation where a god doesn't want to exist so if you do renounce anyone else it probably should be him. In fact, you'd actually be giving him more mercy than he ever had in his heart."

Gordoon stroked his chin contemplatively. He did enjoy being the creator, and only hope of gods, but was also a good and kind person by nature. He understood that gods could suffer in the same way as humans and keeping Falacer trapped in his present form was wrong. Standing he outstretched his arms "Falacer! I renounce you. Return to oblivion and I hope you find happiness, or at least eternal peace." Then, falling silent, he gave God a concerned look "Did it work?"

God shrugged. "No idea. I don't have the ability to see into the domains of other gods, or even tell if their versions of Heaven have remained or disappeared, but I know a way to find out and can check. Leave it with me." Looking at His companions He stood up, causing them to stand up out of politeness as well. "Well Lady and Gents I think it is time for us to leave this place. Roxy, would you be so kind as to safely escort Mr. Simpson back to Colorado? He has had a long and interesting day and I'm sure he has a lot to think about."

"God, what about St. Michael?" enquired Dedan.

"You have a point. We have been pertinaciously ignoring his cries for assistance ever since the end of Hor'idey and her banishment, so I think it only right that we rescue him from his predicament and get him back to Heaven."

Crestfallen Dedan stood up. "Okay God, if you say so." His voice full of reluctance. He proceeded to roll corpses over until he found what he was looking for. Picking it up his colleagues saw him lift up a heavy duty, but ornately decorated, double headed axe and rest it on his shoulder. "This should do the trick. An ideal can opener." Then he began to walk towards the prostrate saint.

"Dedan," a matter-of-fact tone in God's voice "you do realise that the axe is unnecessary as there are leather straps on the side of his body armour? All you have to do is unbuckle him and he would be free from his gilded cage."

"I know that God. I know!" Continuing his walk towards St. Michael, giving his axe a playful swing in the air, "but where's the fun in that?"

36 - Returning to a New Normal, in 3, 2, 1...

Gordoon Simpson's return to Heaven, on the way back to Boulder, had been brief. It had afforded him just enough to time to change out of his clothing that had been soiled by the battle and to settle his own nerves, before he had to go back to Earth once more. While he'd been in Angelica's office, he had tried to get hold of some sort of souvenir that he could show to other people as a way of proving his story. As far-fetched as his tale might have sounded something tangible could have given him an element of credibility with his audience. Unfortunately, his attempt at petty larceny had not been that successful. All he had been able to get hold of, and swiftly stuff into his pocket, was a cheap disposable pen that had been left on Angelica's otherwise gift free desk. Even if it did say 'Welcome to Heaven – Have a nice day' he doubted that such an item would be seen as cast-iron evidence of his adventures and be sufficient to stop him being considered a lunatic and getting locked up for his own safety.

Checking the corridor, fire escape stairway and then his apartment Roxy ensured that there were no demons, or errant South American souls that had somehow managed to escape disintegration, hanging around waiting to complete a mission that no longer had any purpose or value. Happy that her ward was safe she escorted Gordoon into his room and watched as he gave the place a quick inspection to see that everything was in place. He tried to look at his carpet without making it too obvious and was relieved to see that the Heavenly clean up squad had done an excellent job in his absence. Any evidence that there had been a dead demon, inconsiderately making a bloody mess on the carpet, had disappeared. The angels responsible for it were experts and had centuries of experience of removing any tell-tale signs of angel and demon interaction so not even a faint blood stain could be seen. He wondered if they would be utilised to tidy up the mess in Bolivia, as images of container wagons full of bodies being removed by articulated lorries, filled his mind.

Despite his attempts at subtlety Roxy noticed him examining the room for any remaining evidence of the assassination attempt. "Don't worry dearest, our lot know what they are doing. There won't even be a rough demon hair or flake of skin for any Police forensic department to collect some DNA. As far as anyone knows absolutely nothing untoward happened here." Seeing his relief, she walked up to him give him a tender hug and gentle kiss on the cheek. Despite him being young, awkward, gauche and foolish Roxy had grown fond of him and thought that he had potential to do great things. "Be safe my friend. The world can be a complicated enough place as it is without you adding to the confusion and mixing a pinch of chaos to the order so, please, no more sudden looking up long forgotten deities. Go and live your life but please treat your gods well, being a High Priest is a great responsibility and, from the smell of the hallway, you are not the only one that is high today." Gordoon's heart was full of sadness at the thought of losing all that he could be part of, he'd had a taste of excitement and was hungry for more, but the smile that accompanied Roxy's words gave him a glimmer of joy and optimism.

"Thank you Roxy, for *everything.*" He now understood that there was a world outside of his room, one that didn't involve the internet and virtual reality. The reality he had just witnessed was virtually impossible, but it was real.

Without any warning, or visible signals that Roxy had summoned it, there was the now familiar, almost imperceptible, rectangular sheen to the air as the dimensional portal opened close to the far wall in his bedroom. Gordoon stared it glumly knowing that Roxy had to return but he didn't want her to leave him; or at least not so soon. There was much that he wanted to ask, things he needed to know, but had to accept that his unbelievably beautiful new friend, had to leave. As she approached the portal, he managed to blurt out one last question. "Will I ever see you again?"

She turned back to look at him and gave the lonely looking human a kind smile that, to him, seemed to light up the whole room. "Oh Gordoon, I am sure we will meet again. Hopefully not too soon but, if you are good, then definitely later." The words accompanied by her index finger pointing Heavenwards. "Ciao my little brother." And with those sweet words she stepped through the portal and was gone, then before he'd had time to blink, the almost non-existent door disappeared as well leaving just the part time destroyer of gods and full-time university student alone in a room that had witnessed so much.

37 - Home So Soon?

On his return to Heaven Dedan had declined the invitation, from Bob and Paul, to go and find a quiet bar and get stinkingly blind drunk, or as drunk as it was possible to get in Heaven. The alcohol there tasted better than anything available on Earth and left the drinker with a wonderful warm feeling, but it was not designed to put anyone into to stupor or to leave them with a hangover, the next day, that made them think that they'd somehow woken up in Hell. Be it a twelve-year-old single malt whisky, or the worst bathtub gin, there was little chance of having someone else telling you about the legendary exploits you got up to while under the influence but couldn't remember the next day. The lack of such effects was another reason why Dedan preferred to spend as much time as possible on Earth. Instead of unwinding with his friends and having a few drinks he decided that he'd much rather divest himself of his blood, mud and God only knew what else, splattered battle clothing. That was followed by a long and, bubble filled bath before he realised that he had to go and report to God. He hoped that the meeting would involve him getting a new mission to Earth, but was worried that, in Angelica's absence, he'd have to do some paperwork. And to him that was tantamount to being sent to Hell. After drying himself off he dressed and checked the mirror. He looked tired but, as he'd left Angelica on some distant battlefield merrily decapitating demons, he saw no reason to try harder to make himself look any better than he did. God had seen him in far worse states and wouldn't care about his appearance.

Without knocking Dedan pushed open the door to 'The Room' walked straight in and was surprised to see Angelica sat at her desk merrily typing away on her computer with a Santana tune playing loudly in the background. "Hello, my beautiful Angel, I wasn't expecting to see you back so soon. Did the war finish quicker than anticipated?"

"It certainly ended quicker than expected for me." Giving him a playful look as if to say, 'I know what you are thinking, but just shut up'. A long sentence to fit into one single expression but she managed it with words to spare.

"Oh, I see. So…" Dedan was enjoying the moment. "How long did you last in battle?"

"Wellllll, it is hard to be precise. You know how it is, time flies when you're enjoying yourself."

"Yes, battles can be like that, but approximately how long do you think you lasted?"

"By my reckoning it was somewhere between 2 and 5 minutes."

"What happened?" The laugh being badly stifled.

The look had changed on her face so that the unspoken message now contained a few more expletives and the rough instruction to go away. "I had managed to despatch a few demons and was busy with another when..." there was a pause as she tried to find a less embarrassing way of ending the sentence.

"Yes? And?"

"When I slipped on someone's eviscerated intestines, that were in the water by my feet. I lost my balance and fell forwards and landed headfirst onto an axe blade belonging to a dead Viking."

"Ouch. You need to be more careful. Those things can be deadly!" The laugh getting ever closer to escaping.

"You think? Now you tell me." Her stern look evaporated and was replaced by a broad smile, which was signal enough to Dedan, allowing him to release his laughter which was soon joined by Angelica laughing at her own unspectacular and unconventional demise.

"Just look at it this way," struggling to get his words out "at least you did better than St. Michael. He was about as welcome as a turd in a swimming pool and as useful as a spoon in a coal mine. He was *not* happy with the way I helped him out of his fine and intricate armour. I think the panel beaters will have their work cut out repairing those dents."

The memory of St. Michael was still fresh and just added fuel to the raucous laugher. The image of him finally being freed from his inelegant position and standing up, covered in the foul soup that had found its way into his protective clothing was something he'd remember for a long time. The shades of reds, browns and oranges making it look like

286

Jackson Pollock had vomited over his clothing and made the angel, and his companions, wish that they'd had camera phones handy to capture the sight for posterity. The expression on the saint's face alone would have been an internet sensation and most of his less than admiring army would have happily given it a 'like'.

On hearing the exuberant jollity in the adjoining room God decided to investigate. As the disguise was no longer needed, He'd decided to change from the African tribesman appearance and revert to His more recognisable form. The white suit and long flowing beard might have been stereotypical but at least when someone saw Him they had a pretty good chance of recognising who it was. On opening the door, leading to *The Room* God saw his two friends and decided not to interrupt their casual banter. He'd seen into Dedan's soul and felt the inner turmoil that had been tearing him up and was relieved that moving on had been a relatively painless process. Admittedly it had taken a war to totally clear the saint of his emotional fog, but God was sure that even without that Dedan would have come around sooner or later. An eternity in Heaven is a long time to be upset at a rejection. Unnoticed He casually leant against the door frame, with His arms folded, watching them like an indulgent father watching playful children. As He listened to the jokes, at the expense of His Field Marshall, He felt that He should interrupt and chastise them for poking fun at St. Michael, but He was finding the jokes funny and was struggling to keep quiet and unintentionally announce His presence by adding His own laugher.

Eventually, after wiping happy tears from her eyes Angelica happened to glance past Dedan and finally noticed the extra person in the office. Feeling that some inappropriate things might have been overheard she guiltily tried to regain her composure and adopt a more serious face. Giving Dedan a wide-eyed look she began to nod slightly, in the direction of the Holy presence behind him. It took a moment for the surreptitious signal to sink in but when it did Dedan instantly reacted. Standing upright he stopped laughing, his face adopting a similar earnest appearance to Angelica's. "And if you could let me have a copy of the final report that would be appreciated." His voice serious as if he was ending a dull conversation and hoping that God had not overheard too much.

"Nice try Dedan, nice try. But I wasn't born yesterday and, come to think of it, neither were you." God's voice was not attempting to join in the game of sounding serious. "Relax, this is Heaven and you are not American Mormons or born again Christians, so you are allowed to have a laugh and be happy."

Turning to face Him Dedan allowed a smile to return to his face. "Oh, Hello Sire. I didn't see you there."

"Obviously. But since when has Me being around stopped you from insulting, being disrespectful or mocking the leader of My heavenly army? I'd be more shocked and surprised if I'd overheard you saying something complimentary about him."

"Don't worry, I find that highly unlikely." To many humans, that had their own blinkered and ill-informed views of Heaven, and opinions on how it should be run if they were in charge, speaking to God in such an informal way would have been deemed to be disrespectful and have caused some mysterious trap door to appear under Dedan's feet sending him straight to the inner circle of Hell. Fortunately for Dedan, and all the other souls in Heaven that wanted it to be a happy place, such bigoted and closed-minded prejudices were more likely to send the bigots to Hell rather than Heaven, so Dedan was able to have a joke with God without suffering a similar fate as Satan.

"Sorry to break up the glee club but would you care to join Me in My room?" God then looked directly at His personal assistant "and I think that, as you are now a fully-fledged field agent and demon killer, it would be nice if you joined us as well."

Angelica had always been welcomed in God's office and was free to come and go as she pleased but this invitation was something new. Over the years she'd spent many hours sat in a comfortable chair in His office chatting but this time it was different. The feeling of being part of a team, with a shared experience, made her feel significant and important. No longer the outsider looking in, instead she was someone more than a bringer of coffee. She wasn't convinced that killing was for her and doubted that she would ask for a transfer to the demon hunter team, but the change of pace and break from her computer and files had been fun.

The three took their seats and made themselves comfortable. God in His large black leather chair at one side of His imposing antique desk and, on the other side of it, the two guests sat in equally comfortable and imposing chairs facing him.

"Drinks?" God had to reinforce the question with an arm gesture to Angelica to emphasise the fact that he was asking them if they wanted a beverage rather than issuing her an instruction to go and put the kettle on. "Dedan, your usual? And you Angelica, what can I tempt you with?"

"Yes please." Responded Dedan enthusiastically, knowing the treat that was in store for him.

Angelica paused to consider her options. "Can I just have a cold beer? The after taste of battle, and the water I accidentally swallowed as I died, needs to be washed away."

Without any gestures, summoning them, three glasses appeared. One was tall, full of frothy beer with a covering of cold condensation decorating the outside of it. The other two were crystal cut glass tumblers with generous amounts of a transparent golden-brown coloured liquid in them. Dedan passed the beer to Angelica and reverentially picked up his own drink. Raising it up into the air he carefully studied the drink, watching as the light passed through it and sent golden rays along the delicate pattern in the glass. There were many words to describe what he was about to experience be they ambrosia, nectar or amrita but, to him, he simply knew it as the finest aged malt whisky that he'd ever tasted. He put the glass under his nose and gave it a long appreciative sniff and the fumes alone were enough to raise him to a higher plane of consciousness. Then the epicurean foreplay ended as it came to final part of the ornate ritual. Taking a sip, he allowed the liquid to rest on his tongue as he breathed in through his mouth. The alcoholic hit making his senses feel as if they were electrified. Then, finally, he swallowed and allowed it to trickle down his throat. The drink was definitely for savouring and not swigging.

Angelica had taken an approach to her drink that was far from Dedan's connoisseur dramatics. Draining the glass in one go she heavily placed the empty receptacle back on God's desk and gave off a loud 'Aaaaah' of enjoyment and satisfaction. If she had done any savouring it had been a very quick process. God pre-emptied any request for a refill and automatically topped it up and passed the full glass back to her.

"So how is the battle going?" Dedan asked, his glass remaining in his hand.

"With the exception of a few minor skirmishes it is all over. The souls have been steadily returning to their respective dimensions and I have already despatched all the clean-up teams to return the place to its pristine natural beauty. Not the easiest of tasks as there are a collection of useless body parts to be disposed of and the water purity is not what it was, but they know what to do."

"Speaking of a collection of useless body parts," Dedan paused to sip his cherished whisky "where has St. Michael gone?"

God gave him an unconvincing stern look as he tried to suppress a smile. "Please Dedan, show some respect. After all he is the supreme commander of my Holy army and despite his many foibles, and complete lack of personality, he is a good General and, if I must remind you, has won many battles without your assistance."

"I am sorry Boss" a hint of genuine contrition in his voice. "So, where is he?"

"Who cares?" Unable to hide His laughter anymore, the dour expression left his face to be replaced with a smile that gave His regal face extra wrinkles. "I suspect he has gone back to his quiet and distant part of Heaven to have a good sulk and take his frustrations out on his unfortunate batman. As we speak St. Michael will probably be having poor Matt polishing boots until he wears the leather out." He raised His tumbler of whisky in the air. "It was all a bit of a mess but on the whole a satisfactory resolution. Hopefully we do not have to go through that again for some god randomly re-created by a bored nerd. Dedan, Angelica, here's to a successful mission!"

His two guests raised their glasses and spoke in unison "To a successful mission!" and then the seasoned fighter and battle novice took appreciative and thankful drinks. Content that the balance of power had been restored.

38 – Time Flies Like an Arrow, Fruit Flies Like a Banana...

The expression about time going faster if you are happy might be all down to perceptions and for humans the unit of measurements of time are always immutable. For example, someone making love might feel like it only lasted a matter of seconds and if they are unlucky it might have, but when done properly could last for much longer than that. Some men have even been known to break the three-minute barrier, even without two minutes and fifty-five seconds of foreplay. Thanks to the constant state of happiness in Heaven the units of measurement are harder to govern and measure. With the six months, following the 'War of the Plane', that passed on Earth seemed to go unnoticed by the angels. Most angels are immune and separate from the affairs of humanity, so they are oblivious to the changes that are always happening on Earth. Seasons came and went unnoticed with the only indications that new wars, famines or plagues had arrived would be a sudden incremental increase in the normally steady inwards flow of souls. Other than those indicators they would be far too busy enjoying themselves to take much notice of anything on the far side of the Pearly Gates.

There are of course exceptions - Angels that see it as their vocation, in death, to protect and guard the human race from their own stupidity or outside intervention, preventing demons from having a free rein, or even reign. Wherever possible trying to steer, or nudge, the right souls so that they take the best actions and do not do anything silly such as pressing big red buttons that result in the end of the world or opening a valve that pollutes an ocean. Then there are some that just like to know what is going on, watching as if the whole planet was some giant soap opera.

The clean-up teams done their jobs well ensuring that all traces of the battle had disappeared, with any human reports of the event became just urban myths and crazy conspiracy theories told by lunatics, attention seekers or idiots. Thanks to the depletion of demons, who'd been killed in battle and therefore temporarily unable to return to Earth and cause trouble, the work of the Angelic demon hunters was reduced - leaving them time to have a rest. But despite the relative lack of demonic mischief there were still things to be done. The wheels on a train might seem to be running smoothly but they still needed to be kept well oiled. That was why Roxy was currently meandering around the streets of Boulder, Colorado, trying to find Gordoon Simpson. She had tried his student flat but had been told by his neighbours that he had started to act strangely over the last few months and dropped out of sight. When she had pressed them to elaborate, on how strange he'd become, all they could say that he had been attending lectures and started to leave his room for long periods. Such behaviour didn't seem that strange to her but to his friends it was akin to having gender realignment to become a female fish or starting to listen to classical music. Eventually she managed to speak to one student that was slightly less stoned than the rest of them and he was able to give her an address that she could try. Roxy wasn't too convinced that the information was reliable but, as it was the only tangible lead, she decided to follow it up. After getting lost several times she eventually found the less than welcoming street leading off Aurora Avenue. Finding the door, that corresponded to the address on the piece of paper, she saw a laminated sign stuck to it with drawing pins informing anyone that cared to read it that they had reached 'The Church of the Three Gods (Worshipping times: Mon, Wed, Fri 7-9 pm. All welcome)'. The sign, on its own seemed fairly innocuous and the word 'Gods' made her suspect that it was more than a coincidence that she had been directed here. Although the use of the number three did give her cause for concern as, by her calculations, there had only been two deities left after he had completed his renunciations of the ones that were off his figurative Christmas card list. The mysterious third appearance created an uncomfortable feeling in the pit of her stomach as she contemplated how the student had not learnt his lesson and conjured up some obscure and unpredictable god or goddess. Pushing at the door it opened freely to reveal a corridor that seemed to be unusually dark compared to the bright and welcoming evening sunshine. Venturing in she caught a faint whiff of the unmistakable odour of burnt incense and wondered if it was there for ceremonial purposes or, as was usually the case for students, was there to hide the smell of joints that had been enjoyed by people that didn't want to make it obvious. Up ahead there was a door that was slightly ajar, allowing bright light to be seen on the other side. She walked towards it and hesitantly put her head through the gap and was met by the sight of eighteen figures, wearing blue robes, kneeling with their backs to her. In front of them was another figure wearing a yellow robe with a hood covering his head.

Lifting small statues, from a plain wooded alter at the opposite end of the room, murmuring inaudible chants and then replacing the figures, he was for too preoccupied to notice the new visitor. Gingerly she tried to move herself silently along the far wall, so that she could remain inconspicuous and unnoticed until she could be sure that she was safe and wouldn't be used as some less than virginal sacrifice. Despite her best efforts she accidentally bumped into a wooden chair that scrapped across the floor releasing a pained screech. The noise was heard by all and any hopes of not being seen were automatically dashed as nineteen people turned their heads and repositioned their cowls so that they could see what had disturbed their solemn meditation.

"Roxy! Is that you?" The words came from deep within the yellow hood and, as it was hastily lowered, she saw Gordoon's grinning face. He was now slightly less pale and had a tidy haircut but other than that he hadn't changed that much. Running past the curious worshippers he approached her and gave her a tight hug which nearly took all the air out of her lungs. "It is wonderful to see you again and I am glad that it is while I am still alive. Come with me." Without waiting for a response, he grabbed hold of her hand and led her to the front of the hall. Addressing his kneeling audience "My friends, this is *the* Roxy."

The introduction solicited a combined "Uuuuh" from his audience and then a polite "Hello sacred and Divine Roxy." The words chanted as if it were a practiced incantation.

"This way, I am sure you have lots of question and I certainly have a lot to tell you." Continuing his journey, he led her through a door by the side of the alter into a small office with a desk and several chairs crammed into it. The confined space didn't leave much room for anyone to actually sit in them but at least it was private. Taking the chair at the far side of the desk he gestured towards one of the other seats. "Please sit down, I am sorry but there isn't much room. We are a new church and, well, you know how it is."

"What happened with… all this?" Roxy waved her hand vaguely in the air, finger raised as if to encompass a multitude of questions into five words.

"Oh, that is easy. I felt sorry for Elsa and Sonja. Having just one disciple was precarious for them and if I were to get hit by a truck they'd turn back to stone and they didn't deserve that, especially after they'd visited me in my dreams a few times and we…. Well, we sort of became close friends!"

'Men!' Roxy thought as she gave him a knowing look. She'd seen Sonja and heard about Elsa so wasn't surprised by his erotic, and probably wet, dreams. She was just glad that she didn't have to clean his bedsheets. "So…you created a church?"

"Exactly! I designed a bit of software that didn't quite work as well as I'd hoped but, somehow, I still managed to sell it to the NSA for a nice sum of money and I bought this place. I put up a few posters and handed out a handful of fliers around Boulder and hey presto I got a smattering of curious people and, since I started, word has begun to spread. Still small but I have ambitions to expand. First nationally and then, who knows, internationally?" His eyes seeming to glaze over as he spoke. "I have told my congregation all about you, Bob and Dedan along with the war. Everything. You are now part of a holy text."

The idea of her being a religious figure filled her with dread. The last thing she wanted was for souls to find their way into Heaven and start knocking on her door at all hours wearing 'I Heart Roxy' t-shirts and asking for autographs. But she doubted that would be a problem for a long time, but she was sure that it had the real risk of happening at some point. To most people his word and ideas would have seemed like the dreams of a deluded madman but not to Roxy who knew Gordoon and somehow suspected that he would turn out to be a cult figure and hopefully a new voice for peace. "There is one thing Gordoon, my dearest" she chewed on her bottom lip as she tried to find the correct words in English rather than her native Italian tongue, "you have called it the Church of the Three Gods. The last time I counted Sonja and Elsa were only two. Who is the third one? I hope you haven't been searching on the web again and come up with some obscure troublemaker that will start stealing souls from Heaven and be wanting another war."

"No Roxy. I learnt my lesson last time. I decided to hedge my bets and make God the centre of the holy trinity. After all He was the other God on the battlefield, and He is good. I am sure He won't mind the company or be jealous. Plus, it gives the believers a choice of three different versions of Heaven that they can choose to go to when they die. It also saves me having to think up new commandments. I simply removed the first four that, in my opinion, seemed to be a bit outdated egotistical and selfish but I left in the ones about not killing, stealing, telling lies or generally being a dick."

Despite her initial concerns, and reservations, Roxy had to admit that Gordoon seemed to have thought about his church and had a few decent ideas. She wasn't too sure how God would react to being included in the new branch of faith, but it seemed to be based on goodness so couldn't imagine Him getting upset about it. After all the days of jealously smiting humans had been Old Testament and He didn't enjoy creating floods anymore; apparently, they caused too much paperwork.

"Alright Gordoon, I am glad you are well, and your new religion is growing. I am sure that Elsa and Sonja will be happy too. The more believers they have the safer they will feel and be more likely to answer your prayers. God tends to get more than He can answer so people have to get up off their knees and actually work for their miracles. As they say, 'God helps those that help themselves!'" She gave him a sweet smile that made him wish that she would join his church and be his high priestess. "I must be going now, take care my friend."

"Ciao bella." Standing he moved to open the door for her.

As she was being escorted out, via the main hall, she paused by the altar. On closer inspection she realised that such a word was giving it a far grander assessment than it truly deserved. It was simply a couple of planks that had been nailed together, varnished and then laid across some breeze blocks at either end. Even such basic carpentry left a lot to be desired, it looked like it had been done by a baby chimp or someone that had forgotten their hammer and used the head of a screwdriver to bash the nails in. Resting on the wood, in the middle, was an unlit candle in a silver candlestick and, on either side of that were statues and figures of varying sizes that depicted females in various clothing styles.

"Do you like it?" Gordoon's voice excited that his friend was inspecting the sacred chancel. "I made it myself."

"Really? A man of many talents." Her voice sounding impressed even if she wanted to end the sentence with 'But none of them involve woodwork'. It was obvious to her that being a computer whizz didn't mean that she'd want him to ever put up a shelf in her home.

"Those figures there" pointing to the figurines "are Sonja and Elsa. Though I had to put imaginary clothes on Elsa as, in my dreams, she was naked. So, I have never actually seen her with clothes on."

"I don't think anyone has!"

"And of course, the middle candle represents God. I am not sure a spear carrying African warrior is how He'd like to be depicted so I was a little more creative and made Him 'The Light'."

Giving him yet another one of her smiles, that made him wish that he was a little older and Roxy a lot less dead. "It looks wonderful, and I am sure the candle is fine." They walked to the door out of the hall, where she gave him a brief kiss on the cheek and, out of sight of his congregation, she hailed the portal, walked through it and disappeared leaving Gordoon Simpson alone with his less than pure thoughts. His religion might not have vows of celibacy, but the object of his desires was not right for him for far too many reasons.

39 – Where it all Began

Despite the narrow streets of Florence being currently being washed by a light drizzle the rain did nothing to deter the tourists from filling the streets as they rushed from one sightseeing hot spot to another. All trying to capture as many memories as possible without the inconvenience of having to stop and appreciate the true majesty of what was in front of their eyes. Magnificent churches, statues and palaces photographed so that the images could be glimpsed at later, rather than the real thing appreciated in the here and now. But there was a casual person that didn't seem to be there just to take snapshots and buy horrendously expensive ice-creams. His dark blue suit and crimson coloured tie wasn't exactly traditional tourist attire, and he didn't seem interested in any of the sights that would have impressed the most cynical of American tourists. But such things were unnoticed by the crowd, they had better things to look at.

Dedan could have worn clothing that was far more casual, and less formal, but he was in a sombre mood and thought that it would be appropriate if he wore a suit. Despite it being made by one of the most talented tailors in Heaven he still managed to make it look as if it he had been away during the fitting. The sleeves were slightly too short and showed a little too much shirt cuff. The jacket itself was also far too big so the overall impression was that perhaps an ape had been measured up by mistake. But even so he still managed to look smart and presentable. After all nobody, or hopefully nobody, would see where he was going. Approaching Piazza del Limbo he casually looked around to ensure that he was not being observed and was glad to see that nobody was taking any notice of him. Although there were tourists walking along the far edge of the square, thanks to it having nothing of interest to any visitors, he was alone and unobserved. He approached a dull and unspectacular door in an equally uninspiring wall and took one last deep breath of Italian air. Then he put his arms against the wood and instead of it either supporting his weight or opening he passed through the solid material. Expecting the loss of his natural centre of gravity he allowed his legs to walk him through it and, once he had completed the unnatural process, he stopped at the other side. Blinking, several times, he allowed his eyes to adjust to the difference in light from the outside. Although the hall had no obvious source of lighting it still seemed to be illuminated sufficiently well for him to be able to see everything clearly. He walked casually along the Hall of Dead Gods giving each petrified and cold marble divinity a cursory look to ensure that nothing was amiss. Eventually he came to the first of the statues on his 'must see' tourist attractions list. Back on his plinth was Falacer, frozen in the position he was in during his renunciation. He was sat in a simple chair, leant forward with his left elbow placed on a small table and his head resting on his hand. An expression of abject boredom carved for, what Dedan hoped, all eternity. Despite him having killed a police officer Dedan didn't feel anger towards the god. He was just someone that was of his time but, once he'd been returned to the right place but wrong era, he'd instinctively known that he didn't belong and had yearned for obscurity again. It took a lot of courage to accept that, and Dedan respected him for it. Giving the god a slight, but reverential bow, Dedan carried on with his casual walk, passing the other statues. Most were given nothing but cursory glances, but he did stop to admire the occasional one that he recognised or whose posture seemed unusual. He had to walk around one several times as it was a female that was on her knees with her arm wrapped around some now absent object and her head leant forwards with her mouth forming a 'O' shape. Dedan had his own distinct ideas about what she was doing when she had lost her final believer. He gave off a sigh of disappointment on behalf of the unknown person that suffered from 'falatio interruptus' and the subsequent inhalation filled his lungs with the cool and stale air of the hall. It reminded him of the atmosphere in a newly opened tomb that had been sealed for centuries and, in a sense, this was what the Hall of Dead Gods truly was. Eventually he found the statue of Ekeko, still in the pose he'd been in when Gordoon's apostasy had taken its effect. Sword in one hand, trying to block the blow from a now non-existent Viking, and the other outstretched clasping frustratedly at thin air. The god's face still full of rage with the angry denial while his final word seeming to escape from his mouth. He walked around the plinth and noticed that although it was now fully intact again the rubble from Ekeko earlier re-animation was still littering the floor. Looking at the back of the rock effigy he noticed the handles of two pistols sticking out of his waistband. The lethal combination of black wood and metal now transformed into harmless white marble. Dedan wasn't sure if Ekeko had taken them with him as a secret 'ace up his sleeve' to be used 'just in case' or as a reminder of all he hated about the world that he was no longer a part of.

Eventually his lonely tour came to its end as he reached his main objective, the target of his search and one time object of all his desires. There, stood on her plinth, Hor'idey was frozen with her head leaning back in mid scream and arms spread wide as if she'd just been shot in the back from close range. Not the greatest pose and not how he wanted to remember her but somehow, he felt that the pose was appropriate for her. He suddenly felt a single tear run down his cheek and his heart began to ache as he thought of all the happy times, so many long millennia ago, that they had once shared. But he knew that despite all the love and laughter there was much more to their relationship than any human couple would ever have to deal with and those tensions, and dark parts, had doomed their marriage from the start. The need for a god to be perpetually, and unquestioningly, worshipped would put a strain on any relationship and when that god or goddess was also a psychotic and egotistical narcissist the chances of it ever working out were zero to the power of ten. As she was stood on a shoulder high plinth, he absentmindedly rubbed her foot. "Well, my love, I tried to give you everything and enough was never enough for you. Even when you got a second chance you still wanted something different to what was offered." Stepping back to better see her face "you were… are still so beautiful. If only your soul had the same quality. Even now you'd probably have had a legion of followers. But like everything you blew it. Goodbye Hor'idey. Hopefully there is more peace to be found under that cold stone surface than when you had warm, soft and such sweet tasting flesh." Reaching up he gently rubbed her bare calf muscle. The surface was just as smooth, but much colder, than when he'd last done that to her. He felt that he should dwell longer where he was but realised that there was little point. He'd said all that he wanted, or needed, to say and looking at her in the current petrified state just filled him with sadness.

Eventually he reached the opposite end of the hall and was relieved to see that all the plinths, with the exception of two, were occupied and that no more gods had disappeared. He contemplated going through the door closest to him, and having a drink with Limbo, but remembered the terrible tasting coffee available there and decided against it. Instead, turning back the way he'd come, he chose to that spend a little more time enjoying 'la dolce vita' in Florence before he eventually had to return to Heaven. After all the Italian coffee, wine and women had their own charms which he was in no rush to miss out on.

40 – Diplomatic Impunity

When Bob initially wanted to make the unusual request, he had thought about it and, thanks to self-doubt, became convinced that he was being stupid, and God would be polite but meet his official petition with a refusal. After all, he'd chatted with Angelica and made surreptitious enquiries with her casual answers not making him feel optimistic. But just because it might be unprecedented didn't mean it was impossible or wrong. To him being the first to think of it was showing creativity and could be beneficial to Heaven so he felt that he had to bite the bullet and ask.

Stood uncomfortably at the desk in the impressive room he looked nervously at God. He awkwardly shuffled his feet, uncertain as to what posture to adopt. Despite the polite offer he had not felt right sitting down so he'd tried standing to attention, standing at ease with his legs slightly apart and hands clasped behind his back and even attempted nonchalance, with arms folded, but each position just felt uncomfortable and wrong. All the fidgeting reminded him of when he was alive and in his early twenties. He had been the same when he'd been infatuated with a woman and was asking his girlfriend's father for permission to marry his daughter. Even though he'd been given a negative, and threatening response, it had been old fashioned but at the time it felt right. Taking a deep breath, he decided to allow the words to flow, see what came out and hope for the best.

"Sire, I have a suggestion."

"Really? What is it?" God sat casually steepling his fingers as He spoke and listened to His visitor.

"Yes. Sonja seems to have shown her intentions, and earnest desire, to stay on the side of the good. I don't think she has any intention of turning bad so I think she can be trusted."

"You think all that do you? I suppose you are right. Her presence on the battlefield was of great benefit and she was on our side, unlike Dedan's ex."

"Exactly," Bob's voice becoming stronger as his confidence grew. So far God seemed interested and that was enough. "But when it comes to

Elsa, we can't be totally certain. She could be like Sonja and accept the situation or she could turn out to be like Hor'idey, or Ekeko, and want more than is available. Therefore, I suggest that we send an envoy to her domain to see how friendly she is and ensure she remain… friendly with us angels."

"To gauge her intentions?" God's voice was casual, but His eyes seemed to be indicating that He knew exactly where the conversation was going.

"Yes, that's it exactly. An ambassador, so to speak." Bob's voice raised an octave with anticipation of success.

"And I presume that you are volunteering to get to grips with her?"

"Yes, yes, yes that's it, exactly. Get to grips with her and ensure that I understand her desires." His voice trying to take on a solemn tone but failing.

God ran his fingers through his long white hair. "Are you sure? It was tried once before, long ago, and the god in question made it hard for the angel."

"No, no, no God. If she makes it hard for me, I am sure we will both be able to handle it properly."

"I don't know." Sighing "Oh, okay."

"But Sire" Bob continued with a serious voice "I genuinely think it is a good idea and that…"

He was interrupted by God putting His hand up to silence the over eager angel. "I said OKAY. As in all right. Off you go. Just remember one thing."

"Thank you, oh thank you. What is it?"

"That you are an angel, not some little demon." God gave Bob a knowing look.

"Of course, Sire. I promise that I wouldn't do anything that Dedan wouldn't do."

"That, Bob, is exactly what I'm worried about." Rising from His chair. "Now if you will excuse Me, I have promised, or rather a young boy that just happened to be in this room once, has promised to go to lunch with Golda Meir so I need to change. I have no intention of shattering her illusions, or embarrassing her, by letting her know who she was really talking to." With those words he instantly transformed back into the form of the 12-year-old boy that Golda had grown so fond of all those months ago. "Have fun and I am sure that Angelica can organise all the travel arrangements."

41 – The Devil May (not) Care Attitude

Having Satan as his boss, and immediate line manager, had a few advantages. It was certainly better than being a soul receiving punishment in one of the almost infinite number of chambers whose sole purpose was to make Hell all that the name suggested. It also kept him away from other demons that might try and rip his limbs off, which wasn't unusual treatment for demons of a nervous disposition like him. The downside was that work was forever being made for him, so he never had idle hands. Ever since the end of the war he'd been kept even busier and was getting tired. There were red journals to be completed, although he had no idea why as Satan had never once been seen to look at them. Notes on each demon's actions, while on missions, were recorded and when they returned to Hell their exploits were rewarded, or punished, accordingly. Those that had fought well and killed plenty of Ekeko's soldiers, or angels once the battle had become less formal, were given jobs that could be seen as easy, or at least easy by demon standards. Those that had been unfortunate enough to get killed, before they could kill, or were deemed not to have been valiant enough were given shitty jobs and all too often that expression wasn't a euphemism. Satan was still in a relatively good mood and was gloating after winning the ersatz war with the Angels, the slight numerical advantage had allowed the game of last man standing to only just end in his favour. But to him a victory was a victory, so the score didn't matter. Unfortunately, this happiness didn't mean that standards had dropped or that Kran was now immune from any displeasure that might arise. Dishing out pain and misery could make Satan just as happy as winning a battle, so he knew that it was best to just do his job and be thankful for surviving each day without getting a fireball in the face. However, despite having tried to ignore it, there was bad news that needed to be delivered, news that could result in him being fired in a very real and painful sense. He wished that he could delegate it but lacking an assistant of his own he had little option but to do what had to be done and hope for the best.

Knocking on Satan's door and getting the usual snarling and bad-tempered invitation to enter Kran began the traditional battle of supremacy with the self-important and belligerent door. Pushing hard he took it by surprise and managed to force it open a few inches before it realised what was happening and refused to move any further.

Stepping back a few feet Kran began to run towards is seemingly inanimate adversary. Not to be outdone by a demon the door simply gave up all resistance and allowed the full weight of Kran to push forwards. Obeying Newton's third law the lack of an equal and opposite force sent the off balanced demon tumbling forwards, legs desperately trying to regain balance and prevent him from falling onto the less than clean carpet. Momentum seemingly joining in the physical comedy and to be having its own effect but, fortunately for Kran, he managed to regain his balance, if not his dignity, and remain upright. Standing in front of the giant desk he tried to act as if nothing had happened and casually placed the thick ledgers on it. Then he stood to attention, a blank expression on his face. Satan was stood by the fireplace staring into the flames and seemed oblivious to the undignified entrance which his personal assistant had just made. But the lack of reaction didn't mean that the door's antics hadn't been seen.

As Kran stood patiently waiting for his master to turn around, and speak to him, he began to listen to the background music that was filling the room. As usual it was Barry Manilow and, from the sounds of it, the crooner was describing how people should keep clear of some tropical islands or they could disappear. Which is exactly what he wished he could do right now.

Satan gave off a throaty growl and turned away from his fire gazing to look at Kran. "Yes maggot?"

"Sir, I have the final reports for the battle." His voice belying that there was more to be reported than all that was encompassed in the books on the desk.

Sensing that there was some unspoken issue Satan moved to his desk. Resting his clenched fists on it he leant towards his assistant, eyes filled with suspicion. "And?" Allowing the word to fill the gap between the two of them, as if the three letters contained a whole dictionary of words; all of which were full of threats and promises of violence.

"Errrr" The terror gripping his throat almost as tightly as Satan could "all the demons have returned to Hell with the exception of seven."

"Seven?" Satan's voice adopting a tone that Kran couldn't interpret. A mix of curiosity with a promise of unspecified violence if the ensuing response wasn't to his taste.

"Yes Sire. They are your daughters, Kelly Kelly, Lisa, Sasha, Chri..."

"Yes," his voice terse "I *know* who my daughters are." Sitting down he stared at Kran, but he was not interested in the terrified demon. The news had given him food for thought and he needed time to chew it over. "So...they have done a runner and decided to stay on Earth?"

"Yes Sir, it would appear so. I sent an army of demons around Hell to double check that they were not hiding somewhere, but they seem to have remained on Earth and left Bolivia. I have no idea where they are."

Satan gave Kran a smile that took him by surprise. "I knew I shouldn't have allowed them to join in the battle, but KK persuaded me. She always was persuasive that one. Oh well. They are demons and they are on Earth so they're God's problem now. Let him deal with them." With that he leant back in his chair, rested his feet on the desk and began to laugh. And if ever there was such a thing as demonic laughter, that wasdidn't fit so I had to find a way to resample it and save as a PDF, which I se it. He looked forward to seeing the angels try and send them back to Hell. One would have been difficult but all seven would need an army, and a lucky one at that.

"Kran, get me the phone..."

Dedications

(And to those who have yet to be mentioned, be patient)

The last few years have not been easy for most people, and some didn't make it, so this dedication is in two parts. Firstly, I want to say goodbye to George, Simon and Gemma. Three avid readers and wonderful people. The world is a lesser place for their absence, and they are missed.

Next there is the 'Without who' people who hopefully know that they are appreciated but have not had the proper mentions, yet:

Bob, Hawaiian bum, grease monkey and dodgy role model. Any resemblance to angels mentioned in any of my books are not entirely coincidental and you deserve to be the King of Hawaii.

Jennifer, high ranking member of the grammar police, hippy and friend. I don't think I would have stopped procrastinating if I hadn't taken up so much time and energy to stop you from doing the same thing.

Rossana, author, poet, honorary sister and guide. Thank you for challenging me and not letting me rest on my laurels. Keep on fighting the demons – I will always provide the cricket bat.

Milton Keynes UK
Ingram Content Group UK Ltd.
UKHW020813280823
427620UK00015B/932